THREE THREADS

RANDAL R. JONES

BookLocker
Trenton, Georgia

Paperback ISBN: 978-1-958877-53-1
Hardcover ISBN: 978-1-958877-54-8
Ebook ISBN: 979-8-88531-323-0

Three Threads is the fictional sequel to Jones' historical fiction novel *Pendulum*. The events and characters in *Three Threads* are purely fictitious and not intended to represent specific persons, individual attitudes, traits, or characteristics. The character relationships are fictional as are the missions and storylines.

Department of Defense (DoD) Office of Prepublication and Security Review and the Intelligence Community (IC) approved *Three Threads* for release / open publication. Concurrence for release does not imply DOD/IC endorsement or factual accuracy of this material.

Cover Design by Alyssa M. Luongo
Review and Edit by Katherine E. Adams

Published by BookLocker.com, Inc., Trenton, Georgia.

Library of Congress Cataloging in Publication Data
Jones, Randal R.
Three Threads by Randal R. Jones
Library of Congress Control Number: 2022915553

Printed on acid-free paper.
Booklocker.com, Inc

THREE THREADS

In memory of my loving mother,
in appreciation of my supportive wife and best friend,
dedicated to my daughters and granddaughter,
and in recognition of the struggle for
women's rights worldwide

Accept no ceilings ... glass is for breaking!

Table of Contents

Part I

The First Thread

Chapter 1
Black Sea, 1988

The southerly Black Sea winds created whitecaps that cascaded into increasingly larger waves and crashed with velocity into the surf. Naked, shivering, and still catching his breath, Matt Bollard grasped for the bottom near the shoreline before the next set of waves washed over him. Each succeeding wave pushed Bollard further ashore, yet he was able to attain just enough stability to see ahead.

The light of a small fire fifty meters in front of him cast the reflections of a young woman, her shadow moving rhythmically with the flames. Perhaps in her late twenties, she cast a pensive glance to the sea, then stared again into the embers. Sparks spiraled upward as she added another log to the fire which created a bright glow.

While the light provided fair vision ahead, it obstructed Bollard's view into the darkness as he peered intently down the shoreline. The situation was dangerous, and he could take no chances especially given that he arrived at the beach operationally sterile.

There was nothing to identify him or his place of origin. He wore no clothing, had no recorded identifying features, no noted scars, no tattoos, no ring, no watch, and even the fillings in his teeth were reworked to reflect the dentistry of the region.

Bollard pushed his way through the surf, stood up, and walked slowly toward the woman by the fire. What lay ahead was unprecedented and the outcome unpredictable.

Months of preparation brought Bollard to this Georgian Republic shore. Federal agencies and joint military planning teams pooled resources and talent to place a single operator on the coast of the Soviet Union. The insertion and his infiltration were thoroughly planned and rehearsed. The operation began with orders and an intense period of isolation at a U.S. Army Special Forces facility at Ft. Bragg, N.C.

Chapter 2
Ft. Bragg, N.C.
Pre-Deployment Orders

Major Matt Bollard opened the folder and carefully read the enclosed orders. Marked "Top Secret SCI" the orders were succinct and omitted more than they explained. He placed them back in the packet and handed them to Colonel Stevens, his Special Forces commander.

"It looks like some of our earlier concerns with the Islamic allies in Afghanistan are starting to get traction in Washington," Bollard said as the colonel grunted slightly and pushed the folder back into the safe.

The situation in Afghanistan was improving as Mujahideen anti-aircraft defenses were gradually reducing the Soviet air advantage and impacting ground operations. While western governments received the intelligence reports of those successes with satisfaction, they were concerned with other disturbing reports of unintended consequences. It seemed the Mujahideen's success might be devolving into Islamic radical aspirations around the world. After all, some reasoned if success could be achieved in Afghanistan, why not elsewhere, with or without the support of the West or worse, in direct opposition to the very countries who trained them and had supported their fight.

Many foreign fighters flocked to the Mujahideen, especially from the Middle East, and there were concerns some would leave Afghanistan to agitate on a global scale. There were indications this was already occurring in the Soviet Union. Interestingly, these activities were not in nearby Central Asia where the people were universally Muslim but much further away, in the Caucasus region.

The Soviet Republics of Chechnya, Dagestan, Ossetia, Georgia, Ingushetia, and Kabardino-Balkaria struggled for centuries for independence from the central power of Tsarist Russia as well as Soviet oppression. The Caucasus mountains provided a natural obstacle that sometimes gave a false sense of protection. Though the peoples of these mountains were often at odds, their one unifying force was opposition to Moscow's governance.

It was important for the West to learn the degree of the fundamentalist movement in the Caucasus and to identify and understand the role of a newly established revolutionary group, the Mountainous Republic of the Northern Caucasus (MRNC). Importantly, the West wanted to identify the origins and means of external Islamic support should it rear its head elsewhere in the world. In addition to its existing technical sources, the United States needed more reliable human intelligence; a person on the ground with experience in the Afghan fight, an understanding of the Islamic movement, knowledge of the Soviet Union, and expertise and instinct to get in and get out alive. Major Matt Bollard fit the requirement.

Bollard was a Special Forces officer whose field tradecraft and operational expertise were tested often. He spoke Russian and spent much of his career in hot spots around the world including Afghanistan where Soviet military forces, GRU, and KGB agents operated.

Colonel Stevens shook Bollard's hand. "They want to spin you up and get you in isolation right away. You'll be there for a couple of months, so make the necessary arrangements. This won't be an easy assignment."

"They never are."

Chapter 3
Isolation

The undisclosed and nondescript building served as one of the Special Forces isolation sites. Located behind two layers of fencing and armed guards, it seemed more like a prison than a classified preparation and pre-deployment site. To an outside observer, the only thing that might differentiate it from a prison was the orientation of the high fence and razor wire, oriented to keep people out. Even so, operational authorities prohibited anyone from leaving the facility and denied access to any potential visitor. Everyone inside the facility was locked down with no communication in or out, except for relevant and classified operational information, which amplified the sense of being caged.

The isolation facility included a fully functioning kitchen, physical training area, briefing and preparation rooms, showers, and bedding and was designed to accommodate as many as twenty operators. This operation required reduced staffing. Bollard the lone operator, Colonel Todd Jacobs the Isolation Chief, and four others responsible for preparing Bollard for the operation were the sole occupants.

Bollard and his team had been in isolation for forty days and all were focused on the single mission of getting one man into the Soviet Union. From the outset, the entire team began the acclimatization process. They conducted their daily activities and preparations in the time zone of the target country. The team members set their watches and ensured the clock in the briefing room was eight hours ahead. Their diet was exclusively the food of the country and region of deployment, delivered on a strict schedule. Every effort was made to replicate the environment and acclimatize to the area of operations, including daily language refresher training. Though Bollard would deploy alone, it was important to the mission that each supporting staff member undergo the same regional preparations; each person should experience similar physiological and psychological effects and stresses. This ensured that the team functioned at its peak at the same time and better prepared the operator for deployment.

Bollard spent hours studying maps of the region, immersing in the language, reading intelligence reports, regional updates, and battle preparation. The latter included physical training, hand-to-hand engagement, weapons refresher, and firing. While he prepared, the military organization and interagency worked to ensure his insertion was thoroughly planned and covert contacts were in place to assure a safe arrival to the area of operations.

After forty days, the entire team was getting restless, and Bollard was concerned. He still had not heard directly from people who had been on the ground.

Chapter 4
Mission Focus

Colonel Jacobs walked into Bollard's room with a quick knock on the open door. Bollard lay aside the most recent intelligence updates and stood up.

"What's up, Colonel?"

"Well, you're going to break isolation."

"Whoa! Outstanding!" Bollard replied, thinking he may have an opportunity for a final check-in with his wife.

"We want you to interview a representative of the Mountainous Republic of the Northern Caucasus from the target area. You'll have to go to D.C. to do it, then straight back."

"It's about time I got a chance to talk to someone from the MRNC. All the way to D.C.? No side trips?"

"No side trips. Actually, it's not D.C. but Springfield. Just south of D.C."

"Yeah, I've stopped there a few times to top off with fuel before going on to the Pentagon or Hoffman Building," Bollard replied.

"Ah yes, the Hoffman Building. Our best bureaucrats at work. Each is ready to help you with your next armpit assignment to Tim-fuk-tu. They have to make sure your career is progressing according to their plans, you've shaved the unregulated mustache, and haven't gained any weight, or at least your official picture doesn't show it." The Colonel pulled an exaggerated handful of flab at his belt line.

Bollard laughed, "I've met them all."

"Janet will accompany you," the colonel said referring to the CIA member of the isolation team. "You'll drive to the first exit after the Richmond toll booths, where she'll take over."

"A bit of chaperoning I suppose?"

"You know, the two-person rule. Well, a two-person rule for you anyway. She has business at her HQ while you're in the interview."

"Sure."

"While you two are out having fun, the rest of us will be here in our luxurious accommodations. But hey, don't worry about those of us still in isolation."

"You know what I'm thinking? The long lines of traffic at those damnable toll booths in Richmond. They're awful."

"Well, there's only one toll booth you need to be concerned with and it's all in the preparation report." Colonel Jacobs handed Bollard the folder. "Have fun," he said as he walked out.

***

"Not so bad," Bollard said as he looked at the lines of traffic lining up behind the I-95 Richmond toll booths. He looked at Janet who was napping fitfully, her head bobbing each time she drifted off.

"We're here?" she asked lifting her head slightly.

"No. Richmond. Just have to get in the correct toll line; last open one on the right."

Bollard pulled to the right and squeezed between two slow-moving tractor trailers. The trailing one expressed his consternation with a loud blast of an air horn. Janet bolted into an upright position.

Bollard laughed, "Guess you're awake now! Sorry about that!"

"Geez," Janet replied, looking to the rear and seeing only the truck's grill and headlights.

"Excellent. We're in a perfect cradle here. Limited visibility to the front and rear."

Bollard followed closely behind the lead truck and pulled up to the toll booth operator.

"I only have a Benjamin Franklin," Bollard said while waiting for the countersign.

The operator opened the cash register, lifted the internal container slightly, and retrieved a stack of bills. "Look again. I prefer Jacksons."

"Oh yes. You're correct. I have a Jackson," Bollard replied.

Bollard handed the operator a twenty-dollar bill and in exchange received a stack of one-dollar bills firmly affixed with a paper clip. He then continued through the toll booth and merged back into the I-95 traffic. He exited at the first off-ramp, checked for any following vehicles, then got back onto the I-95 access lane, pulling to the side of the road.

He leafed through the stack of dollar bills until he found a thin piece of soluble rice paper. He read it carefully, then handed the paper to Janet. "OK, memorize it. That's where we're going."

Janet committed the address to memory and handed the paper back to Bollard.

"Time for you to take over," he said as they walked around the car and exchanged places.

Bollard took a final look at the paper and offered it to Janet.

"No thanks, I'm good," she said and sped off.

Bollard placed the rice paper in his mouth, dissolved it, and swallowed.

Chapter 5
Safe House

Janet departed as soon as Bollard got out of the car. She would return in an hour. He looked at his watch. It was 1920 hours and he was exactly on time. He rang the doorbell. An older lady in her late sixties or early seventies pulled the door open widely and greeted him with a wide smile and a hug.

"Come in, come in," she said and nearly pulled him inside. "It's been so long," she continued loudly so anyone nearby could hear, and closed the door behind her.

He'd never met the woman before in his life. Gray shoulder-length hair, short and a bit plump, wearing a blue dress and an apron with large pockets, she placed her arm under his to direct him. Bollard looked around the room which resembled a country gift shop with southern-style decorations and gingham curtains. He lifted his head instinctively to the aroma of freshly baked bread coming from the kitchen.

As they walked through the house she stopped abruptly at a small doorway and a hall leading to another room. She pointed and indicated he should go into the room. It was an interior room with no windows and brightly lit with table lamps. Bookshelves loaded with old books lined each wall, but not a speck of dust anywhere, ostensibly a reading room with oversized chairs. He noted he left visible footprints on the deep plush carpet. No other tracks were present. A quick look above revealed a multi-layered popcorn ceiling. Interestingly, he didn't recall seeing a popcorn ceiling elsewhere as he walked through the house. There were so many layers plastered on the ceiling, that some areas seemed to bulge from the weight. The room was intentionally designed; its attributes comprised an area perfectly conceived and built for soundproofing and away from prying eyes.

Bollard perused some of the books and pulling a novel from the shelf sat down in one of the chairs. He stroked his fake beard slightly as he looked at the inside cover of the novel; a first edition.

At exactly 1940 hours the rear door, adjacent to the kitchen, opened and two men stepped inside and shuffled in Bollard's direction. He didn't hear the same greeting as he had received; no cheery "Come in" from someone's grandmother.

Bollard stood as they entered the reading room. One of the men was much older, short and rather thin, balding, with wire-rimmed glasses and an intelligent air about him, but otherwise unremarkable; someone you could pass every day on the street and never notice.

"An OSS type," Bollard accurately assessed referring to the U.S. Offices of Strategic Services, a wartime intelligence agency, and predecessor to the CIA. OSS-types easily blended in and gave no outward sign or physical appearance of being anything other than the common man and certainly not a Rambo type, but a bunch of "badasses" as Bollard had once called them.

The other man appeared to be in his mid to late forties. He was husky, a square build and square head with a beard that was more genuine than Bollard's. Nattily dressed in a suit with a perfect handkerchief, and a high shine on his shoes, made him more noticeable than Bollard or the escort would have liked. Most notably, he was under the escort of the smaller agent and wore a blindfold; a headband was pulled over his eyes.

The escort spoke first, "I see you like Melville."

"Moby Dick is my favorite," Bollard replied.

"What edition?"

"First edition."

Then the escort removed the headband from the larger man and pointed to one of the chairs. "Let's sit." He continued, "This is Lors. He's here to answer any of your questions about the MRNC."

Lors blinked in the bright lights as Bollard studied him carefully.

Bollard began, "Lors... that's an interesting name. I can't place the region of origin. Certainly, the Caucasus."

"Ingush," Lors replied while pulling himself up slightly from the deeply cushioned chair.

"What area of Ingushetia?"

"My family is from the Old Malgobek region."

"Well north?"

"Yes."

"Tell me about the Mountainous Republic of the North Caucasus, the MRNC," Bollard continued, referring to the reemergence of the MRNC whose history dated to 1917 and the Russian revolution.

Lors began with a well-practiced introduction, "The MRNC represents the unification of all the freedom-loving people of the Caucasus in our struggle for independence. Acting as MRNC representatives to the international community, we seek the recognition of the rest of the world and status as an acknowledged governmental organization. It's imperative that we have U.S. recognition. Our members cannot return to our homeland, but we can advocate for those who are there and their struggle."

"I have a lot of questions that will help us assess the legitimacy of the MRNC."

"I'm here to answer those questions. But certainly, there seems to be a lot of cloak and dagger for a simple meeting."

"You'd prefer the Hilton? Or perhaps somewhere closer to Wisconsin Avenue?" Bollard replied dryly referring to the location of the Soviet Embassy.

"That would hardly be necessary."

"Well, it was you who decided to take on the same name as the original MRNC. Do you recall how the original MRNC was organized and how it fell in 1921?"

"Yes. After the Tsar was overthrown, the Caucasus peoples organized the MRNC and were recognized around the world. They fought against the Whites."

"They even greeted the Reds as liberators," Bollard replied.

"But the Bolsheviks betrayed us," Lors replied with a snarl.

"Yes. Betrayal seems to be a common theme." There was a long pause, and Bollard continued, "You understand now, why we insist on cloak and dagger. It contributes to the longevity of everyone involved."

"Yes. Security is paramount."

"Let's continue. Do you see the MRNC as a government in exile? How are you organized?"

The man Bollard identified as former OSS leaned forward, listening intently. It was evident he was as interested in the answer as Bollard.

"We've identified and established all the figureheads of the elements of power. They're ready to assume those governmental positions when we achieve our freedom."

"So, a temporary government in exile?"

"Yes."

"Do you have buy-in from the other regions for those figureheads?"

"Yes. Conditioned on future elections."

Bollard was concerned with this answer. He understood that historically the divisions among the peoples of the Caucasus had outweighed their ability to agree on a united front for independence. Only two times had a leader unified the Caucasus for a common purpose. In the mid-1800s they unified under the leadership of the great Imam Shamil against Tsarist control. Again in 1917, they united under the MRNC. Neither was successful.

"Let me get this straight. The Chechens and Dagestanis are unified? The Georgians and Ossetians? What about the others?" Bollard said, expressing some skepticism.

"Yes. Yes. Others?"

"Ingushetia, Kabardino-Balkaria, the regions around Stavropol and Krasnodar."

"Yes, we're in one accord. And the fence-sitters will jump with our success."

Satisfied with the answer, Bollard asked, "What are your current regional activities?"

"We have a military arm, as do others who struggle for freedom. They provide local protection and when necessary, we conduct guerrilla operations to further our goals."

"Are those operations coordinated across the regions or is this authority granted to local decision making?"

"Mostly local decision making, unless they cross borders, or unless insufferable Soviet oppression occurs in a particular region."

"Tell me how they are organized," Bollard drilled in.

Lors paused momentarily.

Bollard stood and walked to the back of his chair, and then looked at the OSS man and restated the question as if directing it to him. "I'd like to know how your fighters are organized. It's essential information that will assist us in assessing the viability of your overall organization."

Bollard's explanation set Lors at ease. "Each region has its military operational cells who carry out direct armed action. They're supported by key elements within the population for movement and logistics. Other members work within the governmental system who conduct sabotage, intelligence, and other services."

"Tell me about the higher levels of leadership. How are they controlled?" Bollard asked as he returned to his seat.

"Guerrilla chiefs are responsible for coordination locally, determining targets, and identifying support needs."

"Are you organized around governmental boundaries?"

"Somewhat. But more so around ethnic and cultural affiliations that cross government boundaries. Each of the elements knows their areas of operational responsibility and don't cross over."

"How do the guerrilla chiefs, local support, and those in the system coordinate?"

"An Area Command controls the activities within specific regions. It's comprised of a leader and representatives from the various groups. For example, there is a Chechen Area Command, Ingush Area Command, same with others."

"Do the Area Commands report to the MRNC?"

"No. The next level is the Regional Command which is in charge overall. Same structure but with representatives from the Area Commands. It's the Regional Commander who reports to us and sometimes we report to him."

"Does the Regional Commander have the support of the Area Commands?"

"Very much so," Lors replied confidently.

Bollard was especially intrigued about anyone who could command the respect of Area Commands from all the diverse regions. "What can you tell me about him?"

"That's the one question I cannot answer; for his protection and that of his family."

"I see," Bollard replied. "For a political man, you seem to know a lot about this aspect of operations."

"I was a member of the Ingush Area Command. You can tell we adapted some of the American unconventional warfare doctrine, operations, and terminology. The guerrilla, auxiliary, and underground organizations comprise the main elements of the area commands."

"Are the roles the same?"

"I believe so. Guerrilla is a term we use for the entire group but organizationally responsible for direct action and operations, while the auxiliary supports through transport, logistics, intelligence, ratlines, and local action. The underground teams operate within established frameworks of industry, military, and government and are responsible for sabotage and intelligence."

"How did you learn this?"

"Passed along over time. Our own long history of resistance, your Viet Nam, Afghanistan, books, stories, and common sense. We pulled it all together."

"Interesting. I have some final and pertinent questions."

"Please."

"What foreign fighters are present?"

Lors looked away then back, a tell. "None," he replied with a nod instead of a shake of his head. Another tell.

"None? You have none? No foreign fighters? I suggest you answer that question carefully and accurately." Bollard's crossed arms were an indication that he wasn't buying the answer.

"There may be some. I've heard ... I've heard it said some arrived in the region."

"From which countries?" Bollard fired back.

Lors leaned back in his chair perceptibly with this line of questioning but said nothing.

Bollard changed tactics and placed both hands firmly on the arms of his chair. "You're third in the leadership succession within the MRNC, correct?"

"Yes."

"Didn't those above you give specific instructions to cooperate with whatever is needed or asked?"

"My instructions are clear."

There was a pause.

Bollard stood and walked to the shelves. He thumbed through a book absentmindedly. Then without turning he spoke in a low and calm voice. "Then why are you recalcitrant to their authority? Why can't you answer a basic question? We are not seeking your support. The MRNC is asking for our support. You understand any determination of obfuscation will be reflected in my report with a recommendation of non-concurrence?"

Bollard used official terminology to make his point.

"I'm not trying to be circumspect; simply pausing to consider what I've heard."

"Go on." Bollard returned to his seat.

"We've been approached by Middle East organizations through third parties who want to provide men, and if feasible, funds and equipment in our struggle."

"And?"

"We never turned it down. I can't confirm anything ever developed from it."

"Which Middle East countries?"

"Take your pick. All of them."

"Are these overtures from governmental organizations?"

"We think some may be from intelligence agencies. The majority are from actors not affiliated with their governments. Some may be fighters returning from Afghanistan. Others are zealots."

"Wahhabis for example," Bollard referred to a conservative wing of Islam found in Saudi Arabia.

"Yes. Some are radical, which is not sanctioned by their government, at least officially."

"Perhaps they've turned a blind eye," Bollard replied knowingly.

"Yes. But from the view of the MRNC, the 'enemy of my enemy' is indeed my friend."

"Is it your desire to set up a theocracy? Would the guerrilla chiefs support a theocracy?"

"We've promised elections. The people must choose. We won't be bound by religion within the MRNC or the Regional

23

Command. If there can be freedom within a theocracy, then some of the Area Commands might support it at their level, but certainly not those in Georgia or Ossetia."

"Do you have Central Asian support? Fighters? Funding?"

Lors now was more forthright in his response, "None that I'm aware of. The Central Asians have their hands full in Afghanistan. Either toeing the line for the Soviets or actively participating with local and individual support of the Afghan struggle."

"What are your next steps?"

"We are collaborating with different representatives and elements at the United Nations for counsel and advice. We must be very careful. We have bounties on our heads."

"Again, that's why you're here and not at the Hilton," Bollard replied. He then stood, indicating the meeting was over and they shook hands. "I wish you a safe stay and success."

"Thank you," Lors replied and turned to face his escort.

The escort repositioned the headband over Lors' eyes, and they shuffled out as they had arrived.

Bollard looked at his watch. He had to leave the safehouse exactly twenty minutes after their departure. Janet, observing from a nearby vantage point, would drive up exactly on time.

He walked to the bookshelf and replaced the first edition as he had found it. There was movement behind him, and he turned. It was the elderly woman.

***

"Sit, Sit," the woman said, gesturing with a tray of freshly baked bread, a dollop of apple butter, and tea for two.

Bollard returned to his chair and sat down. As she placed the tray on the coffee table, he noticed makeup on the sleeve of her blouse. He looked more closely. Portions of a faded tattoo were barely visible on her forearm where the makeup had rubbed away. He looked up at her.

"No questions. In due time," she said as if anticipating he might have several.

He watched as she sat down opposite him. Her mild demeanor belied her past. She was a survivor.

The lady took a bite of the bread, nodded to herself approvingly, then stirred the tea gently. Without looking up, she began.

"It's important to know the finest details of this region," she began, referring to the Caucasus. "It's very complicated with great diversities, histories, and origins."

"Do you have experience there?" Bollard asked and quickly looked at his watch. Janet would be there soon.

The woman smiled. "Your pickup will be here an hour later than planned. I'll see that you're on time."

"Thank you," Bollard replied. "You're familiar with the Caucasus?"

"Others in higher positions felt I should spend an hour with you. Provide you with some history and discuss the religions of the region and other factors you might consider."

"The man who just left seems to think despite the complexities, they are united. What do you think?" he asked.

"They are united until they are not. Today, yes. But tomorrow, who knows?"

"What is your association with the region?"

"I was born in the Caucasus mountains of Kabardino-Balkaria. So, to answer your question, yes, I know the region."

"I'm surprised. I'm aware there are different ethnic groups but thought most were Muslim. I wasn't aware of a Jewish population," Bollard said, searching for more information about the lady, who still had not identified herself.

"It's difficult to miss, isn't it," she replied holding up her arm, applying a little saliva, and revealing the tattoo. "I was a member of the Gorsky Jewish population."

"Mountain Jews?" Bollard translated.

"Yes, Mountain Jews. Historically, many settled well in the mountains in remote regions and far from potential threats. We established ourselves principally in the eastern and northern Caucasus, perhaps a lost tribe. Our history shows some of our roots are from the Persian empire well after the defeat of the Babylonians. Others came out of Assyria and settled in the Georgian regions."

"A dangerous proposition, given the circumstance of other religious groupings?" Bollard questioned.

"There is always potential danger for Jews. But the Mountain Jews integrated well and formed a regional *teip*."

"A teip?" Bollard asked, genuinely stumped.

"It doesn't translate well. More like a tribal or clan organizational structure. They represent their people among the other teips, regardless of religious affiliation. Set rules, expectations, et cetera."

"The teips are part of a governing system?"

"Yes, you could say that, but more a code of conduct, behavior, and expectations. It's part of the *Adyghe Habze*, the traditional code of behavior. It includes ad hoc councils and courts. Each teip is focused on such things as honor, compassion, and assistance. You know, never surrendering a guest or someone seeking sanctuary. The Soviets tried ridding the region of the practice but couldn't."

"If I might ask, where were you sent during the war?"

"Bogdanovka and Domanevka," she replied quietly, looking in the distance.

Bollard paused a moment, then continued, "That's quite a distance to the east and few survivors."

"Many Mountain Jews escaped or never felt the sting of Nazi occupation because of their remote villages. But the Nazis occupied Kabardino-Balkaria and those remaining were stuck."

"Started the roundups?"

"Initially. Berlin had original plans of giving the regions their autonomy. They didn't understand the region or the people. We and the other teips, including the Islamic teips as part of their perceived Adyghe Habze responsibilities, spread the word the region was comprised of diverse populations with a variety of religions. The leadership of the teips insisted that the Jewish population was native to the region and merely practiced elements of the Jewish religion but were not Jews by descent, not ethnic Jews. It was a good cover story."

"Adyghe Habze," Bollard repeated.

"Or just Habze."

"And how long did the ruse last?"

"In the early days of the German invasion, Habze didn't help me or others. They arrested and deported me right after the invasion. But ultimately the ruse worked for many. In typical Nazi fashion, they began a racial investigation to determine the genealogy of the population, but too late. The Soviets forced them out before they could ascertain the truth. Many of those who the Nazis sent to concentration camps and survived, returned to their original enclaves. So, there are still wartime survivors."

"So, the Soviets liberated the region from the Nazis, but didn't Stalin send nearly the entire regional population to Siberia, after their so-called liberation?" Bollard asked.

"The Soviets didn't exile my people as a group. However, Stalin exiled the other teips and the surrounding populations. He was suspicious that they had collaborated. They had not, but it didn't matter. As Jews, we certainly didn't and couldn't be perceived as having collaborated. There was never a consideration we would collaborate with the Nazi forces and therefore weren't exiled. Many returned from the war to their separate enclaves."

"Do those enclaves still exist?" Bollard was surprised.

"Yes, and they are distinct. The Mountain Jews of Chechnya are distinct from those of Kabardino-Balkaria regions, who are distinct from the Georgian and the Azeri Mountain Jews."

"Azerbaijan?"

"Yes. There as well. The nature of being in remote enclaves evolved over a long time and resulted in variances in the Jewish enclaves, including local language, and even religious practices.

"Do you know where those enclaves are today?" Bollard asked.

"I anticipated your request," she replied as she pulled a folded map from her apron and handed it to him. "I believe this is accurate. It doesn't include all of the enclaves, but certainly, some might be useful."

"Thank you," Bollard replied and placed the map in his breast pocket without looking at it. He continued, "And you? How were you liberated?"

"I survived Bogdanovka, and the Nazis sent me to Domanevka where I escaped as the Soviet military approached. The Romanian and Ukrainian populations obviously could not

27

be trusted. But they were more terrified of the approaching Russians than the ramifications of helping rather than killing a weak Jewish girl, who might vouch for them. I used their fear to my benefit on a couple of occasions. I was malnourished and weak but made my way to the Soviet lines. I rationalized that if I tried to return to my home, I would either starve or possibly be shot by the NKVD, the Soviet People's Commissariat for Internal Affairs. Instead, I joined the military and served in a communications unit, for 'a meal and a cot'. Isn't that what you soldiers say?"

Bollard smiled. She had seen through his civilian attire and fake beard.

There was a pause and the woman continued, "The Germans captured me, but I was able to conceal my identity. There were so many thousands captured, but I slipped through. I was one of the few survivors who the Allies liberated and I wasn't forced to return to the Soviet Union. My Jewish background was what saved me. Just as being a Jew saved our people from deportation after the Soviet liberation of Kabardino-Balkaria."

"Quite a turnaround, given what was occurring to your people throughout Europe!" Bollard commented.

"I guess the point of all of this is that there are immense complexities. It was Muslim and other regional teips who contributed to a great ruse that saved so many Jews. They came together, despite what others unfamiliar with the region might think. Watch for those types of alliances. They can be beneficial."

"Who could have foreseen any of it?" Bollard wondered aloud.

"Indeed." She looked at her watch. "Come, I'll walk you to the door."

As they walked through the hall and toward the main entrance, Bollard noticed a suitcase just out of full view. He hadn't seen it when he arrived. As he opened the door, Janet pulled up. The elderly lady stood back from the doorway and smiled, then shut the door as quickly as Bollard was clear of it.

Bollard was curious about something. As he sat down in the car, and they drove away he got his answer. He saw a black sedan and its driver parked at the side of the house with the parking lights on.

Bollard smiled knowingly - she didn't live there and most likely was on her way to the next safehouse. Perhaps plans for another batch of homemade bread.

Chapter 6
Molly

Bollard's return to Ft. Bragg seemed to take an eternity. Heavy traffic and the nagging realization he would drive within a few miles of his wife and children without a visit darkened his mood. There could be no contact. He knew it. He understood it. He didn't like it. But strict procedures were necessary.

Bollard's final days at home weren't the best of departures. Bollard's wife Molly met his announcement of a pending mission and departure with the reception of a root canal. She was a solid and stable Army wife but constant deployments of long duration with no contact weren't part of the original bargain. She had been supportive most of the time, but each mission resulted in increasing difficulties at home.

"What do you mean you have to be away? How long?" she asked, crossing her arms defiantly.

"Not sure, but it will be several months," Bollard said carefully looking at her every facial feature for a sign everything would be all right. He didn't get it. Molly's frown grew darker.

"You know what pisses me off? All of it! You'll go into isolation for some time, only God knows. You're only a few minutes away. All the wives know it."

Bollard raised an eyebrow.

She saw it. "You think we're stupid? Of course, we know you're nearby. But we can't see you or talk to you. It's nonsense!"

"You know we can't take a chance something will slip out. Even if you saw the time on my watch, you could narrow down the time zone where we're operating. Nothing can slip."

"Give me a break. You speak Russian for God's sake."

Her logic was impeccable, but there could be no debate. Bollard simply shook his head.

"You haven't been home long enough to catch up with the kids, let alone our parents. And now you're leaving again! If you haven't noticed, we have two children, and they need both of us!"

"I know it's difficult. We could call your ..."

"Don't even go there! We're not calling anyone. You're the boss, why do you have to go?"

"Because I am the boss is why it has to be me," Bollard replied. What he didn't state was, given the nature and sensitivity of the operation, he couldn't pass this mission on to anyone else.

They jockeyed back and forth until Molly hit the 'nuclear button' – "I'm pregnant."

"Huh?"

"You heard me. I'm pregnant."

"How did this happen?"

"What the heck does that mean?"

"But we weren't trying."

"It happens, Sherlock, and it did happen! I just found out and I'm not far along – two months. I was saving the perfect time to tell you. This wasn't the way I wanted to give you the news."

They sat silently for several minutes. Bollard scratched his head, "Okay, we have to get support from either your family, mine, or both. We don't have to do this alone."

"You mean me alone." Molly's tone diminished, and she seemed more sullen than in previous times. "Again."

"We have time. Let's work through it."

"Yes, we'll work through it, or I'll work through it."

Several days passed as plans and backup plans were set. It wasn't easy, but each plan had to account for every contingency. Family support was never a necessity for Molly or most military spouses. Absence was simply part of the job, but having family nearby made separations more tolerable. Molly would accept any assistance offered. Coordination with family members to determine willingness to support them; travel plans, vacations, outings – it all had to be readjusted as calendars were marked and remarked.

Just before Bollard's departure, Molly announced, "Matt, if we have a girl, I want to name her 'Nora'."

"That's my mom's name."

"I thought it would be nice to name her after your mother. And if we have a boy, I want to call him 'Finnigan'. My grandmother was a Finnigan."

"I like 'Riley'. Let's call him 'Riley'."

"You want Riley, I want Finnigan. Whoever is here for the birth will name him. So, if you want 'Riley' you better make sure you're here."

Bollard simply shook his head and hugged her.

The discussion quickly ended with no resolution, other than Molly's ultimatum. Bollard knew this wasn't a point to push any further.

Their remaining time together was not a scene of fireworks and marching bands but of tense apprehension. Both knew this would be their most difficult challenge. Neither could anticipate the amount of separation this mission would require.

Chapter 7
Exfiltration, Infiltration Planning

As Bollard and Janet walked inside the isolation facility, a young security guard directed them to the briefing room. It was a long, dark, and narrow chamber. An equally long and narrow table with twelve chairs took up most of the space. Yet someone thought it was a good idea to squeeze additional chairs around the edges of the room so that once occupied and seated, an individual was a veritable captive for the remaining time of the briefing.

The team had been in the room for over an hour. Bollard, two special forces officers, an intelligence officer, Janet, and Master Chief Kevin Dixon, a Navy SEAL, sat huddled around the front of the table and focused on the slide screen. The briefer began with the overall exfiltration and extraction plan.

"This is bullshit!" Bollard said suddenly, his eyes fixed on the lone briefer who took a step back from the podium.

"What do you mean, Matt?" Colonel Jacobs asked as he sifted through a stack of overhead slides and supporting intelligence documents.

Bollard particularly didn't like the briefer's wide-ranging hand motions across a much too generic map covering too great an area for any real analysis.

"What do I mean? I mean, who came up with this bullshit extraction plan?"

"It has the best chance of success," a voice replied from among the team.

"Seriously? Do you know how many Georgians have been caught trying to escape through the Black Sea? The huge waves, storms, and prevailing southerly winds keep them within a kilometer of the shore. It's called the Black Sea because of its demeanor. Huge unanticipated storms push in from the south constantly. Unless you have a power boat that can outrun the border patrol and survive the sea, better come up with another exfiltration plan."

The room was silent. Finally, Colonel Jacobs responded, "Okay, Matt. You win. You have to be comfortable with the plan."

"Thanks, Boss," Bollard responded.

Jacobs turned to the others who responded with huge sighs, "Start working on another exfiltration plan."

The exfiltration plan was severely flawed, and Bollard reacted directly to the team and pulled no punches. He turned his attention to the insertion and infiltration planning. "When am I getting the full briefing on the insertion planning? We seem to be further along on the exfil planning than getting into the country!"

"We're still working on the details. We must be sure. But soon," Janet replied.

Bollard agreed, "Yes, we have to be sure."

***

While Bollard sent the team back to readdressing the exfiltration, they finalized the details of the insertion and infiltration. Interagency coordination leading up to the insertion briefing had been thorough and detailed, but Bollard didn't want ill-fated planning to compromise him or the operation. He wanted details.

"Look, guys, I don't want a briefing on the insertion and infiltration plan. I want a discussion." He looked at the briefer, "Bob, you can sit, or you can stand up there and flip slides, but we're going to talk about it first."

Major Bob Townsend smiled and sat down next to the overhead projector, "How about I sit here and be ready with the slides if you need them."

Colonel Jacobs began, "Okay, Matt. Let's discuss the big picture, and then we'll get into the details. The infiltration includes an insertion plan in coordination with the Navy and CIA. You will covertly disembark from a specially outfitted Turkish merchant ship, aboard a Navy submersible with a two-man crew and make your way to a point two kilometers off the Georgian coast." He motioned to Major Townsend, "Bob, pull up the slide of the debarkation point."

Townsend slipped the slide onto the screen and Jacobs continued, "You'll disembark from the submersible at this point and swim to shore to link up with our agents."

Bollard squirmed in his chair and with a frown interrupted, "With all of the thousands of kilometers of potential land entry points, I'm supposed to do a SEAL insertion?" He turned to the CIA officer, "Seriously Janet, this is the best your folks could come up with?"

Janet Jennell had been with the CIA for fifteen years and these were the times she dreaded most, an irate operator drilling in on the details of a low 'probability of success' operation.

"Matt, we've been working hand in hand with DoD for some time to pull this together. You know it's difficult. You're aware we have problems at Headquarters, that security leaks and compromises have occurred."

"Believe me, I've encountered some of the results of those compromises as well as the workarounds."

"We're doing our best to mitigate any risk by avoiding any standardized planning."

Bollard shook his head. "Disembarking a Turkish merchant ship, or trawler, or whatever it is, climbing aboard a submersible, traveling several kilometers to a 'get off' point, and then swimming two kilometers! Hell, let's call it what it is, high risk! Come on, swimming that far in the Black Sea to the Georgian coast to a hoped-for linkup does not sound like risk mitigation."

Janet looked at Colonel Jacobs for an assist, but none was forthcoming.

Bollard continued, "And this is simply the means of delivery to the area of operation. The delivery looks as difficult as the mission itself." He stood and pointed to the submersible drop-off point, "Why two kilometers from the shore?"

Chief Dixon replied, "The submersible operator has a timeline to return to meet with a follow-up trawler and the submersible is at its extended range. I'm afraid a klick and a half might be as close as we can get you to the target given the operational timelines."

Bollard looked pointedly at each of the team members, "This is why we have a 'discussion' and not a 'briefing'. I'm not committing to anything until we've discussed other options. First, cut the drop-off point from shore in half. If there is any offshore breeze, I'd never make it." Bollard looked at the Master Chief, "Come on Kevin, get with your guys and figure it out. Factor in a swim of a thousand meters or less, but no more."

Chief Dixon agreed, "Okay, one klick." He then turned his attention back to the map.

Bollard continued, "Even with a perfect swim to shore, the Black Sea entry has got to be the least optimum insertion."

"What are your thoughts, Matt?" Colonel Jacobs asked.

"Keep it simple. Insert somewhere along the Turkish and Armenian border."

"Normally, that would be the best choice," Janet said. "But the Armenians are a bigger threat to an insertion than the border guards. Still a lot of hatred there. Anything or anyone crossing the border from Turkey into Armenia, whether legit or not, gets immediate and negative attention from the locals and even the outlaws not to mention the border security."

Bollard concurred, "The Armenians will never forget what the Turks did to them during World War I."

Janet shook her head, "It wasn't just World War I and it wasn't battle losses. Losing one and a half million of your population to genocide sticks in a country's craw. No love there for anyone crossing the Turkish border. Regardless, it's out of the question to infiltrate along that border. Generally, Soviet border guards focus on keeping the population inside their borders, but here they focus equally on watching the Turks. We've just been unsuccessful in getting any kind of a ratline together."

"Ok, if not there, then the Georgian border is logical," Bollard continued. "The Georgians have huge black market rings and I'm confident they have their ways to get goods in and out of Turkey." He rose and walked to the map and pointed to a small black dot on the Georgian–Turkish border.

"Adjar?" Janet questioned.

"Yes! The entire region of Adjar is almost like an independent country. They've switched sides so many times from the Ottomans, the Brits, the Georgians, and the Russians they can only be governed as an autonomous republic. The town of Sarpi seems to be a perfect spot. Most in Sarpi aren't even Georgians! They're a Georgian subgroup, the Laz. We should be able to cross there. Surely, you have some teams who are active in that area?"

Janet pursed her lips and shook her head, "The KGB infiltrated nearly every black market ring and cell. The KGB organizes many of the rings and creates multiple compartmented cells. Their cells are like honey pots to draw the local rebellious 'bees'. They operate much like a business and the KGB operatives make and pocket a lot of the money. When they draw too much attention or see any activity that threatens their business activities, they simply roll up a cell or two to satisfy Moscow. They'll arrest or eliminate the cell members and start anew, back in business. Again, infiltration here is too risky."

"Incredible the Georgians aren't sophisticated enough to smell out a KGB operator! I expected more from them."

"There are a lot of Muslims as well as non-Muslims in the region, and the KGB is adept at taking advantage of old animosities. Like most in these regions, greed is the common denominator for all. Both sides weigh the risk but are blinded by the potential for big money."

Bollard thought for a moment, and finally, as if in a moment of desperation, "No chance of a HAHO?"

"Again, no one is on the ground to receive a high altitude high opening insertion. The insertion we've planned, by way of the Black Sea, has the greatest chance of success if you make the linkup. We trust the linkup cells on the ground and they're effective. Importantly, we've been able to compartmentalize them from our headquarters to ensure no compromise."

"Heck of a thing when you have to compartmentalize from your leadership," Jacobs snorted.

Bollard shook his head, "Making the linkup is a ball buster. I've done submarine lock-ins and lock-outs, but a submersible is a new horse for me."

"We've got a thorough crash course for you. You'll be an expert before you go in," Chief Dixon replied.

"Well, what do you think, Matt?" the Colonel asked.

"If the SEALS can get me close enough to compensate for any unexpected offshore winds, we could make a linkup. I presume the linkup and infiltration to the area of operations is firmed up?"

"Are you ready to hear the details of the infiltration planning?" the Colonel said sensing Bollard had heard enough of insertion options.

"Let's proceed," Bollard replied.

Janet chimed in, "We're solid. With the current planning, and a successful insertion and linkup, the folks on the ground will drop you into their ratline. You should be in the target area within thirty days. If you gather the information within a thirty-to-sixty-day evaluation period and a thirty-day window for exfiltration, we'll extract you in time for Christmas."

Janet paused, but Bollard said nothing. She then handed him a stack of folders. "These are the details of the infiltration. They also contain four exfiltration plans in order of priority. You need to know each thoroughly so we can direct you to the best option at the time of exfil."

Janet's brief description was simplistic and accounted for no mistakes. Bollard understood the dangerous complexities of linkups, cells, and ratlines. The Soviets historically were experts at compromising them. They even went so far as to establish ratlines to draw in and capture high-level operators.

"Have you established my bona fides? Has that information been forwarded and understood? How will they know I'm not a mole in their ratline?" Bollard asked.

"Your information and vitals have already been messaged to the guerrillas' Regional Command."

"Looks like everything is in place," Bollard responded.

"It is," the Colonel replied. "You've got to wrap up training and preparations. Black Sea insertion actions are already underway."

Chapter 8
The *Faik Ali*
Insertion

Captain Karakas, captain of the *Faik Ali*, peered intently at the radar and then back to the specially designed sonar screen as his course rapidly closed the distance to a much larger two-hundred-and-fifty meter, six-decker cargo ship to his port bow and northeast.

Still focused on the screens he sneaked a look forward hoping to catch a glimpse of the huge ship. Nothing. Darkness. The night sky and sea merged the horizon into a single black mass with only an occasional interruption of a splashing whitecap, churned in the wake of the other ship. He quickly turned his attention back to the screens and followed the ship's west to east track.

Seeing his captain's intense focus, the navigator marked their exact position, speed, and time and shouted, "We'll overtake them within fifteen minutes at the prearranged time and location."

The captain was experienced, and though he could tell by the indicators on the screens that everything was going according to plan, the navigator's confirmation was reassuring. He flipped a switch to extinguish all the lights on the ship except the red port and green starboard lights at the bow that marked the limits of the ship's beam.

The Faik Ali was built in 1978 under the scrutiny of the CIA and U.S. special operations experts. Having unique specifications, she underwent several years of cloaked construction. At her launching, she was named the Faik Ali and flagged as a Turkish container ship. The ship's name, an unlikely name for a Turkish ship, implied this ship might be more than a standard cargo ship. Named for a Turkish hero who saved the lives of thousands of Armenians from the Turkish genocide of WWI, the name Faik Ali reflected the regional, cultural, and political strife of the countries and republics around and near the Black Sea.

Measuring a little over two hundred meters in length, it carried less than its full capacity of four containers stacked above deck, three below, and ten containers wide. Its silhouette looked the same as other second-generation container ships plowing the Mediterranean, Aegean, and Black Seas. An up-close examination and inspection of the interior of the Faik Ali revealed major modifications including enhanced engineering and stern alterations, increased engine power, and extended operating ranges. The modifications supported the ship's primary mission, which was not the transport of cargo containers. At the stern and in the lowest compartment of the ship, actions to support its primary mission were underway.

Near the waterline of the ship, a support crew hurried about their duties, flipping on several huge red lights which cast a dull hue across a very specialized cargo and the faces of its operational team.

Bollard and two Navy Seals were bending and stretching and adjusting their gear. As the red lights came on, the team sprang into action. Making final adjustments to their wet suits they climbed aboard their SEAL Delivery Vehicle (SDV), a Mark VIII SDV, and positioned themselves for a long, cold, and dangerous ride. Each man adjusted his seat harness, hooked his regulator hose to the inboard air supply, and confirmed earlier checks that the air system and SDV were fully functional and operational.

The SEAL SDV team of two would transport and deliver a single passenger who was on a one-way trip. To succeed, they must push themselves and the SDV to their limits. While they planned for a six to eight-hour operation, they were fully prepared to remain submerged for as long as twelve hours.

The Mark VIII SDV was a behemoth at nearly seven meters in length. She was centered in the open cargo area at the ship's stern; the staging area for the SDV's cast and recovery operations. With a top speed of six knots, an operating depth of six meters, and with only one passenger instead of the normal passenger capacity of four, the SDV's range extended to thirty-six nautical miles; more than sufficient for this mission.

Using the SDV's Doppler Inertial Navigation System (DINS), the team's mission was to navigate precisely for fifteen nautical miles, cross an international border, maintain depth to avoid patrol boats, and still manage crew dive tables while dropping off their passenger at an exact location. Using their rendezvous and docking system (RDS), they would return before daylight when a westbound cargo ship, identical to the Faik Ali, would recover them. Failure was not an option, but contingency plans were in place if the unimaginable did occur.

If the cargo ship failed in its extraction of the crew, a helicopter backup was in place purely as a rescue plan for the two-man team. They would scuttle and sink the SDV. As for Bollard, there was no backup plan. Once released, he was on his own.

On the bridge, the captain directed the helmsman to bring the cargo ship closer to the starboard side of the larger ship. Their approach was much closer than normal when overtaking another ship and in the intense darkness much more dangerous. Though the night watch of the larger ship noticed the Faik Ali overtaking them, there was nothing yet to necessitate an alarm. The debate to awaken their captain resulted in a shrug and a wave of the hand at the helm, despite standard operating instructions to advise him of nearby contacts. The Faik Ali crew counted on their inattentiveness and indifference.

Once the Faik Ali was parallel and slightly forward of the larger ship's stern, the captain ordered the helmsman to drop speed to match that of the other ship. This maneuver allowed the captain to mask his ship's silhouette and limit observation of his ship from the north.

***

In the darkness of the Black Sea, Captain Karakas remained glued to the sonar and radar screens while responding to the operational preparations of his passengers at the stern of the Faik Ali. Matching the speed of the adjacent container ship Captain Karakas signaled the Executive Officer with a thumbs up. The Executive Officer turned from the large array of video monitors of the stern and flipped a switch to alert the operational support crew.

The crew stood by as two clam shell doors at the stern of the Faik Ali opened slowly with a low audible hum of the hydraulics, revealing the dark sea and the wake of the ship. As the doors opened, a ramp extended slowly down and into the water. A cograil ran from the center of the staging area down the middle of the ramp to support the casting and recovery of the SDV. Once the SEAL team gave the 'all ready' the operational support crew signaled the ship's captain. Captain Karakas immediately dropped the speed to three knots to ensure the smooth entry of the SDV into the wash of the ship's propellers.

Once satisfied it was safe for entry, the support crew initiated the cograil which carried the SDV to the water's edge. As the SEAL team released the latches securing the SDV, they slipped silently beneath the surface as the dark waters washed over the crew. They glided to a depth of three meters behind the ship and turned the SDV due north to cross under the wake of the other container ship. The entire operation took barely four minutes to complete. Only a well-prepared and pre-warned adversary would note that a special operations team had just deployed.

As the SDV dropped to operational depth, the cool chill of the Black Sea swept over the team but was instinctively ignored. Each member settled into his respective position. The two Navy SEALs, one working as an operator and the other a navigator, put all their training, skills, and professionalism to the test.

Bollard was along for the ride; his test would come at the delivery point. He slouched down into his harness and shut his eyes. Despite being in full SCUBA gear he drifted off into a restful sleep, the final opportunity for rest before the linkup.

***

The SDV moved on a direct track northeast, silently. The darkness of the sea was eerie and broken only by the sea's luminescent plants which stirred with the passing of a large fish. The team, operating an open breathing circuit, emitted a large bubble path that reflected the ambient light of the stars and night sky. A keen eye on the surface could readily mark the direction and speed of the SDV by the shimmering trail of bubbles as they floated to the surface from the SDV and crew's open loop/circuit breathing system. At the ready, and in response to any passing ship or patrol boat, the team was prepared to activate the Mark 15 closed loop/circuit mixed gas breather.

The Mark 15, known to some operators simply as the 'rebreather,' circulated mixed gas in a loop and produced no bubbles to give away the location of an operator. Its carbon dioxide scrubbers represented a significant evolution over the Emerson and German Draeger pure oxygen systems. Given the life and effective duration of the carbon dioxide scrubbers, the Mark 15 range was limited to a few hours of operation. As a result, the SDV team waited until the final approach to the target release point to activate the system.

As they passed into Soviet territorial waters the SDV team leader announced in Russian, "*Iskra,*" the code word for "switch circuits." While the internal communications were felt to be secure, there would be no English spoken during this operation.

Bollard rose slightly in his harness as simultaneously, in a well-rehearsed movement, the team switched an onboard lever from the vertical to horizontal position initiating the advanced Mark 15. With no telltale sign of bubbles, the SDV plowed ahead imperceptibly.

Three hours after being cast from the container ship, the SDV's DINS navigation system indicated the team arrived at their release point a kilometer off the Soviet Union's Georgian coast. The southerly winds had increased earlier and now the waves were increasingly choppy. Too dangerous to surface, the SEAL team tried to hold the SDV at neutral buoyancy at three meters below the surface, moving as little as possible.

The navigator announced quietly "*Krasnii,*" the team's codeword for "drop point."

Bollard shifted from his passenger compartment and began a difficult aspect of the deployment that he had rehearsed numerous times – getting out of the wet suit while staying tethered to the regulator hose and SDV. Throughout the journey and between naps, he flexed, stretched, and did isometrics to manage the final stage of the delivery. Even with those exercises and the preparations, Bollard found the slight movement of the SDV along with the tightness of the wet suit made it nearly impossible to remove the suit.

He struggled but was getting nowhere. Instinctively he pulled his dive knife from the sheath on his calf and inserted it deftly at the neck of the suit. Cutting like a surgeon's incision he sliced the suit down to the groin and then cut away both legs. The cut released the pressure of the suit, and he pulled the remaining pieces off and placed them in a black bag. He tied everything securely to the passenger harness. Taking a breath of air and maintaining a long line tether, Bollard swam to the surface and oriented toward the northeast and the shore.

There was a flicker of light. Another flicker as he bounced in the waves. There again, the flicker! He could see his signal, the splatter of light from a small fire. He returned to the SDV, stowed the tether quickly, then tapped the SEAL navigator twice, indicating they had arrived at the exact point of the release.

Returning to the surface, Bollard took a final look down at the SDV. It loomed like a large fish turning slowly on a new heading to its recovery point. The SEAL Team completed their delivery perfectly and would soon be on a westbound Black Sea container ship.

Bollard was now alone. The success of the last phase of the insertion as well as his fate hung solely on a distant spark of light and those who awaited him on the Georgian shore.

Chapter 9
Contact

A red Russian Lada pulled up to a wide spot in the road on the hill just above the shore. A lady and man exited the vehicle and walked within a hundred meters of the water's edge. After removing gravel and rock and creating a circular hole in the ground, they piled some twigs, sticks, and logs in the center and started a small fire. The man walked several times to the edge of a forest and returned with enough logs to keep the fire burning for at least three hours. Careful to check for peering eyes, he stacked a pile of clothes, some jewelry, and a pair of shoes at the edge of the fire. Then leaving the woman alone, he walked back to the top of the hill where another car stopped briefly, picked him up, and sped away. The woman watched the car's lights disappear, stoked the fire, and looked pensively toward the sea.

***

Bollard treaded water and assessed the prevailing current and the position of the campfire to determine the best approach to the shore. With the southerly winds and the waves pushing him due north and directly ashore, he swam toward the firelight with only minor adjustments. Forty-five minutes later the surf washed over Bollard as he scraped the bottom. He stopped and held his position in the surf directly in front of the campfire.

Lying in the cover of the surf Bollard watched as a young woman was tending the small fire. He looked up and down the shoreline for any threat but saw nothing. After catching his breath, he emerged from the water naked and walked directly toward the woman and the fire.

His coordinated approach was simply to walk to the edge of the fire and begin putting on the clothes piled in a heap. Though there was a fully developed cover story there was no sign or counter sign for this linkup. No one would come naked out of the Black Sea except the American operative. Only the

45

linkup, a lone woman with a fire, would be at this point on the shoreline.

Saying nothing, Bollard did not walk to the pile of clothing as planned but walked directly to the woman. He embraced her, kissed her passionately, and lay her gently on the ground. She said nothing.

Bollard rolled on top of her and pressed his nude body closely. Speaking Russian in a well-practiced Georgian accent he whispered in her ear, "Slap me. Get angry!"

She slapped Bollard and pushed him off screaming, "Asshole! You think you can take a long swim in darkness, worry me to death, and then want sex! Not tonight!"

The linkup location was seldom patrolled. But tonight, two young border guards had wandered away from their normal route and were making their patrol less boring by drinking a half bottle of vodka. They had seen the fire and watched Bollard walking naked from the water. At the edge of the reflection of the light of the fire, one guard elbowed the other and pointed to Bollard. They figured their evening was about to get a lot more interesting.

It was the border guards' movement at the edge of the light that attracted Bollard's attention. Bollard had to alert the agent by the fire. His only course of action was to approach her directly.

After being slapped and scolded Bollard arose and walked to the other side of the fire and began to put on the ring, watch, and perfectly fitting clothes from the pile. The two border guards approached laughing.

"No luck tonight, huh?" one of the guards smirked.

Bollard shrugged but said nothing and began putting on his shoes.

The woman replied, "He may never get lucky again! He's been swimming for an hour in the dark and he scared me to death."

"You probably shouldn't be here," one of the guards replied, unsure of his location.

"Oh, we're leaving all right. I'm fed up with this one," she shouted.

"Do you have papers?"

"Sure," Bollard replied. "I could use a drink," he continued, pointing to the half-empty bottle.

The border guard handed him the bottle. Bollard took a drink and handed it to the other border guard. They passed the bottle around the group a couple of times and the border guards forgot they had not looked at the papers, though they were in order.

Finishing the bottle, Bollard kicked some rocks on the fire, and he and the lady shook hands with the guards who staggered back in the direction they had arrived.

Walking up the hill to the car, the lady said nothing until she sat down behind the steering wheel. "It's nice to meet you, Tamaz," she said referring to his codename. "That was well done on the beach."

"It's nice to meet you too, Alyena. You played your role well. I suppose we'll be husband and wife until the drop-off. How long do you think it'll take to get there?"

"It's only an hour's drive. You should rest. It will be a long night."

"I will," Bollard replied, never mentioning his concern that only the extremely wealthy or Communist Party members would have a car such as this.

Chapter 10
Handoff

The Turkish freighter, the SDV, and the long swim to shore might have been the easy part of the insertion. The infiltration into the area of operations would be more difficult. Bollard and his young contact sped along the Georgian coast then turned sharply northeast and into the mountains. He forced himself to sleep. After an hour Alyena awakened him with a tug on his arm. He sat up in the seat alert as she handed him a black cloth bag.

She gave clear directions and pointed to his hand, "Give me the ring, you won't need it. You can keep the watch. Put the bag over your head. We're almost there."

He pulled the bag over his head as Alyena turned off the main road and onto a dirt road. After a few hundred meters she stopped the car and turned off the lights.

Bollard could hear another vehicle, a truck, moving slowly, and stopping adjacent to the car. He then heard the low murmurs of several men.

In this country and given the operational environment, detailed planning was paramount. Another party, unknown to most and in support of the auxiliary forces, established the ratlines to ensure each clandestine cell was independent of the other. Even the slightest screwup could compromise the cell and its operations. The ratline was the only secure means to covertly move personnel or products through the region. Each linkup and each of the handoff procedures were compartmented from site to site. Should one cell go down, the entire operation would not be compromised and eliminated. Because of the necessity of accuracy in any exchange or physical interaction, this was the most dangerous of the cell's activities. A level of extreme caution and firm but controlled trigger fingers ensured a secure linkup.

The most dangerous of the ratline's operations was the potential that the ratline was established by the KGB itself or the accidental admission or deliberate enemy insertion of a mole. Bollard's treatment would be sharp, deliberate, and premeditated with each handoff until the controlling cell confirmed his identity.

Someone opened the car door, dragged Bollard from the car, and held him on the ground while another searched him. Satisfied, both men lifted him and pushed him quickly into the back of the truck and against a wall. They followed him inside.

"Sit there and don't move," one ordered.

The other, somewhat more civil, directed, "Leave the hood on until after the next stop and we've gotten out of the truck. The vehicle will be parked for several hours. Someone will direct you after that. Do you need a drink of water?"

Before Bollard could answer, the truck lunged forward at high speed. Trying to remain upright in the careening truck, both men began pushing wooden boxes around Bollard. One kicked Bollard's feet to force him into a smaller space for concealment. Knowing he would be in this position for some time, Bollard attempted to salvage as much room as possible.

After what seemed like an eternity, Bollard guessed two hours had passed, the truck came to an abrupt stop. The other occupants began to shift about as the truck then backed up and parked. He could hear some voices and the driver's door closing. The two men opened the rear door, got out and slammed it shut.

Bollard sat for a few minutes then removed the bag from his head. He tried to see in the darkness but nothing. He surmised he was in a panel truck but was unsure what kind. Bollard stretched as much as possible and dozed for a couple of hours. He estimated it was 0430 hours when he was startled by a cacophony of familiar noises. It was cattle; likely dairy cows announcing the arrival of a farmer or morning work crew. Given the number of cows, it had to be a large dairy; perhaps a collective.

As the morning advanced, the cows grew quiet. Daylight began breaking through the cracks of the truck. Bollard could see he was indeed inside a panel truck. The empty crates around him appeared to be milk crates.

He didn't have to guess for long as the rear door opened with a jerk, and someone entered with the clinking of milk bottles in a crate. He bent adjacent to Bollard's hiding place, then pushed a bottle through an opening along with a loaf of bread and a piece of hard meat. Nothing was said as he made repeated trips to load the truck. Bollard could hear others talking and loading other vehicles nearby. Soon engines started and trucks were on their way to make morning deliveries.

Bollard swallowed the dry bread with difficulty, made only possible by gulps of the fresh milk. He would save the meat until later and shoved it into his pocket. The truck started and moved slowly forward then picked up speed as it turned onto a paved road and toward the driver's scheduled stops.

With each stop Bollard could hear shouts and laughter, followed by the opening of the rear door, the removal of crates of milk, and the clinking of the empty bottles. The truck made twelve stops, each taking one or more crates of milk until the full ones were nearly gone. At the last stop, something was different. Bollard listened closely. No laughing. No shouting.

The voices started at a low pitch and then erupted into fierce, angry, frustrated shouting. Something was seriously wrong. Bollard pressed his ear to the side of the truck. The shouting was about him, the "package." They were discussing what to do with him.

Bollard was no stranger to this situation, and he knew the danger. Any deviation in the ratline, any threat to the auxiliary cells who comprised or supported it, or any package who posed a greater threat than benefit was subject to elimination. So, it came as no surprise when he heard the words "kill" and "dispose." One of the men fervently argued against this; he cursed. It didn't sound as if he was cursing the men, but other, unseen parties. Then the men stopped arguing. They walked away as the driver opened the door to the truck.

Bollard was poised. He instinctively grabbed two milk bottles and was prepared to break both and use them as weapons. He wouldn't go out without a fight.

The driver stuck his head just inside the door. "We have a problem. Our route is shut down. I'll take you to a place and talk to you about it."

That didn't make Bollard feel much better about the circumstances, but at least he didn't have a life-or-death fight on his hands, not yet. He relaxed back into his hiding spot as the driver set off again in the opposite direction. A few kilometers later he pulled off a side road. He lifted the hood of the truck as if he was having an engine problem, then walked to the back of the truck. Again, he peered inside.

"Are you okay?"

Bollard replied he was fine. He was ready for anything.

"We only have a few minutes. It's going to be a long day. I'll remove some of these crates so you can stretch and piss. But only a couple of minutes."

Bollard stood but said nothing. Greeting him at the door stood an old Georgian with a short-billed hat cocked on the side of his head. A smile crept across his face revealing a couple of broken teeth, earned in a drunken fight weeks earlier.

"You better be who they say you are," the man said.

"*Tochna!* Exactly!" Bollard replied as he stepped around the crates and placed one of the bottles to the side. He jumped from the back of the truck and walked to the side where he urinated a torrent while holding the bottle in one hand and keeping an eye on the old man.

"It's the Ossetians. They're bastards. I never trusted them," he said, then unleashed a flood of Georgian curses Bollard had never heard before.

"What's the problem?" Bollard asked. He knew the regional history quite well, including southern Ossetia's push for autonomy from Georgia. It caused a considerable amount of contention, to say the least.

"They shut down our lines of communication, supply, and packages. They're unpredictable like that. They're always starting and stopping operations, fighting, wanting more money, or trying to leverage their position with the political leadership."

Ossetia was located astride the north-central portion of Georgia and often served as a shortcut between portions of Georgia and other parts of the Caucasus. It was a key part of the planned ratline.

"And we have to pay a price for it," the old man continued to snarl, "and don't get me started on the Armenians! Now you're stuck and I'm stuck with you because of those Ossetian bastards. I'll have to work with our people and find an alternate route. So, you'll have to do exactly as I say and be patient. It's dangerous to everyone and no one can be trusted."

Having relieved himself, Bollard turned and walked back toward the old man. "Whatever you want or need from me," he said cautiously. "I understand that you must take precautions."

"There's a reason we have so many precautions. Most of us don't know who is with us or against us, so trust is never factored in. We trust in the process and rely on not knowing, on dropping off and picking up without knowing. The process is safer than the people who operate it."

"Of course," Bollard replied as he got back in the truck and sat down.

"You'll be safe with me. Just do what I tell you to do." The old man gave Bollard a final look and positioned the crates around him.

Bollard watched him carefully; the old man's eyes belied his words of assurance. There was little Bollard could do. He opened a bottle and took a long drink of warm milk.

Chapter 11
Redirection

Bollard was losing track of time. It was for the best that he didn't dwell on how many months he'd been away. Three months in isolation, two months to link with and deploy from the freighter. It had been two more months since Ossetian intransigence and refusal to support the ratline forced the guerrillas to look for alternative routes.

Now he sat in a cellar. It was well equipped but still a windowless cellar with a wooden floor, rock walls on each side, stairs, and a trap door leading to the outside. As he waited for the guerrillas to complete a new ratline he read books, ventured out to exercise at night, and was nowhere close to his objective. He wasn't confident any of the earlier mission intelligence he'd received was still viable. There had certainly been no opportunity to send the prearranged radio signals. He wondered whether the support elements were still monitoring or whether they had made the decision to count him as a loss, as they'd had to do with operators previously. Yet, there was no option but to follow his original instructions, put his life in the hands of strangers, and continue toward completing his assigned mission.

He was leaning against a cool wall when he heard a vehicle drive up. There were exchanges and the sound of feet running in his direction. The trap door swung open.

A man Bollard had not seen before peered into the cellar. Medium build, the man had a bushy mustache and wore a wide-brimmed hat pulled low on his forehead. Interestingly he was dusty and dirty. He tossed something into the cellar with a shout, "We have to go. We have transportation and must go now! Everything is coordinated! Take your shirt off and put this one on."

Bollard quickly jumped to his feet and put on the shirt without question, but he remained curious. He climbed up the stairs and followed the man down a slight rise to a dirt road and was surprised. The vehicle awaiting him was a rickety coal truck with high wooden sides and appeared to have a nearly full load of coal. The man, covered in coal dust, stopped beside the truck's cab and looked inquisitively if not suspiciously at Bollard.

"I'll take you through several villages on my way to deliver this load," he began. "We'll stop in an hour, a little before dark. Stay hidden in the back. I'll tell you when to get out and will give you final instructions at that time."

Bollard said nothing and turned to look for his hosts who had hidden him for months, but they were either gone or remained out of sight. He climbed into the back of the truck, tried to get as close to the cab as possible, and attempted the impossible task of getting comfortable. He now had a general idea of where he was. His previous hosts heated with a coal furnace, and he heard routine sounds of heavy trucks moving on the nearby road. His current transport, the coal truck, had a full load of coal and was moving him to the next destination. Given the general southerly direction of movement since Ossetia, he was confident he was now in the north-central region of Armenia. This region held the Antaramut-Kurta-Dzoraget coal fields. If he could keep his bearings, he might determine the proximate location. The truck pulled onto the main highway and at high speed careened northeast.

Bollard wanted to shout, "Northeast... Azerbaijan!"

Chapter 12
The Well

Bollard shut his eyes and recalled his insertion was difficult at best. A surge of anger welled up as he thought of the Ossetians' unwillingness to open a long-established ratline, forcing the guerrillas to reestablish the entire ratline. Bollard's operation was months behind schedule as the new ratline routed him out of Georgia and toward Armenia in the safest way possible; hidden in a coal truck.

He sat against the front of the cab uncomfortably. As the coal truck bounced along, the driver seemed intent on hitting every hole in the road, sending Bollard into the air. They passed numerous other coal trucks. Bollard noted those moving east slogged along with heavy loads and those returning west traveled at high speeds, sending a cloud of coal dust overhead.

Bollard braced himself as the coal truck came to a sudden stop at an intersection with a dirt trail. The driver yelled to Bollard to get out quickly. Though his instructions were hasty, the driver was explicit. Bollard must parallel the trail for a half kilometer until it turned at a ninety-degree angle. That's where he should find a well which the driver described in detail. After providing the instructions, the driver sped away as quickly as he had stopped.

Bollard clambered up the hill until he could see the outline of the well at the side of the trail. It had a waist-high wall on all four sides with an old roof that served the purpose of keeping out debris. A heavy wooden bucket hung from a hemp rope wound around a horizontal bar and attached to a hand crank, exactly as the driver had described it. It was the four-inch piece of brown string he handed Bollard and his instructions to 'load' the signal that was both unique and compelling.

The guerrillas used a hybrid combination of dead letter drop and live drop to move people through their ratline. A live drop was simply a meeting between two individuals clandestinely to exchange information. A dead drop called for an innocuous signal or 'load' indicating something had been placed in a prearranged location and was ready for pick up. In this case, it wasn't a package ready for pick up but a person to be routed through the ratline.

Bollard clutched the piece of string tightly. Losing it would be disastrous. Following his instructions, he lowered the bucket into the well. As it settled, he unwound the remaining rope to within a half meter of the end. He then tied the string securely around the rope. He wondered whether the color of the string meant something or if it was simply brown to blend with the rope. Rewinding the rope, he raised the bucket out of the water and back to its original position.

Following his next set of instructions, Bollard moved further up the hill one hundred meters from the well. With limited visibility, he searched left and then right. He squatted slightly to use the skyline of the hill to assist his night vision. Just at the end of a slight rise, he could see the fallen tree that the driver described to him. It looked as if it was rotted throughout and worthless for any wood gatherers.

"Perfect," he thought.

Walking to the downhill side, he crawled up under the log as he was advised at the last stop. The fallen tree created a natural void; a space two by three meters and one and a half meters high. It was perfectly suited for a sitting or reclining person to be somewhat comfortable but obscured from prying eyes and sheltered from the elements.

Bollard settled in and tried to take stock of the position, but it was futile in the darkness. Riding atop a truckload of coal for an hour had created more aches and pains than he could have imagined. He quickly fell asleep.

After a long night, he awakened when streaks of sunlight shone through two gaps in the shelter on the east side. This provided natural lighting and the gaps appeared to have been deliberately cut through the dense brush that obscured the interior. He noted a similar opening on the west side. Above him, he could see the auxiliary organization and the ratline support team had placed a black piece of plastic over the entire void, then concealed it with dirt and debris. It would protect from rain and wind and keep the chill at bay.

Bollard searched for the can of food that was supposed to be hidden near the entrance. Moving some twigs aside, he could see the top of the can lodged between two branches from the main tree. The can was nondescript with no markings to indicate its contents. Bollard continued to search, but there was no can opener.

"I guess they didn't think of everything," Bollard frowned and examined the can closely. He squeezed the middle slightly with his thumb while rotating it until he had dented the can entirely around the circumference. Repeating this process over and over, he eventually saw a break appear in the can. He held it up and emptied the liquid contents directly into his mouth. He then continued squeezing until the can gave signs of weakness; he broke it open like an egg and a portion of the mystery meat fell on the ground. Bollard picked it up and ate it without a second thought. He then ate the remaining meat in slow measured bites. Every morsel was important, and he licked each section of the can thoroughly, careful not to cut himself.

It would likely be a while before his contact and escort would arrive with food and water. He pushed himself out of the sun's rays and settled in for a much more restful sleep.

Chapter 13
Phiroza

At nineteen years old, Phiroza was a veteran of the ratline. She was small, with wide dark eyes that seemed to absorb every point of light yet flashed brilliantly when she was angry or focused. She knew the signs and countersigns, dead drop procedures, load and unload signals, the routes, and all the techniques for moving people through the ratline. Despite her experience, she had conducted only one exfiltration; a relative who had crossed a nearby clan and earned a price placed on his head.

Phiroza ran to her father's house and stood nearby as he split a block of firewood. He smiled as he saw her, but she did not return it. Her face was solemn, and her eyes flashed. She then signaled slightly with her hand, raising a finger up and then down.

Her father put the ax down and embraced her as she slipped a single piece of string into his hand.

"So, it's true," he said. "The alert was real. A transfer from another ratline. This never happens."

"We must have someone in our hide site right now," Phiroza whispered.

"No one knows of this?"

"Of course not," Phiroza replied with an incredulous look.

"Excellent. You know the importance of keeping quiet."

"There are rumors we have an American."

"I've heard that, but it's hard to believe."

"I want this mission," Phiroza declared immediately.

Her father frowned. "It's too dangerous. Especially if we have an American."

"It's either you or me, and your leg slows you down. If it's an American, I may be able to practice my English. Besides, you'll be missed, but I can establish an alibi," Phiroza reasoned.

"How so?"

"It's an overnight mission if we move him. You and mother will have to come up with an excuse for my absence. You could say I went to visit my aunt. Within such a short period no one will miss me."

Phiroza's father thought for a moment. "I don't like it."

"I know, but we have no choice. I'll go gather food and something to drink. Our guest will need it."

Her father relented. "Be safe and don't take any chances!" But she was already walking away with a smile. "I love you," he said quietly.

***

A slight whisper from the entrance of the hide site awakened Bollard, "Hello, inside."

Bollard responded immediately, "Hello, Anna."

"How's the family?"

"All are sick."

Phiroza crawled into the hide site and joined Bollard.

"I'm Phiroza," she said, not using her codename Anna.

Bollard shook her hand, "Do you prefer Anna or Phiroza?"

She didn't reply but held his hand and then turned it to expose the bottom portion of the sleeve of his shirt. Bollard hadn't noticed it was frayed. Phiroza held up the string from the well to the frayed portion to match both the length and color.

"Good, it's a match. You can call me Phiroza."

"I'm glad to hear that. I'm Tamaz," Bollard said as he looked at the frayed sleeve and considered the ingenuity of the identity process. It explained why they had him change his shirt before getting on the coal truck.

"We'll leave as soon as it's dark. We have a long way to go."

"Okay."

She handed him a loaf of bread, a container of cheese, and two salamis. "The water isn't so good," she said as she pulled two bottles from the basket.

Bollard didn't care if it tasted like piss, he needed it.

"This might be better," she said as she produced a bottle of red wine. "We can share it and the water tonight on the journey."

Bollard's eyes lit up as she handed him the bottle of wine, its cork loosely attached. He pulled the cork gently and took a sip. He swished it lightly allowing the fragrance and body to take full hold of his senses. It was excellent. He took another drink and savored it recalling Armenia as the cradle of wine production for over six thousand years.

"It's the best I've ever tasted. Thank you."

Phiroza smiled but she would waste no time. "We understand you are an American?"

Bollard said nothing but looked at her intently.

"You needn't worry. No one will compromise you. If they did, it would draw the government's attention to us and compromise our ratline. The ratline's importance cannot be overstated."

This was a dangerous acknowledgment. Bollard said nothing initially and after a pause, "I've made no claims of being anyone other than a proud Georgian on the wrong side of the law."

Phiroza was undeterred. "Regardless, I have lots of questions. Many questions. I intend to ask my questions in English. So, let's pretend you are an American. How would you answer my questions?"

"I'm not sure I can answer hypothetical questions about another country or another language, but I'll try."

Phiroza's eyes flashed and narrowed slightly. "I believe you can answer my questions. They are important questions. Important to me. The answers will help me determine how much assistance I can give you."

Bollard was surprised at her directness, her threat. He decided he would answer her questions indirectly, without admitting anything.

"Okay. Let's hear the questions."

Satisfied, Phiroza began earnestly. "America is confusing to me. We are told there is immense poverty. But when the news shows an American story, you can see the background. It doesn't look like poverty. And there are so many cars. Does everyone have a car? Can you travel wherever you want?"

"I hear that most have a car. What do you mean about traveling anywhere?" Bollard scratched his head.

"Well, if I lived in Washington could I just drive to Hollywood without a passport?" Phiroza's eyes widened as she imagined Hollywood.

"Yes, I understand Americans only need a passport to leave or enter America."

"We don't have that privilege. I suspect you have documents showing you are Georgian. But those are worthless here unless you have travel authorization documents to enter the Armenian Republic. Tomorrow morning, we'll cross into the Republic of Azerbaijan, but neither of us has authorization. Getting caught and being compromised is not an option."

"And if we do?"

Phiroza lifted her jacket revealing a small revolver, "Three rounds. Two for you and one for me. We cannot be captured and tortured into revealing this ratline."

"I'll provide you with an easy target if necessary. Is that all of the questions?"

"No, I'm just beginning. Is it true you have many grocery stores and department stores in every town, and not just in the capital cities or Hollywood or Washington?"

"If I were an American, I'd answer yes to your question."

"But don't you have shortages, hunger, limited produce, and long lines?" she said as if expecting his reply.

"I'd answer no to that question if I were an American."

"It's so hard to imagine. How can this be?" she asked, completely surprised at such a thought.

"Perhaps God has blessed the Americans."

"We are Christian, and we are blessed, but not in the ways you are. Are Americans Christian?" Before Bollard could answer, she continued, "Then why is it Americans take body parts from babies?"

Bollard was familiar with this piece of Soviet propaganda accusing Americans of adopting foreign babies for harvesting body parts. Believed by the naïve, more easily manipulated, and more isolated populations, this disinformation campaign led to charitable organizations focused on children's healthcare being targeted, and well-meaning people being murdered.

"This is a lie. But let me ask you, would you or your people allow such a thing to happen here? Probably not. So it is in

61

America. Would a Christian, Muslim, Jew, or Hindu standby and allow this to happen? No."

"I didn't think this was true, but it was in the news."

"Do you believe everything in the news?"

"That's why I'm asking you these questions. I have some doubts. Does everyone have guns and are there still cowboys in Texas? I've seen them on television."

Bollard smiled. "I understand that those who want a gun can get it. And yes, there are still a lot of cowboys."

"Do you have religion there? Are Americans Christian?" she asked.

"Some are. There are many religions in America."

"This is something I don't understand either. How can so many religions coexist in the same region and country?"

"It seems America was founded on having freedom of religion, any religion, or even no religion. The government at any level can't interfere. Each respects the other's right to believe the way they want and so they coexist."

"It seems like a magical world," she said dreamily as she closed her eyes.

"Don't you coexist here? Even though there's supposed to be no practice of religion in the Soviet Union."

She frowned. "If the Turks couldn't take our Christian faith, the government certainly can't. But coexist is hardly an acceptable word. We always have apprehension, not just from the government. Pogroms occur unexpectedly."

"Pogroms? Against Jews?"

"We don't have many Jews here. But we have pogroms. Azeri Muslims have conducted pogroms in recent weeks near Baku and Bina region, near the Bina Airport. They rounded up the Armenian Christians. They beat, expelled, executed them because of tensions."

"Tensions?" Bollard asked, recognizing that tensions in this part of the world were commonplace.

"They used Nagorno-Karabakh secession demands by the Armenians as an excuse. But they seldom need an excuse for a pogrom. Sometimes we'll conduct a retaliatory pogrom. I don't support it, and we watch for it to steer clear of the agitators. The authorities always threaten decisive action, but none is taken. I think the authorities like the tension. It helps them manipulate both sides."

"Perhaps."

"But you Americans have your pogroms," Phiroza insisted.

"Not sure that is true," Bollard shook his head.

"We saw it in the news. Black Christians were blown up in their churches, a pogrom against the black Christian slaves."

Bollard took a drink from the bottle of wine, slowly savoring it. The questioning was getting difficult, and Phiroza had obviously stewed over her thoughts for some time. "First, Phiroza, I don't believe there are any black slaves in America; slavery ended in the 1800s."

She looked at him incredulously. "I've seen news reports of blacks being beaten, sprayed with hoses, and attacked by dogs and police. We don't have blacks here, but I don't think we'd do that unless they were slaves."

"What you were seeing are legitimate protestors demanding the rights they are entitled to when others would try to deny those rights. That was many years ago and times have changed."

"I saw it on the news again just last week," she replied adamantly.

"It's old news. Twenty years old."

"Tell me about the pogroms of blacks."

Bollard tried to explain. "Americans don't have pogroms in the same way you are referring here. A pogrom, at least to my understanding, is an organized mob of agitated groups of the population attacking and killing another, usually with no consequence to the mob."

"Yes. I'd agree with that. But in the news, the whites burned down a whole town."

Bollard was stumped. He knew she was referring to Tulsa, Oklahoma and he paused, reluctant to call it a pogrom. "That was in the 1920s, a long time ago. In America today, hatred fueled by racism leads to attacks by cowardly groups, who the Americans call terrorists. Then these terrorists are brought to justice."

"Then a pogrom is terrorism. I don't see a lot of difference."

"Uh-huh," Bollard replied, unsure how to answer.

"The pogroms are why this ratline exists," Phiroza continued in an even more hushed voice.

"How so?"

"It's our history. My forefathers, many great-grandfathers ago, fought alongside neighboring Azeris in support of the Tsar in the Crimean War. They became steadfast friends. After the war and the death of some Armenian Christians, many in our town united in conducting a pogrom on the nearby Azeri Muslims. Many of the Azeris were my great-grandfather's friends. He warned them and they escaped to hide in the forest we will travel through tonight."

"Soldiers make lifelong friends," Bollard said smiling.

"Not just with one another, but their friendship was carried on through subsequent generations. During the great genocide of Armenian Christians by the Turks, when millions died, our family escaped along tonight's route and were hidden by the same families of our great grandfathers' Azeri friends. Over the years and generations, we and our Azeri friends have provided secret warnings, support, and sanctuary to one another during the most dangerous of times. Both sides update and use the ratline. We owe much to one another for our very existence."

It was information Bollard didn't need to know. "Phiroza, I'm not sure this is something you should share. It could be dangerous."

"I confided in you. And now you are among the few who know. But I know you are an American. I also know you aren't supposed to be part of this ratline and we inserted you as a favor to another group. Some were opposed. They even quoted Matthew from the Bible and said you were 'new wine in old wineskins', and the ratline could tear just as easily."

Bollard shifted, the comparison to the dangers of new wine placed in an old and already expanded wineskin did little to set him at ease.

She continued, "You must understand the concerns of our people, our history, and the importance of the route we'll take. Equally important are the people who will move you to the next location. It's not just your life or theirs, but this ratline will continue to be a lifeline for future generations. Do everything that we ask and do nothing that will compromise it. Pray I don't have to use the revolver."

"You're a remarkable young woman, Phiroza," Bollard said. He had every confidence that she would indeed use the revolver if push came to shove. He handed her the bottle of wine.

"Remarkable?"

"Yes."

Embarrassed by such praise, Phiroza blushed and took a drink.

Chapter 14
Trail to Azerbaijan

The sun's rays entered the holes in the southwest side of the hide site and slid along the interior floor until they disappeared into the evening. Soon darkness enveloped everything. Bollard sensed Phiroza as she maneuvered in the cramped space. She squeezed his foot slightly and whispered, "It's time to leave."

Bollard leaned forward, and crawling on all fours, followed Phiroza through the tight opening. It was good to stand and stretch momentarily. He'd been inside the hide site all day and the previous night. Phiroza had remained motionless in the cramped space and was now bending and stretching.

"Tamaz, you'll have to stay close to me at all times. The trail is narrow and steep in some areas with sharp turns. It's not difficult to get separated. In fact, it's quite easy to get lost. If for some reason this occurs, remain in place. Don't continue forward. I'll come and find you. Worst case, return to this hide site."

"Don't worry, Phiroza. I'll be right behind you."

"It's not far away, but we must move slowly and deliberately. We'll arrive before daylight, and I'll take you to a safe house. I have no idea what will happen after that, but you'll be in trusted hands."

The two set out on a steep ascent above the hide site to a slight plateau and then turned sharply. By Bollard's estimate, they were moving due north toward the northwest corner of Azerbaijan. Soon, they were moving along a narrow trail. The trail split many times in different directions with animal paths intersecting at sharp angles. Fallen trees and limbs blocked the trail, and thick underbrush obscured it. Visibility was so poor, that Bollard bumped into Phiroza several times. As dangerous as it was, Phiroza produced a small light to get over, under, or around each obstacle. Each time she did so, they had to stop and regain their night vision before they could continue.

The dim moonlight and the night's forest sounds made the trek seem surreal. The outlines of the trees took on a life of their own, creating an atmosphere of mystique. Bollard could only wonder at the generations of stories hidden beneath its canopy. The forest's infinite impediments, nearly impenetrable obstacles, and maze of confusing trails were the very attributes that secured those who sought refuge. Bollard knew none of its secrets and Phiroza was emphatic in her warning that separation would be disastrous. The forest would tolerate no errors. Bollard questioned whether it would withstand his presence at all or was he, as Phiroza described, "new wine in old wineskins" even for the forest? He moved even closer to his indispensable guide. After several hours, they could see a faint wisp of light to the southeast, and to Bollard's relief, the trail was becoming more visible. The increasing visibility carried a warning, dawn was upon them.

"We must hurry," Phiroza said as her pace increased.

Soon, they came to the edge of the woodline. Bollard could see the outlines of buildings located well below them.

"Put these on," Phiroza demanded as she pulled a pair of glasses from her pack and handed them to Bollard. The glasses appeared to be welding goggles with side panels of darkened glass. "Take these off only when I direct you. It's for your protection as well as mine."

Bollard put the glasses on and was swallowed in darkness. Phiroza grabbed his arms and led him hurriedly down the hill. She broke from the trail and began a circuitous route, deliberately misleading Bollard as to their direction and distance traveled. After several minutes they stopped, and Bollard could hear the grinding of a heavy door. Phiroza placed her hand on top of his head and pushed it down slightly as she led him down a creaking staircase. The door closed behind them. The coolness and dank smell were certainly of a cellar or basement. She led him through a false door and narrow passage and into a separate room. She seated Bollard, then struck a match to light a candle.

"You can take the glasses off now."

Bollard removed the glasses. A small candle provided barely enough light to see. He sat on the only chair in the tiny room. A bed of straw was nestled against the wall and a slop bucket was in the corner.

"You'll remain here. When you hear three knocks on the door, you must put on your glasses. Someone will enter and bring food, water, and a blanket. When you hear two knocks, they have left the room and you may remove the glasses. You must always be blindfolded when dealing with the people here. Do you understand?"

"Of course."

"Tamaz, the people here believe you are as you say, a Georgian. But we both know the truth. I want to thank you for telling me about your country. It sounds wonderful."

"Phiroza, thank you for risking your life for me. I won't ever forget it."

"And I won't forget you," she said as they shook hands. "There are people by the door, so put your glasses on now, please. After I've left, you should try to rest." She pointed to the straw.

Bollard sat back down and put on the glasses.

Two knocks.

Chapter 15
Holding Area

Bollard slept fitfully as the straw gouged his neck and face each time he moved. Regardless, it was better than the cold dirt floor of the last hide site. As he struggled again to get comfortable, he heard three loud knocks on the door.

The flicker of the candle did little to help as he searched in the straw for the dark glasses. Finding them, he sat upright on the straw as someone entered the room. They said nothing, but he could smell the aroma of food. They placed a tray on the floor, then left the room and knocked twice.

Bollard was happy to see it contained bread, cheese, *kuku*, and a small pot of tea. He had heard of kuku but never tried it. It reminded him of quiche or an omelet but was more substantial. A Persian as well as Azeri dish, it was prepared with vegetables, herbs, and meat with eggs and cooked on both sides. His stomach growled loudly in anticipation.

This was first class; they were truly treating him as a guest. The food was the best he'd had since coming out of the sea months earlier. He was famished and ate it all heartily, finishing the entire pot of tea. So much so, that he hardly noticed the blanket. Picking it up, he walked to the makeshift bed. He knew he would be moving at night, so he needed to get as much rest as possible. He covered the straw with the blanket and lay on top of it. Except for a trip to the slop bucket, Bollard slept well into the evening when three knocks announced the return of his host. He quickly put on the glasses and sat in the chair.

A man entered and asked if he was well. Bollard replied he was fine and thanked him for the breakfast.

"I have a dinner tray for you. You should eat as much as possible. We won't eat again for a while. I hope you're rested."

"Yes, I slept most of the day."

"Good. We'll be leaving shortly. There will be a lot of handoffs and it will be stressful and tiring. If all goes according to plan, tomorrow evening you'll be completely out of our ratline, and we'll be able to get you back into your original network."

"Original network?"

"As you are aware, we're simply serving as a bypass to get you back to your original organization. They'll take over at one of the handoffs. Coordination has taken place in advance of your arrival. Things should go more smoothly in the future."

"I understand."

"When you are finished eating, knock three times on the door. Your escorts are standing by outside and you'll depart. Again, keep your glasses on at all times."

The man left, knocking twice.

***

Bollard ate a hearty meal of lamb and something with green garnishing on rice and another pot of tea. A final trip to the slop bucket and he knocked on the door. Two men entered and escorted him to the top of the stairs, led him to a parked truck, and positioned him between them in the backseat.

The truck moved along an unpaved road, swerving routinely and occasionally slamming into the potholes. With each pothole, the passengers bounced violently to the ceiling and slammed back in their seats with loud groans and curses to express their displeasure toward the driver.

After several handoffs and three truck transfers, Bollard was out of the last truck sitting on the side of a dirt road. Once the truck was away, a voice called out.

"Okay, take off your glasses. It was a long night, I'm sure. You're fine now. Everything is good."

Bollard removed the glasses and squinted in the morning light. A small force of armed men surrounded him. A tall, thin man, with his hands on his hips and a no-nonsense air, spoke without introduction.

"We have a six-hour trek. This afternoon our patrol will link up with a supply column and you'll be among your people again. We'll move out shortly."

A young man approached Bollard with a smile. He had a speech impediment and spoke in short deliberate sentences. He handed Bollard a bottle of water, "You need this. I'm escort."

Bollard walked to the edge of the road and let loose a stream of dark yellow. He then drank the entire bottle of water.

The escort gave him another bottle. He then handed Bollard three pieces of hard meat and two biscuits.

Bollard smiled appreciatively. "Thanks! Breakfast?"

The escort laughed, "Breakfast, lunch, and dinner."

"So, link up this evening?"

"Yes. Supply column. You join them. No problem. My friends!"

"Friends?"

"You'll see! No problem."

71

Chapter 16
Journey to Chechnya

After several more hours and well into the evening, much longer than the escort earlier advised, the patrol arrived at their destination. As men moved to their positions Bollard followed his escort up the side of a hill. He watched as two of the young men moved off the hillside and into the middle of the trail. They seemed unimposing to the casual observer as each was unarmed. They milled around nonchalantly and spoke casually to one another. It was this easy-going and unthreatening nature that the small force wanted to project. Not immediately apparent, heavily armed men waited in concealed positions, above and below the trail and a small distance forward. Other armed men were positioned above and along the anticipated approach of the linkup column.

The two young men served as the bait and would determine the legitimacy of anyone entering the linkup area as well as the kill zone of their ambush. If the planned linkup was compromised or individuals proved to be other than those expected, the two men would simply bound over the side of the hill, and all hell would break loose from the hidden positions.

"A well-organized ambush," Bollard thought as he settled in behind a large boulder with the escorts by his side. While he understood the escorts' mission was to secure him, which meant to shoot him if he did something stupid, Bollard was now more relaxed knowing their mission was also to protect him should things go to shit during the linkup.

Bollard and his escort sat on the hillside for two hours waiting for any sign of the column. He wasn't sure what it would look like or how to respond once it arrived. Everything was in the hands of the escort who kept repeating, "Normal. No problem. Normal." Not as confident, Bollard pressed for the type of recognition signals that they might use. "My friends will be in front. Normal. No problem."

Soon they heard sounds of movement and the clomping of hooves on the dirt road. Each peered down the road, and a broad grin streaked its way across the escort's face.

"You see? My friends! No problem!" the escort said as he jumped into the middle of the road signaling Bollard to follow.

The rebel column stopped, and the escort and several men embraced. There was nothing quiet about this encounter as their joyous voices overlapped. They were younger than Bollard anticipated for such a mission. Like many in the region, they sported mustaches or the makings of one. More than a few were olive-skinned betraying, their Persian lineage. Everyone was wide-eyed and laughing, except the leader who watched the activity from a distance but made no effort to interrupt.

Bollard waited behind the escort until the leader acknowledged him and motioned for him to follow. As they walked toward the rear of the column, Bollard counted nine mules. All except two were fully loaded, and those two carried empty hemp bags. There were sixteen rebels in this group and most took advantage of the stop to drink and rest. Bollard noted there was no security placed out on the flanks.

When he came to the rear of the column, the rebel led him to a man who was finishing a long drink of water. "This is your man," the rebel said and without further introduction turned and walked away.

As the man pulled the bottle down revealing his face, Bollard exclaimed, "Abdul! Are you shitting me?"

Abdul laughed and embraced Bollard. "Omar! Who else would you expect to see in this hell hole?"

"I can't believe it. It's a long way from Berlin! By the way, I'm not going by Omar. Tamaz will work for now!"

"Okay, Tamaz," Abdul replied. "It appears the Ossetians got a bit grumpy and this route was more difficult than we could have ever imagined. I'm just shocked the linkup has finally come together."

"But how the heck did you get here?" Bollard asked not expecting an answer.

"We've got our ways too." Abdul grinned even wider in true CIA form.

Bollard had a hunch he wanted to play despite breaking protocol. "Caspian?" he asked quietly.

Abdul simply winked. "Despite all the hype about the tight Soviet borders, they're pretty porous if you're coming into the country. They spend so much time trying to keep their people from getting out, that they don't consider who might be coming in."

"Right. Who in their right mind would be trying to sneak in?"

"Well, there was one... I think his name was Rust, and he could barely fly a plane. Yet he flew under the Soviet radar and air defense last year with a single-engine airplane and landed right by Red Square. What a shit storm that was, especially for the Soviet military!"

"Yeah. Several top generals got relieved over that one. But back to your point, if they're more focused on keeping people inside their borders than keeping people out, it's more like a prison than an international border."

"Right. We're seeing more and more people from different countries on a one-way trip, sneaking their way to Chechnya. You have one in this convoy. I'll tell you about him shortly. Though we're months behind schedule, the delay may have worked out for the best, given the makeup of this column."

Bollard cocked his head to the side. "Easy for you to say. I've been wandering around like Moses in the desert for way too long. Now, after talking to you about porous borders, I'm going to have a long talk with your counterpart at HQ. She pushed for the most difficult infiltration with no planning considerations for the mercurial Ossetians."

"We knew you could do it." Abdul slapped him confidently on the shoulder, but his smile faded. "But I agree, the direct route through Ossetia would have been much shorter if they had cooperated. I see you've still got that limp from your old jump injury. How are you holding up."

Bollard shook off his frustration with the Ossetians, focusing on the mission at hand, "My leg is fine, I'm used to it. What's the plan now?"

Abdul shifted gears as well, his tone becoming crisp and professional. "I return to my start point and leave you here. You're still under escort and they won't give you a weapon until you're cleared by the guerrillas. Before they move out, get in front of the mules. They shit and fart incessantly. If you drop to the end of the column, well, it ain't pretty."

"Worked with those critters before. Mules, mule trains, and muleskinners. All indispensable," Bollard replied, recalling that the military used over fifteen thousand mules in the WWII Monte Cassino campaign alone. He looked down the column of mules. "When do you suppose we'll move out?"

"In a few minutes. The group will move well into darkness until the trails become dangerous. There aren't a lot of Soviet patrols or police in this region. The government forces stick principally to the towns and main roads."

"How far along this route are you going?"

"This is it. No further. You and this linkup are my mission. I need to warn you about a member of this column. He's dangerous."

"How so?"

Abdul put his hand on Bollard's shoulder and led him to the other side of the road and away from the others.

"Says his name is Saud and he's from Saudi Arabia. Apparently, he has connections within the Ministry of Interior, and he's loaded a mule with large crates. I didn't get a chance to see what was inside. He's a Wahhabi, and his proselytizing is second nature. He's bent the ear of a few who seem eager to listen, but others simply shake their heads."

"Yeah, I saw a few of the Wahhabis show up in Pakistan and Afghanistan. Total pains in the ass."

"Key to remember, as you already know, they're not friends of the West or our country. So, watch your back with him."

"You bet. Is he using a translator?"

"No. He has a working knowledge of Russian. However, he's memorized all the necessary Koran dictums quite well to move his radicalized agenda."

"No surprise there."

"By the way, and most importantly I have a message for you from the rear."

"Yeah?"

Abdul's signature grin returned. "Very short. Riley *and* Finnigan."

Bollard paused for a moment as the gears in his head ground to a halt. "AND?"

75

"That's it," Abdul said cheerfully. "I was told to emphasize *and*."

"Holy shit!" Bollard exclaimed. For the first time in a while, he allowed himself to think about his family back home. His wife. His kids. It must have shown on his face.

"You okay, guy?" Abdul asked as he tugged on Bollard's shirt, forcing him to regain focus.

"Yeah, I'm okay," Bollard said, swallowing the sudden lump in his throat. He looked up the hill as the column was preparing to depart. "I hadn't realized I'd been away so long! I'm not sure I can compartmentalize this."

"I hope this isn't a black box issue." Abdul looked at him intently and referred to a place in a soldier's mind where the horrors and tragedy of war reside and were seldom if ever opened. Veterans of WWII returning from the war rarely discussed what was inside the box that permanently marked their souls. Only in their later years and after much prodding did they reveal the pain. Unlike then, the Special Forces units employed psychiatrists and psychologists who evaluated a man's capacity to undertake certain missions such as sniper training or prolonged periods of being alone. Bollard was fine with that aspect of psychological evaluation and interviews but rejected the standard mining many psychologists forced.

"I'm no sociopath," Bollard once said, staring down his psychologist. "I simply don't wear the things I've seen, the things I've done, or the things done to me, on my sleeve. You open the black boxes and shake them like a snow globe, intrigued by the flakes and the way they fall on the little village inside, but you're protected by the outer glass that separates you from the reality we know. For us, it's like a dog wallowing in a rotten carcass; it doesn't make us cleaner. It just brings out the stink we've filed away for years." The psychologist would invariably make a note and the discussion would move on.

"No, not a black box," Bollard reassured him, realizing Abdul had no idea what the message meant. "I've just got to compartmentalize." He paused again and cleared his throat. "Family."

Unlike the black box, an operator could open the family compartment, but only after an operation was over, a critical skill during dangerous operations. There was no room for distraction. Some people are better at it than others. The more intense and dangerous, and the more complex the mission the greater the need.

Leaders know a homesick soldier is a vulnerable soldier. It reflects in his face; it reflects in his posture; it reflects in his actions. A survivalist often breaks, not because he has no food, water, or shelter, but because he fails to compartmentalize those things which distract him from surviving. Home and family top the list for distraction. The news from headquarters forced Bollard to open a compartment and peer at the most important part of his life, his family.

"You okay?" Abdul asked again pointedly. Normally the response "Family" would be sufficient, and one would pursue no further, but Abdul had to be sure Bollard was focused.

"Twins," Bollard said with only a slight smile. "My wife was pregnant when I left. Riley *and* Finnigan, she's telling me we have twins."

"Whoa! That's great news." Abdul laughed and slapped his knee. "As I recall, this makes four children for you. Congratulations!"

"Yeah, thanks. Gotta stay focused on the mission."

"Given the nature of this mission, you have to lock it away," Abdul agreed but stated the obvious.

"Yep." Bollard paused. He counted on Molly to get help from the family. Twins would be a challenge. His head swirled quickly with other thoughts, but there was nothing he could do. He took a deep breath. "Done. Socked it away," he said suddenly.

"You need to complete this mission and get the hell out of here."

"Right. You can bet I'll exfil the minute I complete this mission," Bollard said.

"Well, speaking of that and a final point, we're still working on your preplanned egress. Lots of complicating factors. If you don't hear from us, go with the first exfiltration and extraction plan."

"No shit." Bollard shook his head as a movement of mules signaled the time of departure.

"I'll see you on the other side," Abdul said as he handed Bollard a backpack. "Not much to this, but enough to keep you warm and dry, and some dried meat for the trail. They have a cook so you'll get a warm meal once a day. Do you have any messages for the rear, for your family?"

As the two men shook hands, they held their grip a moment longer. "Tell them I love them. Tell them I think of them all the time," Bollard said.

Then he slung his backpack over his shoulders and followed the column even deeper into the region.

Chapter 17
Hinnies and Mules

Abdul joined three rebels and two mules already moving in the opposite direction. Bollard started moving forward up the hill. As he did, he saw Saud, the Wahhabi, struggling with a mule at the front of the column. His inexperience radiated as he violently jerked at the mule's lead ropes, which entrenched the mule even more.

An older man with a floppy hat stood nearby, monitoring the mules with a practiced eye. He tapped his leg with a switch, pursing his lips and making barely audible kissing noises to encourage the pack animals. He occasionally called the name of a mule as it passed and instinctively tugged at the cinch of each mule's sawbuck pack.

The sawbuck consisted of two X-shaped protrusions extending above a barely distinguishable saddle positioned on a heavy blanket. Each held heavy but soft-skinned containers which Bollard estimated to total about one hundred and twenty pounds. While the mule could carry thirty percent of its weight, the old man appeared to have kept it less.

"Better to add another mule than overburden just one," the old man told a guerrilla earlier in their journey. After ensuring the load was secure and evenly distributed, he touched the mule slightly just forward of its hip and again made a low smooching sound.

"The muleskinner is on top of every aspect of these animals," Bollard thought.

The skinner looked ruefully at the Wahhabi but offered no assistance. It was clear the skinner was a caring master of the mules given his restrictions on the pack sizes. He used a hemp harness for each mule and no bits that might cut their mouths. None of the mules were shoed; their hooves were strong enough to navigate the terrain, were quieter than steel shoes, required no complicated upkeep, and were a lot more agile on narrow rocky trails.

Bollard was confident if Saud tried to use a whip, the skinner would intercede. Force and whippings have the opposite effect on mules and confuse and ruin them. Bollard stopped, and saying nothing to Saud, took the lead rope and stood by the mule's shoulder, and whispered, "*Tisha. Tisha.*" The mule settled down and visibly relaxed. Bollard, still standing at the shoulder turned his head deliberately toward the hip and reached back, tapping gently while making a kissing sound as he'd seen the skinner do. The mule leaped forward without braying. Bollard patted it and praised it, "*Molodyets. Molodyets.*"

"As I would have expected," Bollard thought as he looked closer and saw a slight scar on the throat of the mule. These mules would never be able to give away their location with the usual braying of a pack animal. The skinner had cut the vocal cord on each animal, a standard procedure of most special operators.

Bollard handed the lead rope back to the Saudi. "Be gentle and patient. If you do, they'll trust and obey you. They have long memories."

Saud said nothing and led the mule forward.

The skinner acknowledged Bollard's effort with a broad smile.

"They're not mules, but hinnies?" Bollard asked.

Bollard didn't pronounce the word well. It sounded like "horse." The skinner shrugged his shoulders, obviously not understanding.

"It's a hinny, not a mule," Bollard said again, and again it sounded like "horse."

The skinner laughed, "*Loshak, loshak,* not *loshad.*"

"*Loshak,*" Bollard repeated the word. Bollard was familiar with hinnies from other missions. Though slower and smaller than mules, hinnies were more methodical and better suited for steep, rocky terrain, and moving in loose gravel and dirt.

"Yes, loshak!" The skinner stepped closer to Bollard and shook his hand. "My family has mastered the breeding of donkeys and horses over the years. You see the mule and hinny take their traits and strengths from their mama. For a mule, we want the traits of a horse, which is the mama. For a hinny, we're more interested in the traits of a donkey."

"So, the strength and traits are determined by the mother."

"Yes, but it's more difficult breeding to get a hinny than a mule."

"I guess a small donkey would rather not be mounted by a large horse," Bollard replied, smiling.

The skinner laughed. "But both are pretty choosy." He squatted down to some tracks on the trail. "The tracks of a hinny are narrower and more oval than round, and more vertical."

Bollard had never really looked at the difference in the tracks of a mule and hinny, and tracking was one of his specialties.

"Excellent, excellent," Bollard said. He thought about the analogy to tracking a person, the difference in a woman's track and a man's; a woman's track is narrower, smaller, and more oval, depending on the shoes, pointing more forward than outward with the weight on the toes.

Bollard then turned to tug slightly on the sawbuck X-frame of a passing hinny. "They have better endurance too, correct?" he asked, though he already knew the answer.

The skinner beamed at the opportunity to talk to someone about his animals. "Much more endurance and are certainly far better than horses, donkeys, or mules for what we do in these mountains. But they're all the same to most of these men. They don't know the difference. They call everything mules, but you're familiar with them," he said more as a statement than a question.

"I'm familiar enough to know I have to get in front of them on this trail," Bollard replied good-naturedly.

The skinner laughed and slapped Bollard on the shoulder, "I'm Vsadnik. We'll talk again."

"I'm Tamaz," Bollard replied shaking Vsadnik's hand. "I look forward to talking again," he said as he moved forward.

"Indeed," the skinner replied and moved alongside the last hinny as Bollard moved forward of the supplies and pack animals. In this environment every piece of information was important, but every personal relationship was even more critical.

Bollard smiled. He had made a friend.

Chapter 18
The Auxiliary

The sounds of the column echoed from the hillsides as men, hinnies, and equipment slogged up the steep and narrow passages of the trail. The guerrillas took little notice of the noise and appeared to pay even less attention to their immediate security. Bollard attributed it to a very good intelligence system that kept constant track of the locations and movements of government forces. Perhaps, he thought, guerrilla security forces might be moving with the column, but unseen and at enough distance to provide a warning. Either way, Bollard habitually studied his surroundings and was prepared to bound over the hill to safety should an ambush or confrontation occur along the trail.

While the column had been on the march most of the day, Bollard joined in the afternoon and was fresh and alert. As the evening dragged on, he noted the column seemed to slow perceptibly as fatigue began to take its toll. He watched as a gap began to grow between the lead hinny and the second hinny that the Saudi prodded along. The Saudi ran ahead to close the gap before slowing again, dropping further to the rear. Each time he did this, an accordion effect occurred at the end of the column, exhausting both men and hinnies. Cursing from the rear prompted one of the guerrillas to run back to the Saudi and grab the rope lead forcefully. He too cursed and after bringing both man and beast back to an acceptable distance to the lead hinny, he directed the Saudi to maintain the pace.

Soon the column began to pick up speed indicating they were coming close to the end of the day's movement and rest would be forthcoming. They rounded a steep curve in the trail that turned sharply toward a point where two mountains came together. A small creek was the demarcation between both. Though it was not yet dark, Bollard could see several lanterns, and he heard voices as the front of the column linked up with a group of men and women. The group welcomed each person as they entered an area under a dense forest canopy and beside the stream.

Someone motioned for the skinner and the handlers to move the hinnies well forward of their location. The auxiliary had dug a watering hole for the hinnies and placed several bales of hay nearby.

Vsadnik stretched a long rope along the edge of the bales of hay and watering hole, anchoring the rope to trees at each end. As handlers finished unloading the cargo and placing the sawbucks in a position to readily reload, they led their hinny to the skinner. He acknowledged each with a nod of the head and then stroked the hinny's muzzle, calling it by name. He bent down and tied the front and rear legs with a loose rope that passed under the main one he had just anchored. This allowed the hinnies to move somewhat freely along the main rope to water and food but prevented them from running away if they were spooked or overly anxious. Given the long day's march, it was unlikely any of the hinnies would want to stray far from the food and water.

A woman's voice, slightly uphill and deeper in the forest, called the men forward and toward several lanterns hanging in the trees. Bollard was shocked to see an improvised table holding large pots of soup, loaves of bread, a variety of pastries, as well as a huge jug with a long dipper containing some flavored water. Several men, a child, and a couple of younger women stood behind the table to serve the food. A robust older woman stood in front with her arms crossed and a frown that was pure theater. Her melodic voice belied her sense of drama.

"Okay, boys line up on that side and work your way to the left. If you break a dish, there will be hell to pay." She paused. "Welcome! Eat all you want. We know your journey is difficult."

Bollard watched as men quickly formed a line and exchanged familiar greetings. He was astonished. This kind of coordination and support could only come as a result of a thoroughly organized and mature auxiliary force.

The auxiliary was the element within this unconventional warfare environment responsible for supporting the guerrillas with transport, logistics, intelligence, ratlines, and local action. They were not only well organized but their synchronization and coordination reflected a broad-ranging communications capability. Bollard noted there seemed to be no real concern for Soviet security forces as the guerrillas relaxed and talked freely.

Bollard was last in the serving line and took a ration of everything the servers had to offer. His plate was heaped with as much as it could hold, though he couldn't identify specifically what it was. It didn't matter. It was only important that each man eat as much as he could when he could. As Bollard took his first bite, the leader made a loud grunt, acknowledging the arrival of eight guerrillas walking toward the group.

These new arrivals didn't look like the group with whom Bollard had spent the day. They were older, dressed in camouflage with full scraggly beards, and heavily armed. Their eyes and demeanor betrayed their heavy combat experience.

Their arrival was met with no banter as Bollard's initial linkup had been. Two of the men walked up to the leader as the rest went to the table and began filling up their plates, ignoring the stares of the other guerrillas and the auxiliary. Bollard surmised they were either replacements or additional security. Either way, it appeared a handoff of the escort mission was about to occur.

After a few minutes, the convoy leader addressed everyone. "We'll spend tonight and tomorrow here. The food will remain with us throughout tomorrow. Those of you who have been in this convoy for several days can return to your homes. These men will take over your roles." He waved his hand in the direction of the camouflaged men who continued eating, barely acknowledging him.

"I'll file reports with your leadership regarding the support you provided. You'll receive new guidance and instructions on your return. You may leave now or spend the night and depart in the morning. Be safe, and Allah be with you."

Two of the guerrillas stood, grabbed their packs, and moved to join the men and women of the auxiliary.

"As for the rest of you, get plenty of rest. Soviet security gets tighter from here forward. We'll travel at night to avoid Soviet overflights. The next leg will be the longest of the journey. Tomorrow we must travel nearly thirty kilometers over difficult terrain to get to our safe area. We'll be moving quickly and stopping once every hour for ten minutes. Our experience is the further we go, the shorter our stops will be due to soreness and cramps. Ultimately, we'll stop for no more than five minutes or less. We want to be at our target before daylight. Once we depart, I want you on full alert, weapons at the ready. I'll provide detailed security procedures before we depart."

Bollard took another bite and looked back at the serving table. He was surprised. Everyone was gone, including the two escorts who had stood with their packs. No one had noticed. The auxiliary simply slipped away during the leader's briefing, taking the lanterns with them. They would return the following night to gather the table, plates, and pots and sanitize the area from any indication of an overnight stay.

"Well done," Bollard thought. "Yes, very well done."

***

Bollard woke as the morning sun had just begun to streak across his face. As part of his routine, he moved his bedding after dark and set it up in a different location. Facing the southeast, he ensured the morning light woke him earlier than the others. More importantly, the new location provided a good view of most of the force and observation of his previous position.

Several of the guerrillas were moving about. One of yesterday's new arrivals, acting as security, stood adjacent to the same trail they would take on their departure later in the day. Some stirring to Bollard's left caught his attention. He rolled slightly to see Vsadnik moving toward his pack animals. The skinner cupped both hands together as if holding a bee, then blew between his thumbs, emitting a high-pitched owl-like sound. Bollard smiled because he used the same technique to signal his children to come inside for dinner or to locate them quickly. Each of his children recognized their father's special signal. Vsadnik whistled again. The hinnies stopped grazing and turned their attention to him in anticipation of the daily ritual of currying and the careful examination of their hooves.

Bollard stood and looked at the campsite. There was little camp activity except for the skinner. He placed the poncho he had been using as a blanket back into his pack and walked toward Vsadnik. He cupped his hands and made a sound like the skinners, but much lower so as not to confuse the animals. Vsadnik turned with a big smile.

"So, you know my signal?"

"Indeed, I use it to locate my children. When they hear it, they come running."

"These are my children when we're on the move," Vsadnik replied as he stroked the neck of one of the pack animals.

"Looks like you're one of the first to rise," Bollard said.

"No, they're the first to rise," Vsadnik replied with an outstretched hand toward the hinnies. "I get up when I hear them stir. I need to be the last person they see at night and the first they see in the morning."

"They're your babies," Bollard grinned.

"Indeed. They always respond to me. Regardless of how bad a handler might be," Vsadnik's eyes narrowed slightly. "I can coax them to do whatever I need. I have to keep it that way. They know I'll always take care of them," he ran a loving hand along the neck of one.

"Can I help you, Vsadnik?" Bollard asked.

"Usually it's me alone, but sure, check the areas on their shoulders and back where the sawbuck rests. Sometimes, the blanket underneath cinches up and creates some rubbing. It can create an open wound. Apply this when you see a raw area. I saw at least two when I curried them." He handed Bollard a jar of a thick yellow substance.

"Looks like honey!"

Vsadnik smiled and stuck two fingers in and out of the jar and placed the yellow substance in his mouth. "Yes. It's honey," he confirmed. "Try it."

Bollard did the same and smiled in return. "Delicious!"

"It has some antibacterial properties," Vsadnik assured him.

"I guess it keeps the wound moist as well."

"It provides a bit of a protective barrier. It all contributes to preventing infection," Vsadnik said, checking the leg of one. "It's an expensive ointment but worth it. Just a bit messy."

Bollard examined the hinnies and finding two with abrasions, applied a liberal amount of the honey. He watched as the skinner finished tending the animals.

"Didn't need much. Just a couple with abrasions," Bollard said as he handed the skinner the jar.

"That's because I keep the loads lighter than most. If these guys had their way," Vsadnik pointed to the guerrillas, "they'd load them till their knees buckled and the sawbucks would rub them raw. I'm not going to let that happen." He took the honey and packed it away. "Much appreciated," he said as he walked away to break open a bale of hay.

Bollard returned to his original bed site and sat down. He observed six of his earlier escorts placing food in their packs. Their mission was over and within minutes they were moving away in the direction they had arrived. Their gait was almost airy. They were going home.

***

Bollard had grown so accustomed to dealing with the extreme elements, that he wasn't surprised when a cloud front moved in midmorning to block all the sun's warm rays. The region grew dark with overcast skies and the men bundled up as the temperature dropped. Bollard put on his poncho and exercised occasionally to keep his muscles from tightening in the chilly weather. An agitated voice from among the guerrillas caught his attention. It was Saud.

Saud was speaking sternly and appeared to be lecturing several of the younger guerrilla escorts with whom he had traveled earlier. Bollard figured it was unlikely he would talk to the eight camouflaged guerrillas who had arrived yesterday in the same tone. He wasn't sure, but it appeared to have something to do with the midday prayers. Saud had completed his prayers, but none of the others had joined in. The guerrillas were annoyed, but none responded and went about their activities ignoring him. Bollard observed the group closely, and an hour later they moved to a position to pray as Saud looked on. Midday prayers are to be conducted when the sun is at its zenith, but it was hidden. Something had occurred to confound the young Wahhabi, and Bollard had an idea what it was.

Chapter 19
Night March

It was still a couple of hours until twilight, but the leader was anxious to get moving. With such a long distance to travel, an early start would be the best start.

"Pack up," he said to the hinny handlers who got up slowly and began loading the animals. The skinner untied the legs of the hinnies and ceremoniously handed the reigns to each handler.

Bollard packed quickly to ensure he was ready to depart at the same time as the others. He didn't want to draw too much attention to himself. While his cover story of being a Georgian was enough for the original escorts, he wasn't confident it would stand the scrutiny of the others. It certainly hadn't been adequate for the young Armenian girl.

When everyone appeared ready to depart, the leader presented his security plan to the group. Given the increasing danger of the next movement, Bollard wondered whether he would organize the group operationally or simply move out in a file. With twenty men and seven hinnies, it would be a long file. Thankfully, it turned out to be an operational movement.

The leader identified two of the guerrillas to maintain a timed distance of five minutes in front of the convoy and two others to follow five minutes behind. Each would act as point and rear security, respectively. He then directed seven men and three hinnies to make up the first element. The second element was larger and comprised of nine men and four hinnies. Curiously this element had two hinnies with hardly any load, one with Saud's boxes, and one with a heavier load which Bollard thought might be loose ammunition. Bollard further noted the eight bearded guerrillas were equally distributed with two front and back for security, and two accompanying each element. Experience and expertise had been strategically dispersed throughout the formation.

The leader gave directions to conduct a movement with a five-minute interval between elements, with each capable of supporting the other. The lead element would stop every hour until the arrival of the second element, and depart after five minutes, giving them a ten-minute break. After five minutes, the second element would depart followed by rear security five minutes later, and so on.

Each element had to maintain the five-minute interval rule which ensured each moved at the same rate of speed. This allowed for maximum coordination, rest, and security. Importantly, it did not create the exhausting accordion effect of stopping, waiting, and rushing forward.

***

The sun began to disappear behind the mountain top, casting a long shadow deep into an adjacent gorge. Each man strained to move quickly to cover as much distance as possible in the remaining light. As darkness set in, the column slowed noticeably with the limited visibility cutting their speed by half. Each man and hinny had to feel their way along the trail by establishing a sound footing before taking the next step. Going uphill was difficult but going downhill had bigger challenges and pitfalls. Loose rock and gravel created an unstable pathway causing many to lose their balance and fall forward along the slope of the trail. Most maintained discipline. Only a few curses were heard.

Bollard was relieved to look over his shoulder and see the clouds moving to the northeast, revealing a half-moon. The moonlight soon brought the trail and the steep edges of the mountain into clearer view. The terrain had changed, some of the rocks on the trail jutted upward at sharp angles, while others created small crevices between them; painful should someone fall, and dangerous if his foot became lodged in between. The pace of the column picked up with the new light as each member gained surer footing and maneuvered around protruding rocks.

They progressed relatively well for the first several hours with only minor deviations in the five-minute intervals. After midnight the hours and kilometers began to take their toll. The intervals began to grow until ultimately, the second element was a full ten minutes behind. The leader dropped back to meet with the second element's leader, and he wasn't happy.

"You have to keep up," he said. "We can no longer stop for ten minutes. People are cramping. After five minutes the younger ones are going to sleep, and I have to prod them. We can't wait for you for an additional five minutes. At the next stop, we'll rest for five minutes and then move on, whether you've caught up or not."

"We have one that is struggling," the second element leader replied.

"Then kick him in the ass but keep up! Regardless of how far we're separated, the contingency response to support each other remains the same. You know the way. If we don't link up again, get there by daylight! Regardless of what it takes."

The leader then departed with the lead column, as the element leader strode toward one of the hinnies. Bollard watched as he grabbed the arm of one of the handlers, Saud. Bollard figured he must be getting the same lecture as he had previously, to stay close to the hinny in front and maintain his pace.

It was a short rest. By the time the element leader finished admonishing and encouraging the group to pick up the pace, it was time to set off again.

Chapter 20
Saud

Saud had struggled ever since his arrival in Azerbaijan. He had gone through countless arduous hours of physical conditioning in preparation. But an airconditioned gym in Saudi Arabia was not the environment he found himself in as he moved through Azerbaijan or the Caucasus mountains. The routes were difficult, and the damnable mule was a constant source of irritation. The leader directed each person to assume responsibility for their baggage, and Saud was carrying a big load. Saud felt certainly there were lower caste persons, other than a relative of the royal family, who should have been employed to manage this beast of burden. If the hinny wasn't enough of a problem, Saud was now moving in terrain he was unaccustomed to, mountains, trails, sheer cliffs, and narrow passages. He found it difficult to keep up. He was exhausted, and the column leader had just threatened him by saying he would dump all his baggage and put his sorry ass on the hinny if he had to.

As they continued, the hinny pulled ahead of Saud slightly, instinctively following the hinny in front. Previously, when the hinny pulled ahead, Saud yanked at the rope to slow it down. This time, Saud left the rope loose and slung his arm around the sawbuck allowing the hinny to carry him along. The hinny struggled but kept the pace. When Saud put all his weight on the sawbuck, the hinny couldn't handle it and stopped until Saud released his weight.

The skinner could tell something was wrong. He stepped to the side and squinted toward the commotion. He saw nothing in the darkness. He moved slowly but deliberately forward until he saw the stopped hinny and the animated Saud at its side.

"What's wrong?" he demanded.

"Nothing. Lost my footing," Saud lied.

The skinner didn't believe him. He'd seen this play out before with others. "Don't hang on to the hinny. The baggage is balanced. Any more weight is dangerous."

"I'm not!" Saud replied angrily.

The skinner said nothing. He stepped aside and allowed the rest of the hinnies to pass, then resumed his position in line.

Saud trudged along doing his best to keep up. The trail soon leveled out. He was in pain. His knees hurt, his back hurt, his feet hurt, and he was too inexperienced to put the pain out of his mind. This level piece of ground allowed him to stand upright and catch his breath. Neither leaning into a hill nor staggering down one was a welcomed respite. After five minutes, he wondered whether they were nearing the end. He soon got his answer.

In the distance, a dark shadow loomed blocking the stars. Hoping it was a cloud, Saud's heart sank when he realized it was more mountains. They had been walking in the middle of a saddle, the level ground between two mountains. Now the steep ascent began again. The thought of another mountain drained every bit of his spirit and energy. His mind raced, he never volunteered for hardship. If he could only get some sleep. He closed his eyes and simply held on to the rope, allowing the hinny to lead him on.

A stumble brought him back. They were in an area of dangerous sharp rocks and crevices again and he tried to regain focus. The hinny didn't slow, and Saud started to fall back. He looked over his shoulder. The skinner wasn't there, but at the end of the column. He reached forward and hooked his arm around the sawbuck as he had done multiple times before. Saud tripped and stumbled and put all his weight on the sawbuck.

The sound was distinct and excruciating and could be heard up and down the column. The hinny attempted to regain its footing, but with Saud's additional weight and thrashing, the hinny fell with its hoof locked inextricably in a crevice. The leg snapped below the knee with a loud and sickening crack.

Bollard stopped and hurried over, but the skinner was already there. The hinny struggled. With its vocal cords cut, it could only let out desperate gasps of air from deep within its lungs. The skinner cursed, as a flashlight was turned on and revealed the disaster. Saud was under the hinny but protected by a boulder. Shattered bone protruding through the skin was all that was left of the hinny's lower leg. The skinner took the light and held it down toward the sawbuck. The situation was clear. Saud's sleeve was wrapped and entangled on the cross portion of the sawbuck. He couldn't free himself and thrashed about causing the hinny to fall.

The hinny continued to struggle and made horrible, panicked noises. Vsadnik called it by name, "Natasha," and soothed it. He placed his jacket over its head and gently squeezed the area of the jugular between his thumb and forefinger until the vein protruded. He cut the animal's jugular vein sending long spurts of blood into the air. He continued to talk to it until it died. Once it was dead, he turned his attention to Saud.

"You son of a bitch!" Vsadnik shouted, and the knife blade flashed in the light.

Bollard and the others were confident Vsadnik would cut Saud's throat. No one interceded as he lunged toward Saud. But then he inserted the blade under Saud's shirt sleeve at the shoulder and ripped the entire length of the sleeve, freeing him from the sawbuck. Saud slumped back in relief, as did the others.

Vsadnik then turned to three men who already had their knives out. "Quarter it."

Bollard watched in astonishment. They had planned for the loss of a hinny, or at least the redistribution of weight in an emergency. The three men including the leader began quartering the hinny, paying no attention to Saud who was still under the animal. Bollard and another then pulled Saud out and away from the animal.

The guerrillas quickly removed the sawbuck and Saud's baggage from the dead hinny. Bollard helped load it onto another hinny.

With experienced hands, the guerrillas rushed to field dress the animal, cutting away and packing the organs, hams, shoulders, and tenderloin. They loaded the packed meat onto one of the hinnies that previously carried no cargo and distributed the remaining portions among the other pack animals. They quickly dragged the carcass to the edge of the precipice and pushed it over.

The leader stood in the middle of the road with his hands on his hips. "You," he growled to Saud. "Come here!" He finished ripping Saud's torn sleeve from his arm and wiped the blood from his hands. "You'll stay with me. And stay away from the pack animals," he ordered.

Saud appeared visibly relieved to be rid of the hinny.

"Vsadnik!" he shouted. "Who's leading this mule?" he asked, motioning toward the hinny now carrying Saud's baggage.

Vsadnik quickly pointed out Bollard, who was already standing by the hinny. "He can do it."

"It's yours." the leader said immediately. He then turned and shouted over his shoulder, "See if you can keep up. No mistakes."

"I'll take good care of her, Vsadnik," Bollard said as the column moved out at a fast pace to make up lost time.

After twenty minutes the group stopped momentarily as a guerrilla from the lead column approached. Recognizing him, the column leader directed the column to continue the march.

The guerrilla wasted no time, "Where have you been? I'm supposed to tell you how far back you've dropped." He looked at his watch. "They're an hour in front of you and they're not waiting. That means in case of a crisis neither of you can react in support of the other."

"We're each on our own," the leader replied. "We'll press on with no further breaks."

Indeed, the hourly breaks had become increasingly difficult, and the leader limited them to five minutes. The column continued without pause until they started down a gradual slope. Ahead the morning light revealed a crumbled brick and rock structure; an old building bombed out in a previous war. It sat adjacent to the trail with a small field extending down the slope. The hinnies from the first column, tied to stakes, were grazing in the field. There was no other movement.

The leader met them as they arrived, but no one else stirred. Formless shapes marked the positions of exhausted men lying in and around the bombed-out structure.

"What happened?" he demanded.

"Lost a mule."

"Okay, we'll cook some of it for lunch."

"Everyone is too tired to eat breakfast."

"The area is relatively safe and not in an overflight zone. I've placed a couple of men forward on the trail. After four hours, your group will pick up security. Get the mules fed and watered and get some rest. Move your guys to the other side of the building."

The skinner, Bollard, and the other handlers were already moving toward the field. It had not registered with Saud that he was still responsible for his baggage. He moved to the far side of the structure and collapsed, asleep as soon as he sat down.

Bollard unpacked the hinny and dropped the baggage. As he examined the hinny, he watched the leader walk with two others to a cache, concealed by a pile of rocks at the edge of the forest. They removed the rocks and gathered supplies before returning to the group. Bollard then turned his attention to Saud's baggage.

He forced a small opening in the corner of the baggage, stuck his hand inside, and pulled out paper – Saudi Arabian riyals.

Chapter 21
A Negotiation

A small fire and the shoulder of the hinny roasting on a spit created a mixture of inviting aromas as the men began to awaken. The sun beat directly on many members of the force. Those not already moving toward the spit began to shift and rustle from their positions.

Bollard walked to the edge of the field to join the skinner who was watching over his pack animals. The green grass and fresh water invigorated them.

"Looks like they're doing well," Bollard said as he approached. "The handlers are still resting."

"Yes. I have plenty of time to interrupt their leisure. We still have a long distance to go." However, the skinner had no compulsion about interrupting the sleep of one member of the group. He continued, "I can't afford to lose another. I'm going to speak with the idiot. He owes me restitution for killing my hinny."

"Well, Vsadnik, not just for that hinny but the generations of its offspring," Bollard said lightheartedly.

The skinner smiled, "Yes, the loss of the future generations is indeed substantial." He winked and walked toward Saud who was beginning to stir.

The skinner stood directly over him, purposefully not blocking the noonday sun.

"You killed my hinny, and you have to pay for him," Vsadnik threatened.

Saud threw his hand up to block the sun but could only see the outline of the man standing before him. The cold voice and the floppy hat sent a shiver through him, and he stood immediately.

There was a flurry of activity and Bollard could see a heated exchange of words, with the skinner on the offense. Saud led the skinner to his baggage and retrieved a few paper bundles and offered them to the skinner. There was further shouting as Saud pushed the bundles back into the baggage before retrieving several other bundles. The skinner took them and walked away, passing near Bollard.

"All this time he's been carrying a load of worthless foreign currency. Tried to pay me with it. Only rubles will replace my hinny," Vsadnik grumbled.

Bollard shook his head.

"By the way," Vsadnik said, looking over his shoulder and eyes twinkling. "Three generations!"

Chapter 22
End of the Road

With the steeper terrain Bollard could see the trail on the far side of the next mountain, but it took hours to get to it over a long and circuitous route. At some points, the distance between the two mountains was extremely close. He wondered why he'd seen no effort to bridge the short distance. His answer was forthcoming as the front of the column halted.

The skinner walked by in a hurry. "Move the hinnies forward."

Bollard and the other handlers obeyed. Just ahead there was a one-hundred-meter expanse between the near and far side mountain. A steep crevasse lay between.

"Unload the hinnies," the skinner demanded.

After unloading the packs, Bollard watched the far side as another skinner and his handlers drove a three-mule team forward. As they did, a rope tied to the harness on the mules and anchored on the near side, appeared to pop from its concealed position in the valley. Soon the rope along with a hauling line was taut and bridged the expanse. The process took less than ten minutes.

"Attach the baggage to the traversing rope and the hauling line," the leader shouted to the group.

After they attached one bag to the traversing rope and sent it across, they returned the hauling line to the near side. Then they attached the next bag and sent it across. In this way, the men quickly secured all of the baggage on the far side.

"This will give my hinnies a break. It'll take six hours to get to that location on the far side and the terrain is difficult," the skinner said to Bollard.

"Very smart and efficient," Bollard replied.

The group set off again, with the hinnies showing new energy. Halfway through the route, they stopped once and joined with three young auxiliary men at a cache site. Bollard noted their enthusiasm and professionalism as they assisted in loading new provisions. After some discussion and coordination with the auxiliary members, the group continued ahead.

Having traveled for over six hours, they arrived at the baggage crossing site where a security element was waiting with their packs. The security element had hidden the traversing rope and the hauling line in their original location and the three-mule team and handlers were gone. The group reloaded the hinnies and began its final push through Chechnya.

As the insertion was nearing completion, Bollard's real mission would be underway. He anticipated he would join Chechen guerrillas and had prepared himself accordingly. However, if they were comprised of multiple groups and ethnicities, he would have to be more deliberative in everything he said. As he contemplated these issues, he felt a hand squeeze his shoulder. He turned to see the skinner now walking beside him and pointing to a field in the distant mountains.

"My home!" Vsadnik beamed. "We'll stop nearby and get grain for the hinnies. From there we're only a day's march to the base camp."

"It looks very nice. I expect you're anxious to return home," Bollard said politely.

"Yes. I wish we had time to show you the horses and donkeys and the young hinnies."

"Me too," Bollard replied. "I can see the outlines in the field."

Vsadnik squinted. "They're grazing. My son would be watching them. They're too valuable to be left alone."

"Perhaps someday I'll get to see them. I'm sure they're excellent specimens!"

"The leader won't stop except to resupply and to overnight. But that's okay, he has a mission to complete. Me? I'll return home as quickly as possible!"

He was correct. The pace again picked up as the column moved closer to the base camp. The leader stopped the column three times. The first stop was to give the remaining meat from the hinny's shoulder to several from the local auxiliary, the second to pick up grain for the hinnies, and the last to resupply a cache site. Bollard noted they made no effort to conceal the location of the caches from the others. After a long march, the convoy closed in for the night. As they did, Bollard sensed a higher level of attentiveness and anxiousness. Up to this point, the group had little interaction and paid only cursory attention to him and Saud. Now, the focus seemed to shift completely to them.

"From here forward you'll be under escort," the leader told them after bringing Saud and Bollard together. He walked with both to a large boulder. "Tonight, I want you to rest here and stay together. We'll be providing security and you should notify the guard before moving about."

The next morning, they ate breakfast under guard and began the last day's hike to the basecamp. Before they arrived, the leader stopped the column and directed the guards to blindfold both Saud and Bollard.

Part II

The Second Thread

Chapter 1
Chimkent, USSR
1977

Theirs was not a journey of convenience but necessity. The hope of a new life free of oppression offset the concern for the treacherous route and the many dangers along its way. Thirteen-year-old Sulundik's family was determined to depart their homeland of Chimkent, the Kazakh Soviet Republic, for the religious freedom they sought in Afghanistan. Chimkent had been their home for centuries, but they were of Afghan origin with strictly Muslim heritage. Now, the atheistic government of the Soviet Union had yet again increased its efforts to suppress religion in the region. It considered Islam a threat and inconsistent with communist doctrine. As a result, the central power imposed varying degrees of repression throughout the Central Asian republics, especially in Chimkent.

The beautiful city was a crossroad connecting European Russia and Western Siberia with Central Asia; a city that blended the cultural influences of each of the regions as their people passed through or traded in its center. It was this intersection of cultures that concerned Soviet apparatchiks. They perceived the cross-pollination as a threat and were concerned that Islamic influences in Chimkent might take greater hold among the population at the expense of Russian dominance.

Historically, Chimkent was one small stop of many on the crossroads comprising the old Silk Road of the Far East. It was in these towns and along these routes that legitimate business thrived between the country villages and larger settlements. But another economy operated in the shadows. Age-old roads and trails, largely unknown to outside populations, emerged from the Silk Routes. These ran adjacent and parallel to the well-traveled trade routes. As old as the Silk Routes themselves, they afforded black marketers, thieves, and robbers a means of cloaked approach to vulnerable caravans as well as an ideal means to elude pursuit into the mountains.

Randal R. Jones

It was these lesser-known routes that Sulundik's family traveled to find a new home in Afghanistan.

***

In Kunduz, in the northeast region of Afghanistan, they would join other family members who previously settled there in the hope of escaping religious persecution. Kunduz was a place where they could practice their *Hanafi* school of Islamic faith without repression. Hanafi regarded far broader considerations for Sharia than other forms of Sunni teachings. Their faith recognized the Koran, the teaching and practices of the Prophet, consensus, legal analogy, juristic views, customs, and culture in determining their practice of Sharia. The Afghan government was inclined to leave the tribes and peoples to their beliefs without interference.

The long journey covered eight hundred kilometers over hazardous terrain that deliberately cut the seams of the borders of Uzbekistan and Kyrgyzstan. It traversed the shortest route along Tajikistan to the Kunduz region just across the Soviet border into northeast Afghanistan. Sulundik's family joined an uncle and two of his sons on this journey.

Uncle Bolat was a half-brother to Sulundik's mother. A likable man, tall and lean with a thin mustache and easy smile, his neighbors greeted him enthusiastically whenever he joined a gathering. A trader who plied his wares, some legitimate, some illicit, along the Kazakh-Afghan route every four months and was, therefore, familiar with the peoples and dangers along the way. The dangers were often unique to the region as tribal and clan factions with historic ties or animosities required a careful eye and art of negotiation, compromise, or reason and as a last resort, force.

Armed with a hidden knife, Sulundik escorted two older sisters and a younger sister everywhere in public or away from home. On this journey, as in Chimkent, Sulundik's role was simple but came with its own set of dangers, to protect the sisters. They could move nowhere by themselves and their whereabouts were known and secured throughout the journey. The threat of bride kidnappings was a constant in their travels.

106

This was a concern especially in the Kyrgyzstan region as young males sought out future brides, sometimes by violence. Sulundik was adamant this would not happen.

***

Uncle Bolat's eldest son, Erasyl, was anything but the "noble hero" his name implied. Indeed, those outside the immediate family referred to him as the "lazy one." Sulundik often found Erasyl lurking about and near the sisters' safe zone; far enough away to deny an allegation, but close enough for Sulundik to consciously reach for the knife hidden in the loose-fitting tunic and to maintain a wary eye on him. Rumors persisted that Erasyl had a particular interest in young boys; more than one matriarch scurried her children inside when Erasyl was in the area.

Sulundik's Uncle Bolat, seeing a future opportunity, had a secondary and discrete mission on this journey. He directed Sulundik to learn the route; not only to memorize the terrain features in front of the group but look rearward often and pick out distinct and key landmarks. This would assist in navigation while returning along the same route. At one stop he pointed to a bent branch along the trail. The branch was bent but not completely broken and had grown downward.

"You must watch for these limbs," he said, taking hold of it. Looking around he pointed to three rocks stacked away from the trail. "You should always be on your guard on the route. A tree branch bent toward the ground indicates danger and caution should be taken. If you see three rocks stacked nearby it indicates a violent confrontation occurred here."

Sulundik didn't see the rocks at first. Uncle Bolat pointed again and warned, "Three rocks always mean a confrontation even if there is no bent limb. When you have an issue with the local tribes or individuals along the trail, ensure you bend a nearby branch. If it results in violence or the locals are violent you should stack the rocks to warn others. However, if we establish a good relationship and the bent branches or rocks say otherwise, you should cut the limb and kick the rocks apart. We don't want to approach local populations in a hostile manner because of old trail markings. Do you understand?"

"Yes, Uncle."

"Good," he replied. "Now take your knife and cut the bent branch off the tree and go kick over the rocks. I have established a working relationship in this area, and they are no longer hostile." Sulundik quickly did as told and returned to relieve the family patriarch of the protection of the three sisters.

The caravan moved slowly along the trail, relying on an established infrastructure of support. Usually, they walked. Each person carried their personal as well as Uncle Bolat's trade goods on their backs. Stooped and moving slowly they eased their way along the rocky trails of craggy mountains with open areas and sections of interspersed pine. Each new member searched the trail ahead for a road and where a truck might appear, while the experienced watched for bent branches, stacked rocks, or the threat of robbers who might be lurking along the narrow passes.

Occasionally, Uncle coordinated for a truck to transport the group. Sitting in the back of the truck was a respite from so much walking. They huddled together and fell asleep immediately. The group took on the appearance of a single mass bouncing along the narrow dirt roads. After the truck transported them over the mountains, the caravan members unloaded and shifted the cargo to waiting horses or donkeys as Uncle paid the truck driver in saffron, tea, and a small brick of an unidentifiable brown substance.

The group spent their evenings rearranging packs and eating the tiny rations of food. They spent their nights curled around a campfire that provided barely enough heat. Guards armed with knives and rifles stood at the approaches to the camp.

Uncle Bolat occasionally stopped the group at pre-established trading points located off the main trail. He and the experienced travelers bartered for the finer cotton on the Uzbek border, leafed tobacco in Kyrgyzstan, and sheets of aluminum and canisters of oil in Tajikistan.

This pattern of life continued until, eventually, a waiting family member met them near the Afghan border. Loading into a creaky truck the caravan rode the final ten bumpy kilometers around the KGB border positions and across the porous border to Kunduz. There, they excitedly greeted and embraced family members as others apportioned cotton to the waiting matriarchs. They divided and distributed oil, silk, tobacco, and saffron to the other relatives, leaving the sheets of tin and remaining products for Uncle Bolat to trade locally.

By any measure, the feats of Sulundik's family to escape communism were extraordinary and born of necessity if they were to worship freely. They proved that in times of necessity, extraordinary is simply remarkable, and remarkable isn't given a second thought as unimaginable challenges must be overcome if aspirations are to be fulfilled. Driven by necessity, the family proved the desire for freedom surmounted all obstacles.

Chapter 2
Kunduz, Afghanistan

Life in Kunduz was a unique experience for everyone. While the family loved their new life with family members nearby and the newfound religious freedom was electrifying, Sulundik was not so sure. In the Soviet Union Sulundik's range of interaction, socially and culturally, was large and varying. Here in Kunduz, Sulundik's activities were limited to the immediate family, the town itself, and of course the Mosque.

Sulundik missed being in school in Chimkent. Though required by Soviet law for universal education, Sulundik's father kept the sisters at home. Sulundik attended school with Russian students and established relationships with the Russian youth as well as the Kazakh and family community. They played sports on groomed fields and enjoyed one another's companionship before, during, and after school. In Kunduz, the field was a dusty, rocky maze, full of potholes and few understood the world outside Afghanistan. Sulundik studied many topics across broad areas in the Soviet Union, but here in Kunduz the subjects were limited, and the Koran was at the center.

Sulundik didn't miss many of the Russian boys. They were a vulgar lot and their language reflected it. Sulundik was careful not to utter these words lest a slip and repetition in the presence of the Islamic community resulted in an unbelievable beating. It was from these youth that Sulundik learned the meaning of the most disgusting words, the jokes about girls, the desire to screw as many as possible, and the flagrant disregard for a pregnancy that could be readily remedied with a visit to "Dr. Blood."

Among the Russian boys, Georg Ivanov was Sulundik's best friend. Though taller than the native Kazakhs, Georg's black hair and dark features set him apart from the majority of the light-skinned Russian children. A natural leader, Georg organized the games to be played and his word was usually final in a disputed call. Sulundik admired the exuberance Georg displayed for everything with his quick wit and ready smile. Georg's mischievous dark eyes lit up when plotting some activity that would surely land everyone in trouble.

He taught Sulundik how to play chess and soon the young Muslim student was the school champion. A small chess board, a gift from Georg, was the one personal item Sulundik was permitted on the family's journey to Kunduz.

Georg was never boring. Importantly, he was never vulgar and that was important to Sulundik. Where you saw Georg, you would see Sulundik.

"You some kind of faggot?" a young boy called out to Sulundik when the two embraced at the end of a tough soccer win. Sulundik bristled with anger. But Georg, with fists drawn, immediately turned on the young provocateur who quickly fled. Sulundik was faster but much smaller than the others and Georg often served as a protector. This was important to Sulundik because a physical confrontation with a Russian boy would be futile. Not just because of the size difference but because it could escalate into an even bigger issue between an ethnic Central Asian Muslim and an ethnic, officially atheistic Russian. More than once, other Tajiks or Kazakhs prevented a friend from physically settling a dispute with an ethnic Russian. It's why a close friendship with an ethnic Russian could be dangerous and why Georg and Sulundik's relationship was unique.

Sulundik's father warned against becoming too close for all these reasons and more, and Russian parents warned the same regarding the Muslim community. When it came to religion, there was a fine line between what was legal and what had to be reported to the state. The more one knew of another's religious practices the more likely a report would be filed. This was the reason Sulundik's family and others worshipped in the secrecy and privacy of their homes and why the Mosques were in a state of disrepair or systematic destruction. The Communist government had a quick hammer in the zealous arm of a brutal police force and a sharp sickle for the tongues of those who failed to report an infraction of state policy on religion. The family's presence in Afghanistan made this aspect of Soviet life a distant memory.

But Sulundik never forgot Georg.

Chapter 3
Erasyl

One member of the family was especially happy to be in Afghanistan – Sulundik's cousin, Erasyl. After arriving in Kunduz, he disappeared into the mountains occasionally for several days at a time. The rumor was that he met with another tribe, headed by a degenerate old tribal leader and warlord. There, after receiving a small sum, the tribal leader provided a source that satisfied a peculiar interest – *bacha bazi*.

A Central Asian practice, bacha bazi catered to the interest in young boys. Dressed as girls, these boys danced to seductive music and were the victims of sexual exploitation by their tribe and others. The tribal leader wasn't concerned about the legal or moral ramifications. An approach to a woman, whether married or not, could result in death and blood feuds; not so, with young boys. The abusers paid a high price to the tribe and families of these boys and there were no complaints. The practice of bacha bazi was much more lucrative and safer in Afghanistan than in Kazakhstan where punishment was quick and severe, much to the pleasure of Erasyl, whose life had now become much easier and less dangerous.

Comfortable and relaxed in the safe environment of Afghanistan, Sulundik did not always accompany the sisters to get fresh water from a small spring on a nearby hill. Ulbolsyn, three years older than Sulundik, went alone on occasion. After one such trip, she returned with little water and sat quietly by herself, refusing to speak to anyone if she did not have to. Sulundik questioned her but she said nothing. Two months passed and Ulbolsyn asked Sulundik to accompany her to get water. Sulundik rose and walked ahead of her to the spring.

Ulbolsyn called to stop and pointed to a small ravine away from the spring, "This is where Erasyl killed me." Her hands dropped automatically to her stomach.

Sulundik walked back to her and touched her arm. "What do you mean?"

"He raped me here and now I am pregnant. I'm dead."

Sulundik raged, "I will bring him before the elders and shall kill him with my own hands!"

"You must settle yourself. You know this isn't possible," Ulbolsyn said sadly. "He'll say I brought it on, that I enticed him with my eyes and by being here alone. It's my word against his and the elders will believe him. I'll be condemned and certainly stoned. My fate is sealed."

Sulundik was furious but knew she was right. Sulundik was the one to be shamed. Allowing the sisters to go to the spring unescorted was a mistake and irresponsible.

Sulundik protested, "But you're pregnant..."

Ulbolsyn interrupted, "You've forgotten the rules. I'll be forced to have the baby and wean it, and then I'll be stoned. They'll say it's the only way to purge my sin."

"You're right. Let's sit. We must think," Sulundik said turning away as anger and frustration welled up to a torrent of tears. This would require the strategy of a chess player, each move must be carefully thought through well in advance. After several minutes Sulundik broke the silence, "We must return to Chimkent right away."

"What?" Ulbolsyn asked.

"We must go to Chimkent while you are still early. No one besides me needs to know about this. Do you understand?" Sulundik's brain was racing and full of thoughts and plans that far outpaced what one would expect of a thirteen-year-old, and certainly beyond Ulbolsyn's comprehension.

"Understand?" Ulbolsyn questioned.

"No one should know you were raped, or that you are pregnant! No one!"

"But I should warn my sisters about Erasyl!"

"No! No one! You told me and you didn't tell them. You trusted me, so trust me now. I'll give clear instructions to all of our sisters about traveling as a group including to the spring."

"If God wills it."

"I assure you God wills it! You needn't fear. If you listen to me, you won't be stoned and I won't have to kill a cousin."

"What will we do?"

Sulundik was happy Ulbolsyn said "we." It meant she had relented and was now placing her life in Sulundik's hands.

113

"There are Russian doctors in Chimkent, and I have friends among the Russians who can be trusted."

"But why this journey?"

"Are you being deliberately naïve? We have only one choice, and you must not question it or me in making it. Is that clear?"

"But what are you saying?" She paused. "It's a life and it's a sin! God will not forgive me."

Sulundik replied instantly, "You are not the sinner here! The eldest son is Satan. Is it God's will you have demon seed in you?"

"But..."

Sulundik had heard this discussion among Russian friends on multiple occasions. The average Russian woman used abortion as birth control and had as many as four or five abortions over their lifetime. The pros and cons of the sin that Ulbolsyn was to undertake were clear. A case for it had to be made, but on grounds that went beyond the religious and moral side.

"Do you wish to see my death as a result of Erasyl's sin?" Sulundik asked.

"Of course not!"

"If we do not undertake this course of action, three of Allah's children will die unnecessarily. We are all dead. You'll be stoned. I'll kill Erasyl. Our uncle will kill me for having killed his son. Besides, if this isn't God's will, he will provide an alternative."

Ulbolsyn had not considered the cascading effect that might unfold. "As Allah wills it," she replied quietly lowering her head and realizing the full impact of Sulundik's decision and method to save their lives.

They returned home with their containers of water and Sulundik walked straight to a gathering of men outside the home. "Father, I would like to accompany Uncle Bolat on his next journey to Chimkent."

The father was taken aback and did not respond; this had not been discussed previously and appropriately in private. Before he could reply Sulundik continued, "If I accompany him, we will increase our share of goods and can add to our stocks before winter. Uncle taught me the routes, as well as the signs and the dangers."

Sulundik's father looked at Bolat, who politely and appropriately said nothing, but nodded his head in agreement.

"So be it," he replied and walked away from the group.

Sulundik walked alongside him. "I'll want Ulbolsyn to accompany me."

"Why? She's not the oldest."

"She's stronger, works harder, and is more obedient to my direction. She'll make more money for us."

Sulundik's father couldn't argue with the logic and agreed.

Chapter 4
The Road to Chimkent

Uncle Bolat, Sulundik, Ulbolsyn, and three neighbors gathered on the dusty road in front of Sulundik's home. Conspicuously, neither of Uncle's sons would make the difficult journey, reaffirming every negative thought Sulundik had about the cousins. They were dangerous and lazy. One of the neighbors led a small donkey that was barely visible under a large load of carpets, protected by burlap and plastic. The other struggled with another donkey burdened with hides and pelts tied into squares and strapped down by a heavy hemp rope.

Uncle Bolat showed Sulundik a curved nushtar. "This will be better than your small knife should you need to protect yourself or Ulbolsyn."

Sulundik was familiar with the tool. It generally had a single blade affixed to a handle meant for scoring opium poppies. It was a simple enough design. A tin can cut in half and attached to a handle would do the trick. However, this nushtar was of the highest quality. It was handmade of metal with a curved blade, scooped toward the inside to catch raw opium, and narrowing slightly toward the base. It was perfectly balanced and seated in a well-crafted wooden handle. Sulundik noted, unlike other nushtars, that the blade line on this nushtar followed its curve as well as the greater portion of the forward edge. It was as sharp as a razor.

"Thrust with it this way," Uncle said as he demonstrated a strong thrusting motion from the center of his body carrying his full weight into the thrust. Sulundik had never considered a nushtar might be used to stab but could see how this one, given its sharp blade, could be much more effective. It appeared Uncle Bolat had more than one purpose in mind when he made this nushtar.

"When striking an opponent, hold it like a dagger. Ensure when you strike you miss with the fist and allow the nushtar to strike the person in the face or throat. The resistance of the force is against the fingers and not the thumb." Uncle demonstrated again, throwing a strike from right to left and following with a left-to-right movement of the hand.

"Now you do it," Uncle demanded as he handed Sulundik the nushtar. Sulundik tried twice. "Good," he said approvingly and smiled. "Keep it on you at all times."

Sulundik placed the nushtar inside the loose-fitting tunic alongside the knife and grunted loudly while picking up the assigned pack. The load was extremely heavy with the pack straps already cutting into the shoulders. The pack contained five disassembled rifles; each part wrapped in a thick cloth like a precious metal. Ulbolsyn's pack was somewhat lighter, but awkward, and slid from left to right on her shoulders. Her pack contained handmade jewelry, tightly drawn packets of spices, including hard-to-find saffron, and an unwieldy collection of kitchenware. The other neighbor and Uncle Bolat each carried a rifle. Their packs were light but more valuable, containing brown bricks of raw morphine among other things.

Uncle Bolat preferred raw morphine to all the other products he bartered or sold. It was readily available in Afghanistan, easy to transport, very valuable, and in high demand. Other traders sought it because Uncle's was in its purest form. Removed from the bulk of the opium, the raw morphine allowed the purchaser the option of further refining it into heroin or simply using it for medicinal purposes. Caution was the rule for trading in this product. The penalty was severe and could result in execution or a lifetime in prison. This doubled its value.

***

The trail became increasingly narrow as the group moved higher into the mountains. The slope of the mountain pass was barren, too steep to support the growth of plants. Sulundik looked over the edge and noted the only patches of vegetation were in the valley below. The view was dizzying, and Sulundik cautioned Ulbolsyn to keep focused on the trail to her front. As their route began to level and walking became somewhat easier, Uncle announced they had crossed into Tajikistan. After an hour he signaled everyone to stop, as he moved off the trail and walked up a small draw to an open area. Several Tajik marketers were waiting by a fire. A pot of water was nestled in the coals and steam curled off in an inviting and serpentine way. Recognizing his contacts, Uncle walked up to them and embraced the leader, then acknowledged each of the other five Tajiks. The leader was high-spirited and laughed often, flashing a row of dark and missing teeth. He walked with Uncle Bolat who signaled for the rest of his group to come forward.

"Come! We'll have tea," he shouted, greeting them gregariously.

Uncle Bolat and his group of traders walked into the camp as the Tajik men embraced everyone except Ulbolsyn. She and one of the neighbors stayed near the donkeys while Sulundik sat with Uncle and the men around the fire. They swapped stories of experiences in the region, issues with authorities, and opportunities as they slowly savored the tea. As casual as it seemed, this process was the beginning of a ritual, an expectation, and therefore a formality. It was the prelude to the successful consummation of any deal.

When they finished the final sip of tea and dispensed the pleasantries, Uncle stood and motioned for the Tajiks to follow. They walked over to the donkeys and opened the burlap to show off the carpets and some of the pelts. The men were uninterested.

The leader laughed again and turned to Uncle Bolat. "These are beautiful carpets! Fit for a king! But we need rifles and ammunition."

Sulundik started to pull some of the rifle parts from the large pack but stopped abruptly with Uncle's quick response. "We don't trade in guns. What else do you want?"

The Tajik leader's rotted smile took on an edge. "Sell us the guns you are carrying."

"That's impossible," Uncle replied.

"We need more guns and know your people could provide them."

"That's something we could discuss, but the price would be high."

"What's in the pack?" The leader asked, pointing to Sulundik.

"Kitchen goods, which we've promised to others along the journey. Are you interested in looking?" Uncle asked gesturing for Ulbolsyn to open her pack.

Uncle lifted the pack and gently poured the contents onto the ground. The Tajiks looked carefully at the pots, pans, and utensils made from aluminum Uncle Bolat had received from the same Tajiks in a previous trade. The Tajik leader chose several pots and pans and directed his people to lay out the various collections of fruits, vegetable oils, and thin sheets of aluminum.

After several rounds of negotiations, they loaded Ulbolsyn's pack with exchanged goods to be bartered, sold, or eaten along the way. Uncle embraced the Tajik leader before leading the caravan away, promising to stop again in six to seven weeks.

A few hours and several kilometers away, Sulundik approached Uncle Bolat when they stopped to rest. There was something about trading with the Tajiks that didn't seem right. "Uncle, with all respect, I want to understand the trading process. Why didn't you sell the Tajiks a gun, or even some of the morphine?"

Uncle Bolat, cutting and eating a piece of an apple he had just traded for, quietly replied, "The Tajiks are poor. They are constantly fighting one another, have no money, and can't pay the price for morphine though they need it. They could use their aluminum sheets to make utensils as our family does, but they choose to focus on other things. They don't want the guns for hunting, but to use on one another, or even on us if it suited them."

"So, you don't trust them?"

"Not a question of trust, but opportunity and temptation. Never give a snake the venom that might be used to strike against you, and don't give it a reason to strike by revealing the value of your packs," Uncle said matter-of-factly.

"How do you know what you can trade or sell to the different tribes?"

"As you travel from region to region with me, you will learn the different wants and needs of the people as well as the things they might have to offer. You need to understand the complexities so you know if it can be worked to your benefit or your detriment." It was more than Uncle had ever spoken to Sulundik.

The trek continued. Every so often, Uncle Bolat motioned for Sulundik to come forward and identified signs along the trail as he had previously. At one spot, he pointed to a small draw that led back to a concealed position above the trail they had just walked.

"If you get the sense someone is following you, or you have issues with the other traders, conceal yourself in that kind of position. From there you can observe without being noticed and you can determine if someone is up to no good. Then watch the trail for at least thirty minutes to an hour. If you're followed you can get an idea of their intent by watching their actions, how they look forward, checking for tracks, and how fast they move. Then you'll know how to respond."

"What do you mean, 'sense' we are followed?"

"You have to develop every sense, not just what you can see and hear. You must develop a sense of feeling for things around you, and how to think with the nape of your neck, especially when something seems wrong. Allah gives us this sense, but few understand it or most importantly don't act on it."

"Like with the Tajiks? Something seemed wrong."

"That's very good Sulundik. What did you notice about the Tajiks?"

Sulundik thought carefully, "The Tajik leader smiled, laughed, and talked a lot, but the others of his group were solemn, and no one smiled."

"Good," Uncle said approvingly. "You observed it, but you sensed something did not seem normal. Look at our group. Everyone picks up my mood and adjusts to my spirit at the time. When I relax, they relax. When I'm tense, they're tense. Even when I pretend to be feeling something else."

"So, the leader was tense?"

"His actions were a ruse, and his followers knew it. He was trying to get close to us, to distract us. Perhaps to see if we dropped our guard, snatch a rifle, or simply size us up for the next trip. When a group is overzealous in how they mimic their leader, it also betrays their intentions. What did you notice about our group?"

Sulundik was unsure how to respond.

"There was always someone at a distance from the trading," Uncle responded when Sulundik paused. "Usually behind a donkey with his hands on a rifle. Each of the men watched my demeanor which didn't change to the Tajik leader's prodding and responded accordingly."

"I'll watch you and the traders more carefully," Sulundik said, having missed all the signs.

***

They traveled several more days before undertaking a long trading session in the region of Kyrgyzstan. They bartered most of the heavier carpets and utensils and picked up a load of tobacco. Sulundik still carried the weight of the rifles, having not traded any, and observed the Kyrgyz were different than the others with whom they traded.

"Hard to figure sometimes," Uncle had confided.

The young Kyrgyz men were not discreet in how they looked at Ulbolsyn. Angered, Sulundik saw this and kept Ulbolsyn close by and was happy to leave for the Kyrgyz border.

Uncle Bolat called Sulundik to sit. "In two days, we'll meet with the Uzbeks. They're friendly and no threat. There will be several women trading as well as men. They don't mind dealing with men or women or even youth if they think they can get a good deal. I'll trade with the men for their finest cotton. I want you to trade utensils and tobacco with the women for more saffron and tea."

"So, we'll trade some of the tobacco we just got from the Kyrgyz?"

"Correct. In Ulbolsyn's pack are a few small tin toys to trade. I'll give you a small amount of morphine and a bottle of sweet liquor to sell as well. The liquor is rare. Find out how the women value each of these items."

Uncle explained the negotiating process for conducting the trades, which Sulundik had been watching for quite some time. Focusing on Uncle's directions Sulundik didn't know whether to be insulted at being relegated to trading with the women, or proud Uncle Bolat had such a level of trust.

121

Chapter 5
Side Trip

Sulundik noticed Uncle Bolat's bright mood as they got nearer to the Uzbek trade site. Uncle unexpectedly loaded his pack onto a donkey and directed Sulundik to do the same. Sulundik was confused but followed his instruction.

"The men know where to go for the night and will be nearby for trading tomorrow. You and I will go to town and get food." He looked at Ulbolsyn, "You needn't cook tonight." Uncle then picked up another pack that contained tobacco and morphine and handed it to Sulundik.

They left the group, walked down a mountain trail, and arrived just outside a small Uzbek town.

"We have to enter the town cautiously. We have no documents for traveling internally or externally and any prying eyes could put us in a bad place. I have a friend who's a butcher with a small restaurant and a back room. We'll enter from the rear of the building, and he'll prepare meals and drinks. You and I will eat here and bring the rest of the food to the others. He'll be a good person for you to know in the future."

Uncle Bolat's comment struck an important note. Sulundik never considered black marketing and trading goods were going to be more than a single endeavor. Uncle seemed to have other thoughts; that Sulundik might take up the business as well. Now was not the time for that discussion.

***

They entered the town and walked directly to the back side of the butcher shop where Uncle knocked on the door. A squat, bald man greeted them enthusiastically and, placing an arm around Uncle Bolat, showed them to a waiting table. The man's wife walked to the door of the inner room, smiled, and waved.

There was one table in the room and three in the outer room, but no guests. Sulundik could see meat hanging from hooks in the front with a large body of flies swarming around each. The severed heads of a horse and goat looked down with black eyes on the tables below. The wife waved a dish rag vigorously in their direction each time she passed, shooing the flies from the heads and the drip pans below.

Sulundik's stomach growled incessantly in anticipation of the meal, as the appetizing smell of well-seasoned shashlik wafted through the room. Soon the wife emerged with three large plates of food as the bald man joined them for the meal.

The two men laughed and traded stories between gulps of tea and roasted mutton. Regardless of the topic, each story came back to the local government apparatchiks and the police and the men's utter disdain for them.

"They are dumber than this dead goat and more obstinate than my wife," the man said referring to the authorities. He slammed his hand on the table, laughing at his own joke, and shouted for his wife to produce another round. Getting down to business he said, "We've coordinated with the police and they'll be gone tomorrow. Your share in the cost of getting rid of them, as usual, will be a brick of morphine. Between all of the groups, it is enough to ensure a good day of trading, legal or illegal."

"My payment is a fair share, one brick," Uncle Bolat said as he finished eating.

Satisfied, the three of them pushed back from the table for a breath before the man produced a bottle. "At least the Russians are good for something," he said as he poured a small amount of Russian vodka into three tiny glasses. "Though we don't have to drink like them! This will help our digestion," he said with a slight twinkle in his eye.

Sulundik had never tasted alcohol. Strictly forbidden. Sulundik hesitated, but Uncle's elbow was a reminder of the proper protocol. They clinked glasses and drank in a single gulp. It was fire and it went all the way to the stomach. Sulundik coughed and struggled to catch fresh air. Uncle and the man howled in laughter.

"We'll keep this between the three of us," Uncle laughed, then seeing the wife laughing at the door, "Okay, the four of us!"

"Here, this is for you my friend," Uncle said as he handed over the pack full of tobacco, a brick of morphine, and a piece of jewelry. "Enough for you and the police."

"You know how to keep a man out of trouble," the man laughed as he handed the necklace to his wife. "You're more than a fair trader and always welcome here. And that goes for you too," he said to Sulundik. "Maybe the next time you'll enjoy this fine vodka!"

Sulundik laughed and thanked him. They departed, carrying enough food for the others for that night and the next day.

Chapter 6
Uzbeks

Rest, a hot meal and a cup of tea were like an elixir for the group as they excitedly prepared to meet the Uzbek traders.

"We'll give the Uzbeks time to set up and let them wait a bit. We want them eager to trade," Uncle Bolat said as they untied the donkeys and began to load their goods.

Soon the group walked into the village where the Uzbeks were waiting to trade. It was a well-organized bazaar with two rows of local traders, each on opposite sides of the road and they were already engaged. The organization, coordination, and synchronization were even more evident as another group of traders arrived simultaneously from Kazakhstan and in the opposite direction as Uncle and his caravan. Normally, this might be an issue and cause a real competitive stir, but not here. Each group brought goods unique to their specific regions and countries. Uncle's goods were more diverse with Afghan, Tajik, and Kyrgyz products which gave him the ability to mix and match and bundle multiple items for a better deal.

Uncle Bolat organized his caravan carefully, assigning each member of the group a specific role. Sulundik was to determine the value of liquor, morphine, and the tin toys. Uncle Bolat directed Ulbolsyn to sit on the neatly spread carpets that concealed Sulundik's pack of rifles. Uncle ordered another to watch the donkeys and maintain vigilance, as the other determined anything of value that could be taken to Kazakhstan. Uncle Bolat would negotiate for cotton.

Having given Sulundik a small bag containing the trading items, Uncle pointed to the end of the street and the brightly dressed Uzbek women. "They're your new associates," he said. "But first, I want you to come with me."

Sulundik followed as Uncle picked up another bag and walked in the direction of the cotton traders. He stopped just short of them.

"I want to show you something. What do you see in the market?" he asked, waving a broad arch of his hand.

"This is the area they trade cotton," Sulundik responded, not sure of Uncle's intent.

"Men are trading at the far end and women trading at this end. I trade with the men. I'll tell you why later. But first, look at the women trading cotton and the women across the street in the market section. What do you see?"

"The women here are a bit more stooped, they are more tanned, and their clothes are more worn."

"Very good. As we walk past, I want you to look at their hands."

Carpets lined the side of the road and the women stood in front, clearly in charge of their little section of the bazaar. They neatly displayed their cotton samples on the carpet and stacked the bales directly behind. The women held their best cotton samples high for all to see and engaged everyone who passed by in a well-practiced sales pitch.

After walking by the women, Uncle Bolat asked, "What did you see?"

"Their hands are scarred. It looks like they have scars on top of scars, and some have fresh scabs."

"What does this tell you about the women? Their suntanned skin and scarred hands, and they're hunched over?"

Sulundik hesitated too long, and Uncle answered. "It tells you that they themselves pick the cotton they are selling. They stoop in the fields all day under the hot sun. Their clothing reflects their labor. The sharp edges of the cotton bolls cut into their fingers and around their nails as they try to pick all of the cotton from each boll. Ultimately, their hands and fingers become callused and scarred."

"Then why not trade with them?"

"Always look at each person and group with whom you deal. Examine them carefully. They are different and all have a story. It's the story that will lead you to the best deal. Think carefully about how you described them. These women labored and labored hard to harvest the cotton. They value it more, and they bled and sweated for it. So, they place a higher value on it. Also, some of the women glean the cotton, so the quality is not as good."

"What do you mean?"

"They move into the fields after the main harvest of the crop and pull what's left of the bolls, which isn't the best cotton."

"The men aren't farmers?"

"The men are mostly middlemen. They work trades and deals before we get here; they all know one another and can better negotiate the price for cotton than we can. They'll add a little bit and resell or barter. They don't place the same value on the hard labor to harvest the cotton as the women. As a result, we can negotiate and barter our goods for a better deal with the men."

Sulundik started to walk away but Uncle wasn't finished. "Remember, a good deal is one in which everyone is satisfied. There's always 'puffing' or exaggeration in what is said and in facial expressions and hand movements, but the eyes will tell you if they're satisfied. Other indicators are handshakes, back-slapping, and laughing. In trading with these women, it would be difficult for all parties to be satisfied. Anything less than what they want might be viewed as an insult. At the same time, we want the best return on the trade without overpaying. We have other options that are better for us."

"So, the women, not the men, are the tougher traders," Sulundik declared as if breaking a code.

Uncle Bolat smiled at the comment and agreed.

"The men are always here, each time we come. We've developed long-standing relationships, some good and some not so good. The women you see today aren't necessarily the same women you'll see in the future due to the intense labor. Relationships are difficult to establish, and you want to do so for the long term."

Sulundik looked again at the women and Uncle continued, "You've had your lesson here, now follow me."

Sulundik followed closely behind as Uncle walked determinedly to an old man who stood in front of four bales of cotton. The old man smiled as Uncle Bolat approached and they greeted one another traditionally, but Uncle's expression did not change.

"How many years have the two of us traded goods?" Uncle asked.

"I believe five years."

127

"In that time have I ever cheated you?" Uncle Bolat asked, his jaw set.

"Never," the old man responded without fully understanding.

Then stepping behind the cotton bales, out of the direct vision of the street, Bolat poured the contents of his bag on the ground and whispered, "Then, why would you shortchange my weight of cotton?"

The old man looked in disbelief on the ground at a large number of brown and greenish un-ripened cotton bolls and two rocks. "What is this?" he stammered.

"This was inside just one bale of cotton I got from you on the last trip. It was the same for the others as well. Because of our long relationship, I didn't run a rod through the bales to check each for such trickery. Now, I'm telling you privately because I feel you're honorable and a better man than this."

Concerned, the old man replied, "I should've run the rod myself when I picked these up. Putting green bolls of raw cotton in a weighted bag is an old trick, and I didn't know about it. Adding rocks inside demonstrates dishonor and the lowest of thieves," he continued, becoming increasingly agitated. "I assure you I know who did this and I'll make this right with you, and they'll pay the price."

"I'm here now. How are you going to make this right?"

The old man calculated, "You bought four bales, which weighed twenty-eight kilograms." Putting the bolls and rocks back in the bag he placed it on a small scale. "The thievery," he emphasized the word, "appears to be one kilogram per bale if you agree. Overall, four kilograms were taken from what you paid." He pondered, "As Allah wills it, seven times your loss, and I will add to it. Take one bale at no cost."

Uncle Bolat agreed, "You are a good and righteous man. But it's more than enough."

The old man pulled a bale from the pile and gave it to Uncle Bolat, "I promise you the man who caused this dishonor will more than pay the cost of the bale. On your way back to Afghanistan I'll have the finest of cotton, properly weighted, waiting for you."

Uncle shook the man's hand, then directed Sulundik to a line of Uzbek women selling produce from behind a series of tables. "Go see what you can trade with those women across the street."

The Uzbek women were shrewd negotiators with a unique perspective of what was and wasn't of value. Complicating any negotiation was the fact that they delighted in seeing if they could get a better deal than their friends. Though serious, it was a kind of game between them. Although only thirteen years old, Sulundik would not be given a better deal than anyone else.

Sulundik asked one woman for the price in rubles for the saffron, then asked about the rice, tea, and spices. In each instance, the woman was firm initially. After fierce negotiation, Sulundik realized the price would drop one-half to three-quarters of the original asking price. Since Sulundik had no money and no intention of purchasing the items, the negotiation laid the foundation for establishing the comparative value of the goods to be bartered. The woman was getting frustrated when Sulundik pulled a shiny and intricate toy puzzle out of the pack and held it out to the lady to examine.

"I'll take three packets of saffron in exchange."

"What is this?" the lady asked.

"It's a toy puzzle, a set of rings. You see, this is the way you unravel it," Sulundik replied giving the rings a couple of twists and they came apart. "And this is the way you put it back together. It's a puzzle." Sulundik reattached the rings and handed the puzzle to the lady.

"Ha! I'll give you nothing for this trinket!" she replied firmly. "The last thing we need in our house is a toy to distract my children from working." She held it out to another Uzbek lady. "Perhaps she can afford toys for her children to play with!"

The second lady took it, examined it, and laughed, "Sure, we'll trade you the equivalent of many hours of our sons screwing around!" She handed it back still laughing and asked, "What else do you have?"

Sulundik sheepishly put the toy back in the pack and pulled out the bottle of brandy. "Well, this is certainly

129

something you might find interesting." Sulundik handed the bottle to the first lady. "I can pour some if you'd like to try it."

The lady laughed even louder. "I don't need or want a drink. Vodka is cheaper. Besides, if my husband were to get this, he would drink it in a single sitting, and I'd get no work from him!"

Sulundik argued, "But you can trade for even higher value!"

"Humph!" the first lady snarled. "Who will I trade it to? My husband? Her?" she said to the second lady who was quite frankly enjoying the spectacle.

Sulundik returned the bottle to the bag and looked at the first lady. "I only have medicine left here but I can get pots or utensils if you like."

Now Sulundik had the attention of both ladies. "What kind of medicine?"

Sulundik whispered, "Morphine."

Both ladies crept forward. This was serious business. Sulundik pulled a cake of morphine out, laid it on the pack, and cut it into four pieces.

Changing strategy Sulundik said, "I know this is useful to those who must work but who might be injured. You can get more work even when someone is hurt. It's also easily traded." Sulundik had their full attention and added a slight trading barb, "But unlikely you can afford it."

"How much in rubles?" the lady said trying to get the value.

"Do you have rubles?"

"We can trade the equivalent."

The hook was set. They wanted it. Sulundik had it.

"Perhaps more than you can manage, but twenty-one packets of saffron is the trade for one-quarter square," Sulundik said, remembering three packets of saffron were worth five rubles and recognizing the value of a full square at one hundred rubles. Sulundik's offer left plenty of negotiating room.

The first lady went into her well-practiced theatrics while the second watched intently, her eyes gleaming while attempting to conceal a smile. The back and forth continued until the deal was sealed at fifteen packets of saffron, equivalent to the true value of a quarter square, with the first lady saying loudly, "Done!"

It was finished, everyone was satisfied and Sulundik was about to leave when the second lady said, "What about me? How would you like to deal with me?" It was both a challenge and an effort to best her friend's deal.

Sulundik stopped. "What do you want and what do you have?"

"These are the finest spices which I grind myself and I have some saffron. I want a quarter square."

Sulundik played the game of being uninterested, smelled the spices, tasted the peppers, and appeared bored, then doubled down on the spices and pushed for more saffron. The game continued back and forth but no agreement could be reached. They had stalemated at twenty packets of spice and twelve packets of saffron – the equivalent was just shy of the breakpoint of fifteen packets of saffron and Sulundik didn't want the lady to get a better deal than the other Uzbek trader.

"Sulundik!" Uncle Bolat called out. It was time to go.

"Okay, we must close a deal quickly. I'll drop to eighteen packets of spice, twelve packets of saffron..." Sulundik looked around the table, seeking to close the deal. Seeing an old cup at the side, containing a small amount of tea continued, "... and your cup of tea!"

The lady laughed loudly and shouted, "Done!"

Sulundik drank from the lady's cup and said, "To future trades!"

They all laughed as Sulundik ran to join Uncle and the group to report the relative worthlessness of the liquor and toys among the Uzbek women and to show off the worn but prized cup.

"Casualties of a pragmatic buyer," Uncle Bolat called the items. Due to the necessities of life, the Uzbek women were laser-focused in all their trading. The toys were a superfluous indulgence and the liquor a dangerous distraction. For Uncle Bolat, the utility of those items was better served as gifts to special trading partners.

Chapter 7
Chimkent USSR

Several trading stops and ten days later the group arrived in Chimkent and entered the homes of extended family members. Here, all resident documents were in order and any brush with authorities would reveal nothing of the earlier departure to Afghanistan. Yet, this was not a time to relax, Uncle Bolat wanted to return in one week. He had buyers for the rifles in a nearby town and would net three to five hundred rubles each. The sale would fund purchases to ply along the return route and to pay the others of the group. Sulundik received a few rubles and some kopeks to pay for food and some contributions to the family. This was not nearly sufficient for what lay ahead for Ulbolsyn.

"Uncle, is it possible to get an advance of rubles in case it's needed while you're away selling the rifles?"

"There are no more rubles and you must make do."

"I have a couple of quarter bricks remaining. Please allow me to use these if an emergency arises."

Uncle thought for a moment and replied cautiously, "That's possible. But remember we are not at an off-trail trading site, and punishments here are severe!"

"Yes, Uncle."

Eager to see Georg again, Sulundik left Ulbolsyn with the extended family and ran the entire way to the soccer field. Though it had been a short time since leaving Chimkent, there was not a familiar Russian face on the field. Sulundik waited for two hours, enough time for school to be over, yet Georg was nowhere. Giving up and walking back toward the relatives' home, Sulundik met Asel, a Kazakh friend.

Asel was animated, jumping with such excitement, and wanted to know everything that transpired since last being together. Sulundik was coy, and deflected the conversation, "Asel, where is Georg?"

"Gone. Almost all the Russians went back to Moscow or wherever they came from. Their parents were replaced with new Russians," Asel replied referring to the transitions of government workers to different regions.

"I didn't know Georg's family was part of that move." Sulundik's eyes began to well.

"What's with you and Georg anyway? Look at the way you are acting! Were you loooovers?" he laughed.

Sulundik flushed. Georg was more than a schoolyard friend and more than someone to help find Dr. Blood. Sulundik had genuine affection for him. Recovering, Sulundik lied, "Look Asel, I owe him two rubles from the last time we were together."

"Oh well, better for you," Asel laughed.

"I have to get back to my family. I'll see you later at the soccer field," Sulundik said, putting some distance between the two of them and ending the discussion of Georg.

***

Out of sight of the Kazakh, Sulundik sat down on a bench and wiped away the tears. Everything was going wrong. They made the long journey for one reason and that was Ulbolsyn. Sulundik was deeply disappointed Georg was no longer there. Besides that, it was always in the plan to get Georg's help, or the assistance of a Russian friend to find Dr. Blood. No one in the Muslim community would know anything about who this person was and certainly not Dr. Blood's profession. While the Russian women were getting abortions, the Muslim women were having five to seven children. Only the Russians would know anything about getting an abortion.

Sulundik walked away deep in thought, ignoring the waving of the Kazakh now on the other side of the street.

Chapter 8
Babushkas

The next morning Sulundik took Ulbolsyn by the arm and announced they would go to the bazaar that day. Indeed, they would go to the bazaar, but not to buy food. There were a handful of old Russian women there, *babushkas* – translated as grandmothers, but generally referring to older women. In this case, widows of public servants, long since passed away, who stayed in Chimkent rather than returning to Moscow.

Sulundik and Ulbolsyn walked along the market until they saw the ruddy complexions of several ladies dressed in floral scarves and printed dresses. There were six of them, looking so much alike that they could be mistaken for sisters. Their hardy laughs were accented by the sun glistening off their full mouths of gold-capped teeth. Their smiles and laughing belied a certain toughness.

Sulundik feared and admired these Russian women but mostly feared them. More than once Sulundik observed a drunken Russian husband doubled over as his wife twisted his ear nearly off, beating the hell out of him for being drunk. It wasn't something you would see in Sulundik's community at all, a drunken husband or a demonstrative wife.

A careful approach had to be made to just the right Russian woman or all hell could break loose. The two young travelers sat down a distance away from the Russian women where they could watch without being easily seen. They looked for any indication of anyone who might be kind to two young Muslims. The Russian women sat behind their tables of fruit and vegetables, coming out on occasion to talk to a friend or negotiate with a buyer. Each time they did, Sulundik sat a little straighter and watched keenly.

It seemed to Sulundik that the women's smiles were for Russians only. Several took on a hardened look when an obvious-looking Central Asian approached the table. Their sales were often firm and allowed no wiggle room. One ran down the street to inform a passing policeman of some infraction. Sulundik ruled out these women.

The sun started sinking behind the buildings and Sulundik was desperate. When everything seemed lost, an old woman, a pensioner, walked slowly along the stalls and looked but never begged. At two of the stalls, the saleswomen flailed their arms sending her away. She had no better luck at the stalls where the Russian women were selling until she came to the last stall.

Sulundik's eyes were focused on their interaction and managed to catch the subtle motion of the Russian woman. It was a slight nudge that resulted in an apple falling off the table and onto the ground. The old woman looked at it and back at the Russian woman who nodded slightly to her. The old woman picked up the apple, smiled, and walked away. Then, Sulundik saw it; the Russian woman turned while making a discreet hand motion. Sulundik had seen this before among some of the Russian community. It was the sign of the cross. She was a Christian.

***

The bazaar was closing, and each proprietor was busy breaking down their stall and loading their carts with the leftover produce. No one noticed as Sulundik and Ulbolsyn approached the stall of the Christian lady.

"Excuse me," Sulundik began as the Russian woman interrupted midsentence without looking.

"I'm closed and have no time."

"We need your help."

The woman acted as if she had eyes in the back of her head. "I have no time for children."

"My sister is in a bad way, and we need assistance."

The woman turned and slowly looked them over. "She is much older than you. Why are you doing all the talking?"

Sulundik didn't want the woman to deflect the conversation.

"I'm responsible for her and she needs help." Before the woman could interrupt again, Sulundik quickly continued, "I know you are a good woman and can help us with information."

135

"You must be Muslim. Why don't you get help from your own community? Besides, how do you know I'm a good woman?"

Sulundik responded, "We cannot get this kind of help from our community. Though she is innocent, she would be accused of moral indiscretion and killed. I know you are a good person because I saw what you did for the old woman today. While we are of different religions, I know you're wearing a cross, and I know it is your sign for something good."

The Russian woman was stunned by the answer. "Killed?" she asked incredulously, and in a near biblical response, "What is it that is required of me?"

"My sister is pregnant by the hand of a relative."

The lady shook her head at such a predicament.

Sulundik continued, "I must find Dr. Blood, and no one can know about it. The Russian boys have talked about him."

A small smile etched in the lady's eyes. "Dr. Blood?" she asked. She had not heard this one before but could imagine the young hooligans making the irreverent reference as if it was an actual name.

"Yes. Dr. Blood. To help my sister."

"Do you realize this procedure could result in your sister's death?"

Sulundik responded, "If we don't do this, then death is the outcome anyway."

The lady started, "The authorities..." then stopped. It was a waste. "Help me load the rest of the produce and follow me. I'll take you there before he leaves for the day."

They quickly loaded the produce and then followed the lady at a respectful distance. After a short while, she stopped the cart. "Someone must stay here and watch my produce."

Chapter 9
Nadyezhda and Doctor Blood

The Russian lady from the market and Sulundik entered the building and walked into a tiny reception room. The stark room had cracked and peeling blue walls and a single calendar hanging in the corner. They walked up to the desk of a very bored receptionist who was filing her nails.

"We're closed," the receptionist said without looking up.

The Russian lady was quick, "You tell Pyotr that Nadyezhda wants to see him - now!"

Sulundik brightened at the name *Nadyezhda* – Hope.

The receptionist stood at the forcefulness of Nadyezhda's voice. She went to the doctor's door, "Doctor, Nadyezhda is here to see you."

Nadyezhda pushed past the receptionist with Sulundik in tow and shut the door. The doctor was sitting with his feet up on the desk with half of a bottle of vodka on the table.

"Sit, sit Nadyezhda. How are you? And who is your young friend?" He poured a good shot of vodka into a second glass and passed it to her.

She held the glass up. "To your health!" She threw it back and downed it in a single gulp. "My young friend has a sister who needs a procedure. It must be done with complete discretion."

"Discretion, is it? You know that costs extra. You have to pay for risk," the doctor said very seriously. He looked directly at Sulundik. "You know the dangers?"

"Yes, we have no choice! What is the cost for this procedure?"

"Ha, that's a question you should have asked someone before you came here! The procedure is thirty rubles and discretion will cost you ten rubles – forty rubles. Unlikely you can afford it."

Sulundik felt like a trader back in Uzbekistan dealing with the ladies at the market and quickly settled into a mindset of negotiating. "Rubles are hard to come by in this town. Perhaps something else?"

The doctor took his feet off the table and leaned forward.

Sulundik continued, "You are a doctor. I could provide you with some medicine that might assist in your work."

"What kind of medicine?"

Sulundik produced a quarter-brick of morphine. The doctor was taken aback, "You know the authorities could jail you for life for this? Where did you get it?"

Nadyezhda stared at the young dealer in disbelief.

"It's not important where I got it. We have no rubles and it's all I have to trade for the procedure," Sulundik lied, having a second brick well hidden. "It's worth far more than the cost of the procedure and discretion."

Uncle Bolat would say "In negotiations, it's never lying. That would be a sin. It's simply 'puffing' which is using the brain Allah gave you."

The doctor looked at Nadyezhda quizzically. She shrugged.

"Okay, bring your sister in a week and..."

Sulundik interrupted, "It has to be done right away; it's too dangerous for us to wait. The family is getting suspicious." Indeed, their departure to Afghanistan was in three short days.

The doctor slammed his fist on the table, "Damn it!" He dug into the trash can retrieving the cap for the bottle of vodka, "I'm done with this for the night." He twisted the cap on the bottle. "Shit. Have your sister here at 7:00 a.m. before the receptionist arrives. She'll be here all day. And bring the morphine without one piece missing!"

Their business concluded, Sulundik and Nadyezhda departed and joined Ulbolsyn on the street. Nadyezhda looked at both of them and said something in old Russian Sulundik could only translate as "What a piece of work you are."

Sulundik responded, "You are a good woman. May Allah fully bless you."

The lady smiled. "May the blessing of Christ be upon you, and may God forgive me," she said as she pushed her cart away.

Chapter 10
A Very Long Day

It was the longest day of Sulundik's short life. Checking the time on a clock in a nearby store window, they arrived a few minutes before 7:00 a.m. as the doctor had ordered. Seeing them from inside the office, the doctor quickly opened the door and pulled Ulbolsyn inside. He pushed Sulundik away. "You stay nearby until I call you, which won't be until this evening at the earliest."

Sulundik walked across the street and sat on a bench. It was terrible, waiting, waiting, waiting. Only an hour had passed and Sulundik's stomach was tied in knots. Not knowing, clear dangers, ramifications if something went wrong, and love for a sister pounded simultaneously with every heartbeat. Sulundik tried to focus on other things and dug around in a nasty garbage can, finding an old copy of a TASS newspaper. Same old shit propaganda, pictures of some peasant looking in the far distance, a harvester in the background, quotas that may or may not have been truly met.

"Probably looking for the mountains of Afghanistan and routes out of here," Sulundik smirked and reflected on the family's journey. The question Sulundik pondered most was, "Why haven't so many more done what we've done?"

Sulundik started to turn the page of the paper, but the old date on the front page leaped out as a reminder. It was Sulundik's fourteenth birthday. There was never anything that was expected or done in recognition of a birthday. That would be self-centered. The day was still special and allowed Sulundik's thoughts to wander from the present for a moment or two.

Plucking a few stones from the gravel, Sulundik tossed them one at a time at the slow-moving flies on the side of the garbage can. Ten dead flies and another hour passed. The doctor said to remain nearby; not even lunch could force Sulundik from the vicinity of the doctor's office. Late in the afternoon, Sulundik took a nap under the shade of a tree adjacent to the bench, then awakened to the sound of market carts creaking along the road, signaling the end of the workday. Sulundik stood in time to see the doctor open the door and motion to come in.

Ulbolsyn sat in a corner chair with her head down. Sulundik touched her gently as she forced a smile.

The bottle of vodka was open, and the doctor had thrown the cap into the trash can. "Your sister will be fine. Everything went well and she rested most of the day," the doctor said as he downed a quick shot.

"Is there anything we need to do? Will Ulbolsyn still be able to have babies?"

"The emotional toll can be as great as the physical the first time. She will need to rest. And yes, she will be able to have as many babies as she wants."

Sulundik handed the doctor the small brick of morphine.

Satisfied, the doctor smiled. "If you can provide medicine such as this, perhaps I can be of other services to you in the future."

"I'll remember that and what you did for us."

"Perhaps another time and another deal."

"Yes," Sulundik replied. Indeed, a buyer and at an optimum price.

The two exchanged an awkward handshake.

Chapter 11
Return Journey

Ulbolsyn said nothing and shuffled along slowly as they walked down the road. Sulundik noticed her pace and was concerned.

"Ulbolsyn, there is no dishonor here." Sulundik tried to comfort her. "If there is doubt or any feeling of dishonor, then let Allah place it on me."

"It had to be," she replied without looking up. "But I'm scared and have been thinking. I'm not a virgin now."

Sulundik stared at her blankly.

"You know when I marry, my virginity will be tested. The new in-laws, they'll check my sheets," she insisted, "and there will be no blood."

"You worry too much," Sulundik scowled.

"But what if it does happen?"

Sulundik was getting annoyed but continued. "Okay, then plan for a white sheet test. Hide a small knife, either in your hair or near the bed, and cut yourself slightly. You'll get the result you need."

Ulbolsyn was struck by the frankness and devious logic. "How do you know these things?"

Sulundik looked at her quizzically. "Ulbolsyn, what you did today saved our lives, but you must stop fretting and compose yourself. Everyone, including Uncle, will know something is wrong if you don't act normally. Even if you must pretend, lift your head."

She lifted her head and forced a smile.

"We have one day before we depart, and you'll need all of your strength."

***

Coordination completed, preparations made, packs and donkeys loaded, Uncle Bolat and the group made their way out of Chimkent the next morning before sunrise. Moving discreetly, they traveled up to the old smuggler trail a couple of kilometers out of town.

Ulbolsyn struggled with her pack. Sulundik, keeping careful watch, fell behind her and quietly began repositioning some items and transferring the heavier ones.

The trip was increasingly difficult for Ulbolsyn as days passed. Sulundik added tobacco to her pack to lessen the weight while making it look heavier than it was, and again transferred the heavier items. A day later and a few kilometers after trading with the Kyrgyz, Ulbolsyn stopped with a small groan.

"I'm bleeding," she whispered.

Sulundik stopped the group and approached Uncle who was further ahead. "Ulbolsyn is in a woman's way."

Uncle Bolat was not a man who shied away from adventure or even danger, but the words "woman's way" froze him in his tracks. Women's problems were a conundrum he didn't understand, didn't want to discuss, and were better left to others... to anyone except him. He put his hands on his hips, walked in a circle, and kicked some rocks leaving a symbolic plume of dust. Finally, he frowned and pursed his lips. "You take care of it. We can't stop. There will be a truck waiting for us midmorning tomorrow. We must get to our campsite before dark to meet in time. If we miss it, we'll have to walk up the next mountain."

"I understand. I'll stay behind until Ulbolsyn is better and catch up with you at the campsite."

"If you aren't there, you'll have to make it back alone. Do you understand?"

"We'll be there even if I have to carry her."

Sulundik returned to the donkeys and pulled a large amount of cotton from a pack before they moved on. Handing some cotton to Ulbolsyn, Sulundik turned away as she changed the cotton padding. Sulundik stuffed the remaining cotton in Ulbolsyn's pack.

"We'll rest here for another thirty minutes. Tell me when you feel strong enough to move again."

Ulbolsyn sat down and slowly leaned back on her pack. After a while, they arose and began moving up the trail, but they fell increasingly behind the main party. Soon they were well out of sight.

Chapter 12
Kyrgyz

The sound of voices drifted up as Sulundik turned to see a Kyrgyz teenager and a middle-aged man. As the two men approached, both were animated, laughing, and joking. Sulundik, wary and remembering the Tajik leader's deceptive animation, dropped the heavy pack as the duo approached.

"Where are you two young ones going by yourselves? Have you lost your group?" one teased.

The teenager jumped around like a fool, and pointed to Ulbolsyn saying, "You should come with us and have a much better life than carrying packs like a donkey."

"A donkey?" the other snickered. He brayed, and both laughed like hyenas.

The Kyrgyz hoped Sulundik might join in or change demeanor, but Sulundik remained stoic, consciously locating the nushtar.

The man became more forceful. "Come with us pretty one! We'll have fun, and you can be with a full-grown man." He reached forward and grabbed Ulbolsyn's arm giving several tugs.

Sulundik's movement was swift. In the blink of an eye, the nushtar was stuck deeply in the man's forearm. He pulled away screaming in shock. Then in blind anger, he lunged forward. Sulundik caught the lunge with an effective thrust of the nushtar deeply into the man's chest. The man fell, while the teenager brandished a knife and managed to sink it into Sulundik's shoulder.

Sulundik whirled around, as Uncle Bolat had taught, and threw a right cross deliberately missing with the fist to connect with the nushtar. The teenager screamed as blood from the superficial wound poured down his face. Sulundik poised for another round, but the teenager grabbed the unconscious man and began pulling him down the hill.

Ulbolsyn had not moved and was simply staring in a state of disbelief.

"We have to go now," Sulundik said and quickly stacked three rocks atop one another in several locations and bent a small limb from a tree.

They grabbed their packs and moved hurriedly up the trail, but Sulundik's wound continued to bleed, aggravated by the chafing backpack. After a kilometer and anticipating the Kyrgyz would come in force, they found a ravine that cut behind and up from the trail, exactly what Uncle said to look for in such an event. They moved up the ravine, then back above the trail a couple of hundred meters.

Both dropped their packs and sat down, exhausted. Ulbolsyn helped remove Sulundik's blood-soaked shirt and examined the wound. It was deep. She opened her pack and pulled out a single leaf of tobacco. Cutting a quarter of the leaf, she folded it tightly, then inserted it into the wound. It burned intensely as the tobacco cauterized the wound, but Sulundik remained quiet.

"It seems you've saved me again," Ulbolsyn whispered. "What would they have done?"

"You would have been a bride and my death would have been the dowry. There were no options."

"Just the same, you showed great strength."

Ulbolsyn placed cotton on top of the wound and held it tightly as Sulundik watched the trail for any sign of pursuit.

They didn't have to wait long. Within a few minutes, they could hear rocks being kicked and the grunts of four Kyrgyz moving up the trail. Sulundik watched carefully, a hand tightening around the nushtar. An older teenager carried a long, sturdy stick. The second with the bloody gash etched from his ear to his mouth, carried a knife as did two older men. There was no lunatic laughing or joking now as they passed by quickly. They were out for revenge.

Ulbolsyn and Sulundik watched the trail intently. Nearly an hour passed and as the sun began to set, they could hear loud voices. Sulundik peered over the edge to see the silhouettes of the Kyrgyz returning to their town. There were only three. Trailing far behind, the teenager who bore the mark of Sulundik's nushtar searched the path for any signs of the two travelers. He continued slowly down the hill and out of sight.

Sulundik and Ulbolsyn didn't dare move until ten minutes had passed.

Under the cover of darkness, the two moved back to the main smuggler trail. It would be a difficult trek to Uncle Bolat's camp. Even Uncle Bolat didn't venture out at night and understood that with limited visibility, a single misstep could result in losing the main trail. There were no other options for the siblings.

After seven hours of slow movement and a grueling night of slips, falls, and backtracking Ulbolsyn and Sulundik could finally see the light of Uncle Bolat's camp. It was 3:00 a.m. and they approached carefully, calling out to one of the guards. As they came into the camp, Uncle Bolat greeted them enthusiastically having been awake all night anxiously awaiting their arrival. The entire group circled the fire to hear what had occurred.

Ulbolsyn sat down beside the fire and fell asleep, completely exhausted. Sulundik gave the details of the Kyrgyz encounter. "I think I killed one of them," Sulundik said measuring Uncle's response.

"Then he deserved to die. He dishonored your sister, and they would have killed you to get her."

"I marked the trail with the stacked rocks and a bent limb, but I'm afraid they were pretty stirred up when they came looking for us. Even if I didn't kill the older man, I fear they won't settle down anytime soon. You'll know the younger if you see him in the future, a single nushtar scar along his right cheek and face."

Uncle Bolat shrugged. "They know the rules and they know the price. They learned we won't tolerate anyone disrespecting our women. Any attempt to kidnap a bride is disrespectful to us and our family. It was a mistake for me to split up our group. But thanks be to Allah, you responded properly to the threat and it's a warning to us to never divide our group again, especially when our women are with us."

"Yes, thanks be to Allah."

"You are more than you appear in more ways than one Sulundik," Uncle Bolat said with great praise and a raised eyebrow. "We move early. Get some sleep." Uncle then directed the guards to push a little farther away from the camp to ensure an earlier warning should any trouble appear before their departure.

***

Thirteen weeks after Uncle Bolat and the caravan departed Kunduz, they returned with fresh supplies and currencies. The women began unloading the bundles of Uzbek cotton for distribution while the men gathered around Uncle Bolat and the others. Sulundik and Ulbolsyn dropped their packs as Ulbolsyn embraced her sisters and mother. Their father collected their share of currency and goods as they walked to their home, exhausted.

These two siblings had completed a heavy-laden, round-trip journey of mixed transport for hundreds of kilometers. They faced the same trials and dangers as adult travelers and confronted personal challenges unheard of in their Islamic community. Yet their young ages were of no consideration; they were no more elevated in esteem than any other. They simply did a job with the expectation that they would be successful. Both ate a simple breakfast, and after a change of Sulundik's bandages went to their separate sleeping areas to rest.

Chapter 13
Awakening

Sulundik sat with the young men listening to a local gathering of the community patriarchs. They discussed the increasing presence of other tribes in the town and the impact it might have on crime and commerce. Several women sat in a segregated section, within earshot but not participating.

Something was not right. Since returning to Kunduz, a sharp pain had started to seize Sulundik's gut, twisting inside like a vise as the week went on, tighter and tighter. This morning had been particularly bad. Struggling to pay attention to the proceedings, Sulundik glanced down and stilled. The pain was forgotten and replaced by sheer panic, as the young teenager sprang up and dashed home without bothering to make any excuses.

If that day in Chimkent, waiting for the doctor to complete Ulbolsyn's treatment, was the longest in Sulundik's life, today was the worst day.

"Mother!" Sulundik shouted from the door of the house.

Knowing the day had come, she ushered Sulundik into a back room so they could speak privately.

"I'm bleeding," Sulundik said, dejected and horrified.

Sulundik's mother, however, remained calm. "Yes, we knew this day would be coming soon."

"But I'm not ready," Sulundik protested, with tears welling.

"Your time has come, my dear. Your actions and strengths were so very important to your father, to me, and especially to your sisters. But the time has come. You can no longer be a *bacha posh*."

Sulundik's mother and father had no sons. In their tradition, they identified one daughter to take on the identity of a boy, a bacha posh, until the first menstrual cycle. Until then the bacha posh, Sulundik, acted in every way like a boy and a man; played sports, attended school, and prayed with boys and young men, but most importantly, cared for the other women.

147

Sulundik was the parents' last chance for a son who would be old enough to help with the older sisters. Regardless of gender, her parents chose her for this role long before she was born and gave her the name Ulzhan, "Soul of a Boy." All of the sisters reflected the parents' desire for a son; Ulzhalgas, "Next Will Be a Son;" Ulbolsyn, "Let It Be a Son;" and younger sister, simply Dariga, "Pity."

Sulundik had dreaded this day her whole life. The anger and tears welled up inside her. She had bested many boys in sports; was a champion chess player; could read and write and was educated in the Russian schools; learned the Koran and prayed with the men; she had killed one man and wounded another in defense of her sister. She had been a contributing member of the patriarchal society for so long. Now, becoming a second-class member of the community and relegated to the role of a woman was repugnant.

In her frustration, Sulundik screamed, "You don't bind a falcon with a cloak or a cheetah with a yoke!"

Her mother raised her hand to strike her, but Sulundik instinctively caught her arm in mid-air. Their eyes locked. In that instance, Sulundik realized change had come. She released her grip, dropped her hand to her side, and bowed her head to be slapped. Instead, her mother embraced her, drew her near, and whispered, "Your words are dangerous. You mustn't apply a proverb to our dress or our roles. You must be careful. We have no option but to tell father."

Sulundik buried her head on her mother's shoulder to smother her sobs.

"Come, we'll get some cotton and I'll show you what to do."

Sulundik sat alone all day, sullen, angry, and in dreaded apprehension of the coming discussion. Seeing her father approaching the house for the evening meal Sulundik knew to say nothing until after dinner and at her mother's direction.

After dinner, she stood outside the entrance while her sisters sat in their section of the house. A dim light illuminated their father's face as his wife approached him.

"Sulundik's time has come," she said bluntly, sealing Sulundik's fate with four words.

Her husband called out, "Sulundik! Come inside."

Sulundik entered and stood beside her mother.

Without circumstance or any consideration, her father directed her to immediately give up her identity as a bacha posh and take on the role of a woman; assuming her actual name, Ulzhan, dropping Sulundik forever.

Of the many changes, the most repugnant to her was the hijab, and how it marked her as a woman. All external interactions must change accordingly. Male and female interactions became so much more complicated. Always, she had looked men in the eye, interacting as an equal. Now gazes, glances, and every interaction would be layered with new meaning, if not a dangerous new meaning.

Sulundik, now Ulzhan, had never challenged her father before, but if she didn't speak up, she would lose the life she loved.

"Father, there must be a way I can remain a bacha posh. Please," she begged, "why does it have to be like this?"

"It is our way, and I have spoken. You will take on a husband and have sons just as your sisters will. Tomorrow Ulzhan will be an obedient daughter, who will reside with her sisters, move only with her sisters and do as you are directed."

"Yes, father," Ulzhan replied, broken. She walked outside, sat down on a rock and wept.

The next morning Ulzhan entered her sisters' room. They began to fit her with the clothing acceptable to a Muslim woman with excitement and laughter. Only one was solemn. Ulbolsyn sat quietly and watched the pain etched on Ulzhan's face.

Chapter 14
The Dowry

Several weeks passed and Ulzhan was not fully adapting to her new role but resigned to a fate she considered inescapable. Though two of her sisters were older, they continued to look to her for her strength of will and decisiveness. That admiration was borne in no small part to Ulbolsyn's relating of the story of the fight with the Kyrgyz, confirmed by the deep scar on Ulzhan's back and the fact she continued to carry the same nushtar used in the encounter.

Late one evening Ulbolsyn whispered to Ulzhan that Uncle Bolat was outside with their father, and they were in great deliberation. She had heard Ulzhan's name mentioned. Ulzhan moved within hearing distance.

Uncle Bolat spoke as if he were negotiating for a rifle. "Ulzhan has proven to be resilient and would be a fine addition to my family."

Ulzhan's blood boiled. They were negotiating her marriage! As improbable, if not impossible as it was for a member of her tightly knit Islamic family to marry an atheistic Russian, she often fantasized about being married to Georg. Sometimes her closeness to Georg was met with jeers by the other boys who knew nothing of her bacha posh status. Now, what she heard dashed that fantasy into gut-wrenching reality.

Father argued with his wife's half-brother, "I have other daughters who are older and without a husband. Surely, you could select another."

Uncle Bolat was equally adamant, "It must be Ulzhan. We just need to discuss the dowry."

"Dowry? You know her value. You know what she has done on the journeys to and from Chimkent."

"But I trained her. I taught her everything!"

"Exactly, and that is why her value is higher than any dowry I will provide. She far exceeds cooking and having children. Besides," father continued, "you and I know your eldest son will demand the extra work and labor only Ulzhan could effectively provide. The dowry is that he's getting the best of the lot!"

Ulzhan's anger nearly erupted. "The eldest son? Erasyl? That lazy lover of little boys! Rapist! He should already be dead by my hand, and he will never share a bed with me!" She shook her head, "So, this is why Uncle took such great care in training me. He wasn't training me, he was manipulating me, to take on the provider role of the next generation for his lazy son!"

Ulzhan pulled away from the door and walked back into the room. Saying nothing to anyone she picked up Sulundik's clothes hidden under a mat and slipped away. She was determined to return to Chimkent. She knew the route and needed to leave right away before her father and uncle could consummate a deal.

Standing a short distance from the house, Erasyl waited for his father. In the darkness, he saw Ulzhan leave the house. He followed at a short distance as she made her way through the village and up into the mountains. At the top of a steep precipice, Ulzhan stopped and stripped naked as she prepared to put on boy's clothing. Erasyl could see Ulzhan's nude body clearly in the moonlight.

"Where are your clothes Ulzhan?" he said, the grin on his face reflecting a small white streak as he stepped out of the dark.

She whirled around, her anger outweighing any surprise or fear. "I'm Sulundik! You will never see Ulzhan again."

"You are not Sulundik!"

Ulzhan glared with deep hatred as she continued to put on her clothes.

"Even if you are Sulundik, then I get the best of all worlds! A little boy's energy and a virgin girl!" Erasyl pressed in close to her.

"Then you are indeed an abuser of children. As I and everyone thought!"

"You're mine now or later, makes no difference. I need not wait for a dowry or a wedding night. I'll teach you to be obedient now," he said as he knocked her to the ground.

Sulundik tried to get up, but he threw her back to the ground and pinned her.

151

He released one hand to pull his trousers down. That was a mistake. Sulundik grabbed a rock with her free hand and smashed him on the head. He fell back unconscious.

The anger welled up and thinking not only of her current circumstance but of her sister, she picked up a larger boulder and smashed his skull. With adrenaline pumping, she smashed him again; just as Erasyl would have done to Ulbolsyn had her pregnancy been discovered. She dragged his lifeless body to the edge of the precipice and pushed him over the side. His body fell for a long time, with a wet thud and distant echo when it landed. If the animals didn't get to him first, his death would hopefully look like an accident.

She put Ulzhan's clothing back on and slipped quietly back to her home.

Seeing Ulbolsyn nearby, she whispered, "We must start a rumor that Erasyl had a lover in Chimkent and ran away rather than marry."

It was late and Uncle Bolat and father were still in discussion. Though dinner was long past, their mother was preparing an onion pastry. Ulzhan quietly began to help. As she did, her mother said nonchalantly, "Your father and Uncle are making the final plans for your marriage to Uncle's son."

"I will do as father wishes. But I don't believe his son wants me for a wife," Ulzhan said without looking up. "I've heard him say during our travels that he is in love with a girl in Chimkent. You can check with Ulbolsyn."

Mother looked at her, the message was certainly going to be passed to father and Uncle. She handed the pastry to Ulzhan to carry to the two men and thereby sealed her alibi.

Over the next few weeks, Erasyl remained missing and the story he had returned to Chimkent took hold, until a startling discovery.

Chapter 15
Discovery of Erasyl

A young herder leading two large mastiffs by their heavy chains entered Ulzhan's small town. Numerous goats trailed behind him in a meandering and curious mob chewing on anything that didn't move but were always within earshot of the herder's whistles. The largest of the goats followed closely behind, struggling under a flimsy harness, and dragging a makeshift travois. One of the locals ran up to scold the herder for bringing his herd of goats into the village. She stopped short and simply stared at an indistinguishable pile of cloth and a gray furry heap tied to the middle of the travois.

Ulbolsyn was nearby and saw the young herder stop and talk to a group of old men. Someone pointed down the street and he moved in the direction of Uncle Bolat's house. A small crowd formed and followed, but well behind him.

Ulbolsyn hurried to find Ulzhan, taking her by the hand, "Come quickly!"

They ran with the crowd, but an overwhelming stench confronted them. They worked their way through the crowd to see what was happening.

"They say you are an elder who is missing a member of your family?"

"That's true," Uncle Bolat replied barely containing himself and looking over the shepherd's shoulder.

"Maybe you can look at these clothes."

It was a grisly sight with bones, ripped clothing, and a dead gray wolf that was severely underweight.

Uncle Bolat used a stick to move aside shreds of gray cloth, quite common in the area. It could be anyone. He pushed the stick again and under the gray cloth, he discovered what appeared to be ragged strips of a burgundy tunic. Burgundy was not a common color, but it was Erasyl's favorite. He wore a burgundy tunic on the day he disappeared.

Uncle screamed and lashed out; he moved to pummel the herder with the stick but stopped short. "What happened? How did you find this? Where?"

"It was northeast of here," he said pointing a shaking finger in the direction of the Soviet Union.

"But we looked for him. We couldn't find him! How did you find him?"

The herder pointed to the gray wolf, "He was starving and dangerous. He kept getting closer to the herd. When I had the chance, I released the Mastiffs who were on him quickly. He looks like a scavenger wolf. Probably forced out of its pack."

"But what about this carcass?"

"As I examined the dead wolf, I saw something hanging from it; a piece of burgundy cloth."

"Hanging from it?"

"Yes, from its ass. The wolf had eaten cloth with the meat."

The crowd gasped as Uncle Bolat shrieked again. Ulzhan and Ulbolsyn looked at one another. Wide-eyed they turned back to the herder whose horrific story continued.

"I knew this wolf or a pack had killed someone. I moved my goats in the direction I had seen this wolf earlier. I could see the cloth and bones in a ravine and was able to collect everything you see here. Scavengers must have scattered the rest."

"Why did you bring this mangy wolf?" one of the bystanders asked incredulously.

"I wasn't sure what to do about who or what might be inside. What would be proper, or that ..." he said as he pointed to the burgundy cloth hanging from the wolf's anus.

Uncle Bolat pounded his chest and screamed to anyone who would listen, "Burn the wolf! Let it burn in hell! We must bury Erasyl properly right away."

Several men unhooked the goat from the travois and sat it down to consider their next step. The herder, his dogs, and goats simply walked away as they had come into the town.

Ulzhan and Ulbolsyn turned and walked toward their father's house, their heads bowed as they stared at the road ahead.

Ulbolsyn whispered gleefully, "Erasyl is wolf shit."

"Quite proper," Ulzhan replied with a smile. "Quite proper."

Chapter 16
1979 – Soviets

With Erasyl dead and buried, Uncle Bolat sought to establish a second arrangement for his middle son. He wanted a return on his investment in the time spent training Ulzhan.

Ulzhan received word of Uncle's scheme and made her plans to silently leave Kunduz. But fate sometimes intervenes to redirect one's life entirely.

Early in the morning before daylight, everyone woke to shouts and agitated voices. A group of men mostly strangers, approached Ulzhan's house and shouted for her father to come outside. "We must discuss something of urgent importance."

Agitated, father responded, "What do you want at this hour?"

"The Soviets have invaded. We need everyone, including you to join us as we move into the mountains and organize a resistance."

"I'm an old man and I'll slow everyone down. Besides, I have daughters and a wife."

"They must fend for themselves. We are at war, and you are either with us or against us!"

"I'm too old," father pleaded.

The men were not satisfied and didn't relent, threatening to drag him off. As they argued, Ulzhan heard everything and seized the opportunity. She moved quickly. With Ulbolsyn's help, she grabbed a pair of scissors and quickly cut her hair. Taking soot from their fireplace, Ulbolsyn rubbed it lightly on Ulzhan's cheeks, neck, and above her lip resembling a light growth of facial hair. Donning her trousers, shirt, and hat, she walked out of the house and stood next to her father who passionately pleaded his case.

"Father, why should these men disrespect an elder of our family when your son is happy to go with them and fight!" Her father was taken aback. He looked wide-eyed and in astonishment at Ulzhan.

"Yes," he paused. "My only son Sulundik is fifteen years old, strong, and will serve with honor. He is of much more value than an old man."

The men agreed. Father went inside the house and came back with an old single-shot pistol. "Sulundik, this is all I have for you. May Allah protect you."

Sulundik tucked it inside her tunic alongside her nushtar. She embraced her mother and sisters, turned, and walked away with the men, never to see her family again.

Only Ulbolsyn smiled as Sulundik disappeared in the distance.

Chapter 17
1984 – Mujahideen

The war with the Soviets pressed on for five years. Rumors persisted among the Afghan tribes as well as the Soviet military that a young bacha posh led a large guerrilla force against the Soviets and reported only to Massoud, the legendary leader of the Mujahideen. This bacha posh was rumored to be fluent in Russian as well as multiple tribal languages, and a champion chess player. She was a master strategist who inflicted heavy casualties on the Soviets through effective coordination, concentration of forces, and maneuver against vulnerable points rather than leading her force into costly direct assaults.

Twenty-year-old Sulundik was indeed a leader within the Mujahideen. She never confided her gender, although some knew she was a bacha posh which added to the allure and reputation of her exploits. Rising to a leadership position had not been easy. After countless battles and numerous casualties, the scattered resistance elements began to organize and consolidate power. With larger and more concentrated forces the resistance could inflict heavier damage on the Soviet occupiers. However, this concentration created bigger targets for Soviet artillery and air power. This is where Sulundik excelled. Unlike many guerrillas senior to her, she understood the battlefield, how to maneuver forces with less risk, and made recommendations to ensure successful operations. With each success, the command promoted her within the resistance structure. Ultimately her capabilities came to the attention of Massoud who selected Sulundik for his operational staff. Only once was a challenge raised.

Massoud gathered his staff and leadership, including tribal elders, at his headquarters to plan future operations. There was much debate, especially among the elders, as to a particular strategy that required movement through one of the villages and around another. Massoud asked Sulundik directly why the strategy was better than other options. Sulundik was about to answer but she was immediately interrupted.

An older brutish man confronted Massoud directly. "Why do we have some bacha posh making decisions? Our mission requires a full man; not a half man - half woman."

Sulundik fumed, cutting Massoud off before he could speak. "You dare challenge who I am as well as my expertise?" she shouted. Before allowing an answer, she continued, "My contributions in the fight against the Soviets may be principally in understanding the enemy. However, my capabilities to fight on the battlefield are equal to all and certainly superior to your own."

The man rose, and pulled out his knife, "Then prove your superiority here and now."

Massoud's raised hand quieted the group. He gestured for the man to be seated. "It's you who questioned Sulundik's capability and who she is," he said as he directed Sulundik to continue.

"When was the last time anyone here fought hand-to-hand or used a knife with a Soviet?" Sulundik asked. No one moved. "Certainly not. We fight with our firearms and at a distance. So, if you want to challenge my capability to fight the Soviets, then let's do it with rifles."

The circle of men agreed, as did Massoud. He was glad for a bit of entertainment in this potentially high-stakes game and had every confidence in Sulundik.

Sulundik stood, grabbed her rifle, and turned to her challenger. "Come with me and we'll see who is more able to kill a Soviet."

Two young men ran ahead and were preparing a target on a level piece of land one hundred meters away.

"Not here!" Sulundik shouted. "This would prove nothing. We fight in the mountains, and we do it at long range."

The challenger happily agreed to the change, not realizing Sulundik had baited him.

Finding a spot on a very steep part of the mountain, Sulundik turned to the two young boys, "Put a tunic on a stick and place a rock on top where the head should be. Place it at three hundred meters down the hill."

The boys hurried down the steep mountain and did as Sulundik directed. They backed off and squatted down at right angles to watch the target.

Turning to her challenger Sulundik said, "You've challenged me and my ability to fight. We'll now see if that's true. Four rounds. You first!"

The challenger smiled and taking four rounds from his pouch, lay down on the ground in a prone position. He loaded one round into the chamber. Taking careful aim directly at the target, he squeezed the trigger.

The two boys did not see the impact of the round, but the crack in front of them indicated it was well long. The men at the top of the hill laughed as the two young men scampered behind a rock. Sulundik smiled as well. Her smile was not at the young men, but that her gamble had paid off. A whiff of dust behind the target proved the challenger had little understanding of shooting in the mountains. While he was certainly a good shot on level ground, her gamble that he didn't understand geometry or the dynamics of shooting in the mountains was correct.

The challenger chambered a second round and again aimed directly at the target. He overshot again. Chambering the third cartridge and dropping his aim, the round impacted closer to the target.

"Miss and long," the two young boys shouted. A look of panic crept across the challenger's face. He chambered the final round, repositioned, took careful aim, and fired much lower.

The two boys approached the target to check the tunic. "On target! Top center!" It was a solid chest shot.

Satisfied, the challenger stood, giving the firing position to Sulundik. She sat down and steadied her rifle by resting her elbows on her knees. This was a less stable position, but she was making a point. She chambered a round and fired. The rock atop the target exploded - the first round was a headshot.

The challenger was sullen.

She shot again and the challenger's demeanor brightened as he heard the relayed message, "Miss!"

Sulundik fired again. "Miss!"

The challenger became downright gleeful at the two announced misses attributing the first shot as pure luck. Sulundik maintained an assured smile. She fired again. "Miss!"

The men started to walk away. Before the challenger could boast Sulundik called out, "Wait! We're not finished here!" She motioned for the boys to bring the tunic to the top of the hill.

As the boys arrived, the challenger and the men pushed in to see. "Why did you say I missed the target three times?" Sulundik asked.

The boys looked carefully and saw nothing. The challenger himself lifted the tunic higher and into the light. There it was! Three rounds, each within an inch of the other, neatly centered, and targeted on the crotch!

Instead of becoming enraged, the challenger laughed and let out a loud groan as he pointed to the groin area and the close-shot group. Everyone laughed in unison as the challenger turned to Sulundik, "Let no man challenge you or who you are again if he knows what's good for him!"

Indeed, no one ever challenged Sulundik again. The event that day added even greater allure to the reputation of a bacha posh whose true identity was known to only a few among the Mujahideen, and perhaps a young Afghan sister, Ulbolsyn.

Chapter 18
1985 – Raising the Stakes

Sulundik's experience with the Soviets made her invaluable in developing the defensive and offensive strategies of the Mujahideen. She was so respected among the tribes and within the Mujahideen leadership that Massoud ordered her to Pakistan for a crucial strategic meeting. It was Sulundik who set the stage for the order.

The Soviets were increasingly effective in the use of combined arms and air power, and Sulundik insisted the Mujahideen open a second front. She sat among Massoud, his staff, and senior leaders. She placed a small chessboard in the center of the leaders.

She explained, "In chess, there is only a single queen and a single king; each must be protected for distinct reasons. Lose the king, lose the battle; lose the queen and lose maneuver for the final kill. But the queen is limited by the placement of the others." She pointed to the other pieces and explained their relative importance. She held up the two knights. "It's the two knights who are slightly less valuable than the bishops but represent the true maneuver and deception on the board." She moved one of the knights and demonstrated. "The knight moves in multiple ways and is less discernable. Working together, the knights represent two offensive fronts. Working in coordination, the main thrust may go undetected or could shift depending on the successful maneuver of the knights."

Several shifted in their seats, and the military leaders remained focused on the board. One member of the staff argued the relevance of a game when confronting a behemoth like the Soviet Union. Massoud remained silent and indicated for her to continue.

"Its relevance is that the Soviets are operating with more pieces and greater flexibility." She took several pawns, a rook, and a bishop off the table to demonstrate. "Our ability to counter is limited already, but when I take a knight away," she lifted one of the knights and placed it to the side, "our maneuver capability is halved. We have no ability for diversion, only a single front, and that front is easily detected."

Massoud understood and asked, "How do we apply this understanding and what are you recommending?"

"We have to use both knights. We must go after the Soviets in an unexpected direction on another front."

One of the military chiefs replied, "Our insurgency covers all of Afghanistan. Another front here may be of tactical or operational importance, but I'm not sure of its strategic significance."

Sulundik agreed, and presented the main thrust of her argument, "We must open another front, not within Afghanistan, but the Soviet Union itself and among other sympathetic Islamic peoples."

Massoud became immediately animated and conferred with the more senior members. Others in the room began multiple side-bar discussions. Some questioned Sulundik directly and the noise became even louder.

Massoud's senior staff operations officer quieted the group and brought up the Soviet Central Asian Republics. "Each of the republics and their capitals, from Almaty to Tashkent and Dushanbe, are comprised of Islamic peoples who long for religious freedom."

"The Central Asian republics are under tight control by many different Soviet organizations and military. Most if not all of the peoples are uninterested or don't have the stomach to bring the wrath of the military into their communities as has occurred here in Afghanistan," Sulundik replied.

"Remember, we are fighting because we were invaded by a demonically atheistic and oppressive country that threatens our way of life and the practice of our faith. The republics have lived under domination for over seventy years," another adviser said grimly.

Sulundik agreed, "This is true. However, there is a group of Islamic people who have historically rebelled against the powers in Moscow, the Murids of old. They are the modern-day Chechens, Ingush, Ossetians, and the people of Dagestan."

The operations officer continued, "Foreign fighters who arrive by the scores press us to advance Islam. They encourage us to commence insurgencies in the republics once we vanquish the Soviets. Their purpose is more about their influence than our freedom."

Sulundik acknowledged the presence of foreign fighters, and the overzealous Saudis who didn't understand that the Mujahideen were fighting for their lives and not a Saudi agenda.

"But Sulundik, what you're proposing is different. Are you suggesting we commence operations outside of Afghanistan or Central Asia in advance of a Soviet withdrawal?"

"Precisely. My position is if we assist with a second front in the Caucasus region, we might have a higher degree of success than anywhere in the Central Asian republics. We'll be better positioned to move our knight," Sulundik replied as she held up the chess piece.

"They're halfway around the world!" one of the staff members protested.

"They are republics of the Soviet Union that have fought against the central powers since the Tsarist days. They have the stomach for the fight when they are not fighting one another," Sulundik said raising an eyebrow and looking at the others. The comment drew laughter from around the room.

She continued, "We receive support from around the world, so communications with the Chechens and that region should not be impossible. If they are convinced to unite and commence or even renew insurgent operations, they might sufficiently distract Soviet attention to turn away from Afghanistan. We may be able to force them to shift some of their forces and resources."

Massoud assessed the situation. "We know the Soviet leadership is under increasing domestic pressure as the bodies of their soldiers pile up. They are unable to hide their losses anymore. Another front, especially internally to the country itself, would indeed create domestic pressure that might be favorable to us."

After several minutes of discussion, Massoud agreed it was worth a try.

"Sulundik! You have one week to hand over operational and staff assignments to your number two," he said as he glanced at Sulundik's lieutenant. "We'll make arrangements for you to travel to Pakistan and meet with our international contacts. You may undertake whatever you feel is necessary to bring about this second front. Keep me apprised at all times. May Allah be with you."

"And with you," she responded, recognizing the sheer magnitude of this mission and the honor Massoud had granted her.

"A final point," Massoud said as he moved out of hearing of the others. "There can be no pretenses. You must travel to Pakistan as a woman with all that it means. You may reassume your bacha posh identity whenever you want after working with the Pakistanis."

Sulundik concurred, then gathered her chessboard and departed with her lieutenant.

Chapter 19
Pakistan

Sulundik was not the first to report to the headquarters of the Pakistani Inter-Services Intelligence (ISI) for an assignment abroad. The ISI had plenty of experience in such deployments in Jammu and Kashmir, and importantly, in the Soviet Union.

The headquarters was a non-descript concrete building in the middle of Islamabad. It resembled others in the area and only the presence of armed guards at every access point betrayed its purpose as an important government building.

An ISI agent escorted Sulundik through the main entrance and as they walked, she counted five locked doors and gates with guards at each. Long corridors and windowless side rooms indicated the outside windows were veneer. As she entered a small room, the agent seated her in front of a long desk and departed. The two waiting ISI officers stopped talking and sat down behind the desk.

"Welcome. We're so glad you're here and interested in joining our operations. I'm Colonel Khan and this is Mrs. Syed."

Mrs. Syed, a middle-aged woman in business attire began, "We've reviewed your record and you come with the highest recommendations of the Mujahideen as well as our ISI services."

The colonel spoke pragmatically. "Your mission will be difficult at best and dangerous, but we understand its importance to you and the Mujahideen," he began, looking up from the stack of papers developed from Sulundik's profile.

Sulundik said nothing but eased somewhat in her chair.

"What do you know of the Movement for the Restoration of Democracy, the MRD?" he continued.

"Nothing," Sulundik replied and shook her head.

"It's the parent organization of several subordinate parties including the Communist Party of Pakistan and a similar organization, the Awami National Party (ANP). The KGB has infiltrated most of these organizations and co-opted some of their members, or as they say, 'useful idiots'. Each is focused on undermining our national involvement in countering the Soviet occupation of Afghanistan."

Seeing Sulundik's puzzled look, Mrs. Syed explained, "Sometimes these organizations prove beneficial to our counterintelligence services."

The colonel continued, "At the same time the Soviets seek to undermine our national policies, they are increasing investment and influence in Pakistan. Both of our countries are now maneuvering toward an economic cooperation agreement which has led to numerous trade and investment exchanges of delegations across the government."

Mrs. Syed stood, stepped between Sulundik and the desk, and then sat on the edge of the desk with her arms crossed to emphasize what she was about to say.

"Our plan for you is twofold: preparation and insertion. For the last several weeks, we've developed your bona fides. Through our MRD agents and covert channels to the Soviet Union, we identified you as an 'unregistered' ANP member, and secretly, a communist sympathizer."

Colonel Khan provided the official line. "Simultaneously, and in a government-to-government communique, Pakistan's Ministry of State for Foreign Affairs identified you as a member of our trade council with a focus on the oil and energy sector. That delegation will meet with their Soviet counterparts in the next three weeks."

Mrs. Syed returned to her chair. "You have three weeks to assume the new Pakistani identity. I'll be with you throughout your stay here. We'll assist you with the development of your ANP history and ensure you've met certain members of the MRD to further develop your profile as a Soviet sympathizer. We will also assist you in gaining sufficient knowledge of the oil industry, specifically its administrative aspects, to be an acceptable member of our trade council."

Sulundik was uncomfortable with the complexity of the preparation, not the least of which was the language barrier. "Are you satisfied that my language expertise in Urdu is sufficient for a member of a trade council?"

"It's acceptable," Colonel Khan replied. "Your mastery of Pashto is excellent, so we've ensured those closest to you on the delegation will speak Pashto. Most of the meetings will be in Russian and use interpreters. I know you're fluent in Russian and that could be to our benefit. But you should refrain from engaging in conversations, especially alone, unless it's in Russian. You'll be assigned two handlers who speak Pashto and will ensure you are directed according to our planning."

"What specifically is the role of the handlers?"

Mrs. Syed smiled. "They're your security blanket. They are responsible for managing your travels. They'll assist in your preparations, act as members of the delegation, and accompany you throughout. They'll also intercede if the Soviets become too, shall we say, friendly. In essence, they will backstop your activities to ensure your cover isn't blown," she said, referring to those supporting the cover story. "You are their primary focus, and they'll assist in the final infiltration. Ostensibly, and as far as the Soviets are concerned, the male handler is your boss as well as escort and acts to protect your dignity as a Muslim woman."

Sulundik nodded in agreement but wondered at the great amount of effort put into her infiltration.

"You undoubtedly will be approached by the KGB, most likely a woman. Given your membership in the ANP, they'll likely pass along messages or give you instructions for future plans."

"How do you recommend I respond?"

Colonel Khan opened Sulundik's profile and looked at three pieces of paper the size of business cards. An address and a phone number were handwritten on each piece of paper. "Give them this. Engage no further. Advise them it's safer to contact you in Islamabad rather than on the delegation."

Mrs. Syed continued, "In addition to your male handler, you'll also have a female handler, and there are two other women on the delegation. You should always be in the company of one of these people. However, circumstances may arise when you are not, and you must be prepared. We'll establish a sound bona fides for you."

"I presume I'll be provided with the correct attire?" Sulundik asked.

"Yes. You'll wear a specific dress and always wear a dupatta scarf. Use the scarf to cover a portion of your face as will the others. You should appear to be more modest than the rest."

"I'm confident I'll be prepared when the delegation departs Islamabad. As you know, my focus is Chechnya. I'm unsure how going to Moscow is going to support this plan."

Colonel Khan closed the file. "The delegation is part of an economic council, and we are returning to follow up on previous visits to Baku, to discuss mutual research and development in the oil industry. Our intelligence team will brief you on what to expect once the delegation has arrived in Baku."

Mrs. Syed cast a serious look toward Sulundik. "There is much to prepare and much to learn in a brief time."

"Indeed."

Chapter 20
Moscow

It should have been a direct flight from Islamabad to Baku, but Soviet authorities were strict if not paranoid that foreigners entering the Soviet Union do so via its point of entry in Moscow. This was especially true of Pakistan, who despite the various trade arrangements, continued to support the enemy of the motherland in Afghanistan.

The Pakistani delegation moved as a group through the Sheremetyevo Airport to the right of the long lines of tourists and unofficial visitors. Then they formed a line in front of the diplomatic processing booth. Sulundik noted the KGB officer manning the booth was older and most likely senior to the other KGB officers. She could not see his rank from where she stood. His expression never changed, he made no comments, and he looked between each individual and their passport three times before he indicated they could proceed.

"Ah yes," she thought, "they do have their processes."

She looked around at the building. The structure was modern, especially compared to her experience elsewhere. Considerable work and expense had gone into lining the ceiling with vertical cylinders with lights interspersed within the cylinders. Yet, despite the expense shelled out for the building and its modern ceiling, it seemed the Soviets could never get enough lighting or brightly colored paint to change the atmosphere of the structure or the mood of the people. Everyone moved about in a monotonous shuffle.

The KGB official cleared the next person and with an unenthused wave motioned for Sulundik to move forward. Sulundik stood directly in front of the KGB official and noted he was a major; a conspicuously senior position to be simply processing diplomatic passports.

He looked at her carefully as she pulled back the dupatta scarf to reveal every feature. He looked at the passport photograph carefully and then again at her.

"That's twice," she thought.

As he turned his attention back to the passport, he spoke only loud enough for Sulundik to hear, never lifting his head, and barely moving his lips, "Welcome. We have mutual friends who will reach out to you soon."

A third and final look and he waved Sulundik along with no change in his expression.

Sulundik joined the others in retrieving their suitcases. After their customs processing, they took a short bus trip across the way to the Sheremetyevo Hotel where they checked in. Fully aware the KGB would rifle through their luggage, the delegation left their suitcases unlocked. They departed in a smoke-spewing, carbon monoxide-emitting bus to the Pakistani Embassy to meet with embassy staff.

***

The Pakistani Embassy in Moscow looked like any other with a national flag hanging from a drab institutional building. The entrance consisted of a gate of vertical steel bars welded to a huge frame. A gray concrete outer wall encircled the compound.

The bus entered the gate as the ever-present tail cars pulled off to await the delegation's exit. Nearby there was a flurry of activity as KGB monitors refocused their attention on the numerous embedded listening devices implanted throughout the embassy.

The delegation entered the embassy and exchanged greetings with the embassy staff. An administrator led the noisy group to a briefing room and directed several to sit in specific chairs away from the other members. Sulundik's seat was in an empty row at the rear of the group.

As the ambassador made perfunctory opening remarks, two ISI agents sat down on each side of Sulundik. They opened a satchel and placed several papers on their laps. No words were spoken. One agent handed Sulundik a nondescript paper bag. She opened it and looked inside to see neatly folded clothing similar in appearance to those she wore. Soviet citizenship identity documents were also inside.

The agent wrote on a piece of paper, "Change into these before you leave the embassy. Leave the other clothing." She acknowledged the note and placed the bag at her feet.

The agent then handed a sheet of paper to Sulundik. "Operational Update," she began reading. The paper contained updates on linkups, challenges, passwords, and operational procedures previously established in Pakistan.

The ambassador departed and a bureaucrat stepped forward to conduct the briefing. He expounded on the oil and gas opportunities and future potential for the USSR and Pakistan in enhanced bilateral relations with a focus on Baku.

"Very nice," she thought. "Oil and gas 'opportunities' designed for the monitors and eavesdroppers, a cover for the agent briefing."

The second ISI agent handed her a stack of photographs of significant points in Baku, critical to Sulundik's insertion. She looked at them carefully, turned some to the side, and viewed them from a different angle. Two photographs caught her attention. She looked carefully for an identifying feature or something to define its relevance to her mission. Finally, she wrote on a pad, "What are these? What is the relevance?"

The ISI agent took the pad and wrote rapidly, "This is the access to the market area adjacent to the train station and this entrance is the location of your insertion."

She looked carefully at the insertion point, raised an eyebrow, then smiled broadly. Both smiled in return. One shrugged his shoulders as if to say, "Any questions?"

Sulundik shook her head, smiled, and left to change her clothes.

Chapter 21
Azerbaijan

Though normally a direct flight, the Soviet government inserted a connecting flight and an overnight halfway into the Moscow to Baku trip. The connection with multiple 'weather' delays resulted in more than double the normal amount of time, but sufficient for the KGB to observe the delegation under stress. The group attempted to get comfortable on the final leg of the trip, but most were too tired to sleep. Sulundik stood, stretched, and walked about the cabin. No one, not even the KGB paid attention.

"A glass of water would be nice," Sulundik thought as she moved toward the rear of the aircraft where curtains separated the passengers from the flight attendants.

She pulled the curtain aside to see five flight attendants, three playing cards and two deep in thought over a small chessboard. One had a small dog in her lap with a red leash dangling to the floor. The area was unclean and cramped.

"Could I get some water?" Sulundik asked, hoping not to interrupt the concentration of the chess players.

"Sure!" One of the younger attendants hopped up to fill a cup of water and handed it to her.

Sulundik took the water and thanked her. She was surprised at how quickly the attendant had responded and her friendly behavior.

The attendant smiled. "Do you play 'Durak'?" she asked, referring to a favorite Russian card game with the winner being the first to discard all the playing cards.

Sulundik had played Durak often as a child in Chimkent, but now was not the time to get too familiar or friendly. She resisted the urge to study the ongoing chess plays. "No, I don't play," she replied as she noted the other flight attendants fixated on their cards. She was intrigued to see their hands were dirty and there appeared to be grease under their nails. It was apparent these women pulled triple duty as maintenance, baggage handlers, and attendants.

"I can teach you to play," the attendant said as she sat back down and picked up her cards.

Sulundik noted the attendant was the only one with clean nails, yet she was the youngest. "No thank you," Sulundik smiled and walked away.

As she sat down and pondered the dirty attendant area, she wondered, "Who among those might be KGB? Perhaps the friendly one with the clean nails."

***

Sulundik woke with a start as the aircraft bounced on the runway, came quickly to a stop, and turned toward the terminal. She had slept through and missed her breakfast meal but was glad to finally be in Baku.

Baku was like Moscow with its high degree of activity, however, each city had a distinctive character. Life in Moscow seemed to be an unending spasm of slothful and oppressive motion. It was a typical capital city; dour-faced bureaucrats, apparatchiks, official cars, people pushing and shoving, each grappling for a position on a bus or metro before it sped away.

Baku had a different feel and spirit. It was frantic if not chaotic. People scrambled about with what appeared to be a vested purpose, hustling, and opportunistic. Sulundik loved it. It reminded her of Chimkent, not just the activity, but the people. Unlike Moscow, they were like her; dark-skinned, with dark hair, and dark eyes. She fit well in Baku.

Accompanied by the KGB guides and interpreters, the trade delegation moved quickly to their hotel. On each floor a *dejournaya* sat behind an oversized desk; dejournaya - a sophisticated word for an unsophisticated position and an over-inflated attitude to go with it. The old ladies who served as dejournayas were ostensibly administrators for each floor who also filled a vital position for the authorities; to report on the activities of their guests. On occasion, the dejournaya might drive away an unsavory character with something to sell, or more likely allow access to an approved purveyor who provided an upfront cash incentive.

Sulundik and her roommate signed in and walked together up to their room. It was hot and she attempted to raise the window which was sealed shut by many layers of paint. The thin panes of glass did little to mask the sounds of people and vehicles below.

"What did the dejournaya say about showers?" the roommate asked Sulundik.

"We can get hot water twice a week. Wednesday and Saturday."

"So, cold showers?"

"Yes," Sulundik replied as she peeked out the door at the bathrooms at the far end of the hall. She shut the door and walked around the room looking in each corner. "Why is it that in a country like this, when they know there are two to a room, we have only one towel? Wouldn't you think they'd do better?"

"Really!" the roommate replied. "We have two hours before our first meetings. Maybe we can rest."

They were well on their way to a good nap when there was a knock at the door. Sulundik answered. It was the dejournaya.

"You requested another towel?" the old lady asked trying to peek inside the room.

Sulundik started to ask how the dejournaya knew, but the answer was obvious.

"Yes, we do need another towel. Thank you."

The dejournaya returned to her desk with a big smile, more elated with the thank you than having considered how she had learned of the need.

The roommates looked at one another and rolled their eyes.

Chapter 22
Double Agent

The delegation was going to be in Baku for four days. They attended multiple meetings and discussed how Russia and Pakistan might enhance oil and gas production, how they'd improve its export, how they could better utilize the Caspian Sea to move products through Central Asia, and what Pakistan might provide in return.

Sulundik had little interaction with the Russians or Azeris and was always in the company of her escorts. However, the KGB made several attempts to separate her. The ISI wanted Sulundik to make the connection but at the right time.

Saturday was the final conference meeting and Sunday was a free day with a scheduled departure in the afternoon. On Saturday, during a debate on oil extraction procedures, when all attention was on the panel of speakers, Sulundik stood and walked alone outside the conference room.

She walked to a small counter inside the building where cheese, kefir, black bread, blue cans of caviar, candy, and otherwise nondescript snacks were for sale. A freezer with pictures of various kinds of ice cream was just behind the counter. The clerk ignored her as she stood looking through the glass counter at the cheese. One of the guides walked behind the counter and the clerk quickly disappeared.

"What would you like," the guide asked in Urdu.

"I'll have ice cream please," Sulundik replied in Russian.

The guide turned and reached into the freezer for a container of vanilla ice cream. As she handed the ice cream to Sulundik she placed a small sliver of paper in her hand with a list of names. "These are the names of those we want you to recruit in Islamabad. They are vulnerable," she said quietly.

Sulundik took the paper. She then handed the guide payment for the ice cream and passed a note with phone numbers and whispered, "Use these phone numbers in Islamabad. They'll arrange a safe house when needed."

Each of them passed the necessary information, but with more spoken aloud than normal. They were alone, so both felt at ease to elaborate. Just as they were about to finish, a member of the Pakistani delegation walked in. The guide raised her voice and said loudly in Russian, "Would you like some ice cream as well?"

"No thank you. I must talk to my friend," she said directly.

Sulundik and the delegate walked to a corner where the delegate pretended agitation and scolded Sulundik for leaving the conference room. The two walked back inside to the conference.

This completed stage one of the insertion. They would complete stage two, the actual deployment, the next day.

Chapter 23
A Recruit and Insertion

Aynurova was a young Azeri woman who longed for adventure and an escape from the confines of Baku and specifically the Soviet Union. Her name, meaning daughter of moonlight, typified the Turkic and Arabic multiethnic and cultural background. Her longing to break the confines of the region as well as the culture was not something to discuss among friends or relatives lest she would be labeled a subversive, though many shared the desire.

Her parents were long divorced and far away, her brother was killed in Afghanistan, and there was nothing to keep Aynurova in Baku.

The ISI identified her while she was still a student at the university. Their approach was simple and began with an innocent enough conversation on a park bench.

"Wouldn't it be wonderful to travel around the world?" asked the ISI agent, who was also attending the university.

"Oh, yes," she replied.

The ISI agent met with her routinely and began the lengthy process of grooming her for a future ISI opportunity. The agent told her of the excitement that awaited in countries around the world. She focused on the beautiful sights and the opportunities, far removed from the oppression of the Soviet government, and how life could be so much more enjoyable.

"It sounds so wonderful," Aynurova said closing her eyes as if imagining such a place. "It's just an impossible dream."

"As you know, officially it's not permitted, but there are ways," the agent replied.

"I would go if it were possible. Even if not permitted."

"If you're serious, there may be a possibility. But don't discuss it with anyone and we'll talk later."

And so, the ISI put into place the final phase of a multi-year grooming effort. They identified, groomed, and recruited Aynurova because of her intellect and long-term potential. However, their selection of her for this mission had nothing to do with either.

***

Sunday was the Pakistani delegation's final day. They coordinated well in advance to go to the market near the train station. They wanted to buy fresh fruit and flowers, as farmers brought in their produce from the countryside. The guides were more than happy to accommodate them rather than the typical dull museum visit.

They walked along the market vendors looking among the various tables for the ripest fruit and nuts to take on their return journey. One delegate bought a dozen apples that she stuffed in a net bag. Sulundik purchased a large bouquet of multicolored flowers.

Aynurova shopped across the street and watched as the delegation and the guides moved from vendor to vendor. She was watching intently and finally saw the large bouquet of flowers among the delegation, which confirmed this was the contact group. She walked briskly across the street in front of them and entered a hallway, then disappeared.

As planned, the delegation continued down the street walking past the same hallway that Aynurova had entered. Suddenly they stopped, turned around, and walked back. As they entered the hallway, the guides struggled to catch up.

An overpowering stench filled the hallway. It opened to a multi-stalled public restroom. An old lady stood at the door with a wet cloth swatting at a fly. A plate, containing a couple of kopeks, was on a small table near the entrance.

Sulundik placed the flowers on the ledge above a dirty sink and walked to the last stall. The Russian guides stood by the door, entering just far enough to take a cursory look inside.

A delegate stood in the aisle to the stalls, blocking immediate access as another began screaming at the bewildered old lady standing at the door.

"You want money for this place? For what? What do you do? It's filthy. It's stinking!"

Though confused, the old lady wasn't intimidated and screamed back, swinging her nasty wet cloth at the antagonistic delegate. Two of the guides rushed in to separate them.

Another delegate dropped her bag of apples, spilling them all over the floor.

"No one can eat these now!" she shouted and joined in with the others in a chorus of chaotic screaming.

It was a suitable distraction.

Sulundik rapidly pulled off her dupatta scarf and turned it inside out to reveal a floral pattern. She pulled it over her head and tied it under her chin. She then pulled on Velcro fasteners, releasing her dress. She turned it inside out, put it back on, and reattached the fasteners. Within seconds, she stood completely redressed with a floral kerchief and dark blue dress.

Two stalls down, Aynurova did the same, except now she was wearing a dupatta scarf and gray dress. She pulled the scarf up to her face and stood ready.

The guides managed to move the old lady to a neutral corner and the delegation's instigator shouted, "We're leaving, and you can keep the apples."

Aynurova stepped out of the stall and joined the delegate in the aisle. She picked up the flowers and they all departed.

Sulundik waited a few minutes, squatting at the open hole. She recalled the chuckles of the ISI agents at setting up the exchange in a restroom. She read the graffiti as she waited; mostly pronouncements against Jews, denunciations of Armenians, and even a poem, "I sat on this cold seat, and cried for a bit; I had little to eat but took a huge shit." Sulundik smirked, "Hooligans!"

After a few minutes and hearing others arrive in the other stalls, she stepped out. She left the bathroom quickly but remembered to drop a kopek on the plate of the still incredibly angry and perplexed old woman.

***

Sulundik strolled down the street, passing by the final tables of vendors. Again, she purchased a handful of flowers and then walked to the train platform adjacent to the station office. She moved a little farther down the platform and stood next to several other commuters who were awaiting a train to the suburbs.

"Aynurova!" a voice shouted from behind Sulundik.

An older woman ran up and embraced her. "It's been so long, Aynurova! It's so good to see you!" she said as she took Sulundik's arm. They walked arm in arm as old friends along the platform, past the others, and even further from the station office. The woman spoke constantly of her family, never giving Sulundik a chance to speak.

The sound of the coming train caught everyone's attention. The woman slipped her a piece of paper with a number on it and whispered, "If you ever return to this republic, call this number and you will be picked up."

Sulundik slipped the paper into her pocket. Each looked for the optimum spot where the door of the passenger car might open.

"I don't have a ticket," Sulundik said.

"Ticket?" the lady asked in turn. "Don't you have identity papers?"

"Well, yes."

"Ha! Great! Nobody buys a ticket! The conductor won't even ask for a ticket unless he wants a good ear-tugging and thumping he'll never forget!" The lady laughed again.

The train stopped and Sulundik and the woman jumped aboard, standing between cars among the many other passengers. The woman did not attempt to find a seat. That might actually require a ticket. The train moved away slowly, taking Sulundik on the final leg of her insertion.

Somewhere between Baku and Moscow, the real Aynurova peered from the jet window at the earth passing below. Though the ISI groomed Aynurova as an agent, they didn't select her for this operation because of her intellect, aptitude, or political motivation. They chose her because of her uncanny resemblance to Sulundik. Now, she was on the first leg of her adventure with a new identity as a member of the Pakistani delegation and to another life; far from the Soviet Union.

Part III

The Third Thread

Chapter 1
1985 - Major Grigori Asimilov

Grigori Asimilov, Major in the Spetsnaz, Soviet Special Purpose Force, under the control of the GRU, reported to his commander with a brisk salute.

The commander returned a casual salute and gestured toward a chair adjacent to his desk. "Take a seat Grigori. You have a new assignment."

Major Asimilov sat down. "Yes sir. Go on."

"We need someone to get inside the Chechen rebel organization and assassinate one of its principal leaders. I don't need to tell you this is a difficult assignment. Winning the confidence of the rebels, joining them, getting close enough to conduct an assassination, and escaping back to friendly lines is a substantial risk."

Grigori was not the type of operator to shy away from a mission because it was risky. "I'm sure you've considered the target to be a high return given the low probability of success?"

"Indeed. The leadership evaluated risk, probability of success, and target value."

"Have they undertaken any operational planning? Do I have a backstop?" he asked.

The Spetsnaz commander was unconvincing. "Frankly, they've compartmented the mission, and I have little insight. It's a long-term mission. It's a GRU operation, planned at the highest levels. I'm sure they have a solid plan and will backstop your operation. You'll receive much of the information in Chechnya." The commander described the planning to which he was privy. "You'll be assigned to an Army logistical center and operate inside a storage facility. You'll take on the identity of a corrupt supply sergeant, *Starshina* Davidov."

The commander explained that Starshina Davidov would establish inroads with the Chechens by illegally trading and selling military goods. As his ability grew to provide goods to meet the ever-growing demand, so his integration would solidify among the rebels. It was a plan of action developed with many details yet to be hammered out.

Grigori was now less than diplomatic with his superior. "Some fat asses in a cushy office and far away from regional realities likely came up with this plan."

"They know greed on all sides is a motivating factor. It's a prescription that works. Besides, we all know you're ideal for such a dangerous effort."

Indeed, Grigori was perfect for the cover story. He had a lifetime of experience wheeling and dealing, black marketing, and simply surviving.

Chapter 2
The Early Years

Grigori Asimilov was a Moscovite. He, his parents, and his brother Dimitri lived in a high-rise apartment building, like so many that marked the Moscow suburbs. A product of Khrushchev's modernization vision, the government carried out mass residential construction with cheap labor, prefabrication, dangerous structural design, and an eye toward communal living. Colorless and sterile behemoths these structures seemed designed to antiquate as soon as construction was finished. Malfunctioning elevators, unreliable heating, and questionable water lines were the least of the construction issues. The distinct netting near the tops of the structures gave the buildings and skyline a sense of perpetual disrepair. The builders installed these nets immediately after construction as a safety precaution to catch falling debris, bricks, and stucco; an unintentional paradigm of socialism and the morose living environment for millions. Yet, the apparatchiks crowed of their achievement that the socialist goals were fulfilled.

Grigori lived in a two-room apartment with a living room and bedroom. His family shared a communal kitchen and bathroom. Two old and overstuffed chairs with floral slipcovers took up most of the space in the living room. A TV on a broken stand was in the corner next to a cracked window that looked out on the street six floors below. The bedroom was slightly smaller than the living room. A blanket hung from a rope that divided the room creating two sleeping areas: one limited to a single mattress for the two children, the other with a bed, nightstand, and dresser.

The kitchen, shared with two other families, had a table and three chairs, a sink, a two-burner gas stove, and a hotplate. It was a room Grigori's parents seldom used and certainly not a place for Grigori or his brother to linger lest they suffer the wrath of an irate neighbor. Ideally, the neighbors were other family members, but not in Grigori's case.

The shared bathroom was located at the end of the hall. The most important day of the week was the day their building had hot water. The allocation of hot water was a planned event and rotated between multiple buildings including hotels in the center of town. A hot shower was of little significance to Grigori. He and his brother took showers when neighbors complained about their appearance but only when every adult had finished or after the hot water ran out.

Grigori's parents were alcoholics and worse they were neglectful and abusive. They provided just enough life support to avoid arrest or to lose their children but not enough to fully sustain Grigori and his younger brother Dimitri.

Grigori was Dimitri's principal caregiver. Whenever they went outside, he held Dimitri's hand, pointed to passing cars with a word of caution, protected him from bullies, and carried him on his back when it was necessary. He scrounged, worked the streets, and accepted any handout which he shared with Dimitri. Grigori talked to Dimitri constantly looking for a response that would give hope; any hope for his little brother who continued to suffer from fetal alcohol syndrome.

Now four years old, Dimitri's functionality was limited. Normally a child such as Dimitri was given up or taken at birth and placed in an orphanage. Though most chose to give up such a child, Grigori's parents did not. An admission of Dimitri's condition might create greater problems. It would certainly draw attention to the alcoholism in the family. If the hospital and neighbors didn't report, why should they? It was easier to ignore it and hide the diagnosis. The authorities simply overlooked Dimitri. Besides, the parents reasoned, they had Grigori to provide for him.

***

There was never enough food. Sometimes at the end of the day, Grigori's parents returned home with a few morsels of food but insufficient for two growing boys. Quite by accident Grigori developed a means to add to their diet.

While walking along the street with Dimitri in tow, Grigori felt a forceful hand on his shoulder. It was a babushka holding tightly to a net bag containing cabbage and beets.

"What are you doing?" she asked directly.

"Nothing," Grigori replied not sure what was coming next.

"Good, then come with me." She led them to a long line of babushkas holding their produce and net bags, each looking around nervously as if they had another place to be.

"You stand in line here and wait for me." She then turned and announced to all that Grigori and Dimitri were holding her place in the long line.

Grigori had just entered the most complex if not logical and semi-organized shopping system in Russia. It represented an informal but recognized way the babushkas could do all of their shopping quickly and before the produce ran out.

Standing in the long lines for produce or at an entrance to a store one babushka held the position of another or handed off to a third, as each ran and repeated the process in another line. Once established in multiple lines, the babushka then serviced those lines. Much like a trapper continually setting and running a trap line and then returning for the pelts, the babushka checked each position relative to the front of the line and affirmed the other shoppers were fully aware of her position. The process had to be managed carefully; it was important to remember whose position you were holding and who was holding your position either directly or through third parties. Once the person holding a position was at the front of the line, the babushka returned to take her place.

Grigori and Dimitri were ideally suited for holding someone's position. They had nothing else to do and Dimitri stood completely unaffected by the activity around him. They stood in line, waited for the babushka to return, and on occasion served as the third party for others. While the babushka system was done without payment, Grigori expected and often demanded payment in produce. He might receive a couple of potatoes, several carrots, or any other produce he could negotiate. Money was not an option. Not only could the babushkas ill-afford to pay even a kopeck, but Grigori knew they'd be mugged immediately for any currency. Whatever

Grigori received, it was important they eat it immediately or hide it, but not take it home. They'd made that mistake once previously when they shared with their parents and received the short end of the deal. They wouldn't do it again. One of Grigori's worst beatings came from a fight over food.

***

Grigori's father was excited. He landed what he considered to be one of the best deals he'd had in a long time. Grigori watched as his father opened a wooden box containing sixteen large tins of shoe polish. His father and a friend had arranged a quick deal with a group of soldiers for a case of shoe polish in exchange for several young and willing women. The father's share was one case of shoe polish. Grigori wasn't sure of the importance of the shoe polish since he'd never once brushed his sorely worn shoes. He was even more confused when his mother came home equally excited with a loaf of bread. Grigori imagined it with a slather of butter, but it wasn't for him.

He and Dimitri stood adjacent to the hanging blanket separating their section of the bedroom and watched as their father opened each tin and placed it on the corner of the bed. Their mother then cut the bread perfectly to fit the opened can and placed it directly on the shoe polish. They positioned the tins in a long line under the bed.

Several days passed and Grigori noted that several tins were on the windowsill. He and Dimitri had not eaten that day. The bread was inviting. Those on the windowsill would surely be missed if taken. Perhaps among those under the bed, one would not be missed.

He pulled one tin from under the bed, sliced the bread in two sections, and gave one to Dimitri. It was damp, but not yet moldy. As Grigori began to eat and watched Dimitri swallow his portion, Dimitri tottered slightly and then lay down on his bed, visibly shaken. Grigori tasted then swallowed. He'd never tasted anything like it. Hot, bitter, and distasteful. The two boys had discovered their parents' special treat that was meant for them alone.

The shoe polish was another means for Grigori's parents to access alcohol. Over a couple of days, the dry bread drew the alcohol out of the shoe polish. It was a treat for anyone craving alcohol. After his parents ate it, they placed the tin in the window so the last portion of alcohol would evaporate quickly into a fresh slice of bread.

Believing the tin and slice of bread would not be missed was a big mistake. Grigori's father found the tin hidden under the boys' mattress and beat both unmercifully. Grigori rued his decision not to stand with the babushkas that day, but life was about to change.

***

Alcoholism was rampant. It was a national scourge. Public service announcements broadcast dire warnings of alcoholism. Before every movie, during radio shows, acted out in the parks by Young Pioneers and theater groups, the ravages of alcohol were a constant reminder of the danger, but to no avail. The stranglehold vodka had on Russia went back centuries. For many, vodka served as an escape from the daily grind of life. For others, it buttressed against the horrors of The Great Patriotic War. A push by the government wouldn't change it.

Both boys were growing, and the parents had a dilemma. Grigori was attending school and they locked Dimitri in their apartment, but this couldn't continue. The neighbors notified the government and with just a couple of inquiries, the authorities determined all they needed to know. Grigori and Dimitri as well as their parents were taken away. Dilemma resolved.

The authorities placed the parents in temporary rehabilitation. Given the fetal alcohol syndrome, the government placed Dimitri in an orphanage for the handicapped and later in life locked him away in an institution; locked away and forgotten by all but Grigori.

Dimitri's life and fate were sealed but Grigori adapted. With alcoholic, negligent, and abusive parents, the authorities placed him in an orphanage with its only virtue being not nearly as deplorable as Dimitri's. To avoid the daily beatings, he simply stayed away. He attended just enough mandatory school to avoid the authorities. As when he was younger, hunger forced him to seek other sources of food, whether at the market or among other street urchins. Only the extreme Moscow weather of heat and cold could force him back to the orphanage.

Chapter 3
Out of Options

Grigori often wondered what became of his parents and he missed Dimitri a lot. He wondered whether his parents might have been rehabilitated. They might be home now, wondering where he had gone. Might Dimitri be with them? He hadn't forgotten the beatings or the neglect, but he understood that both parents were slaves to their addiction. Could they have recovered and are working again to support the family?

Both parents had jobs previously. When not drunk, or for that matter when drunk, his father reported to a job site where he painted, installed plasterboard, and strung inside wiring. It wasn't a bad job compared to the job Grigori's mother held. His mother was one of the millions of women who took on jobs that were normally the domain of men. World War II ravaged the motherland with twenty million dead and not enough men survived to work all of the more physical jobs. She dug sewer lines, laid insulation on underground piping, and moved steel girders.

Grigori started to remember his mother in a different light. He recalled the times she was tender. He recalled how quietly he kept Dimitri when his mother returned from a long day at work and fell asleep in her chair. How she smiled when she awoke. How her expression changed when his father arrived with a bottle in hand.

Though not quite rational, the more he thought of the potential reunion the more excited he became. He was determined to find his way home and hoped to rush into the arms of his mother, to walk with Dimitri among the babushkas. He planned to leave the orphanage permanently and return to his home.

It wasn't easy finding his way but two days later he arrived at the apartment building. The elevator was broken and he walked up six flights of stairs to his old apartment. Breathless from the walk and excited he knocked on the door loudly. A woman in her thirties opened the door and looked at him sternly.

"What do you want?"

Grigori tried to answer but had to catch his breath. The woman shut the door and Grigori knocked again. When she opened it, Grigori stammered, "Parents...? I'm looking for my parents."

"Parents? Do I look old enough to have a kid as old as you?"

"I used to live here and I'm looking for my parents."

"Look, kid. I don't know anything about your parents. I've lived here for months."

Indeed, she was correct. An empty apartment never lasted long as everyone sought better accommodations, made the necessary payoffs, and quickly moved in. Certainly, an apartment on the sixth floor was better than one on the ninth floor.

"Dimitri? My brother?" Grigori continued.

"You need to go back where you came from. I can't help you."

The noise drew the attention of a lady in the adjacent apartment who had shared the same kitchen as Dimitri's family. She motioned to the younger woman who promptly shut the door.

"Aren't you Grigori?" the lady asked.

"Yes. I remember you."

"Why did you come back, Grigori?"

"I'm looking for my brother and my parents."

"You can't stay here. You need to go back to the orphanage."

"But my parents and Dimitri?"

The lady sighed and touched Grigori gently. "Dimitri is in a special place. It's perfect for him. But the officials won't allow you to see him."

"Where are my parents?"

The lady paused and considered how to answer. "They're not here Grigori. They're gone."

"But where are they?"

"They're not here anymore. They passed on... they died."

Grigori was shocked. Everything he imagined previously, the glorious homecoming, being with his brother, and the tender touch of his mother, dashed. "How? How did they die?"

"*Samogon*," she replied gently. Samogon, or homemade fire, was a moonshine concoction that tasted as bad as its name.

"Alcohol...?" Grigori asked making more of a statement than a question.

"Yes."

Alcohol poisoning was a well-known killer among the population. A little vodka, some homemade hooch, and just a little antifreeze to sweeten the potion oftentimes made a lethal brew. Priced to sell, the risk was worth the kick for those who craved the alcohol.

"Grigori," the woman continued. "I know this is sad news for you. But you need to leave. I don't know how you found your way here, but you need to find your way back to the orphanage. They'll have a bed and food. Something you won't have here."

Grigori said nothing. He turned and started walking toward the stairwell.

"If you like, I can try to get a policeman, and he can drive you back."

"No. I can find my way back."

As he walked down the steps he stopped between floors and sat down. He cried. He had never cried for anything except the beatings he received from his dad. This was different. He was empty. There was nothing left for him. No home. No family. No Dimitri.

He began his trek back to the orphanage and the beating that awaited him. He resolved to never look back again. There was nothing nor anyone left to hold on to and there was nothing left to lose.

***

When someone asked, "How are things?" Grigori's response was always the same, "*Normalno.*" Neither good nor bad; just "normal." However, you could not describe his life as normal. He avoided the orphanage as much as possible and found side hustles and entertainment from the numerous drunkards nearby.

Along the banks of a small stream leading to the major estuary of Grigori's suburb, a steady trail of men stole away daily with a newly gained bottle of clear liquid. Lying down as if to make love to a beautiful woman, they suckled the bottle, until every last drop had been drained. Oftentimes they would pass out and sleep through the night. On occasion, one might fall into the stream and drown, get rolled by another drunkard, or freeze to death in the winter. What Grigori found most entertaining was the morning ritual; the morning beating as an irate wife discovered the whereabouts of her good-for-nothing lout of a husband.

Grigori and his friends arrived a few minutes early, squatted in the nearby tall grass, and waited for the morning entertainment, much like a wealthy man might find his seat at the Bolshoi. An oversized babushka would discover her lout, snatch up his skinny ass from a drunken stupor, twist his ear into a knot, whale away at the top of his head with backhand after backhand as she dragged him home, with a few kicks for good measure.

Grigori imagined it was his old man getting the shit beaten out of him. It made the smile on his face stretch even wider. Sometimes, if he recognized the drunkard, Grigori might give him a warning of a fast-approaching wife with the expectation of a reward he would collect later. Other times, he might inform an irate wife of the location of her deadbeat husband, also with an anticipated reward or payment.

It was this ability to survive, manipulate his few friends, and capitalize on any opportunities, as well as his uncanny ability to discern the nature and base drives of others, which shaped the rest of his life.

As the orphans grew older, the orphanage afforded no further opportunities and there was no reason for them to remain. The girls often went to work selling themselves on the streets, while the boys joined street gangs or enlisted in the military. As soon as he could pass himself off as seventeen, Grigori joined the Army.

The military provided Grigori with everything he had missed as a young man; food, shelter, clothing, and camaraderie. The *Spetsnaz* became his home.

Chapter 4
Colonel Medved and the Assassination

Grigori reported to his headquarters in Chechnya to begin the first part of the assassination plot, a mission that was as complex as it was dangerous. He ensconced himself into the role of a greedy and corrupt Soviet supply sergeant. His interactions were initially with lower and mid-level Chechens but eventually spread to the guerrilla commanders. To gain the attention of more senior Chechens, those he believed to be operating from principal guerrilla bases, Grigori had to raise the stakes.

He leaked intelligence about insignificant small unit raids, for a price. As the Chechens pressed for increasingly sensitive information, Grigori demanded higher-level connections and more money. Occasionally, while seemingly under the influence of vodka, he stated his opposition to the war in Afghanistan and his support of the Chechen cause. His ruse transcended from black marketeer to treasonous when he toasted with the Chechens to the defeat of the USSR. There was always the risk that others within the Soviet Military, who hadn't been read on to the ruse, would discover Grigori's activities.

Grigori warned the rebels that should he be found out, he would be arrested, tried for treason, and executed. He demanded assurances, advanced planning, and sanctuary should he be forced to escape and defect. The rebels agreed, provided he maintained his value to them.

Leaking intelligence, selling black market goods, and attestations of empathy were not sufficient to fully win the trust of the guerrillas. Grigori needed to demonstrate his commitment and further solidify his position with irrefutable proof.

The GRU had an answer – Colonel Victor Medved.

**

Colonel Victor Medved, a colonel in the artillery, was nearing the end of a tour of four years in Bonn, West Germany at the Russian Embassy. Upon his arrival, Medved provided information and intelligence to the West.

He believed selling to the West Germans instead of the Americans was subtle and safe. He worked closely with western handlers for four years, providing information in exchange for concealed bank deposits under West German control.

Unfortunately for Colonel Medved, the West German intelligence service was replete with agents operating under the direction of the East German Ministry of State Security, the Stasi. They developed their case and reported Medved's activities to the KGB. The KGB along with the GRU set up counterintelligence operations targeting Medved with tailored intelligence; just enough actual information to make Medved appear legit to his handlers, but never enough information that would truly harm the Soviet Union. These counterintelligence operations continued throughout Medved's tour.

Near the end of his tour of duty, as Medved made final plans for his defection, he had a hiccup in the planning. His wife was not aware of his betrayal. Before he could put any defection plans into action, his wife decided to take a return vacation to Moscow with their children to visit relatives.

"Good," he thought. "Perfect. A final visit to relatives, and then we're set."

The KGB and GRU thought the vacation timing was perfect too. They had new orders for Medved to report immediately to an artillery unit near Grozny, Chechnya.

While the defection would have to be postponed, he felt reassured an assignment to an artillery unit indicated the counterintelligence services weren't aware of his betrayal, and his reassignment was simply a response to the growing Chechen threat. He was wrong.

***

After nearly four years of a cushy assignment in Bonn, Chechnya seemed to Medved to be an absolute shithole. The location was shitty, the job shitty, and he was unaccompanied; his family would meet him only after the assignment. Nothing could be worse.

"Should've crossed over alone," he grumbled. Things brightened when he met a gregarious starshina who helped make life a little more bearable.

"Starshina Davidov reporting," Grigori said, with his most disarming smile. He saluted smartly and held it until Medved returned the salute.

"Why have you asked to see me, Davidov?" Medved said bored and disinterested.

"Colonel Medved, this is a difficult assignment, as you well know, but I have suggestions on how we may improve morale."

"Go on."

"Well, I was able to get my hands on a box of Cuban cigars. I have enough to provide a few senior officers with six cigars each. I presume you smoke and if not, they can certainly be used to barter."

"How did you know I love cigars? How did you get these?" Medved asked excitedly.

"I have connections from Moscow who make the monthly runs to Mozduk," Grigori replied referring to the Soviet airbase.

"That's excellent! Cubans too!"

"I only presumed you might enjoy a cigar," the starshina lied. He had a detailed dossier of Medved's every vice and vulnerability.

For the next several weeks, Grigori gained the colonel's trust as his go-to man. Medved leveraged their relationship to elevate himself among the other officers, becoming the source of hard-to-come-by products and goods, such as meat, cigarettes, and alcohol.

"Colonel Medved," Grigori said after entering the colonel's office without even a hint of a salute. "My friends and I can get a case of western alcohol, specifically scotch, but I need your help. If you come along with me, as an officer of considerable rank, we will surely be able to get the whole case."

"Scotch!" Colonel Medved exclaimed.

"Yes sir. Scotch."

"You continue to amaze me! Do you know what kind of scotch?"

"I'm not familiar with it, but I was told it's something called single malt."

Colonel Medved couldn't contain himself as he stood up and patted Grigori on the shoulder. "Outstanding! I love single malt scotch. When do we leave?"

"I've arranged a driver and can pick you up at 0700 hours. We don't want to attract attention."

"Agreed! I'll be standing by." The colonel reached inside his desk and pulled out a prized cigar as Grigori walked out.

***

Less than a month after his arrival in Chechnya, Colonel Medved found himself sitting in the backseat of a speeding car with a pistol to his head. After a harrowing two-hour ride into the mountains, the Chechen driver pulled off the main road and into a wooded clearing. Ten armed guerrillas quickly surrounded them.

Grigori got out, and then pulled Medved from the car. "As I promised. I brought you a present," he announced. "He's a colonel. You should be able to get several thousand rubles in exchange for him."

The Chechens were delighted and quickly bound the colonel. The Chechen leader was a gruff and brutish man who went by Ugroza; a name that suited him well - Threat. Ugroza turned to Grigori, "Okay, you've kept your end of the bargain. Before we go, please give me your pistol."

Grigori wasn't eager to hand over his pistol, but there were few options. He hadn't yet earned their trust and he would have to prove his value even further.

They trekked up a steep path and arrived at a large base camp. The guerrillas wanted intelligence, the kind of information that a colonel would have. However, Colonel Medved, having arrived less than a month earlier, had nothing to offer the rebels even after several brutal interrogations.

Ugroza was angry; angry with Davidov. "This is it? You're wanted by the Soviets and we guaranteed your defection. In exchange, you bring us this useless piece of shit!"

Sensing the threat, Grigori replied quickly, "He's a hostage and a senior officer. He should bring a high reward."

Ugroza grunted, slapped the colonel, then walked away.

Over the next few days, the guerrillas sent messages with a picture of the bound colonel to the local Soviet commander. The Chechens offered his release in exchange for ten thousand rubles. The Soviets refused.

Again, the rebel commander raged as he looked wide-eyed at Grigori and waved his pistol in the air. "We'll make an example of him. They'll learn we don't bluff."

Two guerrillas brought Colonel Medved to Ugroza, while others stepped away and gave him space to rant. It was the opportunity Grigori had been waiting for.

Grigori stepped forward and reached out toward the raised pistol. "I brought him here. I'll shoot his sorry ass and deliver him back to the headquarters he came from."

Grigori's quick action and eagerness to kill the officer startled the guerrillas. Medved, despite his condition, was also mystified and questioned Davidov's motivation. He was about to get his answer.

Ugroza held out the pistol slowly as if questioning whether he would do it. Without hesitation, Grigori took the pistol and shoved Colonel Medved to his knees. He placed the barrel on the back of his head. "In the name of the Communist Party of the Soviet Union and the Rodina, you are hereby sentenced to death for espionage," he whispered in German, just loud enough for Medved to hear.

Medved's eyes reflected the horror and understanding. The bullet exploded out of the front of his head, and he lurched violently forward. The Chechens looked on in silence. Grigori offered his gun back to the commander.

"Keep your pistol," Ugroza said approvingly.

"I'll deliver his body to the front door of his headquarters tonight," Grigori promised. "A message has to be sent."

***

Now an accepted member of the rebels, Grigori convinced the Chechens that his connections in the Soviet military black market would continue to be useful. As his role grew in importance as a supplier of Soviet rations, medicine, and weapons, so did his reputation and his ability to move among the rebel leadership.

Grigori waited and watched for an opportunity to carry out the assassination. His target was an elusive Chechen who served as the conduit for cross-border communications and coordination between the separate factions. Little was known of the man or his operations. The guerrillas simply referred to him as Nol - Zero. Nol used a system of cutouts and go-betweens except at the most senior levels. Rumored to be highly educated, respected, and well-liked among the senior leaders, he enjoyed privileges that chafed some, especially Ugroza.

Having a penchant for young girls, Nol maintained three houses. Each was outfitted with a caretaker, who was also a part-time housekeeper and part-time sex toy. It was Ugroza's responsibility to provide one of the houses and an attractive housekeeper. He routinely complained about the requirement, the risk, and the cost of catering to the privileged Nol. On one occasion he complained when Grigori was nearby.

The GRU quickly rooted out and recruited one of the young caretakers to report on Nol's activities and his schedule. With this information, it would seem relatively simple to complete the assassination, but Grigori would leave nothing to chance. He had too much invested to simply hand the mission to another operative.

Peering from a darkened room across the street, Grigori and two GRU agents waited for Nol's arrival at one of his houses. Well before dark, a sedan pulled up and parked briefly in front of the house. Two men got out and walked into the house as the car sped away. Grigori was surprised when they arrived so early, and their flagrant disregard for security. Even the presence of the car could draw unwanted attention. There was either an overabundance of confidence or there were countersurveillance operatives already positioned to protect Nol. Grigori couldn't be sure. The presence of two men, one most likely Nol's security, and the likelihood of the sedan returning had complicated his planning.

He directed one of the agents to take a cursory walk along the street in front of the house to draw the attention of any countersurveillance. After a few minutes, the agent returned and reported seeing nothing or anyone out of the ordinary.

Grigori knew Nol was planning to leave the house a little after midnight, which was perfect for a takedown. However, Nol's early arrival could mean there was a change in the schedule. He directed one of the agents to a nearby alley to kill the driver when he arrived. No sooner had the agent hidden in the shadows when a figure stepped out of the house and lit a cigarette. Soon, a sedan pulled up. The figure flipped his cigarette and walked back inside. Grigori and his team sprang into action.

Using a silencer, the hidden agent appeared suddenly from the alley, shot the driver, pushed him aside, and sat down behind the steering wheel. Grigori and the other agent hurried across the street and stood out of sight. They emerged to kill Nol and his security man and quickly stuffed them in the trunk of the car, then sped away. The young caretaker simply disappeared. Grigori returned to the rebel base operating as normal with routine trips in and around the Russian base to buy and trade goods.

The successful assassination and the completion of his mission ensured Grigori's ultimate return to Russian control for other operations. To be completely successful, everything was dependent on a new cover story to explain his disappearance.

A month later, newspaper headlines reported that the authorities captured a Russian traitor, Starshina Davidov who had supported the rebels. The article continued that while being transported aboard a prison truck for interrogation the truck veered off the highway and down a steep ravine. The driver and guard were killed, but the starshina escaped. The article further reported a thousand-ruble reward for his capture. It was enough money to show the government's intent, but not enough to tempt the rebels to go looking either. All of it was a nicely staged GRU cover story and extraction plan for Grigori, and yet, left open the option to rejoin the Chechens at an optimum time. For now, he had another mission to carry out, in East Germany.

This operation would not go as well.

Chapter 5
East Germany

The cold war had reached its zenith, with covert operations and counter operations, proxy wars, the Soviet invasion of Afghanistan, attacks on civilians, assassinations, treason, executions, and near misses that could have led to nuclear war. Despite this, bilateral relations between the United States and the Soviet Union began to thaw as both sides strove to scale back and reduce their nuclear armaments. Not all in the Soviet military were happy with the rapid changes.

Under deep cover, the GRU ordered Grigori to East Germany to assassinate two U.S. military personnel assigned to the United States Military Liaison Mission. Unbeknownst to Grigori, his mission was an unsanctioned Soviet military and GRU conspiracy to sabotage the Soviet policies of *glasnost* and *perestroika*, as well as the new détente with the West.

From his ambush site and thinking he had killed one of the Americans, Grigori held his fire on the other American, a man he recognized. Years before, Grigori was the sole survivor of an ambush in Afghanistan. He watched as this American, with a distinctive limp, shot a Soviet officer rather than allowing the Mujahideen to torture him. That memory rushed back like a punch to the gut, and Grigori slowly eased his finger off the trigger.

The assassination attempt became front-page news, and the conspiracy was revealed to the KGB. They recalled Grigori and his operational commander to Moscow where they arrested his superior, but Grigori managed to evade capture. Wanted by the government and KGB, the former Major Asimilov was on the run.

He had few options and could not remain in Moscow. He needed to return to Chechnya where he had rebel contacts and could be assured a degree of safety. Joining again with the rebels was the only solution. He must reestablish his original cover story, which was now a reality, a man on the run and wanted by the government. It was simply a matter of survival and waiting for political upheaval to open an opportunity for his restoration within the military. Given the political changes occurring in Moscow, this was unlikely to occur.

Grigori had few true friends and the distance from Moscow to Chechnya was long, difficult, and dangerous. He must rely on contacts whose relationships were transactional, based strictly on reciprocal benefits and the best financial value for each interaction. Trust was not necessarily an element of the equation. Few friends and many connections had been a lifelong pattern. To survive now, as a fugitive on the run from the Soviet government and two thousand kilometers from a hoped-for Chechen sanctuary, he would have to maximize every instinct and skill he had honed his entire life.

He pooled his collective skills for a hasty exit from Moscow. That included a surreptitious jump aboard an outbound train, overnights in multiple safehouses, and quick cache stops for cash, clothing, and food. A couple of unmarked and shallow graves along the way and Grigori arrived in Chechnya and among the rebels.

Picking up the well-planned cover story established by the GRU a year before, he produced the tattered wanted poster for Starshina Davidov with a thousand-ruble bounty. This time was different, it was true. He was indeed a wanted man; wanted by every intelligence service of the Soviet Government. Had those services known he was back in Chechnya the bounty would have been many times higher; more than enough to tempt the rebels. But for now, the bounty was low, and his old cover story remained intact.

The rebels interrogated him thoroughly. Satisfied with his answers and given his connections, contacts, and underworld networks, they quickly restored him as the source for much of their supply needs.

Part IV

The Three Threads

Chapter 1
Area Command

The guerrillas led Bollard and Saud blindfolded into a small room with a couple of dimly lit lanterns. They plopped them down into two straight-back chairs and removed their blindfolds. Bollard opened his eyes slowly as the surroundings gradually came into focus. Six figures sitting behind a long table spoke quietly to one another. They sat shoulder to shoulder as the lanterns cast large and imposing shadows on the wall. As he carefully glanced around, Bollard could sense there were ten or so others in the room behind him. It was clear the top leadership sat in front of him.

Two of the leaders, one slightly overweight and the other smaller in stature than the rest, wore camouflage hunting netting over their faces and sat at the right. One of the leaders, leaning back in his chair with folded arms, wore a balaclava and sat to the left. The other three sat in the middle of the table. The three in the center, with mixed camouflage and bare faces, exuded authority. Bollard presumed this to be the Area Command, responsible for the coordination and synchronization of all the guerrilla operations in the region.

As Bollard sat in front of his interrogators, he knew he must focus on answering appropriately while gleaning as much information as possible. This included determining the respective organizations represented in the meeting. It wasn't an art or a gift, but simply an observation that groups took on similar dress, taste, interests, and proclivities which revealed who they were and their operational functions.

Bollard sat silently, understanding this would not be a perfunctory grilling. It would be intense, with an outcome of either acceptance into the force, or worst case, removal and death. Saud was not so patient.

Saud immediately complained about his treatment in broken Russian. "I'm an emissary and my treatment is not good. I've brought huge money. There are even more financial resources with the potential for extraordinary amounts. Yet, you blindfold me and treat me roughly."

In his arrogance, Saud failed to understand how close he was coming to death with each word from his mouth. Finally, the senior commander slammed his fist on the table and shouted "Enough!" Saud's tirade faded to indignant sputtering.

The commander then motioned for two of the men standing behind Saud to come forward. One guerrilla took Saud's right thumb and rubbed it unceremoniously with a coarse piece of charcoal, then rolled it across a piece of paper.

The commander then passed it to a guerrilla at the end of the table, who compared the thumbprint to another. It was Bollard's turn, and they repeated the procedure. Bollard rolled his thumb carefully to ensure a clear print, with the firm assistance of the two guerrillas.

It was vital to the guerrilla's survival that no agent had entered the ratline at any point along the route, hence the fingerprinting at the beginning as well as the end of the ratline. Now any mistake or inexperienced reading of the index lines, arches, or whorls of the thumbprint could result in a swift end.

The commander took the paper and looked at the print and Bollard curiously. He then passed it to the end of the table for comparison. There was a long silence, then the guerrilla verified the identities.

The tension in the room finally relaxed as several removed their balaclava and face nets. Bollard heard whispers of approval from behind.

Satisfied and without introduction, the commander began, "You men have come a long way to join us and we've used many of our resources to get you here. Everyone here must understand why you are here and for what purpose you believe you might serve our cause."

"Uh oh," Bollard thought, "Here comes the grilling."

"First, we'll hear from our friend from Saudi Arabia, then the American."

Saud whirled in his seat. "American?" he gasped. His astonishment quickly turned to fury as he shouted, "American!"

Bollard was not expecting the leadership to divulge his cover as a Georgian quite so abruptly, yet he remained expressionless. Saud began to puff and displayed his inexperience. Members of the leadership team asked some basic questions. Saud prattled on about his relatives in the royal family and his connections rather than simply answering the questions directly.

"I have great access to money and financing, some of which I've already provided. We're able to resource whatever you need to wage your holy war."

The leader rubbed his chin, "Five, where is the funding needed most right now?"

The man who had been wearing the balaclava didn't hesitate to answer. "We're behind in our payments for transportation, fuel, and safehouses. We're also running low on long-term canned goods. We have the support of our suppliers, but they are stretched thin without an infusion of funds. But I'm not sure how riyals will help us."

There was a long pause. Five searched among the rest of the guerrillas, seeking another opinion. "Ten, would you take riyals for goods?"

A voice from behind Bollard responded gruffly, "Rubles or barter only. I can't use anything else."

Five then pointed to one of the men seated at the end of the table, "Two, how can we dispense or use these riyals?"

A thin man with a beard and wire-rimmed glasses pecked on a stack of papers with a pencil, shook his head, and replied, "This is difficult. Any foreign currency exchanged for rubles requires *spravichiki* documentation. We would have to pay a heavy black market fee if the riyals entered here, made their way to a city center, then converted to rubles and returned to us."

Bollard started drawing connections in his head. Five seemed to have authority for logistics, likely the head of the auxiliary force. Two had to be the financial head of the organization.

Five, displeased with what he'd been told, looked intently at Saud. "Explain again how you might provide support?"

Saud's inexperience became even more evident. He sat silent.

The leader turned to Bollard. "And you. What are your thoughts on this dilemma?"

Bollard had considered this issue throughout the journey as he watched Saud freely dispense the worthless riyals. All heads turned to Bollard.

"I believe there may be three options, each with varying degrees of risk."

Saud's blood pressure rose. The utter indignity of this American deciding how he should fund this insurgency. He was infuriated but wisely held his tongue.

Bollard continued, "There are certain city centers where Saudi populations exist as an extension of their embassy. You can exchange through those populations, but you may gain unwanted attention. The best way is directly through the Saudi Embassy which can hide large amounts of ruble exchange and then secret those through other ratlines. This, however, is dependent on the cooperation of the Saudi government." Bollard paused, giving everyone time to turn their attention to Saud. "Do you have the direct support of the Saudi government?"

Saud seethed with anger. With every fiber of his being, he wanted to shut this American down. He knew the impact of lying would eventually catch up with him, so he responded in a barely audible voice, "No. The government is unreliable." Attempting to recapture the focus of attention, he added, "I have connections at the highest levels, but none can respond at the moment or will respond officially."

Just as Bollard anticipated, Saud was a part of the higher echelons of rich Saudi rogue families who had their own political and theocratic agendas. His answer confirmed what Bollard had hoped to hear.

"Then the other option is to exchange riyals for rubles at every capital outside Russian control. Such as those in Africa, the Middle East, and Europe," Bollard continued speaking over Saud's posturing. "Those rubles would then be secreted back to this location via the established ratlines." Bollard paused, then addressed Two directly, "Do these options sound viable?"

Two assured the commander, "These are viable options, but the last is most viable, most secure, and causes the least suspicion."

The commander was crisp with his order, "Then work out the details with Saud and provide a schedule for shipments of the rubles."

One of the leaders said to Saud with a slight edge to his voice, "We invited the American; he's here at our invitation. But you requested to come here yet have provided no motive."

Saud had prepared for this his entire life. The years studying in the madrasas, the memorized excerpts of the Koran, the speeches from the radical Imams, and his well-rehearsed lines prepared to spew forth. It was all lost in the stammering of his wounded pride and anger at the American.

"We," his voice cracked and strained. He cleared his throat and tried again. "We are all brothers," he said with a wave deliberately excluding Bollard. "I'm here to support my Islamic brothers." He continued with more composure and after several minutes he concluded, expressing his desire for Islamic communities worldwide to align and rise against any power except the authority of a central theocratic leader.

The effect of his impassioned speech brought about two different general reactions. Some of the guerrillas offered soft cheers and agreements, others unconsciously pursed their lips and wrinkled their noses like an unpleasant smell had drifted in, particularly at the notion of a theocratic leader.

"But who is this American?" Saud demanded. The presence of a few supporters in the room boosted his confidence. So much so, that he didn't realize he was about to cross a line. "He is a *kafir*, an unbeliever. What does he know of us or our faith? What does he know of me and the faith of my people? His people are the most repressive of our faith and our people!" He whirled on Bollard with no shortage of contempt.

Instead of making any reply to the hot and stupid accusations that Saud shot his way, Bollard addressed the Area Commander. "Our Saudi friend's opinion personally makes no difference to me, and I won't pretend what I have to say, relevant to his comments, has any importance to the people gathered here."

The leader, predictably, smiled. Something twinkled behind his eyes. "I would love to hear your response."

Bollard bowed his head and turned to Saud. "I know you are dedicated to your personal agenda and made a long and difficult trip. While you know nothing of my faith, I know much of yours. I know you are a Wahhabi and a *Salafi* going back to the *Hanbali* movement. These people are also Sunni but from the *Shaf'il* school. Like you and other Sunni faiths, they rely on the Koran and *hadith*. But unlike you, they do not view faith through a narrow prism. They must rely on the *ijma* consensus of Islamic Scholars and *qiyas* analytic reasoning to adapt to their tumultuous circumstances, which you reject."

Bollard had begun to draw a line between Saud and the others. Saud tried to interject but the leader stopped him.

Bollard continued, "Everyone in this room understands that not all who support the cause of freedom are necessarily Muslim. Some are freedom-loving men who want no authoritarian power or theocratic power of any kind governing them. Success may ultimately depend on them. I know that freedom is more quickly achieved when there is external support, Islamic or not, such as is underway in Afghanistan."

A member of the leadership with a slight build and whose face remained covered with the camouflaged net tapped on the table. The leader acknowledged, "Yes, Seven. Do you have a question?"

"What do you know of Afghanistan?" Seven asked Bollard pointedly. "Its people, their religion, and their struggle?"

"I know the preponderance of the population is Sunni of the *Hanafi* school. Their considerations for Sharia comprise Koran, hadith, ijma, qiyas juristic preference, and customs. Other than the acceptance of juristic and customs, they are more akin to the Shaf'il school than certainly Wahhabism, which this man represents," Bollard answered shrugging in Saud's direction.

"What do you know of their struggle?"

"I know they are fighting for freedom from the same oppressive regime the people here are fighting. Furthermore, Afghanistan's success is going to be dependent on foreign support including aid from my country."

The room seemed to ripple with surprise as the guerrillas all tried to get a better look at the American. Bollard noticed that a man had moved forward and was standing next to him. Seven stirred somewhat nervously and looked in his direction with some degree of familiarity. He had the physical features of many Russians, stocky and squarely built. He had thick black hair, a swarthy complexion, and mischievous eyes, with a perpetual grin that never left his face despite the circumstance.

The man raised his hand. "May I ask something?" The commander acknowledged him, and the distinctly Russian guerrilla peered down at Bollard and drilled in. "Yes, but what do you know personally of Afghanistan? One would have to be present among those fighters to truly understand the fight."

Bollard recognized the voice from earlier as Ten, the supplier. "I have been to Afghanistan, have been with the fighters, and understand their cause," Bollard answered cautiously, omitting he had barely escaped with his life from those same fighters.

"Was your mission with them the same as your mission here?"

This might have been a trick question to elicit information on Bollard's mission among the rebels. Bollard was circumspect in his answer. "The guerrilla leadership sitting here today understand my purpose and mission. Just as I would keep our mission here confidential, my involvement with the Afghans must also remain confidential. Suffice it to say, in both cases, you have a common enemy and a common cause, in which I and my country may be able to assist."

The supplier searched Bollard's face as if inspecting him, produced an odd smile, and returned to the back of the room.

"The American is correct," Seven said, tapping the tabletop. "He identifies with my mission and that's the unification of all our regional efforts. Accepting as much external support as possible around our common cause is vital and I'll readdress this at the next Regional Command meeting. Thank you, I'm satisfied." Seven then removed the camouflage hunting net revealing a face covered in patches of soot.

Bollard took advantage of the pause and continued. "As you know from earlier coordination my role is quite simple: identify your needs and determine the means to satisfy them in support of your struggle. My country will deny any involvement, my

213

role, and my affiliation should I be captured. I have limited time and need to return to my superiors with recommendations as soon as my role is complete. I can neither lead nor plan armed operations but must serve strictly in observer and advisor roles. That is the extent of my mission and my presence."

Saud pounced at the opportunity. "You have no ties to us and now you say you won't take part in this jihad? You're an infidel."

Six had heard enough of the arrogance of the young Saudi and was eager to hear how Bollard might respond. He waved his hand to Bollard.

"I've explained my purpose for being here. I know you are a pious young man," Bollard began, with Saud initially in full agreement and greatly satisfied. "Yet, you're inexperienced."

Bollard realized he had to proceed with caution. There appeared to be two groups among this Area Command: those who were empathetic when Saud spoke, and those who appeared to be more amused with Saud's inexperience. Saud angrily looked to others for some correction of Bollard's perceived smear. They showed no inclination of support and the Commander simply motioned Bollard to continue.

"I know you are inexperienced because when we crossed from Azerbaijan into the Dagestan region you lectured some of our escorts for not praying at the appropriate time of day. They seemed a bit confused but didn't respond to you as you prayed alone. You see, you didn't realize we had been in a different time zone for several hours. We were no longer in the Azeri time zone. Those men had already changed their prayer time to the new time zone, which by the way, is the same as Mecca." Bollard then baited Saud, "But you didn't notice because at the time of their praying you were negotiating the cost of a dead mule."

Saud responded angrily, "Yes, and I paid heavily for the cost of that mule. It was my duty as an upright Muslim."

"I agree. In fact, as an expression of such piety, you paid three times the cost of the mule in rubles because the owner wouldn't accept your riyals. Perhaps you can explain how you arrived at the negotiated cost of the mule."

"Yes. The mule owner said he would lose generations of offspring and the payment should reflect it. So, doing my religious duty I paid an even greater amount of three generations for the mule's offspring."

Each in the room understood the skinner likely had his fill of the Saudi and had taken advantage of the young man. Everyone, except the inexperienced upper-crust Saudi, knew it was unlikely a mule ever produced a single generation of offspring. It was also unlikely anyone would explain to the Saudi the nuanced life of a mule or a hinny for that matter. There was laughter around the room.

Six raised his hand to quiet the room and to indicate the end of the interrogation. He turned to the heavier guerrilla who had just removed his camouflaged mask, "Four, what is your near-term operational planning?"

Four replied, "I've been coordinating with Two and Five. We are in desperate need of funds. I'll be working with our cells to arrange a raid to retrieve cash from one of the regional government payroll stations just across the Ossetian border. The government disburses cash from that location to regional offices. Before the Soviet escorts arrive from the local airfield, they stop at a small shithole on the outskirts of town for an overnight stay. They secure the money in a vault in the town's constabulary. We plan to relieve the constabulary of the funds."

"Good. What do you need from Three and Five?"

Bollard calculated the numerical code for Three and Five, the underground and the auxiliary.

"Once the payroll officials deliver the funds to the constabulary, Three and Five will coordinate the sabotage of the transport truck that the Soviet security force uses to move the funds for disbursement. That will create the delay we need to complete the mission. Operationally, we've coordinated with Five and the auxiliary to provide us with explosives, keep us apprised of any changes in and around the constabulary, and identify a potential safe house nearby. Also, we'd like an onsite observer to assist during the operations; someone who can move among the population without anyone taking notice.

215

We'll coordinate for signals to indicate whether the situation is safe, or if an abort is necessary."

"Ten, is this something you could do?"

The Russian supplier expressed an affirmative.

"Anything else?" Six asked.

Bollard had a lot of questions, such as why Ossetia, but he held his tongue.

Four replied, "Yes. I want Seven-Alpha included in the operation. I want his input and advice."

The leader looked at Bollard, "That's you." He then leaned in toward Saud, "Do you want Seven-Bravo to go as well?"

"No thanks. He can go with Five," Four replied with a smile.

"Okay, wrap up final coordination tonight and keep me posted through the normal communications," Six ordered.

The Area Command leadership began discussions for long-term operational planning and ended the meeting with the coordination of signals that would indicate the next gathering. The leadership adjourned and exited from the rear of the building as the others left from the front.

Bollard determined that Four was the Guerrilla Chief, organizationally responsible for direct action and operations; Five was the Auxiliary Chief, responsible for transport, logistics, intelligence, ratlines, and local support; Two was Finance and likely subordinate to Five; Three was the Underground Chief, responsible for sabotage, intelligence, and operating covertly within established government and civil frameworks; and Six, the overall Area Commander. He surmised nearly all operations would be comprised within the authority of one of these chiefs.

He presumed the codenames Seven, Seven-Bravo, and his codename Seven-Alpha were set aside as external liaison members. Seven struck Bollard's curiosity as to the individual's background. Excellent Russian, dark eyes, and a face camouflaged in soot. He made a mental note that after removing the camouflage netting, Seven reacted nervously to Ten's presence. He also noted Ten had an odd smile with each of Bollard's previous answers, especially during the discussion of Afghanistan. It was all very intriguing.

As they exited, Bollard walked alongside Saud and whispered, "Change your watch to the correct time. You're still on Azeri time. You're a full hour ahead."

Between clenched teeth, Saud, retorted, "By Allah and in my lifetime, the hands of this watch will never be changed to look like yours... that of an infidel!"

There was no time for a response as Four put his arm around Bollard, "Come with me. We have mission details to plan."

Ten watched their every movement as they left.

***

Ten walked out of the Area Command Meeting shaking his head incredulously. His prior experience led him to many different places in the world and the chance of meeting someone serendipitously in any two of those locations was extremely low. Tonight's meeting broke all the odds. Sitting in front of him at the Area Command Meeting was a man he'd seen in Afghanistan, East Germany, and now Chechnya. He couldn't believe it. But there it was, as the American left the building, a slight and unmistakable limp.

"What do you know of this American?" Ten asked the Area Commander directly.

Six stood up and started walking toward the door. "He's the person we've been expecting and his fingerprints match."

"Do you have any details on him?"

"His presence here was approved at the highest levels, at the Regional Command and the MRNC. We'll watch him and take every advantage he and his country might afford us."

"I agree, but ..."

Six walked out of the building with Ten and then placed a firm hand on his shoulder. "You should feel free to work closely with him to satisfy your curiosity. If there are issues, you should let me know immediately."

"Indeed, I will."

Chapter 2
Rapport

It was dark when Bollard, Four the guerrilla chief, and a handful of escorts cleared the outer and inner perimeters and walked quietly into the guerrilla basecamp. An old woman stirred a large pot of indistinguishable stew over a fire. An even older man squatted beside her, eyes glazed over, and threw in an occasional stick to fuel the flames. Otherwise, the camp was still. Bollard's stomach growled as he caught a whiff of the stew. It occurred to him that neither he nor likely any of the guerrillas had eaten since before noon, well before his introduction at the Area Command meeting. Hunger, Bollard was reminded, is an expected and conditioned result of such operations. If hunger is a constant companion, then a lack of sleep is its mistress. The rule "eat when you can, sleep when you can" is always in play. Now, all were hungry and equally tired.

Bollard waited as he watched the others line up with their dirty and mismatched dishes. Four passed him a cracked bowl and an oversized spoon and motioned for him to move ahead in line. Bollard chose to fall behind the last in line. Four smiled approvingly and stood beside him. As they came up to the smoldering pot, the old woman ladled out the last dregs of gruel and handed them both a small piece of bread. Bollard was tempted to simply lift the bowl and pour it down his throat, but Four gestured to sit beside him at the fire. Bollard seized on the opportunity to establish rapport over a meal.

"Tomorrow will be an important operation for us," Four said, dipping the bread into his bowl and swirling it around. "We're in short supply of everything including food. We need cash. We could simply run a requisition from the locals if we wanted, but that would be self-defeating in the long term. We'll run the operation through Ingushetia into Ossetia."

"Why Ossetia? Aren't we more or less on the same side?" Bollard asked, slurping his stew.

"Same side? They have a long history of resistance, but currently, they see our activities as a threat. They're not cooperating as they've agreed, though we hope that will change. To your point, if we must take money, we prefer to take it from elsewhere. The government's police and military in Ossetia aren't as organized as they are in other areas and they're poorly equipped. It makes them an easier target."

"How confident are you in your intel?"

"Our supplier, Ten, was the initial source. We can't pay him for the information if we don't have money, so he is highly motivated. We've also been monitoring the situation for ourselves."

The old lady interrupted their conversation, handing them each a cup of root tea. Bollard thanked her and took a long sip. It had a slightly bitter taste. He hoped it had no caffeine.

"How big a force will take part in this operation?" Bollard asked.

Four blew on his tea. "Only seven of you."

"Why so few?"

"This is a high-risk operation. The fewer the better. The auxiliary will provide transport if needed, as well as safe houses, and food. If this isn't in line with the instructions of your headquarters, you are welcome to decline."

Four's offer was sincere and astute; something Bollard didn't expect. "I'm in." He crumbled some bread into his remaining stew, stirred it, and took a final spoonful. Bollard continued, "If someone is captured, it's only a matter of time before your base camp is revealed to the enemy. Do you have a contingency?"

"Multiple. One of those is to make sure none of our forces survives," Four examined the bottom of his cup, "but that's the last resort. Should someone be captured, we'll relocate the camp to a predetermined location. Far away from here. That's why I won't be with you."

"You won't be on the operation?"

"No, I have to remain with the main force. Nick, my number two, will lead the operation. He's experienced and a good man. I'm also sending Dukvakha, my nephew, with him. You'll meet everyone tomorrow."

"The supplier... Ten. He's participating as well?"

"Yes," Four eyed him curiously, "he'll participate, but as part of the observation team. If necessary, he'll warn the team of unforeseen dangers. He's known to the locals, so he'll be in the town at an outdoor restaurant. If there's trouble, he'll wave off the operation by smoking a cigarette. You'll watch for his signal."

"So, I'll be watching from a distance?"

"Yes, you and one other. Your job is simply to return to camp and report if the operation fails or if there are issues. You'll get a full operational briefing in the morning."

"Understood."

Four shifted in his seat. "Look, our highest leadership levels requested your presence. We went to a lot of effort to get you here. The Regional Command had its reasons, and we were advised it was relevant to the MRNC, the government in exile. I couldn't care less about a bunch of bureaucrats. I'm glad to have as much support as I can get. Tomorrow and the next few days should give you keen insight into how we operate. I'm always open to discussing anything."

"I want to be of assistance to you," Bollard reassured him. "If I may, there is something you could help me with."

"Go on."

Bollard pulled out a sliver of paper.

"I wrote these items down for you to review. I need to establish communications with my people using these items to set up a transmitter."

Four took the paper and examined the list carefully. "I think we can have these in a few days, possibly by the time you're back. However, I'm concerned about any outgoing radio communications, given Soviet direction-finding capabilities."

"Operationally, no messages will go out that exceed twenty seconds, which should be secure. Regardless, I'll need to identify a location a safe distance from here to transmit."

"Okay, Nick will assign one of his team to assist you. I want to know anytime you leave camp to transmit."

"Absolutely."

Bollard couldn't believe his luck. Attempting to assemble a transmitter and transmit from a secure location without the buy-in of the guerrilla leadership would be extremely dangerous. With Four's assistance, he would be able to carry out a difficult part of the mission, communicating from within the operational environment.

Four stood and handed his cup and bowl to the old lady. "Let's get some rest."

Doing the same, Bollard walked to his makeshift lean-to and lay down. Forcing himself to stay awake until the flicker of the cookfire had died, he listened for the others in the camp to settle in for the night. He grabbed his blanket and quietly moved ten meters uphill and away from his shelter, then settled in for a peaceful night's rest.

Chapter 3
Operation Order

Bollard noted the interruption of the early morning stillness with the stirrings of men around the base camp. Each man moved to a preset defensive position at the perimeter. It was a security precaution practiced by armies for centuries and carried out in anticipation of an enemy's predawn attack. When the practice was not observed, the potential for annihilation increased significantly.

Bollard rolled up his blanket and slipped back to the lean-to, tossing it inside. He sat and watched the activity in the camp. Like clockwork, as visibility increased the inner camp set into its routine of starting fires, preparing meals, washing, changing security forces, and morning constitutionals.

The evening's stew hadn't set well with Bollard. His intestines groaned and gurgled as he made his way to one of the camp's slit trenches. Located a fair distance away and well downwind, the trench was still within the perimeter of the base camp. Less than a meter wide and two meters long, it could accommodate two men comfortably, but Bollard observed three squatting along the trench. He stood by at a comfortable distance until two of them threw a perfunctory amount of dirt into the trench and departed. Bollard grabbed a handful of broad leaves from a nearby bush and took his position over the latrine. He was able to relax. No orders, no requirements, just a moment of solitude at last! His short respite was interrupted as his stomach churned and he released a torrent. This was serious. If the problem continued, he could be a liability to the operation. Taking a glance into the trench, he determined he wasn't the only one with a bowel issue. Either the food was affecting the camp, or worse, the camp was rife with dysentery. He wiped himself with the handful of leaves and returned to the camp.

Bollard joined some of the other men drawing water from a cauldron to wash and prepare for the day. Most of the guerrillas pretended to ignore him. Given the nature of their business, the less known the better. No sooner had Bollard finished washing when a short man with a light brown beard approached him.

"Good morning. I'm Nick. You'll be with me today." He extended his hand.

"Good morning. I guess I'm Seven Alpha. Four said you would link up with me."

"Ha! I keep telling him to save the numbers for the Area Command and dispense with them here. We'll have to do something about this Seven Alpha business. How about Alpha?"

Bollard smiled. The Area Command had identity papers with his cover name, gave him a number, and now the guerrillas were giving him a new name. "I'm good with Alpha if you are."

"So, it is! Come along, and you'll meet our team. They're eager to get their hands on government money," Nick laughed.

Bollard grinned as he followed Nick. He led him to a makeshift table made of parallel limbs wound tightly and attached to a wooden frame. Four men stood around the table, waiting.

"This is Alpha," Nick said, taking a stance at the center of the table.

Each man greeted Bollard, but no one offered a name.

An eager young man jogged up to the table, late and slightly out of breath.

"I'm Dukvakha," the young man said, quickly introducing himself to Bollard before turning to a frowning Nick. "Sorry."

Nick cleared his throat and began, "By now each of you is familiar with the mission, but I'm going to go over it one more time for Dukvakha and Alpha's benefit."

Stepping away from the table, he took a long stick and started scratching images into the dirt. "We are here." He drew a small circle. "We must make our way to the linkup with the auxiliary." Nick made another circle in the ground and dragged a line connecting the two. "At the linkup, they'll take us to a safe place where we'll find some food and water and rest overnight. Well before daylight and before the residents rise, we'll move to an observation point to the east of the town that overlooks an outdoor restaurant and the town constabulary."

Nick sketched a rough layout of the town. "Immediately after the operation, we'll link up at a rally site or an alternate site. I'll identify them along the way. Misha will be carrying the explosives. Alpha and Misha will keep a lookout for trouble." Misha, a young man in his twenties moved alongside Bollard. Nick stared at them intently. "You must warn us if there is a need to abort. Fire three shots in the air at two-second intervals. In such a case, we'll regroup at the alternate site. If everyone has done their job, we'll walk in, take the money, and walk out while the Soviets are busy repairing their payroll truck. Any questions?"

"Is there a cover story?" Bollard asked.

The team laughed. "Our relationship with the government and military isn't so civil as to allow for a cover story," Nick chuckled. "You're dead either way, so it might as well be by our own doing. This is why you and each of us have one of these." He pulled up his shirt to reveal a Tokarev pistol tucked into his belt. One of the men handed an older model pistol to Nick who in turn passed it to Bollard.

Nick frowned slightly. "It's also why Dukvakha is coming along. It's his turn."

Bollard looked a bit confused as he turned to Dukvakha. "His turn?"

Dukvakha pulled a vest from under the table. Two shoulder straps supported six vertical pockets, three on each side of the center connecting strap. Each of the vertical pockets held explosives wired to a battery and a handheld pressure button. Dukvakha put it on and smiled at Bollard.

"Yes, my turn to wear this. I'm the ultimate guarantee the Soviets will take none of us prisoner and I'll take a lot of them along with us."

Bollard studied the young man. Despite the dark implications of what he had just said, Dukvakha's eyes were optimistic and bright reflecting his inexperience. Bollard suspected that Four assigned his nephew to this mission because he believed the team wouldn't need the suicide vest.

Bollard turned his attention to his pistol. It was a Nagan M1895 revolver whose better years were behind it. Despite this, there was a certain comfort with placing the pistol under his belt. He had been behind enemy lines for months, completely unarmed.

"Any other weapons?" Bollard asked.

"The rest of us will have rifles, but we'll leave them at the observation point and carry pistols during the actual operation."

"Do you think we'll need the explosives?"

"Alpha, we always have explosives. You never know what opportunity might arise."

"Okay, I think I've got it, thanks," Bollard said as two young men approached the table.

They carried a pot of warm goat's milk, bowls, and a loaf of bread. Then they distributed three boiled eggs to each man. Nick instructed them to place everything else on the table. Each member of the team took a bowl and poured a portion of the goat's milk. Nick broke the bread in two, then cut five pieces from one of the halves and passed them out. He crumbled the bread into the milk and began drinking it from the bowl, everyone else followed suit. One man started to break a boiled egg.

Nick looked at him and scoffed. "You'll want to go easy on those eggs," he advised. "Other than the other half of this bread, it's all you'll get till nightfall."

Some of the men tucked two of the eggs into their breast pockets and ate the other. "I'm not sure these eggs are going to help anyone's stomach problems," one man muttered.

"You mean our shit problems," another corrected with a laugh.

Bollard looked around at the chagrinned faces of the other guerrillas. That was a question answered.

"Make your final preparations," Nick ordered. "Meet me by the supply point and we'll pick up ammo and explosives. We'll leave in ten minutes."

Then Nick did something rather unorthodox. He took Bollard by the arm and pulled him to the side for a private conversation.

"You may have noticed that among us there are two separate groups. Some are more fundamentalist and militant. They bear watching. They may or may not follow orders. I prefer to leave them behind. Today you will be with Dukvakha, Four's nephew. Four is grooming him for leadership and he sits beside his uncle at Area Command and Regional Command meetings. I didn't want him, but Four ordered him to take part in today's operation. He's young and sways towards the theocrats, the militants. I want you to watch him and tell me if he acts or does anything other than what I direct. Do you understand?"

It was obvious Nick, as the leader of this operation, was leaving nothing to chance. Bollard was surprised at his candor and replied, "Yes, it's very clear."

Chapter 4
Movement to Linkup

It was daylight when the team moved out at a brisk pace. They had to cover fifteen miles of mountainous terrain before twilight and avoid any contact. They traveled light, carrying few supplies. The only person with a pack was the smallest, Misha. A partial opening at the top of the pack revealed several sticks of dynamite. Bollard could only guess at its exact contents. Each man carried a handful of loose ammunition, along with an AK-47 or the newer AK-74 with a full magazine.

The men picked up the pace. Despite their intent for speed, their progress slowed multiple times throughout the day as Dukvakha ran to the side of the trail, dropped his pants, and let loose a stream of spurts. The others seemed to have similar problems but waited for the planned stops; not Dukvakha. Finally, Nick had enough.

"Get over here," Nick growled to the young man. "Bend over!" Dukvakha, confused, complied and bent slightly. Nick inserted his knife into the seam of his pants and ripped it from the ass to the crotch.

"Now, when you must defecate, just pull the seat of your pants apart and let it fly. No more stopping and pulling down and pulling up your pants! And drink more water. We don't want you dehydrated from all this shitting."

Dukvakha was embarrassed, but Nick was right, the pace increased.

***

As darkness set in, the team emerged from the forest at the corner of a small field. A man with a cane and carrying a large bag approached them slowly from the right edge of the field. Nick raised his right arm and extended it parallel to the ground as he walked along the edge of the forest toward the man. The team followed in a single file. As they approached the man, Bollard could see he wore a disguise that included a beard and a hat pulled low.

Nick and the man exchanged a few words. The man, who would serve as their guide, led the group back into the forest and after an hour they approached a barn at the edge of another field. The guide instructed the group to remain quiet and in place as he went forward alone. He returned after five minutes.

"We'll have to remain here for another hour," he said without explanation.

After an hour the guide led them inside the barn. As their eyes adjusted, small streaks of ambient light streamed through the cracks of the walls. A hand flashed its way through the rays of light, providing each man with a large piece of bread covered in lard with small, unidentifiable shreds of meat.

The guide gave careful instructions. "There's a bucket of water and a dipper by the door. If you must take a shit, there are two buckets at the back of the barn. This place must remain sterile with no sign of our presence. Now find a place in the hay and get some sleep. We get up in the morning before daylight. Remain silent. Be ready to depart immediately, but don't attempt to leave this barn unless I tell you. It would be fatal."

There was murmuring as each of the team stumbled around to find a comfortable place to rest and eat. One of the guerrillas went to sleep immediately and his snoring earned him a kick in the side. Bollard snickered to himself, "Just like home." His thoughts started to turn to Molly and the children, but he shut that down before it could go too far.

The insistence on silence and sterilization confirmed something Bollard had suspected. The farmers were not aware the guerrillas used the barn as a safe house; the earlier halt was because they were simply late to bed. This secrecy ensured their safety as well as that of the guerrillas. If the farmers had known, it would have solved the mystery of why their dogs never survived but a few days on the farm.

***

Well before any civilians woke, the guide awakened the team with a gradual and strong grip on their calves. It was a good technique; no one was startled, and no one reacted. There was nothing to gather as each man had followed instructions to remain fully dressed. The team emptied the buckets while others scattered hay to hide any evidence of their stay. The guide gave each team member two slices of bread with lard and a single boiled egg wrapped in newspaper; this would have to last for the next thirty-two hours.

The team departed. Bollard estimated it was no later than 0400 hours. In what seemed like an endless trek of stumbling, falling, and circuitous meandering through the forest, the guide led them to a trail where a man emerged and talked quietly to the guide.

"Going back to the same trail is dangerous," the guide explained. "We're well ahead of where you were yesterday. Given the security risk and potential for enemy elements tracking you, we placed one of our team to monitor the trail. You're clear."

The team continued on its mission. In an aside to Bollard, Nick assessed their overnight stop, "In addition to operational after-action reporting, the good work of the auxiliary will certainly be noted during the next Area Command meeting."

"We received what we needed; rest, food, water, and security," Bollard replied. "Very commendable."

Chapter 5
A Nasty Diversion

As visibility increased so did the pace. After five hours, with the sun at their back, the team moved quickly. To the north, two small hills formed a small saddle. Nick called for a stop. Surveying his front, he whispered, "If things go to hell, the area just below the saddle will be our alternate rally point. There is a small spring there for water. Don't approach the rally point directly. That way you can see if anyone is trailing and form a quick ambush. Understood?"

These were standard operating procedures that each man understood. After thirty minutes the team left the trail. In the distance the sun shone brightly on a small village, streaks of light reflected from the windows at the center of town. Nick moved toward a large hole in the ground just ahead. A tree, blown over in the wind and long since harvested by the locals, left a huge gaping hole with a berm of dirt piled conveniently on the forward side. The team jumped into the hole and crawled to the edge of the berm.

"The money should be in the administrative building adjacent to the Zil-151," Nick whispered referring to the old Soviet truck parked in the front. "The security force hasn't noticed the Zil's right front tire is flat."

Ten sat at an outdoor table of a small coffee shop just across the street from the building.

Nick motioned for the team to drop back down. "We need to move."

Dukvakha started to get up, but Nick grabbed his arm. "Not you. Change of plans. You're staying here," he whispered.

"But I've got the vest."

"We won't need it. Four didn't want you on this part of the operation. Besides, with the seat of your pants cut out, you'd draw attention."

Dukvakha was angry. Being a part of the assault team was a chance to prove himself, but he knew not to argue with Nick and slumped against the berm dejected.

"Misha, drop your demo. You'll go with the team," Nick ordered. "Alpha and Dukvakha, you watch Ten and the guard force as we planned. The rest of us will go uphill, cross over the road behind the town, and make our way to the building, entering from the left side." The guerrillas grunted affirmatives, then placed their rifles in a pile and carried only their pistols. They crept out of the hole and silently moved up the hill.

Bollard noticed Dukvakha grimacing and rubbing his knee. When they jumped into the hole, he slammed his knee into a rock.

"Are you okay?" Bollard whispered.

Dukvakha pulled up his pant leg. The knee was already swelling. Bollard motioned for him to stay in his position and then crawled to the edge of the berm.

He watched Ten sip his cup of coffee and read an old newspaper. The security forces, now agitated having discovered the flat tire, were on the far side of the truck and out of sight of the building's entrance. One member of the security team was cussing and kicking the offending tire. Maybe he hoped kicking it might cause it to miraculously reinflate. As the soldiers formed a small circle to discuss the predicament, Bollard watched the guerrillas nonchalantly enter the administration building.

So far, so good. Nick was relieved when he saw that the sacks of money were already out of the safe, ready to load. A single guard stood next to the window trying to see the activity around the far side of the truck. Nick walked directly to him, shoved his pistol in his face, and disarmed him. The team quickly gagged, tied, and placed the guard on the floor, alongside the others in the room.

Outside, Bollard grimaced as an old Army jeep, a UAZ-69, rounded a town corner and stopped in front of the building. Four soldiers got out. One of them, an officer, marched up to the truck and started giving orders. The three other soldiers milled around the front of the administration building blocking Nick's exit.

Nick heard the officer barking orders and peeked out the window. "Shit!" He held everyone in place. Any exfil at this point would be a shootout. If push came to shove, the guerrillas

231

could take the soldiers easily, but that would bring the entire army down on their heads. They would never escape. Nick listened to see if his observation team would fire shots, as planned, to draw the soldiers away. Across the street, Ten blew puffs of smoke as fast as he could without drawing attention.

Bollard slid down beside Dukvakha. If they fired warning shots, the injured boy wouldn't escape in time. They needed another plan.

He opened the demolition pack. There were some fuses and sticks of dynamite. "Where are the blasting caps?" Bollard hissed. Dukvakha shrugged.

"Damn! No blasting caps?" Bollard improvised. He quickly removed a cartridge from a rifle, then twisted and pulled until he removed the bullet from a shell casing.

Holding a strand of fuse, Bollard asked, "What's the burn rate on this?" Dukvakha, again, shrugged. Bollard added a six-inch fuse, not knowing how fast it would burn. Using a rock, he gently pounded the neck of the casing around the fuse, then stuck it inside a stick of dynamite. It might work or it might not. Either way, the casing would certainly explode.

Grabbing the improvised demolition, Bollard jumped from the hole and crouching, ran down the hill and toward the far end of the town. In the distance, he could see a small shed fifty meters from the nearest building. Approaching the shed from the rear, he cautiously opened the front door and entered.

"Ah geez!" Bollard muttered as he held his breath. He was in an outhouse, a two-holer; the communal shitter, and it was full. He quickly lit the fuse and placed the demolition on the far hole, then turned to run. Just as he was about to open the door, it swung open and a local man came nose to nose with Bollard. Startled, the man froze. Bollard instinctively swung a right cross against the man's cheek, knocking him out. He then dragged his limp body behind a nearby boulder. Bollard expected to take the impact of the explosion at any time, but nothing happened. He sprinted up the hill and ducked back into the hole beside Dukvakha.

The soldiers at the administration building were now smoking and laughing at the efforts of the security forces to change the truck tire. Ten didn't appear to be in a panic but continued puffing and smoking, even lighting a second cigarette without missing a breath.

Bollard looked back at the outhouse, baffled that there was still no explosion. He didn't want to fire warning shots, but circumstances were edging him toward that contingency plan. His initial concern was the fuse would burn too quickly, but that wasn't the case. The fuse was homemade; a cheap mix of string, powder, and an inhibitor; it sputtered and sparked slowly toward the shell casing as Bollard counted down the seconds.

Finally, on its last flicker, the powder in the casing erupted detonating the dynamite. In turn, the dynamite detonated the built-up methane in the outhouse, tripling the size of the blast. The explosion threw shattered boards and debris, as well as spewing shit for a hundred meters in every direction.

"Come on, we've got to get out of here," Bollard said, slinging the rifles over his shoulder and lifting Dukvakha by the arm. Dukvakha grabbed the demolition bag, and with Bollard supporting him, they hobbled to the alternate rally point.

It seemed as if hours had passed since Nick and his team had gotten stuck inside the administration building, but the explosion had done the job. The entire town, including the security forces, the soldiers, and Ten ran in the direction of the explosion. Nick and the other guerrillas slipped out of the building, back up the hill, and dashed in the direction of the alternate linkup point.

Bollard and Dukvakha arrived before they did. Dukvakha pulled up his pants leg and rubbed his knee.

"How are you feeling?" Bollard asked.

Dukvakha seemed more dejected than in pain. "I'm okay," he replied.

"Let me help you with that," Bollard said as he snapped a branch, wrapped a rag around it, and began applying a small splint. "This will make it easier to walk."

Dukvakha stretched out his leg for Bollard to position the splint.

"Look, don't get down on yourself," Bollard said as he tightened the splint. "Nick was right about the cut in the seat of your pants. Something's going on to cause all the shitting at camp. When your knee is better, the two of us can run the length of the stream to the spring. I'm guessing it may be the source of the problem. We can determine if there's contamination."

"Yeah, and the old lady never seems to boil the soup. It's always just warm."

"Yes, that could be an issue."

"Anyway, I'll go with you to check out the stream when we get back."

Suddenly, there was movement below them. They watched as the other team members crossed the stretch of land below them and then doubled back from the opposite direction. No one had followed them.

"What the hell was that?" Nick asked as soon as he was within hearing distance. "I thought I would hear three shots. That was the plan!"

Bollard pointed to the young guerrilla who was adjusting the splint. "We had to improvise and use the explosives with the help of a methane build-up in the shitter. As you said, you never know when an opportunity might arise. Otherwise, we wouldn't have made it out."

Misha was exuberant. "Methane? The American blew the hell out of the town shitter! Methane! Ossetian shit went everywhere!"

Nick laughed. "Okay, let's get the hell out of here."

***

Four stood expectantly outside his tent, grinning as he embraced Nick and Dukvakha when they approached. Four signaled for Five to join them as Nick handed him the bag of rubles. Bollard and the other guerrillas beelined for the old woman who ladled a bowl of soup for each of them. Bollard sat down and took hungry gulps. Dukvakha was correct. She didn't boil it. He took another spoonful and angled his seat to watch the interaction between Four, Nick, and the other leaders. He knew at some point their discussion would turn to him, the distraction, and the shithouse. Their meeting ended and they dispersed throughout the base camp.

Dukvakha picked up a bowl of soup and sat down beside Bollard. "I told you this stuff is warm," he said as he lifted a spoonful to his mouth.

"Yeah. I remember you saying that," Bollard replied. "You did your job well today. Even after you were injured you didn't give up your vest until we were safely back in Chechnya."

Dukvakha's eyebrows shot up in surprise and a smile started to stretch across his face. He was about to speak when Bollard stood up suddenly as Nick and Four approached. Four carried an AK-47 over his shoulder.

Four smiled, "Nick told me what you did to distract the security forces."

"It was a predicament. I did what I had to do," Bollard said respectfully, keeping a wary but hopeful eye on the rifle.

"Well, you've earned this," Four said as he handed Bollard the AK-47.

Bollard beamed as he accepted it. He opened the receiver to ensure it wasn't loaded, inspected it, then held it up to his shoulder. "A nice weapon. Much better than only having a pistol. I'd like to test fire it and make modifications if necessary."

"It's one of our better rifles, and it's yours. Anything you want to do to enhance its accuracy would be outstanding. You can coordinate with Nick to test fire it."

"Thank you," Bollard replied as Nick and Four walked away.

Dukvakha smiled and wasting no time, asked, "When do you want to walk to the source of the spring?"

Bollard carefully placed the rifle down. "Let's finish eating, rest for an hour, then advise Nick or Four."

"I'll catch up with them," Dukvakha said as he sprung to his feet, "and be back in an hour."

Bollard smiled as he noticed Dukvakha hurrying to his uncle's side, with hardly a limp.

Chapter 6
Foul Water

An hour later, Dukvakha returned with his rifle slung over his shoulder. "Here. This is for you," Dukvakha said as he handed Bollard a bag and a coil of thin wire.

Bollard looked inside the bag. It was everything he needed to build the primitive transmitter and included a magnifying glass. He quickly put it in his backpack.

Dukvakha was eager. "Ready? Uncle says it's fine."

"You seem to be in a real hurry."

"I want to fix this problem so I can get a new pair of pants without worrying about ruining them."

Bollard laughed. "I understand."

The stream flowed between the inner and outer security perimeters. They followed it uphill, waving to the two guards as they passed them. Just a few meters outside the inner perimeter, the small stream meandered back towards the camp and just below the outer perimeter. It then moved back again and continued following the slope of the hill.

"Let's stop here. I've got a hunch," Bollard said. He signaled the security guard and walked slowly from the stream up the hill. Midway between the guard and the stream, the source of the contamination became obvious.

"There it is," Dukvakha said as he took a step back from piles of exposed feces along the hillside.

"Yeah. The guards have been using this as their dumping ground without considering the stream. With the rain, it's flowing right into our water source."

Dukvakha cursed.

"Okay, we know what the problem is here. But we need to find the source of the spring, even if it's all the way up the hill."

Dukvakha smothered a grimace as he turned to follow the stream. They walked several hundred meters and saw water flowing from underground between a series of rocks on the steepest part of the hillside. They hiked up to it when a strong stench started to fill the air. The stench led them further up the hill. Something formed a small dam and the water flowed over and around with much of it spilling away from the stream's normal course. Several large bones protruded from loose and decomposing skin and hair.

"Carcass of an animal. Not sure what it is," Bollard said between breaths.

"If the shit from the guards didn't taint the water, then this carcass certainly did."

"You see," Bollard said, picking up a stick and poking the remains. "It caused a dam to form with the leaves and twigs building up."

"Yeah. We're losing water," Dukvakha observed.

"All right, let's remove it and redirect the water so it can flow naturally again."

It didn't take long. They buried the cadaver in the leaves away from the water flow and built up a wall of rocks to redirect the spring to its normal channel.

When they finished, Bollard leaned back against a tree while Dukvakha sprawled on the slope of the hill, looking up at the sky.

Bollard was curious about the young man. "I know your uncle is the leader here, but how did you get involved with the guerrillas?"

Dukvakha paused and his eyes narrowed. "The Soviets killed my father. They wanted information about my uncle. He said nothing, so they killed him." He went on to explain that the Soviets killed his grandfather years earlier and that many of his forefathers died fighting Russians dating back to the Tsarist days. "It was natural that I join my uncle against the Soviets."

Bollard let the young man's story sink in. After several minutes, he asked carefully, "What are you going to report to your uncle? Let's discuss it a bit."

"I haven't thought about it." Dukvakha shrugged. He rolled on his side to look at Bollard. "Aren't you going to report it?"

Bollard shook his head. "No. That's more in line with your responsibility. You should do more than just tell him what you observed. What caused us to go on this trek?"

"Well," Dukvakha began slowly, scratching the side of his face as he thought, "we went on the trek believing the water was causing the shits. We discovered shit from the outer perimeter that was getting into the water. Then we found a rotten carcass in the water."

"Recommendations?"

"Certainly, the guards have to find a new place to shit. I don't know what we could recommend about the carcass."

"It's not often an animal will die in such a small stream. But is it something we should check routinely? If so, how often?"

Dukvakha perked and sat up. "You know, we should check the length of the spring once a week."

"Hey, that's a great idea. I'm sure your uncle would approve. You know, you mentioned something about the old woman's cooking. What was that?"

"Oh, yeah. She's not boiling the water in the soup."

"Yeah. Boiling kills germs."

"I'll tell my uncle she needs to boil everything."

"Wow. That's great. You had an issue. Found the sources of the problem and now have three solid recommendations. Real good."

"Thanks, Alpha," Dukvakha said smiling.

Bollard smiled too. At heart he was a mentor and teacher and watching the young man develop was satisfying. But he needed information, and he angled the conversation to his real motive. "It appears you have two different groups in your camp."

Dukvakha responded immediately, still anticipating and savoring what he would say to his uncle and not what he was telling the outsider. "Yeah. Some want to see a unifying head, an Islamic spiritual commander. They're more focused on spiritual unity than fighting the Soviets. My uncle says there are two factions, militants and guerrillas. You know, guerrillas, like Nick, who are more interested in covert operations and fighting the Soviets. Nick definitely doesn't want a spiritual leader."

"So, you'd say the first group is a bit more radical?"

"What do you mean?"

"Oh, you know," Bollard said casually while wracking his brain for the gentlest phrasing. "They believe the ends justify the means; whatever it takes to get the mission done."

"Well, if the spiritual leader directs it, who are we to question? We'd have no authority to challenge it."

"Your uncle and Nick disagree, I take it. But they're still able to work together."

Some of the boy's enthusiasm drained and he began plucking at his pant leg. "It's about survival. It might change if the Soviet threat does."

"I guess Four likes what Saud has to say?" Bollard asked.

"He likes the message but hates the messenger. So arrogant!" Dukvakha spat. "We've been debating this for centuries. We don't need Saud to lecture us or a foreign Islamic leader to tell us how to kill Soviets."

Bollard was pleased to hear Saud's personality was diminishing his message. He got the confirmation of what he already suspected: two factions, running the same operations with a different end game in mind. Bollard stretched and stood. "I guess we better get back before the old lady starts cooking today's dinner."

"Yeah, I'm eager to tell Four what we discovered!"

They began the short journey back to camp. Bollard was counting on the young guerrilla's excitement and inexperience to cover for his probing questions.

For now, Bollard's highest priority was assembling the radio transmitter. It was his lifeline. He could never let it leave his side once he completed its assembly. He had a lot to report.

Chapter 7
Communications

As promised, Four provided a secure place for Bollard to transmit; a dilapidated single-room hut far away from the camp. An armed escort stood guard outside watching the approaches. Bollard sat in a corner of the hut. The wall behind him creaked when he pressed his back against it. The wood was grey with rot, and the roof leaned dangerously far to the right. It looked as if it could fall at any minute. A small flicker of candlelight had to suffice for the meticulous work.

Using a razor blade, he cut gingerly around the ball of his foot. He peeled back a small portion of what appeared to be a calloused and narrow skin tag, revealing one of several dots that resembled tiny black freckles. He removed it with his fingernail and placed it on a small piece of white cotton. Holding the candle to the side of the microdot he peered through the magnifying glass to see the letters comprising one page of a one-time pad.

He worked meticulously to write down his coded message and include his unique identifier and authentication code, NTIAD. After several minutes he completed the coded message and set it to the side. He opened his pack and removed a small radio and placed it on the floor.

Bollard hovered over the small AM radio, slowly moving the dial for the strongest signal. After briefly tuning between two high-pitched signals, he settled on one that seemed to be optimum. He placed an improvised antenna of wound copper wire and a transmitter on top of the radio and connected a portion of the wire outside to a tree, to serve as a directional antenna. He pointed it high and to the south. The transmitter key to send the signal was a basic design. It consisted of a clothespin-type key with antenna wires affixed to the long ends. By compressing the long ends of the key, the two wires touched, and with the release of pressure, the key sprang back to its original position automatically breaking the wire connection.

Bollard held the short end of the key on the table with his left hand and pushed down on the key's long end with his right index finger, causing the two antenna wires to connect and grounding out the radio signal with an audible hissing sound. When he lifted his finger, the grounding stopped. He began with his unique coded identifier, ssssh sht/ssssh/sht sht/sht ssssh/ssssh sht sht/.

The U.S. support team said he had twenty seconds to transmit his message before a Soviet RDF team could pick it up. He planned for a fifteen-second transmission, and it had to be as concise as it was precise. He knew the method of transmission was primitive and was generally for only short ranges, but the support team assured him the U.S. receivers were sufficiently capable of picking up the signal.

He finished the transmission, placed the microdot on the message paper, and burned both. He squirreled his materials back into his pack, pulled on his boot, and returned to his escort.

The message was a basic situation report; short and to the point: Two competing groups of militants and guerrillas among the Caucasus groups; one Saudi Arabian Wahhabi present providing funds. Interestingly, he reported one Afghan guerrilla present.

He sent nothing regarding the MRNC.

***

When Bollard and his escort returned, they found the camp in motion. Instead of the standard light and noise discipline, flashlights waved like beacons, and people dashed about while shouting urgently to one another. Even from a distance Bollard could make out the blazing campfire and a huge caldron practically boiling over with water.

As he got closer to the fire, he noticed several prone bodies lying nearby. Some let out groans as their comrades treated their wounds. Others were still and beyond help. Bollard turned to see his escort running across the camp toward a pair of approaching headlights. Bollard followed.

A tractor with a trailer large enough to carry produce to market pulled up to the camp at the end of the main trail. The tractor driver sat at the wheel staring straight ahead, jaw set. The trailer was stacked with bodies. Those who were not dead were riddled with bullet and fragment wounds and were being pulled off the trailer. The rest succumbed during the long journey and showed signs of rigor mortis, their stiffened limbs in a grotesque salute. A hasty triage was set up in front of the tractor's headlights. Those capable of walking with assistance were sent to the campfire. The organization doctor, or the closest thing the guerrillas had to one, walked among the wounded, gesturing left and right. A shake of the head or wag of the finger indicated if someone was beyond treatment. He directed the guerrillas to carry the more severely wounded to a medium-sized tent for field surgery.

Nearby, Four and Nick were engaged in a heated discussion. They quieted as Bollard came nearer.

"What happened?" Bollard asked as he was within speaking distance.

Nick quickly brought him up to speed. A skirmish had broken out in a nearby town, Sverny, and escalated into a full-blown battle when a Soviet airborne unit deployed unexpectedly.

"When it got dark, the fighting subsided, and our folks were able to pull the dying and wounded out of the area and onto the trailer. Most of them died on the way here, but we had no other choice," Nick explained.

Four jammed his hands into his jacket and turned to watch the train of stretchers. "Tell him the rest of it," he snarled.

Nick grimaced. "The damn Soviets called in an aircraft and bombed a school," he said quietly. "It didn't matter that the roof had the word CHILDREN painted on it. Killed a lot of kids."

"Nowhere near the battle," Four spat. "They chose a large building full of little children to drop their ordinance." He spun on his heel and met Bollard's gaze, radiating with rage. "There will be hell to pay for this atrocity."

Nick shook his head, and Bollard wondered how Four's comment might play out.

"What can I do to help?" Bollard asked.

"There's nothing you can do, Alpha," Nick said. "The remaining survivors are being treated. We have to bury the dead and inform their families."

Four's angry outbursts subsided as he became more somber with Nick's assessment. "As the numbers of dead in the school are revealed and the dead here are identified, there will be a lot of grieving in that town."

"We've been badly bloodied," Nick said as he walked toward the tractor driver who was still motionless at the wheel.

Chapter 8
Regional Command

There was a certain tension in the air as Bollard walked into a forest clearing that served as a secure holding point. Representatives from the Area Commands to the Regional Command stood in silence as the bombing of the school was on their minds. Recent rain and overcast sky added to the somber mood. A very alert security team searched, checked, and double-checked each representative, then moved them through an open door of an abandoned and rickety barn. The security team was comprised of trusted men from each Area Command. They were organized to minimize the possibility of betrayals or violence between the Area Commands and to protect the Regional Commander and his staff who were already in the building.

Bollard noted there was little interaction between the representatives as he took up a position at the outer edge of the clearing. Ten stood nearby, smirking at something he was watching. The soot-covered Seven stood next to him with a pensive expression that only brightened after Ten leaned down to mutter something. Bollard followed their gaze to see Saud attempting to chat up a non-responsive Area Command representative. Several operational guerrilla chiefs and their deputies were also present, including Four and Nick among others. Dukvakha stood between Four and Nick, looking nervously between them as he shifted his weight from one foot to the other.

The Area Commands were organized along the lines of family factions, and cultural and historical groupings. They weren't structured around the government's republic and oblast standing. Each had a historic grudge against the Russian government going back to the Tsars. They also had their internal grudges against the representatives of the various groups standing in the holding area. Despite their loose organization and a Regional Command, the Area Commands were comprised of regional groups from Dagestan, Georgia, Ossetia, Chechnya and Ingushetia.

Bollard sorted the group and gave each person a name that he could refer to or consider for future reference. One, in particular, drew his attention. A tall, older man with a long neck and beak of a nose never changed his terse expression. He reminded Bollard of an angry stork.

A low whistle from the door triggered a rustling among the representatives as the remaining attendees began forming a single file to move through the gauntlet of security. Bollard shuffled along the muddy trail toward the entrance. Ten and Seven fell into line in front of Bollard. Instinctively, Bollard examined the tracks on the soft ground in front of him. He smiled when he was able to confirm a suspicion he'd had for some time.

As Bollard ducked his head below the low door and entered the barn, he noted the room was far more primitive than his original reception at the Chechen Area Command. The Regional Command leadership sat on logs. Bollard followed Ten to where Four, Nick, and the other representatives from the Chechen Area Command were sitting near the front. Seven, interestingly, flipped a small log on its edge and joined the semi-circle the Regional Command had formed at the head of the room.

Bollard assessed the leadership before him, gleaning whatever information he could. There was nothing to betray the Regional Commander's lineage or cultural grouping, but by his air, he was clearly in charge.

The room was quiet except for some shuffling among the area commands. If there were an agenda, it was known only to the Regional Commander. After several minutes he directed Seven to begin. Seven stood to address the room.

"When I arrived here four years ago you were a scattered and unorganized resistance against the Soviet forces," Seven said matter-of-factly. "Together, we identified the need for a Regional Command to coordinate operations between the Area Commands. As we organized the Regional Command it was you who shouted the name of the great Imam Shamil, who over a hundred years ago, took a disjointed group of vagabonds from these very mountains and forged them into a fighting force that threw off the yoke of Count Vorontsov and his ten thousand

Tsarist troops. You clamored for the same kind of unification. As it was in the days of the Tsar, when you were under the leadership of Imam Shamil, the Regional Command's direction has unified us against the Soviets." Seven swept an arm over the room. "It's this close coordination and our synchronized efforts that have proven effective in hitting key Soviet facilities and troop formations across the region. In just two years our success was marked by the establishment of the MRNC in Paris. We are inextricably linked, and unification is the only effective strategy. We must maintain this unity without exception."

Bollard's ears perked. This was the first time someone had mentioned the MRNC since he had been there.

"The Regional Commander is not Imam Shamil," Angry Stork spluttered loudly and out of turn.

Seven's head tilted at him. "But it was you and the other Area Commanders yourselves who selected him and agreed to abide by his authority. You chose him precisely because he's a direct descendant of Shamil and his ties to Dagestan, as well as his prowess."

The Regional Commander interrupted Seven. "You need not defend me. My authority will not be questioned." He looked directly at the Stork. "Is that clear?"

Bollard had at least one answer to his many percolating questions. It was clever of the guerrilla leaders to find a Dagestani and blood relative of Shamil to lead them. It demonstrated their commitment to the region as well as its unification.

Angry Stork did not change his expression but nodded assent. The Regional Commander motioned for Seven to continue.

"We were effective when we operated cohesively. But now several operational groups among your Area Command," she gestured meaningfully to the Stork, "have ceased operations. This has allowed the Soviet military to concentrate its forces against the rest of us. Your Area Command must reinstate discipline and deal with this breach of our agreed strategy and effectively reengage." Seven's voice took on a hard edge. "This is not a matter of if, but how."

"Holy shit," Bollard thought as Seven took a seat. Seven was not the reserved liaison he had presumed but was one of the founders of the Regional Command, and the MRNC by extension. This meeting wasn't a review as much as it was a kick in the ass.

Angry Stork came to the same conclusion. He leaped to his feet belligerently, but the Regional Commander verbally shoved him down.

"Stay seated!" the Regional Commander bellowed, shaking the rickety walls of the room as his impassive expression flashed to one of cold rage.

The Stork paled, his aggravated demeanor becoming momentarily nervous. It seemed to dawn on him that he may not make it out of this meeting alive. He recovered and forced another frown. "It's me and my people, the people of Alania, who are aggrieved," he insisted.

"Alania?" the Regional Commander asked incredulously, his voice returning to a dangerously neutral octave. "Alania, not Ossetia?"

Bollard's ears perked. He zeroed in on the Stork, his anger beginning to fester. This was the Ossetian Area Commander who had caused him to slog through the Caucasus mountains and hide in cellars and truck beds for all those months!

"You can call yourselves Persian for all I care," the Regional Commander continued. "You need to get your head out of the ass of ancient history and into the present!"

"One of our towns was attacked by this very organization," the Stork accused, volume rising. "The attack on the payroll could only have occurred with the approval of the Regional Commander and his staff. The Russians have played ball in our region until now. They've beaten and threatened everyone in the vicinity of the robbery. Now they've increased their patrols and helicopter flyovers. It's beginning to interfere with our trade."

As he spoke, low whispers and mutters broke out among the different area commands. "You mean your illicit drug and alcohol trade?" someone called out.

"What part of our honor does that fit into?" another shouted.

The Regional Commander waved his hand for silence, then turned back to the Stork. "It's true, I ordered the attack. We used the money to arm and equip one of our better combatant Area Commands. It had to be done to offset your own failed operations."

Whatever Angry Stork had been expecting, it certainly wasn't complete admittance. "They nearly destroyed the town!" he sputtered.

The Chechen Area Commander grinned. "Oh, I believe it's true that the better part of the town was destroyed when they blew up the shithouse!"

There was an eruption of laughter across the room.

Now red-faced and seething, the Stork turned back to the Regional Command Leadership, but before he could speak, the Regional Commander pointed an accusatory finger at him. "It is you who sought accommodation and a favored status with our enemy. While you cozy up with the Russians, we're fighting for our lives and the independence of all."

Another round of angry muttering trickled throughout the barn. Before the tide could further turn against him, the Stork pressed on with his last demand. "We want our autonomy," he declared. "The South Ossetian Popular Front demands it, yet the Georgian Supreme Council spits on the idea."

One of the Georgian representatives snorted a laugh, but the Regional Commander was not amused.

"You are talking about the Georgian Supreme Council whose members are vassals of the Soviets. And you say this to men who are fighting against the same Soviets! We don't care about the Soviet-managed Georgian Supreme Council. To hell with them! They're a distraction from our regional effort for independence from the Soviets. You and the Georgians can deal with your age-old problems after we rise fully, as a cohesive group against the Soviets."

The Stork's deputy spoke, "It's the tallest blade of grass that gets cut!"

"Do you now speak for the Ossetians, you so-called Alanians?" the Regional Commander responded immediately. "You want to spew forth a Russian metaphor? A metaphor of the Russian masses cowering to any show of authority! I'll give you a metaphor, a metaphor of the Caucasus peoples. Look at us!" He pointed to the Area Commanders. "We stand as weeds in a field towering above any blade of grass! Together we defy the Russian sickle. But you! A patch of dead ground, baking in the sun; pissed on by every passing dog. Not a single blade of grass among you!"

The Stork and his deputy said nothing, as the others in the room grunted their agreement.

"We've been cooperating ..."

"Don't come to this Regional Command meeting with a lie and deceit! It's you who has shut down the supply routes, and contacts along the Georgian border. Furthermore, you've closed the ratlines that are critical for our agents and operators and benefit everyone. It took six months to move the ratline around your Area Command. You blackmail us because of a grievance with the Georgians and a desire to gain so-called bullshit autonomy within the Soviet empire. Unacceptable! Is your organization compromised or do you simply seek to be a vassal or avoid Soviet consternation?"

"We are not compromised."

The Regional Commander remained calm and in a near monotone said, "Then you violated our agreements and are accommodating the Soviets. I'm ordering you to open all lines immediately. You will be folded into the next synchronized regional offensive, and you damn well will do your part! Do you understand?" He glared at the Ossetian commander.

The Stork visibly broke into a sweat. He realized his mistake. "I have operational groups who have maintained autonomy to operate against the Soviets as they feel is best for their people in the region," he protested. "By making such an order, you usurp this."

"That's the point!" The Regional Commander's tone took on a new edge. "Their failure to conduct operations impacts everyone and hinders the efforts of the entire Regional Command. By shutting down supply lines, not to mention failing to participate in the last synchronized operation, you've forfeited your autonomy until I direct otherwise."

He scanned the faces of the other Area Commanders. "Are we in accord?"

One by one, each of the commanders raised their hands in agreement. The Regional Commander turned his attention back to the Stork.

"Unless your Area Command wants to face the wrath of each of these commanders, you damn well better comply," he seethed. "Need I remind you, any of these are much more ruthless than the Soviet enemy."

The Stork said nothing. Strangely, that only seemed to make the Regional Commander even angrier. "The same Soviets, on whose goodwill you seem to place such high value, who just two weeks ago bombed one of our schools, killing children, so many children, and their teachers!"

He paused for effect, letting the room become so silent, that one could hear a pin drop. "Do these names mean anything to you... Doku, Bashir, Aslanbek?" He then read a long list of names... Lema, Ayna, Vait, Esila, Deti... as he did, tension filled the air and the expressions of each person present grew darker as they turned their attention to the Stork.

The Stork shook his head.

The Regional Commander finally snapped. "They are the sons of Iskra, and Pozhar... killed fighting near Grozny. They are the wife, sons, and daughters of Dima, all dead at the hands of the Soviet bombing. Look at them," he roared. "Look at Batir, Daud, and Abbas!" He called them by their true names rather than their codenames. "What do you see in their eyes?"

The Stork only looked down.

"Did they die because you've done nothing?" the Regional Commander demanded. "Did they die because you allowed the enemy the luxury of concentrating its forces? Then you will know these names ... Irina, Elena, Bega, Aslan, Fedor, Vano, Zina, Ariana ..."

A visible tightening emerged along the jawline of both the Stork and his lieutenant.

"Of course you do," the Regional Commander said. "They're the names of your own wives and children. When you return to your homes, you will find red paint on the ground near your doorstep. Don't remove it. It's a reminder each time you pass it, as to what has happened to the families of these men. It's also a warning," he continued, pounding his fist into an open hand. "I will hold you and your families personally responsible for carrying out our directives."

The fury building on the Stork's face was surpassed only by the severity of the threat just levied at him, and the families of his men. He remained silent.

"You'll be advised through normal communication channels of your requirements for the next operation," the Regional Commander continued matter-of-factly. "As for now, you're dismissed."

The Stork and his lieutenant, lock-jawed, rose and stalked out. They had been dressed down, humiliated, and threatened and there was nothing that could be done to change it. As the Stork exited, he was shocked to see his security team had been disarmed. Though the other security guards were not pointing their weapons, it was clear that Stork and his team were under escort. They walked well away from the Regional Command site before their unloaded weapons were returned to them and they were released.

Bollard, for his part, had looked on in amazement as the centuries-old history of drama and distrust between regions played out once more.

***

Some side conversations sprang up among the representatives as the Stork departed the meeting, but the Regional Commander was silent. After several minutes he raised his hand and all attention turned back to him.

"I have my concerns," he began.

One of the regional staff members, Bollard thought the operations chief, spoke up, "You should have concerns. It's for no small reason we saw the need to put an escort on him."

"We need to exert more pressure on the population, so they view the Soviets as they truly are, an oppressive institution of thugs," one of the Area Commanders advised.

"We thought the payroll robbery would invite more pressure from the Soviets, and it appears we were right," the Operations Chief replied.

The Regional Commander shook his head, "But, it wasn't enough. We still don't have the level of support we need. Not among the population or the guerrillas at large in that region." He shook his head again. "Now I sincerely question their commitment to independence over acquiescence. They are all focused on gaining autonomy from Georgia. We must consider whether the Ossetians might ally with the Soviets against all of us to gain some scrap of meaningless paper granting just that."

"If the Ossetian Area Commander is any measure of the overall attitude, we need to bring some crushing Soviet retaliatory measures to bear," one of the other regional command staff suggested. "Something that will completely and overwhelmingly alienate the population against the government and demonstrate that we are to be feared more than the Soviets."

"We've had this discussion before. Such extreme measures. Is it time?" the Operations Chief asked without a hint of trepidation.

"That discussion resulted in some drastic if not extremely severe options," the Regional Commander agreed. He stood slowly, then, looking around the room said, "Let's take a few minutes to pause while we ask Ten and our guests to wait outside as we deliberate."

Ten took to his feet and indicated Bollard and Saud to follow with his lead. As they left, the Regional Commander spoke calmly but firmly to Seven. "For this particular discussion, I'll ask you to join our guests outside."

Seven rose and obliged with enough deference to imply real concern. Deliberations were always at the highest security level, but never before had they excluded Seven. Seven understood the next discussion and operational planning would be so sensitive that only those who had known one another for decades would take priority over organizational considerations.

Bollard watched as the Regional Commander dismissed other representatives who filed out. Nothing, in particular, caught his attention with one exception. All of the Chechens remained.

The security element herded Bollard, Saud, Seven, Ten, and the others out of earshot of the meeting. They sat down in various positions as several guards stood a comfortable distance away. There was a period of silence that proved too much for Saud. He tried to engage one of the guards, who promptly rebuffed him.

Suddenly, there was an eruption of indiscernible but angry shouts from the meeting room. The shouts and counter-shouts continued for several seconds until the unmistakable voice of the Regional Commander overrode them. A little over an hour later the meeting ended and the deliberators trickled out of the building.

Four, Nick, and an ashen Dukvakha marched by the now standing group. Without taking note of anyone, Four shouted, "Let's go!"

Bollard and the others shot a questioning look at Nick. He said nothing as they followed, but the expression on his face was both grave and angry.

Bollard didn't need years of training and experience to know something had passed and gone very, very wrong. If some kind of rift had formed between the Chechens or the Regional Command, then the organization was standing on a powder keg.

***

There was a shift in the atmosphere within the Chechen camp in the days that followed. It wasn't something Bollard could put his finger on, specifically, but there seemed to be static in the air. The more militant elements were in a higher state of activity, moving with more deliberate strides, cleaning weapons, and talking in small groups. In contrast, the other faction seemed to be treading carefully, casting wary glances toward the militants, checking their weapons, and speaking in low tones.

Bollard was reminded of two distinct packs of wolves and their interactions as they sized up one another before all hell broke loose. He was confident the militants were preparing for something big, but the other group of guerrillas didn't appear to be a part of it. He watched the interaction between Four and Nick and noticed them behaving more reserved toward each other, much colder. Nick moved routinely among his lieutenants; more so than previously.

Bollard felt the tense situation fester and seep into every nook and cranny of the camp. He kept his rifle at the ready, the old revolver loaded in every chamber. Most importantly, he kept his backpack and radio within arm's reach.

Whatever was about to happen, he was taking no chances.

Chapter 9
Ambush

Bollard was busy repairing a small tear in his pack when Nick approached with Ten, Seven, and eleven other guerrillas. Many of the militants, along with Saud, left earlier that day on a different patrol.

Nick was in a hurry. "Alpha, get your shit and grab your rifle. You're going to accompany us."

"What's going on?"

"We're meeting with the Ingush. They've identified some new leaders and we have operational coordination to complete. I want you, Ten, and Seven to meet them," he said loud enough for anyone nearby to hear and waved a quick hand at the team.

Seven asked whether some of the others should come along.

"I have what I need," he responded tersely. He then turned and set out.

Bollard thought it was an interesting exchange. Nick wasn't himself, and he attributed it to the build-up of tension, already at an elevated level.

Everything had seemed normal initially, barring the fast pace. However, when one of the men ran up to inform Nick that a lagger had turned around and gone back to basecamp, he practically bit his head off.

"Keep moving!" Nick shouted and picked up the pace even more.

For the first three hours, they moved directly west. But after they had hiked down a particularly steep stretch of a mountain pass, Nick turned south. Bollard didn't understand why there was a course change. Their target was located due west. He looked to his rear at the men behind him. No one else appeared to be paying attention. The pace was quick and the level of security he'd seen on prior patrols seemed to have eased. Nick sacrificed security for speed. He had not stopped or looked behind since their departure from the basecamp.

By Bollard's estimation, they had been paralleling the Ingush eastern border when they entered a trail that turned southwest toward Ossetia and showed signs of recent activity.

The turns, doglegs, and thick underbrush reduced the ability of each member of the patrol to support the other and put everyone on alert.

The group slowed its pace. Nick became more deliberate in his steps. Suddenly, he stopped and raised his rifle to his shoulder. Three men peered from behind trees and boulders with rifles pointing down the trail.

Bollard couldn't believe it when he recognized one of them. Saud!

Another head peered from behind a tree at the right front. There was yelling between Nick and one of them, both now pointing their weapons directly at each other.

"What the hell are you doing? Point those weapons in the air," Nick screamed.

"Drop your weapons! You and your men are coming with us," the militant ordered.

"Screw you! On whose orders, you son of a bitch?"

Bollard noted movement along the west side of the trail and heard a click; the sound of a weapon's safety placed in the firing position. They had walked right into an ambush. Pulling his rifle to his shoulder, he backed slowly off the trail while he still could.

"Four ordered you back to base!"

Nick held his ground. "Bullshit! I report directly to Four and I left after you. Where the hell is Adlan?" he shouted, referring to one of the more senior militants.

"He's behind you on the side of the trail." The militant then shouted for Adlan.

Nick turned in the direction the militant pointed, but Adlan was around the bend in the road and did not emerge immediately. There were more angry shouts and cursing coming from the rear of the column between Nick's men and those hidden in the woods. Suddenly, a shot rang out from the rear and then another until it cascaded into a roar along the column and the western flank. Bollard and the others returned fire instinctively at those firing from the brush. In an instant, one of the guerrillas, running for his life, sprinted by Bollard and toward an open stretch of trail between Nick and the militants in the front. In the next instant, there was a deafening explosion and a ball of fire as the designated guerrilla triggered his suicide vest. Trees shattered, men screamed out and friends and foes alike were blown up.

The blast knocked Bollard on his back, his head slamming into the damp earth as the high-pitched ringing in his ears blocked out all other sounds. As a result of the explosion and the concussion of the blast, the shooting ceased momentarily. Then, as the skirmishers regained their bearings, the gunfire returned with a vengeance and crescendo.

Blinking away the shock, Bollard scrambled for his rifle and started crawling toward the hillside behind him. Just ahead he discovered Ten lying on his back. He was alive, though he was motionless. His eyes were fixed as if watching the clouds overhead. A trickle of blood flowed from his ear. Bollard hooked his arm in Ten's pack harness and dragged him up the mountain.

The gunfire slowly started to peter out behind them, most of it coming from the ambushers as they quickly eliminated the column. Seven took cover behind a large tree and fired several more times in the direction of the ambushers before noticing Bollard and Ten. Firing one last shot, Seven pulled back through the smoke towards them. Grabbing each side of Ten's pack harness, Seven and Bollard dragged him up and away from the ambush site and over a slight rise that offered cover and concealment. They didn't stop moving until they were far away, and only then to ensure that no one followed them.

***

Keeping the slope of the hill between them and the road, they worked their way up to a small plateau; a place where they could fire upon anyone who might approach. Ten had long since fallen unconscious. Bollard cut through Ten's blood-soaked shirt and tore it open to reveal a deep, jagged gash. The wound was dirty, with small fragments of rusted steel glistening at the outer edges. He poured water onto the wound and cut away the fragments with his knife.

"I need your cotton," Bollard said to Seven.

Seven remained by the edge of the plateau, eyes trained down the rifle sight.

"I said I need your cotton," Bollard repeated more harshly.

Seven moved back to Bollard and Ten, opened her pack, and produced a handful of cotton. Bollard packed the wound and secured it with a cord tied around Ten's shoulder.

"Is he going to be okay?" Seven asked quietly.

"Not sure," Bollard admitted. "Really bad concussion and the wound is nasty."

"He's dead weight," Seven said bluntly, "and we can't carry him. We've got to get to higher ground and find a hide site."

Bollard agreed. "You continue to watch the approaches. I'll get a couple of poles to make a litter."

He disappeared, returning five minutes later with two sturdy tree branches eight feet in length.

"These are going to make nasty tracks," he said as he quickly constructed a makeshift travois from belts, wooden cross members, and extra clothing from the packs.

"We can attach some brush to the bottom," Seven suggested. "That might help cover the tracks."

"If they haven't started already, they'll be looking for us soon," Bollard said.

Seven glanced over the edge of the plateau again. "I'm not so sure. I know I killed several, and the damned suicide vest blew everyone to hell who was in the front. I'm sure the explosion took Nick out as well."

Bollard frowned as the realization hit him. "Shit. They may be trying to determine who's missing. Or maybe they'll lick their wounds for a while before realizing we're the ones missing."

"Right," Seven agreed.

Bollard returned to the task at hand. "I'll lift Ten's side and you slide the litter underneath."

They secured Ten to the litter and began dragging him up the hill. Bollard paused. "What the hell happened down there? Did you make sense of any of that?"

Seven blinked incredulously at him. "You want rationale? Logic? Perhaps a power grab. Here, motivations are seldom linked to logic."

Chapter 10
Escape

After pulling Ten on the makeshift stretcher for several kilometers, Bollard and Seven stopped to rest near a potential hide site. The site had all the requisites – easy to observe without being observed; a trickle of water nearby; clear open areas to place rifle fire on an approaching enemy; a small clearing with close surroundings, and a canopy of trees with some scrub brush around it. With some work, it could serve as a shelter from the elements. Importantly, it had an animal trail nearby that served as the perfect concealed escape route.

They had been at the site for several hours, but Ten had not regained consciousness and the wound showed signs of rapid infection. This was no surprise to Bollard. He had watched one of the guerrilla teams build an explosive device using rusty pieces of steel and shards of glass, the perfect recipe.

Lying just outside the campsite, watching every potential approach, Bollard looked over his shoulder to see Seven pushing more cotton into the wound.

"We have to get medicine to fight the infection," Seven told him.

"Most of these towns have an apothecary and should have antibiotics. I might be able to break into one," Bollard pondered aloud.

Seven thought for a moment. "There was a lot of confusion in the ambush. I saw the medic get killed. He tried to jump behind a boulder but was shot with such force it knocked him in the air and out of sight behind it."

"Was he shot or killed by the explosion?"

"He was shot. The explosion was afterward."

"Do you know what he was carrying?" Bollard asked.

"He was well-equipped and had been building up his medical kit for several months. I'm confident he had antibiotics."

"If he had the medicine, and his body wasn't discovered," Bollard said slowly, "it would be safer to go back and look rather than trying to sneak into town."

"I can tell you exactly where I last saw him; he was toward the middle of the column."

"It's possible the enemy cleared the kill zone and wasn't thorough in clearing the entire area." Bollard sighed, "I don't like retracing or going back but it's worth a try."

"I should go back. I know exactly where it occurred," Seven said, standing and walking toward the mountain spring to soak a new cloth.

"No," Bollard said. "You should stay here with Ten. When he comes to, he should see someone he trusts, not me."

Seven knelt by the spring. "When will you leave?"

Bollard squinted at the setting sun. "I have to leave soon. I want to go check for the medic's aid kit and still have time to recon the town for a night run if I'm not successful."

"If you find it, when will you return?"

"I'll be back before daylight if I don't run into trouble."

"And if you go into town?"

"It'll take at least twenty-four hours," Bollard said. He looked down again at Ten's limp body. "We need him. I hope he can hang on that long."

Seven returned to Ten's side and pressed the cloth to his forehead. "Me too."

Chapter 11
Return to the Ambush Site

Bollard moved methodically and cautiously through the forest. Up ahead he could see what appeared to be a white line lying horizontally; a line made more distinct in the moonlight. He slowed his pace and crept forward. It was the trail where the ambush occurred earlier. If his calculations were accurate, and if he had offset his route correctly, the ambush would have occurred to his right. He paralleled the trail from the woodline for fifty meters and stopped. Ahead, numerous forms lay on the trail. The odor was the giveaway; the smell of blown intestines, feces, blood, and urine permeated the area. The bloated bodies had been stripped of their equipment and weapons. No one was going to stop for a burial. They left that distasteful duty to the locals.

Bollard looked up and down the path. He listened carefully. Nothing. He crossed the trail and followed Seven's directions until he saw the huge boulder she described. It was darker than the surrounding forest and stood out prominently. He searched carefully behind it. His heart sank.

The bullet-riddled body of a guerrilla lay grotesquely against the boulder, his head twisted unnaturally. Bollard studied the body. Seven had said the medic fell well behind the boulder. He took the dead man's head between his hands and tilted the face towards the moonlight. It wasn't the medic.

Relieved, Bollard began searching in the high bushes behind the boulder. The area was pitch black; he had to feel his way along the forward edge of the boulder. Nothing. He moved to his left and nearly stumbled. He reached down to discover a boot sticking out from under the brush. He felt up the leg to the torso, then to the backpack. Grasping the harness in both hands he pulled it over the guerrilla's shoulders and removed it. He took the pack to a beam of moonlight and opened it. He had to be sure it was the medic's aid kit. The white bandages and multiple bottles of pills inside were his confirmation. Thankfully, everything was intact.

Satisfied he had everything he needed, he put on the backpack, crossed the trail, and started the trek back to Seven and Ten.

Within just a few meters of paralleling the trail, Bollard froze. There was movement ahead, followed by the cracking sound of a broken limb, a crash into the brush, and a moan. Astonished, Bollard watched in fascination as a person continued noisily in his direction. He unsheathed his knife and stood at the ready. At the last minute, he grabbed the individual with one hand on his mouth and the blade at his throat. The person went limp in Bollard's arms. Bollard dropped him to his knees, remaining in total control.

"Speak quietly and answer my question only," he said lowly. "Do you understand?"

The individual nodded.

"Who are you?"

"Dukvakha," the boy whimpered.

Though he didn't fully relax, Bollard allowed his voice to pitch to a less menacing whisper. "It's me, Alpha," he said. "It's dangerous here. Let's move quietly away and we can talk. You walk in front of me and don't do anything stupid."

Bollard took Dukvakha's rifle and slung it over his shoulder, then nudged him along. They walked in the direction of the hide site for fifteen minutes.

"This is far enough," Bollard finally said. "Sit down and let's talk."

They sat down on a fallen tree trunk in a small clearing that afforded enough moonlight to see. Dukvakha's face was bruised and smudged.

"What are you doing wandering around? Do you know where you are?"

"I was knocked unconscious," the boy said. "When I woke up, the others were gone. I got separated from the rest. I don't know where I am."

"You've managed to make it right back to the ambush site. Exactly where you started. You've walked in a large circle." Bollard shook his head at the inexperience of the young man.

Dukvakha hung his head in embarrassment.

"You were part of the ambush," Bollard stated.

"Yes," Dukvakha replied without any pretense or evasion. That was good. It saved time.

"We were together when we robbed the payroll. You and I discovered the contaminated spring water. We worked well together." Bollard took a long pause. "You also had friends who were with me. Why did you fire on me and your people?"

Dukvakha said nothing as he turned his head away from Bollard's stare.

"Look kid, you're a good guy, but you're going to answer me." His tone offered no room for negotiation. "We can do this the easy way or the hard way."

"The others will kill me or my family," Dukvakha finally said.

"The others are either dead or scattered. No one has to know we talked."

"They'll kill me," he said again, shaking his head.

"You just killed your own people and tried to kill me. I'm in no mood for your newfound aversion to death. If you don't answer, I'll kill you," Bollard said as if he were simply commenting on the weather. He leveled his rifle.

Dukvakha was terrified, eyes practically popping out of his head, but he said nothing.

Bollard held up his knife. "The hard way is for me to disembowel you and force you to watch as the wild pigs feed on your intestines. I assure you, you'll talk. Or you simply answer me, and you live with no harm to you or your family. Do you understand?"

"Yes," Dukvakha said in a low whisper.

"It's your last chance. Now, what happened to cause this?"

The boy wet his lips. "We heard that one of your patrol members returned within twenty minutes of your departure from base camp."

"That's true," Bollard said. "We saw that the rear man was missing but Nick insisted we continue ahead."

"When that man returned to base, he alerted Four and the others that Nick and your group were going to warn the Ossetians."

Bollard's eyebrows shot up. "Ossetians?" he asked. "What are you talking about? We were going to meet with the Ingush."

Dukvakha shifted nervously, eyeing the knife. "Nick pretended for your sake he was going to meet with the Ingush. That was never his intent. The others were in on it."

Bollard remained silent and gestured with his knife to continue.

"We found out you were on the way. When Nick's man returned to basecamp, he reported to Four and the leadership and they sent out an alert. We knew the patrol would turn southwest toward Ossetia. We were supposed to stop you and force you back to base camp, but someone opened fire."

Bollard began to piece it together: two factions, short tempers, the buildup of tension, and quick trigger fingers. But he wanted details. "You haven't explained why we were supposed to be warning the Ossetians," Bollard pointed out.

Dukvakha looked genuinely surprised. "You don't know about the Regional Command's direction against the Ossetians?"

"I and the others were sent away, remember? We weren't there for that discussion."

The younger man looped his fingers together and considered how to explain it. "The majority of the Regional Command agreed extraordinary measures were necessary to force the Ossetians to cooperate with the insurgency. Nick, as the number two of our Area Command, objected. Loudly. He was overruled."

"What was the mission?"

"There is a Soviet base just outside Vladikavkaz. The children of the military attend a middle school at the edge of the city. Over a hundred of them. There are Ossetian children there as well, mostly from the city apparatchiks."

A cold weight formed in Bollard's gut. His face grew dark as he began to understand.

"The Regional Command decided to hit the school as vengeance for the bombing of the Sverny school," Dukvakha continued. "Take hostages. Make demands. Ultimately, it was a suicide mission."

"So," Bollard said, with barely restrained outrage, "you were going to kill the children."

"Most of our people would be wearing suicide vests," Dukvakha confirmed. "They planned to rig the school with explosives."

"What was to be gained by this?"

"They were going to make it look like the Ossetians did it. Blame it on them. The Soviets would bring all hell down on them and they'd ultimately be forced back into the insurgency. It also sent a clear message to anyone who decided to cooperate with the Soviets." The boy's voice took on a sickening note of pride.

"So, Nick was on his way to alert the Ossetians?" Bollard questioned.

"Yes, taking you, Ten, and Seven along as part of his plan. You three are considered highly valuable by all the Area Commands. Nick figured your presence would give him standing among the Ossetians. Given your backgrounds; an American, a Russian, and Seven as the liaison, we knew you'd never approve of the Vladikavkaz operation. That's why you were asked to leave the Regional Command meeting." Dukvakha's brow furrowed in confusion. "I presumed Nick told you."

"I was not aware," Bollard told him. "I saw Saud at the ambush site. Why was he there?"

"They told Saud about the Vladikavkaz operation. He supported it. When he learned we were to intercept your team, he and some of the others insisted on joining us."

Bollard said nothing.

Dukvakha continued, "You should be aware, that you won't get a warm reception from the Ossetians. If we were unsuccessful in intercepting you, the Area Command was going to alert Ossetian leadership that your entire team was solely responsible for the Vladikavkaz job."

Bollard knew the severe impact of this statement. Damn it. *Damn* it.

"Why didn't you simply ambush us?" Bollard demanded. "Would have been a quick end."

"The group wanted to run an ambush but our leader, Adlan, had a cousin in your patrol. He wanted to take prisoners more than kill anyone. So, we set up the ambush as a contingency."

"Then someone got trigger-happy in your ambush," Bollard finished. "But no one figured on the bomber."

Dukvakha shook his head.

Bollard sighed and stood. He sheathed his knife and trained the rifle carefully on Dukvakha. "You're coming with me," he said. "Do something stupid, and it's the end. If we find the Ossetians at some point, you can explain. They might let us live."

The two walked slowly through the forest, working their way cautiously through dense scrub, then back into the forest. Bollard wanted to take a different route back to the hide site and moved adjacent to the entanglements of the underbrush. He fell.

It was the chance Dukvakha had been waiting for. Too scared to attack, he fled like a panicked deer; hurtling himself over the scrub, then falling, running, and leaping as fast as he could go. Bollard jumped up and considered aiming a few bullets in his direction.

"It solves my dilemma, I guess," he said to himself. "Ten or Seven likely would've killed him anyway."

Chapter 12
Militants

Darkness set in as the militants formed a small defensive perimeter a safe distance from the ill-fated ambush. Saud was unnerved. He had never experienced any violence in his life and this was his first combat. It had previously been a sterile concept to him; something in which others suffered and died, not him or those around him. There was no plan for the suicide bomber, though it was a standard operating procedure for one to accompany every patrol.

Many of Saud's friends and several other militants were ripped apart by the explosion with heads, limbs, and torsos scattered in an instant. One was standing beside Saud as a shard of steel blew off a portion of his head, splattering brains, bone, and blood across Saud's clothes. Saud himself was thrown backward, and he lay there, splayed out in the mud on his back. Too frightened to move, he listened to the gunfire and screams until the fighting finally ceased.

The militant ambush wiped out Nick and his guerrilla patrol. After a careful search, they accounted for all but four of them – the medic, the American, Ten, and Seven. The latter three, with their connections and influence, were the greatest threat to the militants' push for vengeance as well as their radical plans for dominance in the region.

Unnerved and inexperienced, Saud raged and fumed at the militant patrol leader. "We failed! What are we going to do about the American? We had a plan for the school!"

After sustaining heavy losses and finding a good position, the militant leader, Adlan, had decided to stand down, let his men lick their wounds, and consider his options while opening a can of food. He was a brutish, brooding man with a scraggly beard, always dirty clothes, and a nasty personality to match. He was given a wide berth by everyone except Saud, which was Saud's mistake.

Adlan hurled a volley of insults while digging his grubby fingers into the can. "You wanted to join the big boys. You wanted to be part of the action. You were even thrilled at the idea of attacking the innocents at the school. Look at you now, wild-eyed, shaking in your boots, covered in the brains and guts of far better men who stood beside you."

Saud unconsciously wiped at his face and sleeve.

"Give me your rifle," Adlan ordered.

Saud handed it to him immediately. Placing the can down beside him, Adlan pulled the rifle bolt to the rear, inserted his finger, then held it up to Saud in disgust.

"Just as I thought. You never fired a shot!" he shoved the rifle into Saud's chest, who reeled back a few steps with a wild expression. "Stupid twit! We've lost half of our force. There are eight of us left. Six dead. We don't even have the men to hit the school." Adlan took a calming breath. "Besides, we had a contingency plan. Four alerted the Ossetians that it was Nick who planned to hit the school. We can't hit it now. That mission is off."

Saud made a valiant attempt to look down his nose at the other, much larger man. "There are just four of them. We still have the advantage."

Adlan simply shook his head. "So, not enough blood for you, huh? Consider this. Ten has resources and connections we don't. That increases the odds in their favor. Likely, they're in a hide site just like ours and haven't gone far." He reached forward to yank Saud by the front of his shirt, dropping his voice to a conspiratorial whisper. "In fact, they may be looking for us right now, even if there are only four. Probably not in the mood for taking prisoners. And if they do," Adlan chuckled darkly, "you won't want to be on the receiving end."

Saud gulped. "Me?"

"Especially you. The American seems to have a special dislike for you." Adlan released Saud. "If only for your own sake, you should be worried about our security at this point. Leave everything else to me."

Saud's eyes somehow tripled in size as he flicked his gaze around their perimeter. "I think we should, as God wills…"

Adlan interrupted, "It's too late for your proselytizing! We'll go after them, but when I say so. Not you. Go somewhere else, far away from me, sit down, and shut up." He turned back to his can of meat and said nothing further.

Saud stomped off and lay next to a large, jagged rock. He pulled his rifle to his shoulder and peered toward the trail. The others ignored him.

***

Dukvakha had barely gone a hundred meters after his escape from Bollard. He was exhausted. Sprinting, falling, stumbling through the underbrush, he stopped only to catch his breath. He leaned against a moist, moss-covered tree that served to remind him of how thirsty he was. He ripped off a handful of moss and squeezed it over his mouth. Only a few drops of woody moisture dripped onto his dry tongue. Every little noise and twig snap captured his attention. He fought off the bone-deep desire for sleep as the adrenaline leached out of his limbs. He had to think, but his thoughts slogged across his brain.

The American had said he'd been walking in circles and indeed, he had. How could he be sure to walk in a straight line? In his mental state, no answer was forthcoming. He had to set off again; try to find a recognizable landmark before daylight. The trail? Yes, the trail. It was straight ahead. Or was it to the left? Or behind? No, not behind him! He couldn't run into the American again. That would seal his fate.

After moving several hundred meters he could see that something or somebody had recently disturbed the ground. The militants could have come this way. He moved ahead more confidently.

***

Saud hadn't moved. Wide-eyed and practically clinging to the boulder, he watched the approach to their site, trying not to puke. The phantom scent of dried blood and brains on his clothing lingered. Adlan's words were still ringing in his ears, "They're not going to be in a mood for prisoners." His stomach churned.

Down the trail, there was a snap of a dead limb, the rustle of brush, and a flurry of movement in the darkness. Saud raised his rifle and fired as fast as he could pull the trigger, the shots crackling in the darkness and echoing like thunder off the mountains. Several of the other militants jumped up and began to fire indiscriminately until they realized there was no return fire.

The leader sprinted over to Saud. "Why are you firing?" he demanded, peering down the trail.

"There." Saud pointed with his rifle. "About thirty meters. Listen."

There was a long silence. Then, a moan.

"You stay here and do nothing!" Adlan ordered, before turning to the nearest militant. "Come with me."

The two men crept down the trail towards the sound. Adlan pointed out a man sitting with his back against a tree, holding his stomach and leaning forward, groaning with each breath.

"Damn it!" the other militant cursed. "It's Dukvakha. He's gut shot."

Adlan called for two more men to come and assist. They pulled Dukvakha back to their site.

As Adlan passed Saud, he got in his face and shoved him. "You fool!" he shouted. "You stupid son-of-a-bitch! You've shot one of our own! You shot Four's nephew!"

Saud trembled. Horrified, he looked where they had laid the wounded boy. Someone pressed a cloth to the wound, but it immediately soaked red. It was clear he wasn't going to survive.

"The American ..." Dukvakha gasped between moans.

"Where?" Adlan asked, squatting at his side.

Saud spun and stared in the direction of the trail, raising his rifle again.

Dukvakha sputtered again, "The American ..." and tried to lift his hand in the direction of the trail.

"Where?" Adlan repeated.

"Up ... up." Dukvakha's voice faded.

"Toward the mountain?"

"Yes," Dukvakha replied feebly, closing his eyes. His breath was labored and shallow, then ceased.

Adlan didn't notice as he turned to address his men. "We need to pursue the American and the others. His trail may still be fresh tomorrow." He squinted at the sky. "It will likely rain, so we need to get his general direction right away and move out first thing in the morning."

As his men muttered agreement and prepared themselves, the one who had been tending to Dukvakha approached Adlan a few minutes later. "He's dead."

Adlan drew a deep breath, turned, and snapped at Saud. "Bury him! I don't care how you do it but bury him."

Saud was slow to move.

Adlan grabbed him by the back of the shirt, lifted him, and pushed him in the direction of Dukvakha. "Now!"

There could be no ritual bathing, no shrouding, but praying. Yes, lots of praying, as Saud contemplated how Four might react when he learned of the death of his nephew, and importantly *who* had killed him.

Chapter 13
Mission Complete

The crack of rifle fire rang out nearby and Bollard froze in place. He turned in the direction of the flurry of panic firing. It was coming from only a few hundred meters away. Bollard figured Dukvakha must have stumbled into his friends.

Bollard had a long distance to travel to his hide site and a short time to do it before daylight. Out of necessity, though, he created false trails, backtracked, then concealed his tracks by stepping on logs or rocks wherever possible. His progress was even further hampered by the cloud cover blocking the moonlight. He hoped the rain would begin soon and wash out his trail. His prayer was answered when the heavens opened, and a deluge of rain began to fall. He sat down next to a fallen tree and after an hour, visibility increased. He stood and walked slowly toward the hide site, making no effort to conceal his movement.

Seven watched the agreed-to approach area and saw movement. Bollard held his rifle in his left hand with the muzzle pointed down. Seven peered down the sights of the rifle as the approaching silhouette became clearer, then lowered it after identifying the recognition signal.

"Right here," Seven called.

Bollard came fully into view. "You were right," he said. "I have the medicine. How's the patient?"

"Still feverish," Seven reported. "I created a makeshift shelter to keep him out of the weather. I've given him a few sips of water, which he's held down. We must get the antibiotics into him." Seven took the pack and led Bollard toward the new site, a slight adjustment to their original position.

"I heard shots this morning. I feared the worst."

"I wasn't far from the shooting. I ran into Dukvakha but he escaped. I believe he walked right in the middle of the militant camp." Bollard rubbed the back of his neck. "We can anticipate they'll try to pick up my trail."

"Maybe the rain will take care of your tracks," Seven offered.

"They know we're in the area. They'll start their search after the rain. If we get lucky, fog will follow the rain."

"We have some time before we need to worry, I suppose."

Ten lay prone under a hastily constructed frame made of branches. He shivered against the cool morning air. Seven opened the pack and removed a container of pills. The medic had written "gonorrhea" on the side.

"This must be it; most likely ampicillin," Seven said, handing the bottle to Bollard and then moving to a position to hold Ten's head.

Bollard grabbed a canteen and squatted adjacent to Ten. He opened the container and handed Seven three pills. "This should be good for a start. You can give him more intermittently."

Seven placed the pills in Ten's mouth one at a time, as Bollard coaxed each one down with small sips of water.

Bollard stood and surveyed their position. The makeshift shelter was dry. Seven had taken advantage of a large fallen tree that created a void between it and the ground and added brush and leaves to the edges to block the wind. Though damp, they were as comfortable as they could be in the pouring rain.

"I interrogated Dukvakha before he escaped in the dark," Bollard began slowly. "You, Ten, me, and the entire force were set up by Four, and the other militants."

Seven blinked at him. "Set up?"

"They planned to attack a Russian school in Vladikavkaz, ultimately kill everyone, then blame the Ossetians. Nick was on his way to alert them, with us in tow."

"But we were supposed to meet the Ingush."

"If you recall, we changed direction, and turned south for a significant distance, before we were ambushed."

Seven acknowledged.

"It gets worse, though," Bollard said. "They've since notified the Ossetians that *we* planned the attack."

"Us? A school?" Seven was incredulous. "Why would they do it? I never figured Four to be so stupid."

"He's not. He's under the orders from the Regional Command. Payback for the Sverny school bombing and they wanted to drive a wedge between the Ossetians and Soviets."

Seven's expression morphed from stunned into a thin line of rage. "The fools! They might force the Ossetians back into the fold, but they'll lose every bit of international support they need. The MRNC will disavow us, but that would make little difference as they'll lose all of their current credibility and standing. It will certainly fuel Soviet propaganda. It's all self-defeating!"

Bollard replied grimly, "I agree, but we're running out of options."

"We are?"

"The three of us. They've pinned the blame on us."

The full implication of Bollard's words now sank in on Seven.

Bollard ticked off, "We're in a dangerous mess. The guerrillas are after us. The militants are after us. The Ossetians think we were behind the planned attack on the school. The Russians would love to catch us."

Seven sat stone-faced.

Bollard continued, "We need to consider our next steps."

Seven looked down at Ten's drawn face. "He'll have to be part of the planning."

"I agree. We need him. I think the two of us should discuss this in advance, though. Ten can offer some ideas when he wakes up."

Seven didn't respond.

Bollard shifted. "We need to discuss an escape and evasion plan."

"I'm confident Ten will have some ideas."

"We'll see."

Bollard shifted again. There was a long pause as he leaned against the back of the shelter and pulled his hat over his eyes. The rain continued to pour, dripping into the sides of the shelter. Without looking up he asked, "Seven, what are your plans? Return to Afghanistan?"

Seven startled, jerked up to stare at Bollard.

"Let's not be coy, we have to be straight with one another," Bollard continued. "I know you're Afghan. Your focus on the impact of Caucasus' efforts on Afghanistan and your status as liaison makes that pretty obvious. Despite the soot, you still have Afghan features, and an occasional language slip betrays your accent."

This was a dangerous game he was playing, especially if Seven interpreted it as a threat. Bollard pressed on regardless. "We can't go back to the base camp. By now, we're already on everyone's hit list. If you have an escape and evasion plan to get out of the country or back to Afghanistan, we need to activate it."

Seven stiffened. "An extraction is out of the question. I have a mission here and nothing can jeopardize it. The Soviets must be defeated first."

Bollard finally lifted a corner of his hat to look at Seven. "Your mission is over."

"What do you mean?"

"First, we're wanted by every player in the region. Second, on the strategic level, the Soviets are taking huge losses in Afghanistan, and pressure against the government is building. I don't think it will be long before they pull out. If nothing else, that will end your mission. Even so, there isn't much good you can do here. We've been set up and we need to get out of the region."

Seven fell silent yet again and stared at Ten's chest.

Bollard leaned forward. "The three of us have to work together."

Several minutes passed. Bollard waited and considered his points regarding the reluctant young Afghan, until finally, Seven spoke. "Azerbaijan."

"What?"

"Azerbaijan." Seven looked at him. "If I can get to Azerbaijan, I can get help. There is a plan in place, but I'm not sure how reliable it is. I believe I could disappear into the population."

Bollard thought for a moment. "Okay, we'll see if that can fit into an overall plan after we've talked to Ten."

"What about you?" Seven asked. "You have to have an extraction plan."

Bollard laughed, "I assure you; I have no intention of remaining in this hemisphere. We may be able to work all three extractions into one effort." Bollard squinted at the falling rain.

"We'll hold this position until Ten recovers, but then we have to evade our pursuers and escape the region. We'll need Ten's access to any resources where he hasn't been compromised." Bollard settled back into his seat and closed his eyes again. "This will take a lot of planning."

Chapter 14
The Revelation

"How long have you known?" Seven asked sometime later with a soft voice.

Bollard knew what the real question was but decided to tread carefully. "That you're Afghan? Suspected on the day we met at the first Area Command meeting. Then confirmed later at the second."

"That's not what I mean. You demanded cotton from me for Ten's wounds. How long have you known that I'm a woman?"

Now that she was being specific, Bollard knew he could properly answer her. "I'm familiar with the bacha posh of Central Asia. It wasn't a huge leap after I determined you were Afghan."

"But how did you know?" she insisted.

Bollard sighed and looked sidelong at her. "It was Ten who gave you away."

Her eyebrows shot up. She immediately looked down at Ten's unconscious body. "He has no idea." Her expression quickly grew mortified. "How could Ten possibly know?"

"He doesn't." Bollard shrugged. "But you have feelings for him."

"I..." Seven's protest died on her lips. She was shocked and embarrassed, but she had to know. "Go on."

"At the first Area Command Meeting, you were focused, intentionally. Then Ten came forward to question me. You seemed to lose your focus," he reached out to tap the toe of her boot, "you wiggled your foot continuously."

Seven sent a betrayed glance at her boot. "That's a sign?"

Bollard grinned. "Pretty much in any culture. The baggy clothes and soot on your face are a good touch. I couldn't tell for sure by looking at you. I simply suspected."

Seven appeared to mull this over. "So, I must have slipped; done something to confirm your suspicions?"

"Yes and no. It was your tracks that gave you away."

"My tracks?" Seven asked.

"Your foot is narrower; you don't plod along with your toes sticking out at wide angles. You walk normally with an even balance of weight with a slight angle.

"I know how to track a man, a woman, and a child. I didn't know my tracks were so discernable."

"Normally, they're not," Bollard assured her. "It comes out when you're around Ten. Your weight shifts to your toes, which point more inward. Just before the Regional Command meeting, your tracks in the mud gave you away."

Seven appeared to study Bollard but said nothing.

Bollard arched an eyebrow. "Am I wrong? About your feelings?"

She paused, having never been this frank about her sexuality. "No," she finally said. "I can't explain it."

Bollard wasn't sure whether pursuing the point was a good idea, but now he was curious, "You're a bacha posh. Have you ever had the chance to explore these feelings?"

"Yes, I'm a bacha posh," she admitted. "I fought hard for a position of respect and the opportunity to use my abilities as a man might." She paused. "It would have been unwise to express the feelings I've had, given I had to behave as one." She paused again, then stared out at the rain. The downpour was slowly starting to lighten to a drizzle. Finally, in a barely audible whisper, she said, "And yes, I had similar feelings; but only as a child."

Bollard remained silent and allowed her to take control of the conversation at her own pace. It wasn't so astonishing that such a conversation would take place. It was a distraction from the duress of the situation. Truthfully, it was also the frankness that mattered in such circumstances; a sort of bonding needed for what lay ahead.

Seven paused, internalizing what she had just said. "I had such strong feelings for a boy," she continued. "A Russian, which was forbidden." She brushed back a strand of dark hair from Ten's forehead. "He reminds me of him. I've tried to block them out, but those feelings came rushing back."

"And Ten doesn't know you're a bacha posh," Bollard finished. "Or your feelings."

"That's true." Seven shook her head sadly as she continued to stroke Ten's hair. "And it has to remain so."

"You know," Bollard said slowly, recognizing he was wading into unpredictable territory, "you may have had no options to being a bacha posh in Afghanistan. But here in the Soviet Union, among these men, or in the West, it truly isn't necessary."

Seven wasn't so easily persuaded. Bollard couldn't blame her; he only had the scantest idea of what she may have been through. "I have to maintain my persona," she insisted.

"Perhaps," Bollard granted, "but there are lots of women who are military leaders who don't have to pretend they are men. There are even units comprised of women fighters in numerous countries. As I've said, your mission here in the Caucasus has come to an end. There is no need to maintain a bacha posh persona. Besides," Bollard added meaningfully, "the militants will be looking for Seven, a man."

Seven's head snapped up to meet Bollard's eyes, she hadn't considered this point.

"You can be honest with Ten," he said. "More importantly, you can be honest with yourself. Why not show your feelings? Our probability of getting out of this mess isn't great. What have you got to lose?" His focus became distant for a moment. "I would tell my daughter the same thing. Let nothing or no one stand in your way." He dragged himself back to the present with another shrug. "But ultimately it's all the same to me whatever you decide."

Bollard had said his piece. Daylight was slow to come as the fog began to move its way up the mountain, blocking the morning sun.

Bollard unfolded his legs and stumbled to his feet. "I'm going to move forward to a better position and watch," he said, brushing the mud off his pants.

"Sulundik ..."

"Huh?" Bollard stopped and turned.

"Sulundik," Seven repeated, raising her chin to look up at him, almost in defiance. "My name is Sulundik."

Chapter 15
Sulundik and Ten

Sulundik watched as Bollard disappeared down the hill. He had given her a lot to think about. Indeed, she was a bacha posh. It had been so her entire life except for a brief but miserable period as Ulzhan, and during her insertion into Azerbaijan. If not a bacha posh, she would be breeding stock, married to and subservient to a man she didn't love or respect. She rationalized the purpose of concealing her identity was to ensure she could integrate quickly within the guerrilla force and maintain her position in the Area and Regional Commands. There were no other women at the senior levels and given her life experience, she could not trust she would be treated the same. Now it was all different.

The Area Command was scattered, as well as the majority of the guerrilla force and militants. The American knew her identity. Then there was the matter of the man lying in her arms. Ten might not survive and she wanted him to know. If there were ever a time to explore her desires, without compromising her independence or the core of who she was, it had to be now.

Sulundik gently removed Ten's head from her lap. She moved carefully from the makeshift bed to the spring as he murmured in his sleep. She cupped her hands and gratefully drank the fresh water. Then taking a cloth, she scrubbed the soot and camouflage from her face. She felt refreshed, if not relieved. It felt as though she had shed a skin. She was a woman now, if only temporarily.

When she returned to the bed, Ten's eyes were open and glassy. Sulundik repositioned herself at his head, pulling the upper part of his body into her arms. She gently wiped his eyes with a damp cloth as he stared at her. He lifted his arm and touched her cheek. She froze at the unexpected contact for the briefest moment. She reached up and covered his hand with her own and returned it to his chest, caressing it gently. With a slight breeze and a shiver, she pulled him closer.

***

Ten was in a desert. A barren, unforgiving desert with a searing sun that scorched his skin and made him feel as if he was being boiled alive. The only relief, which was too infrequent at that, was when he plunged into the cool, restorative waters of a nameless lake that would occasionally appear before receding. Just when he thought he couldn't bear the heat any longer he cried out, and the cool waters came like a wave. Despite the infrequency, there was a constant, those big almond eyes with a brilliance that reflected the light, like dark pieces of amber.

Those almond eyes, cresting with each rising wave of relief, beckoned him into the coolness. Sometimes, he reached out, never fully comprehending but wanting to grasp and hold close the untouchable, before returning to the unbearable heat.

Ten drifted in and out of consciousness as the fever rose in response to the growing infection. The fleeting moments when he opened his eyes were not a period of lucidity, but a confusing blur of shapes and colors accompanying the relentless pain of a powerful headache. He dreamed. He dreamed of a desert and water and almond eyes. Nothing else seemed real.

Sulundik was no less transfixed on the patient. As she tended to him, she became even more self-aware. So many years had passed since she was called by any name other than Seven, and she longed for Ten to know hers. She wanted to know his. She moved from the makeshift bed to the mountain spring where cool water burbled to the surface, wetting a cloth to wipe Ten's face and forehead and another to clean his wound. In his delirium, Ten twisted and turned, opening the wound, and giving Sulundik guilty but wanted justification to hold him.

From the minute she met Ten, she was infatuated. His thick black hair, wide dark eyes, and distinctly Russian features bore the legacy of the Mongol invasions. His impish smile lit up his face whenever he took pleasure in something, and his eyes always held an untold depth of mischief. She observed him move with authority among the guerrillas and knew he was a leader and a good one. It all drew her in.

Ten moaned, drawing her focus back to him. He opened his eyes slightly as she laid the cool compress on his forehead. He thought he might have seen an angel in Seven's face. Surely, he must be dreaming.

Chapter 16
Fog

As the fog moved in and reduced visibility, Bollard anticipated the militants might gravitate toward the flats along the hillside, for ease of navigation. He identified several junctures where the flats and his previous route intersected. He found a position that offered clear fields of fire over the points of intersection.

The fog crept steadily up the hill until it was within two hundred meters of Bollard's position. Ideally, should the militants come into range, he would kill the rear man in the column in hopes the fog would muffle the sound and direction of his shot. If successful, the others in the column would be unaware of his accuracy as he worked his way up the column with each of their successive maneuvers. It was an old but effective strategy, and the environment suited the plan, but circumstance can just as easily change the equation.

Bollard forced himself into the kind of calm that came with years of experience in a high-stress environment, but he suddenly felt as if his heart was pounding. The deep thump became increasingly louder, and he realized it wasn't his heart, but the blades of a Soviet helicopter.

In the skyline, behind and to the north of their hide site, a Soviet Mi-8 Hip came into view and landed on an open area on the hilltop. Twenty Soviet soldiers leaped from the helicopter, sprinted to the edge of the woodline, and laid down in firing positions.

Bollard dropped a little lower in his position and tried to determine the direction the detachment of soldiers was moving. He wondered whether this might be the first of several insertions. Just four hundred meters away, any large-scale consolidation on the hilltop would certainly disclose the hide site.

As the Hip departed at low altitude, Bollard was relieved to see the soldiers rise in unison and begin moving in a tactical formation down the ridgeline in the direction of his previous day's engagement with the militants. He surmised the Soviets were responding to the reports of gunfire and fighting in the area. They were likely a part of a larger operation deployed to locate and force the guerrillas into a direct engagement. It was also likely that the Soviets established ambush sites and choke points to support the search and destroy team.

Bollard needed to get the information to Sulundik who couldn't see what had occurred. That would have to wait until the Soviet engagement team had moved off into the distant fog.

***

The Soviet soldiers were reluctant to approach the blanket of fog. It first appeared as a faint wisp of white that grew thicker and thicker, until it completely covered the valley and up to three-quarters of the mountain, forming a great white wave, rolling closer, covering everything in its path and creating a cloak of invisibility.

They understood that weather conditions are a fact of life for a soldier. The conditions may vary, but the common theme is the relative impact on operations. Rain, cold, and heat are the normally anticipated factors; but sometimes, looming unexpectedly, is the blanket of dampness that can envelop an entire operational area - fog. It limits and alters the normal senses; visibility is reduced, odor is enhanced and lingering, sounds are deceptive and muffled, and orientation and bearings become difficult.

"It always gives me the creeps," Private Nemtsev, a young Soviet soldier, whispered to his friend Private Petrov, as they moved down the ridgeline and toward the wall of fog.

"This whole place is eerie," Petrov replied and continued to scan forward.

Ahead of them, Warrant Pavlick moved cautiously, watching for any movement. A Baltic man who had been in the service for fifteen years, he was a veteran of the Afghan wars and had fought in many engagements and numerous battles. Like many of his ilk, he had little stomach for drill and ceremony and enjoyed the freedom his Spetsnaz detachment provided. His superiors turned to him for difficult tasks and

Pavlick's mission to probe insurgent lines was one of those times. The fog complicated everything.

Once Pavlick detected and engaged the insurgents, he and his team would drive them toward choke points and waiting ambushes. He knew the guerrillas, having been in an engagement earlier, would likely be just ahead of them or well hidden. Under these circumstances, his inexperienced troops should not take the point. He moved forward, signaling the young troops to cover his advance.

Halfway down the hill and out of sight of Bollard, the Soviet force stopped. Pavlick didn't like what lay before him. The fog was too thick; visibility so reduced, that it would be near suicide to stumble along toward an unseen or waiting enemy. Now, just short of the wall of white, he turned and organized his soldiers into two-man groups, each capable of supporting those adjacent. They would wait for the fog to move over them, or conditions might change to dissipate it.

Nemtsev and Petrov were positioned back-to-back behind a fallen tree, covering the areas to their right and left.

"The fog is strange," Nemtsev said nervously. "Always did make my hair raise a little; unable to see what is moving on the inside, peering out, us not able to see in." He shuddered. "I'll be glad when it rolls over us."

"It'll sure be colder and wetter when it does," Petrov replied.

"At least the waiting will be over, and we'll be on equal ground with whatever might be in there," Nemtsev offered. "Gotta be careful; it's easy to get confused, having no sun or stars or ground markings to get a fix on our location. They could be on top of us before we realize it. I'm glad Warrant Pavlick stopped when he did."

"Well, whenever it gets here, I'm staying put," Petrov whispered as he crouched a little lower behind the natural breastwork.

"Right," Nemtsev said. "I don't like the feel of it."

Both men lay facing each flank as the damp blanket of white settled over them. Although soldiers were located somewhere to their left and right, they now seemed hopelessly alone. They pulled their collars a little higher on their necks and curled deeper into position. Two hours passed and the dampness of the fog and the cool mountain air chilled them to the bone. Large trees grew within a few meters of their position, but they could see only a blur of an outline.

A twig snapped nearby. They both froze, slowing their breathing to a near halt; straining to hear, to fix the direction of the sound. They understood the dangers. Denied any visual advantage, they had to rely on every other sense and intuition to locate and identify the source of the sound.

Petrov turned his head to the side and opened his mouth to enhance his hearing, much as he'd seen his grandfather do on numerous hunting trips as a youth. Five seconds, an eternity passed, and then the faint sound of a stick or branch being slowly crushed into the damp ground.

Nemtsev heard it too. It was in his direction.

Again, Petrov turned his head to the side, but this time he closed his mouth, flared his nostrils, and inhaled deeply. There! He squeezed Nemtsev's arm, who tensed and raised his head slightly to see the signal, a slight touch on the side of his nose. It was the unmistakable smell of campfire smoke and body odor, amplified by the dampness of the fog and carried by a barely perceptible breeze.

***

At first light, Adlan sent two of the militants to search for any indication of Bollard's trail. They moved out in the direction Dukvakha had arrived the night before. The fog was moving quickly and both scouts returned with no information. Adlan determined the American and his cohorts were hiding somewhere along the top of the mountain.

The fog now enveloped the militants, and despite his reservations, Adlan led the men away from their night site and the shallow grave. Organizing his remaining men in a column, they followed one another cautiously and at a distance to protect the movement of the person to their front. As visibility decreased, they moved closer to one another. After an hour, Adlan signaled for a stop as he heard the muffled sound of helicopter blades; it was difficult to determine its flight path.

He was confident it was simply passing overhead, and above the fog bank.

The militant group moved slowly on. More of a shadow than the tangible form of a man, Adlan probed his way toward the top of the mountain, still hoping to break free of the fog. He stepped, paused, and listened before stepping again. But even that was too fast for the militants nearest him.

The passage of time is relative to the circumstances with which one is confronted. In a more carefree time, their days might fly by. But war is different. War is when the passage of a mere second may seem to last an eternity. So it was with the militants. For it was within that second, that their attention waned. Now Adlan was gone; consumed by the white mist. They could no longer provide the cover for him. One of the militants darted forward and also disappeared into the mist, then another. Within minutes the entire element was separated and dispersed along the hillside. One or two stopped, frozen in terror. Others moved in the same general direction, but no longer in a supporting column as much as a wide arch. The militants were scattered and were soon to learn the effectiveness of their enemy's strategy.

***

In that environment and under those conditions, the well-rehearsed Soviet element's operating procedures were simple. Once in position, no one moves, except the leader who will approach from the rear, and anything that moves is an enemy.

Nemtsev and Petrov crouched, their senses fully alert. The mist, which earlier had been such a fearful and detestable image, now served as a protective blanket. The sound of a measured step, the slow grinding of a stick in the ground, and an unfamiliar odor, followed by a shape just forward and at the edge of their defensive position confirmed what they suspected. Instinctively, Petrov sprang, swinging the butt of his rifle with such force the militant's head burst upon impact, breaking the silence of the forest with the most sickening sound.

In the distance and hidden in the mist the others heard it, the unmistakable sound of death. It was too late to correct their mistake. Unable to see or help the person to their front and too confused to rush blindly forward, the militants froze in position.

Nemtsev jumped over the fallen tree to help Petrov drag the body into their position. The men gasped for breath as the adrenaline rapidly drained away, leaving both exhausted.

To their left, a shot rang out. Adlan met his fate. Suddenly the entire Soviet force opened fire in a mad minute of all-out firing simultaneously to their preplanned zones of coverage. It was soon over, as the militants were either dead or running down the hill. With three blasts of a whistle, Pavlick signaled his men to hold their positions.

Nemtsev rolled the body of the dead militant over and began to remove any papers or personal items with almost lackadaisical practice. Interestingly, the militant's features were not familiar; darker complexion, perhaps a foreign fighter. His pockets contained indecipherable paper and they stuffed it in their pockets. They could never imagine the paper was money – riyals.

As they removed and examined the dead man's watch they noticed it was inexplicably running a full hour ahead of time. The soldier put it on his wrist and set it to the proper hour.

Chapter 17
A Gamble

Bollard watched as the Soviet force moved down the ridgeline and then cautiously enter the fog. He was confident, despite his efforts to conceal his tracks, it wouldn't be long before the militants picked up the trail. The deep ruts from the makeshift litter he and Sulundik had used to move Ten were nearly impossible to hide. But then, he listened in astonishment as a first shot was fired and then the mad minute.

Either the militants had walked directly into the Soviet force or vice versa. The green tracers ricocheting through the fog indicated the former. There were three blasts of a whistle and afterward a long silence. Then a flare, a red star cluster, shot its way through the fog and up the mountain. Bollard looked back to the top of the hill and was surprised to see two men followed by a third. They were sprinting downhill, carrying large ammunition boxes toward one of the Soviet soldiers standing at the edge of the fog. It was likely a supply team and Bollard had an idea.

He made it back to the hide site as Sulundik moved to a firing position.

"It appears the Soviets and militants had a head-on confrontation," he told her. "The Soviets are resupplying, so they likely got the better end of it. You stay concealed here."

Seven lowered her rifle questioningly, "What's your plan?"

"The logistics team appears to have moved down the mountain. I'm going to come up behind their assembly point and see what supplies I can find."

"Won't you be seen?"

"Not if I keep the mountain between us. Make sure you know your target before you shoot. I'm going to try to come back the same way, but it's hard to say given the fog." He gestured towards Ten. "You need to stay with him and keep him quiet. He could give away our position."

"No," she replied firmly.

Her fierce response startled Bollard. "What do you mean?"

"I'm going to go check it out," Sulundik declared. "You retrieved the medicine, now it's my turn to take the risk. Not you. You watch Ten." Sulundik was adamant.

"We don't have time to argue. If it's you, you need to move out immediately."

Bollard sat adjacent to Ten and kept vigil for the approach of Soviet soldiers as Sulundik moved cautiously up the hill.

She was right. It was incredibly risky, but they had only a few morsels of food and needed to take a chance. It was up to Sulundik to see if the gamble paid off.

***

Sulundik, looking from a concealed position, could see four large boxes of ammunition. Adjacent were ten to fifteen smaller crates of rations, some of them opened and scattered. It seemed that the logistics team had picked through them for the better portions. Seeing no one nearby and staying low to the ground, she made her way to the smaller crates. One crate was opened but appeared to contain most of its rations. It was stuck between the other crates and least likely to be missed. She wiggled the crate out and hoisting it onto her shoulder, quickly retreated around the back of the mountain. She didn't get far. Shouts from behind her made her drop to the ground.

She could still see the assembly point. The three logistics men returned, but one of the tactical team was with them. He wasn't happy. Seeing the rations boxes open and spilled on the ground, he began shouting at and beating the other three. They hurriedly began placing the rations back in the crates as the fourth man shouted into his radio for the remaining Soviet soldiers to return to the hilltop.

Shots in the far distance drew everyone's attention. Most likely the remaining militants were running into the preplanned Soviet ambushes. The officer shouted instructions into the radio. Within a few minutes, the sound of an approaching helicopter forced Sulundik to crouch low to conceal herself from observation from above.

The helicopter landed and quickly departed with the Soviet soldiers and supplies aboard. Then, all was quiet.

Chapter 18
Almond Eyes

Bollard watched the helicopter take to the sky when he heard a voice. It was Ten's.

"Almond eyes ..."

Bollard turned to see Ten stir and lift his head slightly. Ten looked left and right and then to Bollard with a dazed expression.

"The woman ... where ...?"

"Seven," Bollard replied, matter-of-factly.

"No ... an angel ..."

"Seven," Bollard repeated. "She's been caring for you."

"She?" Ten fell back onto the bed. "What happened? Why the hell are you here, Alpha?"

"Ambush. You, Seven, and I are the only survivors."

"But ... an angel ..." Ten drifted off.

"Yeah, Seven's an angel all right," Bollard said dryly. "All the details can wait."

***

"There are several days of food here," Sulundik said as she returned to the hide site and placed the rations on the ground. "How's he doing?" she asked.

"He was asking for you," Bollard said as he opened the case and began examining the rations.

Sulundik almost jumped. "Me?"

"Almond eyes, angel," Bollard replied mildly. "I assume it was you. That's what I told him at least."

Sulundik blushed. "What did he say?"

Bollard shrugged a shoulder. "He went back to sleep. I suspect he's hoping when he wakes up again, it won't be me he sees, but you." Bollard glanced up and winked at her.

She turned an even deeper shade of red. After retrieving a wet cloth from the spring, she returned to her original post to tend to her patient.

Bollard finished sorting the rations and made a mental calculation of, at most, three to four days of food. He looked at

Sulundik, "I have an initial plan, but it entails a couple of days' hike. If I'm successful, it'll buy us some time; at least, until we know what Ten can offer. But the plan won't wait for him to get better. I'll go alone; you watch him. I don't think you'll need to worry about the Russians or militants for a while. If I'm not back in five days, assume I didn't make it and that you're on your own. Stretch the rations for as long as you can."

Sulundik had been in enough operations to know the necessity of a contingency plan. "I won't leave until the end of the fifth day," she impressed. "If you return sooner than five days and we aren't here, it means we've been forced from this site. So, we'll need a rally point."

"Correct."

"There was a draw halfway between here and the ambush site. It runs toward the bottom of the hill and a stream junction. We'll be at that junction until the end of the fifth day if forced from here."

"That's a good plan, Sulundik. Perfect." Bollard then settled back and shut his eyes, as his breathing evened out.

He had called her by her given name. Sulundik smiled and marveled at how fast a soldier could fall asleep. She shook her head and returned her attention to her charge.

It was well past sundown when Bollard woke abruptly. He tried to get his bearings in the dark when a voice reassured him. "Over here," Sulundik smiled. In the light of the moon, her eyes glistened. Soot removed and the burden of being a man lifted, it occurred to Bollard that Sulundik was a truly attractive woman.

"You've been in a deep sleep," she explained. "Your snoring was barely audible, and I didn't want to disturb you. Figured you needed the sleep to recover and prepare for your journey tonight."

"Thank you." Bollard stretched and groaned. "Yes, I needed the sleep. How's your patient?"

Sulundik placed a hand on Ten's forehead. "He seems to be doing better."

"I'll be back as soon as possible."

Chapter 19
A Deeper Connection

Sunlight filtered through the leaves and cast a moving shadow across Ten's face. He blinked sleepily and started to shift. The movement woke Sulundik who had dozed off beside him. She propped herself on an elbow and looked down at him. Ten blinked and smiled. The angel was there again. He lifted his hand to her.

Sulundik was about to place it on her cheek as she had done before, but Ten lifted higher. He gently slipped his fingers into her dark hair and tugged her down. She resisted at first, but selfish desire and curiosity made her relent as he pulled her to him. Slowly their lips touched. It was gentle, the barest brush of lips.

It was the first time Sulundik had ever kissed a man. A warmth bloomed from where their lips touched and spread across her cheeks, and her neck, and settled in her core. She pulled back shyly. Perhaps it was an accident. Ten pulled her to him again. They kissed again softly and more deliberately until Sulundik's lips tingled.

Taking Ten's hand in hers, she studied him. Ten smiled dreamily. He was transfixed. Sulundik's hair slipped down and framed her face, accenting her dark eyes. Ten was lost in her.

Sulundik cleared her throat. "Are you feeling better?"

"I am," he replied still staring into her eyes.

"I'll fix something for you to eat if you're up to it."

Ten gave a slight nod and closed his eyes. As Sulundik moved to get up, he mumbled something.

"What did you say?"

He opened his eyes slightly, "I'm afraid to fall asleep. Afraid you won't be here when I wake up."

"I'll be here."

***

Sulundik busied herself with fishing out some rations and pushed the kiss to a far, far corner of her mind. She pried open two small cans of meat, added some water, and heated it over a small fire as it boiled to make a stew. The smell made her stomach growl, but her patient had to eat first.

Ten was now sitting upright and leaning against the back of the shelter. He was still weak. Sulundik nudged him until he opened his eyes.

"Here," she said as she placed the spoon in the broth. "This might make you feel better but eat it slowly."

Ten watched her every move but said nothing.

As she spoon-fed him the stew she asked, "How do you feel? Do you need more?"

He shook his head.

Sulundik returned to the embers where the remaining meat simmered in a can. She ate it in two bites, swirled water in the can, then drank the liquid.

As she placed the empty can in the hole with the embers, she turned to see Ten looking at her with an intense gaze. It wasn't the mischievous sparkle he was noted for, but something else.

Chapter 20
Skinner

Bollard was on his second night of a strenuous march over difficult terrain when he finally arrived at a steep ravine. On the other side, he could see the faint outline of a trail in the morning light. If his calculations were correct, his objective should be over the trail and a kilometer to the southeast.

After two more hours of climbing, he emerged onto the trail and started paralleling it. In the distance, he could make out a pasture and an old barn. He crept closer, then ducked behind a large tree. An old man and a young boy were working in the field. It was Vsadnik and his son.

After a moment's consideration, Bollard cupped his hands over his mouth and blew slightly, making an owl-like sound.

The boy continued to work. Vsadnik, startled, turned in Bollard's direction as each pack animal perked its ears attentively.

Bollard briefly leaned out from behind the tree to show himself to the skinner. Vsadnik directed his son to return to their house and then walked directly toward Bollard.

"It's good to see you, Vsadnik my friend," Bollard said, extending his hand.

Vsadnik shook his hand vigorously, a wide grin on his face. He peered quizzically at him. "Why are you here? What's going on?"

"Some pretty big problems further north, serious chaos among the guerrillas."

The skinner looked over his shoulder to ensure his son had left the field. "What do you mean?"

"You recall the man who killed your Natasha?" Bollard asked, hoping to strengthen his position.

Vsadnik's eyes narrowed, and his jaw clenched. "That bastard! How could I forget? I relieved him of his rubles, but it wasn't worth Natasha."

"Well, he, along with half of the force ambushed the others. A big power grab." Bollard watched Vsadnik for any sign of his knowledge, or betrayal. "I and two others survived, but we were set up and we're on the wrong side of both groups. Now it looks like a Russian force inserted into the area and has everyone on the run." Bollard wasn't sure about his last comment, but it seemed like a safe assumption. "I need some assistance."

Vsadnik scratched his beard and muttered something under his breath. "Two runners came by yesterday evening. They were running the length of the supply route to shut it down. They didn't say why just that all hell was breaking loose. I was told not to run the normal resupply column until things get sorted out. Now I know why."

"Do you know if they were militants or guerrillas?" Bollard asked warily.

"Militants?" Vsadnik scoffed. "You mean the crazies?"

Bollard smiled. "Yeah, the crazies."

"They were guerrillas. I don't think the crazies would even know the supply line needed to be shut down."

Bollard blew out a relieved breath. "I need an assist," he repeated.

"These are dangerous times." Vsadnik placed his hands on his hips and raised his chin. "What do you need?"

"There are three of us on the run, and given what happened, we can't trust anyone."

The skinner arched a bushy white brow. "How do you know you can trust me?"

"You're the only person I can trust," Bollard confessed.

"Well, I suppose so. You're not even armed," Vsadnik allowed while looking behind him.

Bollard was glad he hid the rifle before approaching the skinner. He wanted his assistance without any risk of posing a threat.

"I wouldn't approach you like this but one of us is seriously injured."

"Who are the other two? Do you trust them?" Vsadnik cast a questioning glance.

"They're both guerrillas. One is a woman. We're all in the same circumstance," Bollard replied. At this point, he was fairly certain he could trust Sulundik, but the jury was still out on Ten.

The skinner thought for a moment. "Okay, what specifically do you need?"

"I need a pack animal. Preferably a hinny. And food. We'll bring the hinny back but then we need a place to hide for a day or two."

Vsadnik removed his hat to wipe his brow and looked back at the house. "What you're asking is dangerous. I might be able to give you a hinny for a few days as well as some food. It would go unnoticed since the supply line is closed, but I have guerrillas coming through here all the time. If either side is looking for you and they found you here, they'd kill us all. They'd figure I was a part of whatever went down."

Bollard knew the man was just trying to look out for his family and respected it, but he wasn't going to give up. "If we could find a hiding place nearby but not on your property, it might reduce the risk. We'll be there only long enough for our friend to recover, then we'll be on our way."

"I'll need to think about it," Vsadnik sighed. "When you return the hinny, come back to this same location at the same time. I'll try to figure something out. How long before you'll be back?"

"Based on how long it took to get here and with a wounded man, I'd estimate four days."

"Got it. You wait up against the hill there," Vsadnik pointed toward a thicket. "I'll get some supplies and load a hinny."

This had gone far better than Bollard had dared hope. As he watched the skinner walk toward the house, he wondered if he'd receive the same warm reception later, when he returned with the others. Suddenly, the skinner remembered something and turned on his heel to walk back.

"If you haven't heard, there may be other issues on the horizon," he said when he was back in earshot.

"Really?"

"We think there will be a greater concentration of Soviet forces soon throughout the Caucasus."

Bollard furrowed his brow. "What's happened here to cause an increase in Soviet forces?"

"Nothing's happened here. It's what's happened in Afghanistan."

Chapter 21
Passion

Ten was awake and aware as he watched Sulundik intently. She was busy at the fire, preparing another can of stew and doing her best to ignore him. Neither of them had mentioned the kiss from the day before. Sulundik doubted he even remembered, and she wasn't going to force anything.

Ten cleared his throat. "So, how long have you been a woman?"

The absurdity of the question took her off guard. She raised her head and shot him a quick look. "About three days," she answered. She barely restrained a laugh as Ten went from interest to confusion to concern.

"Is that so?" he choked out, wondering whether he should have asked the question.

Sulundik did laugh this time, louder and much harder than she meant to. After a moment, Ten joined in with a chuckle.

"No... and yes. It's a long story," she said.

Ten squinted up at the afternoon sky. "I think I may be able to spare the time."

Sulundik let out one last breathy laugh. She stirred the stew and considered how she would explain herself to him. When she began to speak, she only meant to explain the concept of a bacha posh, but soon, she was telling him everything. She talked about her sisters, her childhood in Chimkent, her uncle, the crimes of Erasyl, when she was forced into becoming Ulzhan, and how she escaped by joining the Mujahideen.

She continued to talk as she fed him his stew, and all the while Ten listened and continued to watch her. It wasn't the same as the dreamy stare he had the day before, but the deep, inquisitive eyes of someone who cared. Someone she had fallen for, the friend she had always wanted to share everything with and was finally allowed to. It was almost dark when she finally trailed off. It took another few minutes before she realized she was still looking into his eyes. She swallowed and busied herself by playing with the lid of the long-emptied can. "And now, I suppose you know everything," she said.

Ten settled back against the trunk and closed his eyes. "Somehow, I doubt that."

"You do?" she smiled.

They lapsed into a comfortable silence, disturbed only by the rustling leaves of the forest as a breeze drifted over them. "Tell me about yourself," she said softly.

"As far as I am aware, I have always been a man." Ten winked. "Let's save it for another time. When I'm feeling better, I'll tell you everything."

The next day, most of the color returned to Ten's face, and despite Sulundik's concerns, he was able to stand. He walked gingerly around the hide site, stretching and testing his range of motion. His wound was healing nicely, the infection subsiding with the antibiotics.

"I've always been a quick healer," Ten said, flashing a grin that should not have made her heart pound. He only complained of the lingering ringing in his ear and the spike of pain that occasionally drove itself through his head at random.

Enough of his strength had returned for Sulundik to spend most of the day catching him up to speed on their situation and Bollard's plan. They discussed alternatives and contingencies, and who they may be able to call upon for assistance should they get the chance.

The temperature took a sudden plunge as the sun sank below the horizon. Building a fire was too risky at night, and though both Sulundik and Ten sat shivering in their jackets, neither of them wanted to take that risk. Sulundik was resigning herself to a sleepless night, when Ten suggested, "We should share body heat."

Sulundik's heart leaped into her throat. "What?" she asked, hoping the squeak in her voice could be blamed on the cold. Ten opened his jacket and beckoned her in.

Realizing what he meant, Sulundik drew closer. She folded herself against his chest, careful to avoid his wound. The difference was instantaneous. Heat radiated from Ten's body and pushed away the chill. "Much better," Ten sighed.

"Much," she echoed, but it took a little more effort for Sulundik. His scent, unwashed as it was, completely enveloped her. She could hear every breath as he inhaled and exhaled, and every place her body touched his increased her desire for him. It was overwhelming, if not torturous. It was agony, wonderful agony.

If she could hear Ten's thoughts, she would have heard his own agonizing. It had only been three days since he had discovered his friend and compatriot was the intoxicating young woman huddled against him. He couldn't help but feel that it should take longer, much longer, to develop a pull towards someone whom he had considered to be a man for so long. He could blame it on the fever, on her laugh or spirit. Ultimately, he blamed it on those almond eyes, those damnable almond eyes that had haunted him as the infection ran its course and softened whenever she looked at him.

The following sunrise marked the fourth day Bollard was gone. If he did not return in the next twenty-four hours, Sulundik and Ten would move to the alternate site.

"Can you make it to the alternate site?" Sulundik asked Ten when the sun reached its zenith.

Ten, recognizing this was not the time for bravado, lifted a shoulder. "I'm feeling better. I think so," he said truthfully. "But we'll need to try for it regardless."

Sulundik frowned. "Let me see your wound," she said.

Ten offered her a crooked smile. "If you are looking for me to remove my shirt..."

In one of Allah's many mercies, Sulundik managed to keep her gaze level and unamused. Though his smile did not retreat, Ten complied. He sat on the edge of the tree trunk as she bent over him and peeled back the bandage. It had not completely scabbed over, but there wasn't any sign of oozing. Ten's muscles twitched wherever Sulundik's fingers brushed him as she probed around the wound.

When she glanced down at him, she stopped. In the time she'd known him, she'd never seen this expression on his face before. He looked pained, thoughtful, and vulnerable, all at the same time.

"You know," he said slowly, "you kiss very well for being a man most of your life."

Sulundik reacted like she had been stung. She snatched her hand back "I- how?" Her words blended and strangled each other in her throat. Ten caught her fingers and kept her from leaping away from him. "I'm sorry," she finally managed to say.

"What for? There are many worse things in life than waking to the attention of a beautiful woman."

"I-I shouldn't have," she stuttered. "You were ill and confused, I..." Ten started to stroke her fingers and she quickly lost her train of thought. He tugged her closer and she willingly stepped forward. He slipped his fingers into her hair as he had done before and gently bent her head down to kiss him. When their lips met, it was more intentional. He was firm but undemanding, sealing his want into the kiss. Sulundik felt as if someone had ignited the blood in her veins as she responded with desire.

Ten lifted his other hand and fumbled at the buttons of her shirt. She broke his touch. "We can't," she gasped.

If Ten's eyes were dark before, they were the color of obsidian now. "Why not?"

"Because," Sulundik gestured helplessly at the surrounding forest, "there are Soviets in these woods, we are being hunted by our former comrades. Because we need clear judgement, because we are in the middle of a forest and..."

"Seven," Ten interrupted, his voice becoming somewhat somber. "You are one of the best strategists I have ever met. Even if the American returns tomorrow, what's the probability of us making it out alive?"

Sulundik's squeezed her eyes shut. "Low," she whispered.

Ten replied seriously, "We are a man and a woman who desire each other. I don't know how you feel, but I would like to live each moment like it's my last." He removed his hand from her hair and folded his hands over hers. "But the choice is yours."

Sulundik inhaled sharply. She had wanted him for so long, and he was right. She leaned forward and pressed her mouth into his, pouring every last grain of desire and affection she had into that kiss. Ten eagerly met her and pulled her to his chest, barely noticing the pain of his injury. He gently positioned her until she was on her back in the makeshift bed, and he was on top of her. When he went for her buttons again, she didn't resist.

Much later, Sulundik nestled her head into the crook of Ten's neck and sighed. He stroked her shoulder and watched as the stars began to reveal themselves. She whispered something and he felt a hunger and a deeper longing for her.

He drifted off with Sulundik's body entwined with his. It would be easy for him to pretend it was just about the sex, but he knew this was different. It was both exhilarating and frightening as he realized he had never had such deep feelings before in his life.

Chapter 22
Common Purpose

Ten and Sulundik were sanitizing the hide site, removing any evidence of their stay, when the screech of a startled jay sent them both to their rifles. They watched as two jays flew directly overhead from the northeast indicating the direction of the alarm.

They could see movement through the trees. It was Alpha, leading a pack animal in a long zigzag direction. He led the hinny into a draw and tied it to a tree. He removed several containers and unfastened the sawbuck before entering the hide site.

He grinned when he saw Ten standing. "Looks like you're feeling much better!"

"Thanks to the two of you," Ten replied and sat down.

Bollard placed the bags on the ground and partially opened them. "There's plenty of food here, cheese and sausage."

Both Sulundik and Ten greedily reached inside the separate bags and started eating hungrily. Bollard noticed how closely they sat next to each other, knees almost but not quite touching. It seemed an aura had enveloped them. It was apparent the two had come to terms with their feelings. Bollard was happy he had encouraged Sulundik to express her feelings but hadn't considered the potential downside. In another parlance, there was now an in-group of two and an out-group of one, Bollard being the out-group. He sat down across from them and cut a slice of hard cheese.

"So," he addressed Ten, "I take it Sulundik has filled you in on our situation?"

Ten furrowed his brow. "Sulundik?"

"It's my real name," she said quietly.

"Sulundik," Ten repeated the name and regarded her for a moment. He turned his attention back to Bollard. "Oh, yes, not many options. How did you get the food and the mule? Why the mule?"

Bollard offered an enigmatic smile. "Ten, you're not the only one with connections. And the hinny was for you. We can't stay here any longer and I thought we might have to carry you out."

"Thanks to you two, it won't be necessary," Ten said as he flashed a soft smile at Sulundik.

Bollard searched for any tell-tale look or response. He got it. Sulundik blushed, leaned against Ten, and smiled happily at Bollard. Aw, hell. Indeed, there was an in-group.

"Have you two discussed options?" Bollard asked. "Ten, what dependable contacts do you have, and what courses of action do you recommend?"

Ten thought for a minute as if trying to decide whether to divulge his circumstance. "I'm wanted by the KGB and the GRU," he admitted. "The guerrillas, as well as the militants, are after each of us. The Ossetians would like to get their hands on us as well, and we can't count on the Ingush or any others who are part of the Regional Command. I have numerous contacts, but they were only viable when I had value to them. Now my only value is the bounty on my head." He paused for a moment. "I could move south and deeper into Georgia and away from the region," he thought aloud. "But with little hope of success. I'd likely be intercepted."

"What about you Sulundik?" Bollard asked.

"I've stated before if I could get to Azerbaijan, I might be able to elude the authorities."

Bollard was silent, then, "Each of you has said 'I' when referring to an escape. What is your preference? Do we evade as a group or split?" Both Ten and Sulundik shifted and glanced at each other. "It appears to me you two are likely to stay together," Bollard said mildly.

"Yes," they both responded automatically.

"Then where do I fit in? Shall I evade alone? Do we remain a group of three? There are advantages and disadvantages."

Ten considered for a moment. "We've survived well as a group of three. Our combat capability as three is superior. I think we remain strongest as three."

Sulundik agreed.

Ten pressed Bollard, "Do you have a plan?"

"I have a plan. It's difficult," he said, slowly eyeing them. "But I need to be sure you're with me. There's a level of trust I must have, and we need to put aside any pretenses."

"Agreed," Ten said.

Bollard leaned back, satisfied, "Let's start with our names. What are we going to call one another? We can't continue with codenames, especially if we come into contact with civilians."

"Grigori," Ten said simply.

Sulundik repeated his name to herself and smiled.

"Is that your real name?" Bollard asked.

"Yes." Grigori gestured for his turn. "And Alpha, what's your name?"

"Matvey," Bollard replied, using the Russian form of his name. "And it's my real name."

Bollard waved his hand at the two of them. "Is this going to be a problem?" he asked bluntly.

"What do you mean?" Sulundik asked.

"I mean, we can't have two united against the third when we need to make tough decisions. Again, there must be a level of trust between all of us."

Grigori could see Bollard was hesitant and was ready to pull out at any time unless he offered up something real. He had to establish an undisputed level of trust between them.

"You saved my life at the ambush," he told him. "Life takes some ironic turns; you and I have a common past."

Bollard seemed genuinely surprised. "How so?"

"Now I want to be completely forthcoming on everything," he said warningly.

"Go on."

"Indirectly, we've met twice before, prior to your arrival in Chechnya."

"Twice?" Bollard replied without showing his surprise or keen interest.

"Yes," Grigori replied cautiously. "Once in Afghanistan and once in East Germany."

Sulundik pulled back and watched things play out with a wary eye. Things could get nasty, quickly.

Bollard kept his expression blank and body language neutral. "That's hard to believe; that we would cross paths three times."

Grigori leaned forward in an earnest posture. "Matvey, it's true. I want you to know everything so you can rely on my word as we go forward."

Bollard now looked puzzled.

Grigori closed his eyes and took a deep breath before he took the plunge. "From a distance, I watched as you executed a Russian colonel, a prisoner of the Mujahideen. I was injured, hiding among the rocks, and watched from the hillside. If I had a rifle, I would have killed you." He opened his eyes and leveled his gaze at Bollard. "But then I realized you executed the colonel to save him from agonizing torture at the hands of the Afghans."

Bollard could hardly contain his surprise at the revelation. "You said there were two instances."

"In East Germany," Grigori affirmed. "You and your driver were ambushed. I'm the one who killed your driver." His voice wavered for the briefest second, but he forged on. "But I recognized you from Afghanistan. Because of what I saw in Afghanistan, I disobeyed my orders and did not kill you." He let out a wry chuckle. "By saving your life then, I'm alive today."

Bollard was more intrigued than angry. "Spetsnaz?"

"Yes."

As Sulundik listened, she came to the sinking realization that the man with whom she had made love, who had stolen her heart, was once her enemy; and worse, a Spetsnaz. She unconsciously shifted away from him.

"Operating with the Stasi?" Bollard asked.

"Yes," Grigori answered.

Bollard allowed himself a triumphant smile. "I thought so; figured Stasi and GRU were involved. Well, your intelligence was wrong."

Grigori furrowed his brow. "What do you mean?"

"I was not the officer the Stasi or GRU targeted; I was a substitute for another officer that day. The man the GRU and Stasi targeted was actually in Berlin. We exchanged operational positions at the last minute."

"You're joking."

"Furthermore, you didn't kill the driver."

Grigori found that hard to believe. "But I saw him," he protested, "the blood on the windshield."

"You shot him in the arm, and he wrecked the vehicle. He slammed his nose into the steering wheel, splattering blood everywhere," Bollard replied.

"I'm happy to hear it was a bad shot," Grigori said, relieved.

"What was the reason, the rationale for killing two Americans?"

"It was to create a political shit storm between our two countries and end the ongoing arms control negotiations. Stasi chose the targets. My involvement put me on the wrong side of the government and the KGB and made me a wanted man with a bounty. So, I chose to live another day among the Chechens."

Bollard frowned suspiciously. "But why tell us this now? You know Sulundik is Afghan, and you can't be sure of my response."

"You're the one who said to drop the pretense. I don't want to sink our low chances of survival even further. I want you to know everything so we can completely trust each other. If we can't, we need to separate. Then none of us has much of a chance."

Bollard processed this and turned his attention to Sulundik. "Why Azerbaijan? Was it your plan to return to Afghanistan?"

"It was..." Sulundik looked sidelong at Grigori.

Bollard interrupted her. "Perhaps this will help you decide. The Soviets are pulling out of Afghanistan. My contact advised me of this change in Soviet policy."

Grigori shook his head. "That's incredible! This means the military will shift its attention to the Caucasus. This region will become even more dangerous."

"That's right."

All three fell silent, with Sulundik deep in thought. Her mission to Chechnya was to pull Soviet attention away from Afghanistan by assisting with and fomenting revolution in the Caucasus. Was she successful? Had she contributed to a Soviet withdrawal? What now?

She could return to Afghanistan, but how would she be treated? Relegated again to second-class citizenship? Forever a posh? Could she recover from the knowledge of Grigori's past; that the two may have fought against each other in Afghanistan? It wasn't Grigori, she rationalized, who relegated her to a stereotypical subservient position. It certainly wasn't the American. It wasn't he who challenged her ability because of her gender, whether she operated as a soldier, a member of a guerrilla force, or a person in love. Indeed, it was her people, her culture, and her country who forced her into taking on and adopting a false identity. Everything she had achieved was not permitted of a woman.

If Grigori remained with her, the two would never be accepted in her homeland. They could never return. Grigori had been a hated enemy and she had seen and accomplished too much since being away. Grigori was the tie that bound her; Grigori, and her newfound peace with her identity, the person she longed to be. She could never return to Afghanistan, and she was content.

After several minutes she said, "Yes, it was Afghanistan. That was my original plan. But now," she looked at Grigori, "Azerbaijan is the only option."

"Azerbaijan," Grigori concurred.

She took Grigori's arm and turned to Bollard. "We'll remain in Azerbaijan if we can get there."

"Matvey, we've played all our cards, perhaps to our detriment," Grigori said to Bollard. "What's your hand? What's your plan to escape? I know your people would never deploy you here without an extraction plan. Do you agree to a group of three as part of your plan?"

"Yes. I feel we're stronger as three. But if there is an instance when you feel splitting up is better, I won't resist," Bollard said looking at each of them. "Operating as a group, Sulundik shouldn't have to hide her gender," he added. "It might even work to our advantage." Bollard looked over his shoulder at the pack animal. "First, we'll return the hinny, then hide and rest before we make our way southeast to Azerbaijan."

"How will we get food and water?" Sulundik asked.

"When I infiltrated, we used a well-hidden supply route that included caches of food and supplies. I have a mental picture of where those caches are located. Because of the turmoil and infighting, I've learned the guerrillas have shut down the supply route; at least for now. We might be able to take advantage of it."

"Dangerous," Grigori observed.

"Yes," Bollard concurred. "Very dangerous and not a high likelihood of success. But it's the only chance we have. Are we agreed?"

"Agreed."

***

Bollard, Grigori, and Sulundik arrived at the edge of the field where Bollard previously met the muleskinner. Vsadnik was waiting at the edge of the field with several sacks at his feet.

"I thought, based on the timing we discussed, today would be the day," he said to Bollard. "Was hoping you'd get here early."

Bollard noted the look of concern in the skinner's eyes. "Has something happened? What's wrong, Vsadnik?"

"There are three guerrillas in my house. They stayed up drinking last night and are sound asleep." Vsadnik glanced over his shoulder. "They're pretty edgy and expecting three more this evening. They say they'll leave in the morning." He turned his focus back to Bollard. "They won't say who or what they're looking for, but I don't think it bodes well for you." Vsadnik looked over Bollard's shoulder to the others and acknowledged them.

"Well, here's your baby as promised," Bollard said, handing the skinner the reins.

The skinner nudged one of the sacks with his boot. "I've put these sacks of food together. It should hold you for two or three days if you go easy."

Bollard took the three bags and handed two to Sulundik and Grigori. "Which direction will the other guerrillas arrive this evening?"

"I don't know. Probably from the north but couldn't swear to it."

"Do you know where they'll go?"

"I don't know, but you should get as much distance as you can."

"I was thinking we'd return from the direction we came."

Vsadnik offered a knowing smile and winked, "Back to the southwest."

Bollard returned the smile. "Yes. Southwest." Bollard extended his hand one last time. "I won't forget you, Vsadnik, my friend."

"Nor will I forget you." Vsadnik shook his hand, then walked back through the field and up the hill with the hinny in tow, never looking back.

Bollard turned to the others. "Let's go."

"Southeast?" Sulundik asked.

"Southeast."

***

Except for a couple of short stops for water and to check Grigori's wound, they moved at a near run for three hours parallel to but away from the supply trail. Bollard glanced at his watch and a frown crept over his face. It was dangerously past time to stop. They needed to find a daytime hide site and remain there until dark. He signaled for the others to follow and jumped down a steep ravine, away from the trail and well hidden from anyone walking along it.

"We'll stay here the rest of the day and leave as soon as it gets dark," Bollard said. "Eat, rest and sleep. Tomorrow, there may be an opportunity for a shortcut if we stay on this route. We'll discuss it when we get there."

Grigori and Sulundik sat and ate morsels from the supply bags. Then they leaned into each other and shut their eyes. Bollard, for his part, was focused neither on sleep nor food, but on getting a message to headquarters.

"You two get some rest, I've got to send a signal to my headquarters," Bollard said as he picked up his bag and walked to the south side of the mountain.

He looked out over the long steep valley below until he spotted a gap in the mountains. It was as good a spot as he was going to find for sending a signal. Bollard put the transmitter together, cut a microdot from his foot, and created a coded message. He then stretched out the directional wire and pointed it high in the sky and at the middle of the gap in the mountains. Ideally, his transmission signal would 'skip' by bouncing off the ionosphere, and friendly forces would be standing by to receive the message.

The coded message was brief. It included Bollard's identifier and the second part of his mission, the MRNC status. Specifically, he advised his leadership that the Chechen Area Command was compromised, and Ossetia was not participating in unified action. His mission was to retrieve intelligence regarding the MRNC and report on its legitimacy. Whoever made the policy decision to recognize the organization or distance themselves based on his intelligence collection was not his problem.

The sound of a dog barking viciously nearby caused Bollard to quickly end his message with a five-letter code word – OLIVE.

Chapter 23
OLIVE

Technical Sergeant Pablo 'Pancho' Gonzalez, USAF, turned the page in his career development manual, yawned, and cast an eye to the chessboard as his duty buddy was about to expose the white king to a black bishop.

"Jerry, sure you want to do that?" he commented as he turned back to his manual.

His buddy repositioned and took a second look at the board. Other than the routine maintenance start and check of the auxiliary generators, coordination with local Turkish security, and an occasional review of radio signals, it was the most excitement the two men usually got during an entire shift.

Located in western Turkey's Bolu province, rising above the Köroğlu mountain range and just south of the Black Sea, a sixty-four-meter tower barely broke the skyline with its multiple parabolic dishes. Several auxiliary generators as well as supply, latrine, and operational buildings formed a semicircle around the tower. The operational building consisted of two rooms, one housing a wall of receivers, transmitters, and huge computers. It included multiple tape drives and a tape data selector with recorded, stored, and transmitted data. The other room was designed as a planning room which served more as a break area.

The duty was typical, monotonous, and boring. Until an anomalous communications signal interrupted their chess match and triggered an alert.

Pancho quickly yanked on his headphones and sat next to a receiver. Both men were quiet as he tuned in to the radio channel.

Pancho frowned. "I've got a continuous line of static. It must have been a non-repetitive one-time delivery." Without looking up, he raised a hand and made a circular motion. "Rewind the tape to five minutes and play."

Jerry rewound the tape until the display showed the five-minute increment. "Playing."

Pancho waited and listened again to the static, breaks, and interference; standard radio frequency patterns. The alert indicated the static and breaks had a rhythmic pattern over a unique duration. One not seen in nature, but a hand-initiated transmission. Suddenly his eyes widened as he waved to Jerry to record the increment on the tape.

"That's it, morse. Rewind to the start point and begin again."

Jerry initiated the second playback of the transmission as Pancho recorded the coded morse message.

"Here it is," Pancho held up the paper with the code. "I'll transmit this message directly to headquarters and advise a transmission is forthcoming. You retrans the actual signal, just in case."

Jerry was prepared to carry out the instruction when Pancho stopped him.

"Wait a minute. This isn't routine," Pancho said as he read it again and handed the paper to Jerry. "Everything is coded but check out the last group of letters. It's in the clear."

Jerry looked at it. "Live?"

"No, it's set up in five-letter code groups. Check the letter before it."

"O... Olive?"

"Before we transmit, check for a codeword OLIVE in the codebook."

Jerry walked to a safe located in the corner, spun the dial the requisite times, opened the heavy door, and removed a notebook. It was a heavy blue binder, marked with numerous classifications, and three inches thick. He opened it, turned to a section in the middle, and ran his finger down the list of codewords. "Here it is! It has specific trans and retrans instructions. Not our normal lines of communication."

Pancho reviewed the codeword instructions carefully, "It's an extraction!"

Chapter 24
Capture

Bollard had been away for a couple of hours when Sulundik snapped awake. She shot up halfway and surveyed the surroundings. It was a few hours before dark. She wasn't quite sure what had awakened her, perhaps a dream. She pulled her hat further down on her face and shut her eyes momentarily. She was startled awake some moments later to see three men shoving their rifles in her face.

"Hands up!" one ordered.

Another jerked a rope tethered to a large, short-haired dog that began jumping, barking, and snapping viciously at Sulundik and Grigori.

"Good boy, good boy." The dog's owner yanked him back and held him around the neck.

The other two shouted orders in overlapping voices. "Keep your hands raised! Stand up! Turn around!"

With no other options available, Grigori and Sulundik complied and the men quickly tied their hands behind their backs.

Sulundik cast a rueful look at the dog.

One of the men saw it. "That's right! That's right!" he said triumphantly. "He led us right here. Picked up your scent and didn't bark once, until now! Good boy, good boy!"

"We're guerrillas too," Grigori shouted. "What are you doing?"

"We know who you are!" one of them spat. "There are bounties on your heads. Everyone is after you!"

The leader, the one with the dog, stiffened and whirled around. "There were three of you! Where's the other?" he demanded.

"Dead," Sulundik replied. "Died of his wounds."

The man narrowed his eyes. "If he's dead, where's the body?"

"We threw him over the precipice, two kilometers back," Grigori lied.

"You didn't bury him?"

314

"Why should we? So, you could find a grave?"

The leader directed the third man to search the area for the missing person. He gave a cursory glance around and returned. "Nothing."

Sulundik tried another option. "Take us to the Chechen guerrilla chief, Four. He'll vouch for us."

"He has a bounty on you too." The man shrugged. "But you're not going there. We're taking you to the Soviets."

Grigori couldn't believe what he was hearing. "Soviets? What do you have to do with them? Why not to your people?"

Sulundik was equally surprised. "We've fought for years against the Soviets!"

"Exactly." All three of the men smiled greedily. "The Soviets will pay more money! It's all about the rubles."

Sulundik's voice was faint. "You're not guerrillas?"

"We work with them when they need us, or we need them."

"So, you're bounty hunters, mercenaries," Grigori scoffed.

Their leader shrugged. "Makes no difference. Right now, we're going to make a ruble and you're the trade."

Sulundik was disgusted. She'd seen these types of men before, many times. Untrustworthy scum whose principles were available to the highest bidder. "You're right," she said. "Makes no difference because both have two things in common."

"Yeah? Well, what's that?"

"Be careful," Grigori muttered.

Sulundik ignored him and frowned, "They don't get paid, but they always get their due."

The man raised his rifle to slam it against Sulundik's face, then thought better of it. "Shut the hell up and start moving." He stuck his rifle in her back and prodded them up the hill to the trail and headed southeast; in the direction Sulundik, Grigori, and Bollard had planned to travel that night.

***

From afar, Bollard watched as the bounty hunters escorted Grigori and Sulundik from the hide site. He was a hundred meters away, but it was too risky to engage all three bounty hunters. With the potential of a greater force being nearby, the chance of ricochets among the rocks hitting his people, coupled with the likelihood he would not be able to kill all three, discretion was the rule.

He had just completed his radio message when he heard the dog barking and quickly sent the extraction code word. Everything in his gut told him this was more than a wandering hunter or a wild dog stumbling on the hide site. He hid and watched it all play out. They were starting to walk away when the dog suddenly turned and saw him. It didn't bark and Bollard didn't move. The bounty hunter didn't notice the dog's alert and yanked the leash as they walked away.

It was fortunate they were headed southeast in the direction Bollard originally intended, toward a cache site he had stopped on his insertion. He followed at a safe distance watching every step. They moved in a file with the leader and dog in the front, followed by Grigori, the second bounty hunter, Sulundik, and then the third bounty hunter who trailed behind.

Bollard noted the trailing bounty hunter seldom looked to the rear and remained focused on his prisoners. Yet, it would be nearly impossible to rescue them from the rear, Bollard reasoned. It was just too dangerous. He recalled the hidden rope bridge located along the way to the cache site. If he traversed the chasm on the rope, he could save as much as five hours, and could set up an ambush.

After several kilometers and just before dark, Bollard arrived at the crossing site. During his infiltration, he had seen a mule team stretch a rope across a hundred meters of the crevasse between the two hills. The mules kept the rope sufficiently tight for the guerrillas to move equipment across, but no one wanted to cross themselves.

Bollard needed not only to locate the rope but stretch it taut to support his weight without sagging. Unlike the guerrillas, he had no mules to tighten the rope. He recalled where he had seen the mules and the rope on the near and far sides of the crevasse and began searching. He searched down the side of the hill until he found a pile of brush that seemed out of place. He removed the brush and found the coiled rope that served as a traversing rope.

He pulled on the portion of rope that ran down the precipice and to the far side. He thought he might be able to tie a prusik tightening system that would allow him to stretch the rope, slide the prusik knot to lock the rope, rest, then pull again. However, there was simply too much rope and it was too heavy to raise and pull across the chasm. Even if he was successful in moving such a large amount of rope, it would take the entire night just to tighten it enough to cross.

He uncoiled the rope and pulled it around a huge tree to serve as an anchor. He then walked to the edge of the precipice and paralleled it. He tried multiple boulders and fallen trees, but most were too large or positioned too poorly to support his plan. He needed luck, and he got it. A log lay precariously close to the edge and was supported only by a small amount of rock and dirt. He cut off several meters of rope to use later as a harness, then pulled as much slack as possible. He then tied the rope securely to the log.

He pushed on it. Nothing. Working from the backside of the log, he began digging underneath the small portion that was keeping it in place. Using a stick, he dug and pushed dirt through the opposite side, then repeated the process. Two hours later and well after dark, the tree showed signs of slipping. Bollard used his legs to push, but manpower alone would never move this log. It would take gravity, and more digging to move it. He continued for two more hours when suddenly the log gave way and swung around, barely missing him. It plummeted down the precipice. The slack in the rope snapped tight like a guitar string, but it didn't break. It held. Importantly, the traversing rope was taut across the width of the crevasse.

Chapter 25
Auxiliary Encounter

The cache site was located adjacent to the main trail in a relatively protected area at the end of a long crevasse; it was the same cache site where Bollard had arrived on his insertion and manned by three young auxiliary members. The bounty hunters knew it would be well-supplied and offered a safe place to spend the night.

They arrived at the cache site well after dark and shoved Sulundik and Grigori to the ground. Two auxiliary members, servicing the cache site, turned to confer with a third member who had intercepted the bounty hunters and escorted them.

After some hushed discussions, the three stood around the bounty hunters and their captives. A campfire lit the outlines of their faces, revealing the youthfulness of the auxiliary.

"You know you don't walk into a cache site without forewarning the auxiliary, especially if it's after dark," one of the auxiliary chastised.

"We just captured these prisoners and need to spend the night in a safe place. There was no time to notify the command, but we'll make a point of it in the future," the bounty hunter leader replied.

The auxiliary leader approached Grigori and frowned. "These are the prisoners with the bounty on their heads?"

"Yes, we have two of three. The third one is dead."

"I wouldn't advise going too far to the southeast," another of the auxiliary advised. "The Soviets established a temporary garrison across the trail at the Azeri border to support training maneuvers. Don't think they know they've straddled one of our supply routes. Fortunately, we had already shut it down due to the issues with the Chechen Area Command."

"That's where we're going. The Soviets will pay a higher bounty than the guerrillas," the dog handler replied.

Grigori and Sulundik paid careful attention, looking for anything they could use to their advantage, and Sulundik seized the opportunity. "You better have your story straight," she warned. "The Russians have a way of seeing through

318

subterfuge. You'll have to answer how you came into contact with guerrillas in the first place."

"Shut your mouth. It's our business," the leader said, quick to shut her down.

To draw the auxiliary into the discussion she continued, "If even the slightest suspicion is turned this way, the Russians will torture you until you lead them to this very cache site. The entire local population will be suspect. The auxiliary will be shut down in this region, if not annihilated."

Grigori sensed the change in the demeanor of the auxiliary men and sneered, "The Russians have no loyalty to three bounty hunters and they'll want more. These three," he jerked his head toward the bounty hunters, "will compromise themselves and betray each of you."

The bounty hunter kicked Grigori in the head. "I told you to shut up!"

One of the auxiliary members stepped between Grigori and the bounty hunter, pushing him back. "He makes sense! You can't guarantee the Russians will let you leave. They could force you to compromise this location."

"Look, we've been doing this for years." The leader dismissed him, "You three are too young to understand."

This was absolutely the wrong thing to say. "Well understand this..." the eldest of the auxiliary bristled. "You aren't taking these prisoners anywhere until we've conferred with our leadership! We'll be back by midmorning with your instructions."

Sulundik saw another opening. "When you talk to your leadership, be sure to advise them that these three have been arguing how they're going to split the reward."

One of the bounty hunters also tried to kick Sulundik, but a member of the auxiliary stepped between them.

"No, you don't! There will be no more prisoner beating at this cache site." He turned to Sulundik, "Go on..."

Sulundik continued, "They're arguing and fighting among themselves over how they're going to split the reward three ways. We know all funds go to the guerrillas, the auxiliary, and the underground, and then the rest is parceled out. These three can't keep it all, but they have every intention of doing so and violating our rules for disbursement."

Suddenly, the site erupted into loud accusations, denials, and threats. Grigori, head throbbing from the kick, marveled at how well Sulundik manipulated both groups to bring on the ensuing chaos.

As the shouting faded, and the bounty hunters assured them they would follow the rules for disbursement, Grigori added to their confusion and addressed the auxiliary men.

"These three idiots have the wrong people," he cried, adopting a regional accent. "They know the Chechen guerrillas won't pay for the wrong people, but the Russians will pay for information on any guerrillas. My wife and I were picking mushrooms when these three imbeciles stumbled upon us. The people who are wanted are three men. There are only two of us here and one is my wife. They've taken the wrong people!"

This information surprised and confused the auxiliary as well as the bounty hunters. One of the bounty hunters ran to Sulundik and removed her hat and held her face up to the light of the fire.

"Shit," he said as he thrust his hand between her legs and then pushed her back to the ground. "My God! She's a woman! All this time!"

It was as if someone flipped a switch on their depravity and the bounty hunters lost it. One pulled and ripped at her jacket and shirt, revealing her breasts. He then climbed on top of her and buried his face between her breasts.

Grigori shouted, "She's my wife you bastard!"

The leader pushed past the young auxiliary men and knocked the first out of the way. "I'll give her what she needs." He unbuttoned his pants and stuck his penis against her face as she turned her head. He grabbed her and tried to force her toward him.

The auxiliary men had enough. They pointed their weapons at the bounty hunters and pushed the leader away from Sulundik. "We'll kill the three of you right here if you don't stand down! What the hell is wrong with you," one shouted, as the others looked as if they might shoot at any time.

The out-of-control emotions triggered the dog. He growled, jumped, and snapped at everyone. "Get that dog under control or I'll kill him now."

The bounty hunter leader put his hands out. "It's fine. Settle down! No harm done. Just a little over-exuberance. Besides, she's a prisoner and will be dead in a few days. We could even take turns with her," he offered.

"When you come to our cache site you conduct yourselves honorably."

"Understand... understand," the bounty hunter replied with his hands still raised slightly.

"We're going to go to the leadership, and they'll decide what is to be done. In the interim, don't harm or touch these prisoners," the leader of the auxiliary group commanded. "We're not even sure they're the ones who are wanted. We'll return mid to late morning."

"Sure, sure... we'll be waiting."

Grigori cursed himself for revealing Sulundik's gender. He assumed the bounty hunters knew she was a woman, and that it was an angle that might save their lives. He also anticipated the auxiliary would leave one person to remain at the cache site, or even be convinced to release them. Instead, they left Grigori and Sulundik alone with three ruthless men, undeterred by their promises to the auxiliary.

As the auxiliary men departed, the three bounty hunters looked at each other and the leader smiled.

"We'll be long gone before they get back."

"Won't the auxiliary leadership demand an explanation?"

The leader made a dismissive gesture. "It's our word against those three young punks. What could they possibly know? Besides, if we must, we'll give the leadership a share of our money and they'll be fine with it. I have no intention of coming back this way." He then turned his attention to Sulundik. "As for you, we'll rest tonight, but tomorrow night I'll be the first to take you."

His companion protested. "Come on! I found her! I should be the first!"

"Shut up!" he growled. "You two will draw straws for her."

Sulundik stared at them angrily, "The last man who tried to force himself on me... I fed him to the wolves!"

The leader laughed. "You have spirit! Good. This will be an enjoyable tussle." He cast a meaningful look at Grigori. "After tomorrow night, when we've had our way with her, we may decide you're too dangerous to keep around. Remember, the Russians don't care what shape you're in when we turn you over. They just want you alive." He shrugged. "We'll see."

Grigori only glared at him in response. His every nerve begged for a few seconds alone with this man.

One of the men looked over his shoulder, "They could have left one to watch us from the hillside."

The leader smiled, "We'll leave before daylight."

Chapter 26
Payback

Bollard checked the anchor tree and the traversing rope which he had positioned perfectly. However, he had worked for four hours until almost midnight trying to unseat the log and he was exhausted. He would have to rest for an hour to have enough energy to pull himself across. He rested while standing. It was too dangerous to sit or lie down; he might fall asleep and not awaken before it was too late to carry out the rescue.

An hour later, he made a makeshift harness that secured him at the hips and waist. He tied his rifle and pack together and looped them over the crossing rope. He then looped another rope next to it and tied it to his harness. There was no time to wonder if the rope, stretched taut by a log hanging precariously over the precipice, was at its breaking point. Lying back and supporting his weight in the harness, he pulled himself hand over hand on the crossing rope, his feet dangling beneath him. It was a painful process, moving across the deep ravine. Bollard pulled himself one meter, then pulled the rifle and pack forward. He repeated the process over one hundred times until he traversed to the far side. It was difficult and he was cramping in every muscle.

On the other side and just a couple of meters from the ground, he unsheathed his knife and cut his harness, pack, and rifle free from the rope. He paused to take a final look, then cut the crossing rope which sprang like a slingshot and dropped into the ravine behind the once-suspended log.

***

Morning brought greater visibility, permitting Bollard to search for the optimal ambush site. Farther down the trail he found a good position by a steep precipice in the shadow of the mountain. Bollard could see that the trail cut a swath into the mountain and was marked by such steep banks a person could neither go up nor over the side without injury or death. Also, there was little protection or cover from incoming rifle fire. Given the wide swath of the trail, each member of the approaching group would expose their flank to Bollard's position. Bollard raised his AK-47 and evaluated the range. The 7.62mm round could reach four hundred meters, and he practiced routinely for accuracy at three hundred. The range was optimum.

A brief time later, and seemingly out of nowhere, five figures emerged around the bend in the road. They formed a file, exactly as they had the previous evening. They seemed to be moving slower, and an occasional nudge pushed Grigori forward with a stumble.

Bollard took careful aim at the trailing bounty hunter, exhaled, then squeezed the trigger. He quickly pivoted and fired at the second bounty hunter. As the trailing bounty hunter dropped and in the split second of the sound of the gun, the second bounty hunter turned and took the next round squarely in the chest. Both Grigori and Sulundik immediately dropped to the ground and lay motionless. The leading bounty hunter also took cover on the ground.

Luck was still on Bollard's side as the echo of the rifle reverberated off the mountain on the far side of the crevasse. The lead bounty hunter pointed his rifle in that direction. Bollard shot him in the side. The dog barked and pulled at the leash, still wound tightly around the dead man's hand.

Bollard sprinted along the trail and checked each of the dead men before cutting the ropes that bound Grigori and Sulundik.

"We have to get out of here. Now!" he shouted as he cut Grigori's rope. "Grab your rifles from them."

"By Allah! Where did you come from? How did you get in front of us?" Sulundik asked incredulously.

Grigori stood and stretched his arms. "Get their packs! They're loaded with food."

As they gathered the packs and rifles Sulundik studied the dead bodies. Bollard was preparing to drag the dead men to the edge of the precipice when she stopped him.

"Wait! Don't move them! Position these two in the direction of the leader with their rifles up to their shoulders. And do the same with the leader."

Both Grigori and Bollard sent her questioning looks.

"It's an old trick. It might slow down anyone who comes this way as they try to figure out what happened. The auxiliary men saw the three argue and fight with each other. Regardless, we want them to be found so others will take the time to bury them properly."

They followed her instructions, positioning the two dead men, as Sulundik directed. Bollard went for the leader and his dog, but Sulundik stopped him, her eyes narrowing.

"He's mine!" she growled.

Bollard and Grigori watched transfixed, as she rolled the man over. She pulled down his pants and taking the knife from her backpack, cut off his penis. She then tossed it in the direction of the dog which leaped, snatched it out of the air, and devoured it.

Both Grigori and Bollard gasped.

"I told him I'd feed him to the wolves, but his dog will suffice," Sulundik said simply as she fastened the dead man's pants and rolled him back into a fighting position with his rifle at his shoulder.

Both men wisely held their tongues. Sulundik was not in a trifling mood.

Grigori shook his head. "Hell, he'll haunt this region."

Sulundik stood after wiping the blood on the man's pants legs. "I hope he does. I hope he roams these mountains forever, looking for the dog that ate his dick!"

She took the leash from the dead man's free hand and gave it to Bollard. "What about this fleabag?"

Grigori cursed. "What are you going to do with that damn dog?"

Bollard gave the mutt a cursory glance. "We're taking him with us. He doesn't bark too much and could be useful to us. Besides, if things go badly, we could eat him before he gets too skinny."

With their weapons now in hand and the packs in place, the three of them, along with the dog tugging at the leash, set out at a steady pace down the trail and eventually moved southeast into the forest again.

325

As they moved into the woods, Grigori suddenly grabbed Bollard's arm. "We can't parallel the trail anymore. We learned the Soviet military has blocked the trail at the Azeri border."

Sulundik pointed to the looming, jagged mountain range. "We need to go there, deeper into the mountains."

Bollard led them down the hill in the direction Sulundik had suggested. That complicated his plans for getting the others to Azerbaijan, though it better suited his escape plan.

The group moved at a steady pace all day and night, a full twenty-four-hour march. They stopped near the top of a hill where they could monitor any approaches from a distance.

***

With one hour on security watch and two hours off, Bollard tightened the leash on the dog to feel any indication of an alert and shut his eyes. They rested for most of the day. In the afternoon they pulled some food from their packs and Bollard shared a morsel with the dog. He noticed there was tension between Grigori and Sulundik that hadn't been there before their capture.

"I'm sorry," Grigori eventually said. Something in the way he said it made Bollard wonder if this was the first time those words had ever left his mouth. "I should never have told the bounty hunters we were married."

Realizing a private conversation was going to take place, Bollard turned away, pulled his hat over his eyes, and leaned against a tree to provide some semblance of privacy for the two. He still could not avoid overhearing.

Grigori continued, "I didn't know I was revealing you. I thought they knew."

"You couldn't know," Sulundik sighed. "I thought they knew too. We couldn't predict what they'd try to do." She kicked a nearby pebble. "I'm sure they've done it to others."

"I'm glad the boys in the auxiliary were man enough to stand up to them and protect you."

"It was a good attempt to confuse them. A man and his wife instead of three wanted men," Sulundik said.

"I thought the auxiliary might release us. I just couldn't foresee the depravity of the bounty hunters. I wish I had been the one to kill them." Grigori's voice took on an edge.

Sulundik shifted around to face him, grabbing his hand. "Grigori, when I was a posh, I was never threatened. No one would dare. But I was forced to protect my sisters from similar men. As a woman, I was challenged multiple times. Almost as soon as I gave up my status as a posh, I killed a man who tried to rape me. Later, one sought to challenge me because of my gender, and I humiliated him with my shooting capabilities. Now, just as I emerge again as a woman, I'm sexually assaulted and threatened. Life is so much easier and less risky as a posh, as a man. Will I always have to question the motivations of men?" The question slipped out before she could stop it.

Grigori shook his head. "I won't pretend to know what it's like. Why didn't you remain a posh?"

She looked at him incredulously. "Because of you! I wanted you to know me as a woman. Because I'm in love with you. I'm not going back to life as a posh as long as we're together."

He stared at her for a few moments before a slow, bright smile stretched across his face. He raised their joined hands and kissed her palm. "I love you too."

The two embraced and held each other as Bollard casually rose to scout the perimeter, dog in tow. He looked at the distant mountains as the sun set on his back. He studied the ridges, the valleys, and the peaks, and chartered the night's route due east and through even more extreme terrain.

Chapter 27
Gorsky Jews

Bollard knew the best route through the mountains for concealing their movement would be the most difficult route. However, he didn't anticipate the extreme restriction the thickets, briars, and brambles would cause during the final leg of the night.

On their hands and knees in darkness, the group crawled its way up the steep mountain through entanglements that pulled on their packs and bodies and forced them to alter direction repeatedly. Thorns and briars cut at their flesh and ripped their rapidly deteriorating camouflage uniforms. Bollard gave up on trying to restrain the dog as the leash became entangled. Maintaining any control proved futile. He released the dog and put the leash in his pack. Surprisingly, the dog did not take off ahead but fell between Bollard and Sulundik, content to let Bollard break the trail.

In the early morning hours, they arrived at a piece of flat ground and were able to stand. The thick brush remained an obstacle, but they pushed noisily ahead. At the center point of the saddle, Bollard stepped onto a narrow path that continued toward the easternmost hill. It was nondescript enough, it could have been an animal trail. Exhausted, muscles aching, and their knees raw from crawling, he pointed out the trail to the others.

"I don't like paths, but we'll follow it to the other hill and quit for the night."

The others happily agreed. As he stepped forward, he tripped on the dog, who let out a small yelp. Bollard put the leash on and let him lead them toward the hill. The trail cut circuitously through the waist-high brush before straightening out. Bollard noticed the trail became wider with forks at various points. He hoped to see what he anticipated to be an open area near the base of the hill where they could stop. Something caught his attention to the right and slightly down the hillside. It looked like a structure the size of a small house and he pointed it out to the others. Further along, there was another structure on the opposite side of the hill. They moved cautiously forward another hundred meters when the dog stopped and alerted to the rear. Bollard picked up speed and advised the others. He looked for a way to get off the saddle, but the dog alerted again, this time to the front. Bollard halted as Sulundik and Grigori stopped alongside him.

Suddenly, a pool of lights flooded their faces from the front, and they could hear people approaching from the rear.

"Damn trail," Bollard muttered. It had been like a mermaid's siren to a ship's captain, the animal trail beckoned him, and he followed it right into an unknown threat.

Shouting came from behind as well as in the direction of the lights which merged into an incomprehensible roar. It was obvious they should slowly raise their hands. As they did, men from behind seized their weapons and packs. Bollard was surprised by their numbers, eight men carrying weapons. He understood then that the structures he passed housed security. Those security elements alerted others ahead and allowed the trio to pass. With the terrain so extreme, the security forces simply fell in behind Bollard and the others and followed at a distance. A well-planned and rehearsed response to an approach from the west. He suspected such positions were located all along the mountain's approaches. But why?

Their captors shoved them forward and into the lights. Bollard could see the lights were from a tractor and hand-held spotlights with numerous armed men around them. They forced the trio to their knees.

"What do you want and why are you here?" a voice demanded from beyond the lights.

Sulundik spoke first. "We're refugees."

"We want asylum from the other tribes," Grigori quickly added.

Bollard dug deep into his memory. There was a word; a word the old woman in the safe house back in the states had given him. A word to use specifically in such a situation. He paused, then blurted out, "Habze! Sanctuary! We're seeking sanctuary under Adyghe Habze!"

Sulundik whipped her head around towards Bollard at the sound of the unfamiliar words. Whatever it meant; their captors seemed to relax. Bollard noted the change in their disposition. The briefing from the old lady, the Jewish survivor, may have just paid off.

***

Their guards led them beyond the lights which grew increasingly dimmer with the morning light. They walked past the parked tractor, its headlights creating a shimmer as the engine started. Their captors led the dog away and directed them toward a building located to the side of a cluster of houses. Even as visibility increased, it was difficult for them to describe what lay in front of them. Certainly not a town, nor did it appear to be a typical village. No storefronts or shops were evident. People were moving around normally, going in and out of houses, and walking along a dirt road. Those who were outside stopped and took careful notice of the strangers being escorted under guard. Grigori noted the clothing. Several were shoeless and wore a rope for a belt.

"Gorsky Jews," Grigori said lowly to the others, but loud enough to grab the attention of an escort who shoved him in the back and ordered him not to speak.

It was a remote enclave, for sure. Bollard remembered the old lady describing the locations of the enclaves but couldn't remember this one.

The escorts directed them inside a building and gestured to seats at a long wooden table. Grigori took the center seat with Sulundik on his right and Bollard on his left. It reminded Bollard of the night he arrived in Chechnya. The results of the interrogation would likely have the same consequences of life or death.

Adjacent to the building someone started a generator. The lights went from dim to almost blinding, revealing the faces of everyone present. Bearded men armed and with contempt stood in the corners.

Bollard glanced briefly at Grigori and Sulundik who each bore the marks of scratches and dried blood from a night's march in the thorns and briars. He imagined he didn't look much better.

Four men and their guards strode into the room and sat down. Their guards stood nearby. Bollard tried to assess the men across from him. Who's on the left, who's on the right, how did they walk and sit, what are they wearing? All were crucial questions he needed to answer as he assessed their status. In that Grigori sat in the center seat, Bollard presumed the man opposite him was the leader.

Each man sported a curly beard, with one sitting in front of Sulundik hosting a long white one. Bollard studied their hats carefully and remembered a saying from the region, "If you have no one to consult, consult the hat." The man sitting opposite Grigori wore the papakha or astrakhan hat, a traditional Georgian hat. It was a badge of honor and reflected the military prowess of these Mountain Jews. The white-bearded man and the one to his left wore a smaller, less conspicuous hat like a fez, which sat at the crown of their heads, revealing their faces. Interestingly, the latter two men wore rope belts and were barefoot. The fourth man sat stone-faced, wearing no hat, with arms crossed. Bollard sized him up as strictly personal protection for the other three.

The two groups studied one another carefully, no one saying a word. The trio, though certainly captives, didn't act like prisoners. They sat erect and confident with no trace of deceit. The opposite four scrutinized every feature and action. The man with the papakha sitting across from Grigori then spoke with a voice of authority and a twinge of sarcasm.

"Usually, it is my people who must ask for sanctuary under Adyghe Habze. Sometimes it's accepted and sometimes it's not. In my life, it's never been requested of us. Who are you and why are you here?"

Of the trio, Grigori felt he was the most vulnerable, especially if they determined he had been Spetsnaz. Given his training and time in the Caucasus, he had some insight into the Gorsky Jews, certainly more than Bollard or Sulundik. He understood them.

He knew they, like others in the region, adhered to Habze and would cooperate across cultural, religious, and geographic lines despite Soviet aims to undermine those relationships or infiltrate the various enclaves. The strict code of honor under

Adyghe Habze demanded he, Bollard, and Sulundik speak truthfully. Any attempt to deceive or lie would be detected and met with either a bullet to the head or delivery to the Soviet government.

"We stumbled into your village by mistake," Grigori began. "As you can see, we chose the most difficult route to access this mountain to avoid anyone who might think of following us." With his finger, he drew a line along the deep scratch on his cheek, "It was not a pleasant trip."

The leader understood the difficulty. "You chose this site for the same reasons as we did, difficult to access and with a lot of natural protections. But why would you need such a sanctuary? Who is chasing you and why?"

"We're survivors of a Chechen ambush," Grigori told him. "We were betrayed by militants who sought to blow up a school in Ossetia. When their effort went awry, they blamed the three of us for planning the school attack. Now the Ossetians, as well as the Chechens, want us. The Soviets would also like to capture us. We are seeking our way out of the region."

"Chechens, Ossetians, and Russians. Quite a quandary," the man seated furthest to the right muttered, then froze as if he had spoken out of turn.

The older man stroked his long white beard and looked at each person across from him as if pondering a chess move. "You three seem so very distinct."

Grigori gestured questioningly, "What do you mean? We are three individuals."

"You don't look as if you belong together." He gestured to Sulundik. "She is short and dark. You are squarely built, like a Russian." He looked longer at Bollard. "And you are the most distinct of all. Tall and lean, with blue eyes – but I cannot say where you might be from. Yes, you are each very distinct."

Grigori wanted to point out the differences between the men sitting in front of him but held his tongue.

The younger man to the right touched the sleeve of the white-bearded one. "Yes, Dayan. You are correct. They are indeed distinct."

Bollard heard it - "Dayan."

The old man represented the religious authority of this enclave and the region. He was the rabbinical judge. The younger man beside him was certainly a rabbi. Bollard now understood their odd choice of dress.

"Perhaps it's their faith," the dayan continued. "What is your faith?" he asked, which seemed an odd question.

Grigori stammered, "I have no faith."

Sulundik spoke up, "I'm a follower of Islam."

Everyone turned their heads to Bollard who said, "I'm a Christian."

The dayan laughed and slapped his hands together. "I knew it. I knew there was something distinct about each of them. Certainly, they aren't bound by their faith!"

The man directly opposite Grigori, now narrowed down to being either the military or political leader, became even more intrigued.

"How can it be the three of you are together? You have little in common."

Sulundik responded, "We have much in common. It is our hatred of the Soviet military that binds us together."

The dayan spoke from the corner of his mouth to the political leader, "Even their language... their accents are different."

"You are not from the Caucasus!" the leader said with a wide wave. "Where are you from? Where are your origins?"

That question posed a dilemma. They needed sanctuary, and they had to reply, but the truth might not bode well for them.

Again, Sulundik spoke first. "I'm Afghan, sent here to assist in fighting the Soviet military."

Grigori did not want to draw too narrow a focus on himself. "I'm Russian. I was born in Moscow and am wanted as a deserter from the Soviet Army."

Yet again Bollard was put on the defensive as he debated whether to hold to the cover story of being a Georgian or tell the truth. Before he could answer Grigori answered for him.

"He's an American."

That statement sent shock and then murmurs and whispers throughout the room. Grigori had done it on purpose; it was the truth, and it took the pressure off him.

"Your government sent you to the Caucasus to join with the guerrillas?" one asked Bollard.

"That's a question I can't answer. My honor to you and under Habze dictates the truth. My honor otherwise dictates my silence," Bollard replied.

The dayan grunted his approval and looked at Bollard with newfound respect.

The questioning continued. "What was your role with the guerrillas?"

Sulundik answered, "We were advisors to the guerrillas."

"But you've fought alongside them."

"We fought in our defense, but principally we were advisors."

"Who planned the attack on the school?"

"The militants. We knew nothing about it. The militants knew we'd object and resist," Grigori replied.

Two men walked into the room, interrupting the meeting. They placed the packs on the table and one of the men acknowledged everything was in order with one exception: a radio. Bollard watched as they displayed the parts of the radio to their leader. Grigori straightened, he was as interested as the others.

"What's this?" the Gorsky leader asked as he examined the parts and passed them to the others.

"It's mine," Bollard said. "It's an archaic but functioning long-range receiver and transmitter. Its signal is vulnerable to radio detection finders beyond a twenty-second transmission. I use it at a safe distance, so the location of the signal's source is not detected."

"I want to know its purpose. Where are you planning to use it? Here?"

"Currently it has one purpose and that's to initiate a signal far from here and to communicate for my ultimate extraction from the region."

"With whom are you communicating?"

"'Friends' is all I can say to ensure an honorable answer."

334

The four Gorsky leaders talked quietly among themselves, then the leader announced they would adjourn to consider the request for sanctuary. Bollard wanted to press a second point to confirm a hunch.

"I have a question for the dayan if that is permitted."

The dayan gave permission and Bollard continued, "Why is it you wear a rope for a belt and walk barefoot?"

"An easy answer," the dayan replied. "Today is the Sabbath. The rabbi and I, as well as others in this community, wear ropes instead of belts every Sabbath to remind ourselves and others of the bondage of our ancestors in Egypt and God's loosening of those bonds. We wear no shoes to remind us of God's protection and our escape from Egypt and the many years of sojourn with Moses to the Promised Land."

Bollard pressed his point. "Isn't it ironic we sojourners appear on the Sabbath seeking sanctuary? Like your ancestors, we've escaped bondage. You must certainly understand and identify with our despair, as we attempt to sojourn to a place of safety. If not granted sanctuary or safe passage, we will be condemned to similar bondage you know all too well."

The dayan paused, thoughtfully. "We shall see," he said and cast a searching glance at Bollard.

The four men walked away, leaving them alone with the guards. A few minutes later, a man entered with a pot of tea. It was a good sign.

***

Other than a permitted toilet break, the guards forced Bollard, Grigori, and Sulundik to remain in their seats. It was a physically difficult night and the adrenaline ups and downs that came with their capture left them exhausted. Each slumped in their chair or laid their head on the desk and slept.

After an interminable amount of time, the four heads of the community returned with their verdict. The rabbi held the dog's leash. The dog jumped exuberantly and playfully under the rabbi's control as they moved to their seats.

The trio sat up, attempting to shake off the drowsiness by filling their cups with tea.

"We're not a guerrilla community," the leader addressed them, "but, a peaceful village. I am its administrative leader, and my name is Gershon ben Schmuel na-Katan." He touched the shoulder of the man Bollard figured to be a security man, "This is Reuven, my assistant."

Then Gershon introduced the other two by their full names; Dayan Mattathia ben Moshke Nadki, and Rabbi Elisha ben Schmuel ha-Kohen.

Dayan Mattathia began, "We don't support the guerrilla's actions, passively or actively. We've lived here in relative peace for centuries precisely because we are no threat to the government or anyone else unless provoked. Likewise, we don't cooperate or collaborate with governmental agencies against our brothers or neighbors."

Gershon interjected, "Our position is to never give anyone, whether guerrilla, neighbor, or an official any reason to be suspicious of us as a people or our intentions. We desire to practice our faith and grow a community of people with a solid foundation of trust and honor. We aren't naïve. As you've discovered, our security teams are vigilant even at the most obscure community access points. We're vigilant because we won't be lulled into complacency. Complacency makes us vulnerable to local pogroms or infiltration by others regardless of our best intentions."

Bollard took note of "pogroms." A word used many times since his arrival, whether an Armenian pogrom, Azeri pogrom, or Jewish pogrom. It was a manifestation of suspicion, hate, and murder.

Gershon's tone became more ominous. "However, you as guerrillas who seek sanctuary make us extremely vulnerable. Any external knowledge of your presence here would arouse suspicion, distrust, and potential allegations of our intentions, or the motivations of this community. It could potentially spell hostility and even disaster."

It appeared to be a ruling of the four-member board, but Dayan Mattathia spoke the verdict.

"While you represent a potential threat to our community, we will not forfeit our honor under Habze out of fear. We will grant you sanctuary but under strict inviolable rules. Any infraction will be considered a violation of Habze and you will be surrendered to Soviet authorities."

Gershon laid out strict guidelines. The community would provide shelter in specified areas with specific restrictions on movement. The community would identify hide locations in the event external search teams arrived seeking information about them. They would give them civilian clothing and destroy the guerrilla uniforms. They forbade them to undertake any actions supporting the guerrillas or subversive to the government. The offer of sanctuary was good until the leadership confirmed their stories and determined the best and safest manner for their exfiltration; the leader estimated three to four weeks. The leadership would retain the radio and weapons until the sanctuary ended.

Bollard could not have hoped for a better outcome. They would have sufficient time to recover from the days on the run since the ambush, and Bollard could more clearly and thoughtfully plan how he might complete the exfiltration.

"But you must work," Rabbi Elisha said.

"Indeed, Rabbi Elisha is correct," Gershon interrupted. "You'll work while you're here. He will coordinate your work details. Normally, my deputy would exercise authority to manage the work with the citizenry. However, I believe the rabbi's authority with our people would carry much more respect and cooperation among our community than I can provide."

Sulundik spoke up, "Regardless of the nature of the work, I request that you give me the same details as the men. I don't want to be sidelined to less meaningful work because of who I am."

"It makes our management of the escorts much easier," Gershon replied with a smile. He turned to Rabbi Elisha, "I know you may have other plans, but I'd appreciate it if she's given the same tasks as the men."

The rabbi responded, quoting Ecclesiastes, "A cord of three strands is not quickly torn apart." He looked at the trio, "It will be better for everyone." He then handed the dog's leash to Bollard. The dog tried to follow the rabbi and pulled on the leash, but Bollard jerked it back.

Rabbi Elisha hesitated before leaving. "I wonder if I might visit or walk the dog occasionally while you're here?"

"Anytime."

***

Weeks passed and the three assimilated quickly into the community. Initially, the locals regarded the three suspiciously and Rabbi Elisha had to spend a great amount of time convincing the community to allow them to join in the work. They overcame their suspicions as reports came in confirming the trio's story and as they watched them throw themselves into their work.

In the first week, they helped timbering teams cut trees in a section of the forest. Once a tree was down, Grigori cut limbs from the tree. Sulundik choked the tree with a chain by wrapping it around the trunk and attaching it to another set of chains. Bollard then attached the chains to a harness on a pair of mules and dragged the tree to a makeshift sawmill.

It was exhausting work. At the end of each day, they watched as the locals rotated their work schedules. The trio returned to the forest each day with a completely different crew. They cleared the area of all the brush and trees and processed the desired timber without complaint and earned the enclave's respect.

As she worked, Sulundik watched with increasing alarm as several children played dangerously close to the workers. On the fifth day, a tree kicked back and almost crushed them. Sulundik saw the tree kick back and as if in slow motion, fall in the direction of the children. In that instant, she jumped forward knocking one of the children to the ground but away from the tree. Sulundik was pinned underneath one of the larger limbs. After a frantic effort, the men removed the limb and she emerged unscathed. Word of her actions and heroics spread quickly throughout the enclave.

By the third week, the trio moved lumber from the mill to a location they helped excavate by hand, then assisted in the construction of a small home. By that time, their relationships with the enclave had relaxed so much that their assigned escort only accompanied them at night and to and from their work detail. Not only did the locals start to accept the outsiders but engaged them in lively conversations whenever possible. They all wanted to hear the story of the child who was saved.

Bollard was especially keen to understand this unique group of people and how they lived. During a break, he asked several men sitting on the ground and eating their lunch why they didn't have storefronts like other villages. It was obvious stores were common to the enclave. Several men laughed at the question and another thought it simply odd.

"Why would we need a storefront?" one man asked. "Everyone knows where everyone else lives and what they sell from their homes. We just go to the house that has what we need and buy or trade from there."

Another joined in, "We have only one place to buy bread. We know the family who bakes the bread. They've always baked bread. We know where they live, and we know how much it will cost. We don't need a sign to explain anything. And if someone wants to raise their price, they justify it to the leadership."

The logic, as well as the simplicity of life here, was mind-boggling to Bollard.

The relationship with Rabbi Elisha blossomed into a friendship. Work ceased on the Sabbath and the population gathered in their unmarked synagogue. Grigori, Sulundik, and Bollard attended out of respect for the community which also allowed their escort to participate in worship. They sat in a designated area in the rear. They considered taking on some of the adornment of this group. But this might be considered an insult, so they discussed it with the rabbi.

"You said it was permitted for us to go with you to the synagogue, but we'd like to wear ropes for belts like you," Grigori said before they attended their first service. "Is it allowed, or would it be taken as an insult?"

Rabbi Elisha was bewildered. "It wouldn't be an insult if you arrive with me. So, I suppose it's fine, but I question your motivation. Is your request because you want to remember the bondage of my people in Egypt?"

Sulundik smiled sweetly. "Or, perhaps, remind you of our bondage."

The rabbi chuckled. "As I suspected. Your bondage is hardly comparable, but I think it is a good thing for our people to draw the connection."

As a result, the three appeared weekly adorned with their rope belts. However, they never went so far as the rabbi to arrive barefoot.

***

Over the past weeks, Bollard witnessed the tenderness grow between Sulundik and Grigori. Though they never had time to themselves in the enclave, it was undeniably there. It was there when Grigori would mutter a joke in her ear and Sulundik's normally stoic expression broke. It was there when they shared food. It was there when they simply held a door open for each other. Previously, the two of them had been in the throes of newfound passion and romance, now their bond seemed to be developing into something more.

One day, their escort rolled his blanket out on the cot and walked outside the structure to smoke a cigarette. Seeing an opportunity to allow his friends to be alone, Bollard followed the escort. The escort shared a cigarette and the two chatted light-heartedly. Inside the building, a more serious conversation was underway.

Grigori sat down on the side of his cot and asked Sulundik to join him. He took her hands and looked into her almond eyes.

"I love you so deeply," he began.

"And I'm so in love with you," Sulundik said not able to hide her delighted smile.

Grigori continued, "I would love to remain here with you forever if it were possible and if our presence didn't bring danger to the community. I know it's impossible. We're in a bad situation still, and there's no denying it." He reached up to brush her hair out of her eyes. Over the last few weeks, it had grown out almost to her shoulders. "But, despite all the uncertainties we face, I can't imagine ever being without you. As much as being in love with someone is terrifying, the idea of living without you is equally as terrifying."

Sulundik squeezed his hands.

Grigori took a deep, deep breath. "Even with all the uncertainties and dangers ahead... if I asked, could you... think about... would you consider..." The words caught in Grigori's throat, and he barely managed to choke out the rest. "You and me... marriage...?"

Sulundik couldn't help herself, she laughed while thinking of their circumstances and his strained proposal. All she could think about was the look on her father's face if he were to see this. "Are you asking me to be your wife, Grigori?" she finally asked.

"Yes, yes... asking," Grigori replied dumbly, his head spinning. He felt like he had been blown back by the suicide bomber all over again. "Would you be my wife?"

Sulundik gently pressed her lips to his. "Yes, I'll marry you."

Grigori pulled her in for a deeper kiss. There was a tap on the door and Bollard and the escort came back inside.

Sulundik jumped up, but Grigori managed to keep an arm around her waist. "She said she'd marry me, Matvey," Grigori's said, beaming.

Bollard's eyes lit up as he crossed the room to shake Grigori's hand. "Congratulations! Perfect!" He then went to Sulundik and without pretense or reservation embraced her. "I'm so happy for both of you."

She grinned and returned the embrace. "I think you've had a hand in this," she said to him.

Grigori, with a large smile, said, "Then it must be you, Matvey. You must stand with me when we're married."

"It will be an honor to be your best man," Bollard said. "So, tomorrow you'll talk to Rabbi Elisha?"

"As we discussed."

Sulundik gaped at the two of them. They had planned this.

***

Rabbi Elisha was so excited he practically pulled the dayan along the narrow dirt street. "Come see! Come see!" he repeated.

Grigori and Sulundik stood at the door of their building, under a small porch. Bollard and the escort stood nearby. As Dayan Mattathia and Rabbi Elisha arrived, the couple stepped out into the sun to greet them.

"I understand you want to be married," the dayan said, getting straight to the point.

"We have no idea what the future holds. We're in love and want to share our futures together, regardless," Grigori said.

"If it's permitted, we'd like the rabbi to marry us as soon as possible," Sulundik said with a smile.

Dayan Mattathia frowned and pretended to consider it for a while. He turned to the rabbi. "As the dayan, I see nothing preventing it, but they've asked you to officiate. What say you, rabbi?"

Rabbi Elisha laughed and clapped his hands, "I knew it. Yes, I knew it."

The dayan smiled, "Well?"

"A rabbi conducts a marriage ceremony for an atheist and a Muslim with a Christian standing with the groom!" Rabbi Elisha laughed again, "What challenges we bring to God! But what better way for us to show Him our brotherhood and humanity."

"Then you'll do it?" Dayan Mattathia confirmed what he'd just heard.

"Indeed!" the rabbi exclaimed as everyone began to speak excitedly over each other. They all shook hands, patted the rabbi on the back, and Grigori and Sulundik embraced each other. Then Rabbi Elisha interrupted the celebration.

"But you should understand, it will not be a valid wedding under Jewish law, *Halachah*," he said solemnly. There was quiet as they tried to puzzle through what that meant, and they waited for him to continue. Then, as if suddenly receiving a revelation from God, he laughed and exclaimed, "But you are not Jewish, so what do you care about Halachah!"

***

The news of a forthcoming wedding put a new spark in the life of the community. The enclave had grown fond of the strangers who lived under their protection and those feelings were mutual. The excitement was heartfelt as even arranged weddings were few and far between in the little village.

Several ladies pulled Sulundik away from the escort one evening to take her to the house of the village seamstress. It was surreal for Sulundik to be treated as someone special among the women as well as in the eyes of the men. In Afghanistan, she'd looked at the prospect of marriage with dread, but this was different. The exuberance of the other women was contagious, and she embraced the fullness of not only being a bride but of being a woman.

She was away for two hours. When she returned, two of the women accompanied her to the door. They stuck their heads inside to catch a glimpse of the groom. Their eyes sparkled, they giggled, then hugged Sulundik and quickly left. Sulundik was radiant as she entered the room. She glowed as Bollard and Grigori caught sight of her and watched her walk to her cot. The men had a million questions, but she answered none.

***

The flickering candles above and around the synagogue cast dancing shadows that provided the only light inside the dark wooden walls. The rabbi stood at the front wearing a long dark cloak while Grigori and Bollard stood at his side. Dressed in their new white shirts, starched to a stiffness that could cut, and wearing their festive-colored hats, the two men stared anxiously at the entrance.

The synagogue door opened casting new light into the room and silhouetting Sulundik and Dayan Mattathia at her side. As they entered and the door closed, the full radiance of the bride energized the room. Grigori's eyes could barely behold her beauty. He and Bollard were taken by the sight. Both expected the bride to be dressed in white, symbolizing purity. These were Mizrahi Jews, and for such events they dressed in festive colors of yellow, red, and green to represent the joy of the occasion. A wreath of yellow flowers adorned Sulundik's hair which was pulled into a simple but elegant twist. It made her look so very feminine. Hand stitched yellow and red flowers with bright green leaves and vines ran up the sides and arms of a brilliantly white, high-collared dress accented by a rainbow of embroidery. It was her smile that was most radiant of all.

Dayan Mattathia and Sulundik made their way to the altar, joining the wedding party under a canopy that symbolized the creation of a new home. Grigori and Sulundik joined hands as the dayan stood beside the rabbi. It was a ceremony with traditional blessings unique to this particular enclave and handed down over the centuries. It included commitments from both the bride and groom and an exchange of rings. The rings, cut from the brass of a small gauge shotgun shell, were identical and molded to size. In addition to their affirmation of love, both committed to a lifetime of respect and recognition of their individuality. The ceremony ended with Rabbi Elisha's prayer and Dayan Mattathia's presentation of a plate to the bride and groom. When they reached the outside, the couple tossed the plate onto the ground, breaking it and symbolizing their commitment during the difficult times as well as the good times. A cheer rose from those in attendance. Then Gershon and Dayan Mattathia had one last surprise.

Grigori, Sulundik, and Bollard expected to return to their holding building together. Instead, the wedding party and guests led the couple to the small house they had helped construct over the previous weeks. Standing at the front, Gershon announced the couple should spend their first night as husband and wife in privacy, and the house was prepared and theirs for the night.

Gershon then handed Grigori a bottle of vodka and whispered, "This isn't for you. You'll need it later. You'll know when."

"Thank you," Grigori said as he took the bottle.

***

As they lay together an hour after dark, Grigori and Sulundik were startled by loud banging and clanging from outside the front of the house. Grigori rose and went to the door. Outside, a group of twenty men clanged on tin cups and sang the most off-key songs ever to be found among humankind.

"What are you doing?" Grigori shouted. "Go home."

The men instead sang even louder and banged their cups with even greater fervor. One of them stepped forward.

"We'll leave when you pay the singing tax."

Grigori now realized what Gershon had meant.

He held up his hand, ran back inside, and returned holding the bottle of vodka high over his head. Handing it to the man he announced, "A serenade such as yours demands the highest in taxation! Will this suffice the tax for your most outstanding singing?"

The man held the bottle high amid loud shouts of support. The men circled the bottle while holding out their empty cups to be filled. Once they filled their cups, they streamed down the street like a herd of very drunk, singing cattle.

A wedding night serenade, and another unforgettable custom. A custom that was but a minor interruption, for there would be no sleep for Grigori and Sulundik.

***

A week after the wedding Gershon arrived at the entrance to their building and announced there would be no work that day. He directed that the trio make plans to depart the following morning. He pulled a map from his breast pocket and spread it across the table. Bollard leaned over it almost greedily. The Soviet government kept all maps under tight control. Bollard requested and was granted permission to make notes and copy as much of the map as possible.

"We've tried to honor your request to get you as close as possible to the Armenian border." He indicated an area on the map, "This is rugged territory and leads toward the northeast corner of Armenia. It's as good as we can do. We feel we've fully honored your sanctuary request and fulfilled our duty under Adyghe Habze."

The trio agreed with that and attested that the enclave had gone above and beyond their duty. They felt they had become members of the community.

"Your hard labor and willingness to be forthright in all things earned our trust and respect," Gershon told them. "Though you were here under the rules of the sanctuary, we've drawn close to you as friends. Sulundik saved the life of one of our own. We'd like to recognize you this evening at a ceremony and a traditional send-off with you and the town's leaders and elders."

"We would be honored," Bollard accepted as the other two echoed his sentiments.

When Gershon departed, he directed the escort to bring the trio's packs inside and place them on the table. The three opened their packs, took inventory, and discussed the amount of rations they would need for the next few days.

Bollard opened his pack and laid out the radio parts. It was intact. He observed Sulundik look inside her pack, then carefully examine the bottom. It was very curious.

***

Despite all they had seen and all that happened during their time with the enclave, nothing prepared them for the meeting with the elders and a traditional send-off.

As they walked into the administrative office, all furniture was either pushed to the side or removed. In the center of the room, the townsfolk arranged large plush pillows in a circle where the leadership and elders were already seated. The brightly colored pillows were large enough to seat at least two people. Many members of the community occupied smaller cushions located behind the larger ones. Several women who had assisted Sulundik in her wedding preparations were seated behind one of the large pillows. The escort helped them pick a path between the cushions, seating Sulundik and Grigori directly in front of the ladies and Bollard to their side.

After the formal introduction from the leaders, they motioned for several men at the entrance to enter.

Bollard watched as three men, with great ceremony, brought forward an incredibly polished, bronze-looking object a meter in height. It caught the light of the room and reflected in every direction. At first, Bollard thought it might be an ancient scroll, based on its rounded shape, but as they got nearer, he was stunned. It was a brass hookah, a large one with numerous multi-colored hoses.

The men placed the hookah in the center of the circle, placed a brick in the bowl, and lit it with great formality. The smoke slowly spiraled upward; the smell was unmistakable. The leadership and elders picked up the colored hoses but waited for Gershon, who spoke with great aplomb.

"This tradition dates back centuries," he said. "To the early beginnings of our people who escaped from Babylonia to Persia, and well before we migrated to the protection of the Caucasus mountains. Our ancestors brought this very hookah with them during their migration from southern Persia. Generations upon generations of our ancestors cultivated the original seeds and plants that were brought here to produce the leaves we smoke today. This hookah has been used for our grandest ceremonies since time immemorial." He paused and addressed Sulundik. "You're the first woman to join this inner circle. Because of what you've done for this community, for your actions at the logging site to save a child, and because we know the three of you so well, we want to include you. We're honored to have you."

The ladies in the room applauded as the leader took a puff from the hookah. It was the signal for the others to partake. As they smoked, the dayan stood and told stories of their past, their conquests, and the strict adherence to their religion, culture, and traditions. Enclave elders then stood to relate their own stories and pronouncements of feats of the past. Much to her surprise, Dayan Mattathia asked Sulundik to relate the events in which she saved the young child's life.

Sulundik modestly related the near tragedy. As she spoke, the women behind her seemed to straighten with second-hand pride. She took note of the change and decided to end her story with a few thoughts.

"I hope my sitting here among you, in this inner circle, is not a one-time exception for a woman. Perhaps this seat might remain open to others," she gestured to the other women. "You see, what I did was nothing more than what any one of them could have done and would have done in the same situation. The strength of the circle will be tempered and made stronger with that taken into consideration."

The dayan remained silent as Sulundik sat down, but the women behind her touched and patted her shoulder in gratitude. Gershon recognized Grigori's request to speak.

"We came here with nothing but a request. We leave here with much more. Certainly, I leave here with a wife!" Everyone cheered and clapped, forcing Grigori to pause for a moment before he could speak again. "It's our custom to provide a gift, but as I said, we have nothing to offer except the one thing we want you to have."

Bollard stood and asked Rabbi Elisha to join him, Grigori, and Sulundik beyond the rings of pillows. As he did, Bollard signaled the escort to release the dog. The dog barreled toward the rabbi, jumping and leaping around him until the rabbi dropped to one knee to hug and hold on to the dog.

"He's the only gift that we can provide, and we want Rabbi Elisha to have him," Grigori said.

"He came here as a security alert and tracking dog," Bollard explained to the room, "but we fear the rabbi has ruined him. He seems to be the rabbi's pet!"

The people in the room laughed and applauded.

The dog licked the rabbi on the face as Bollard warned, "I don't think I'd let him do that."

Grigori agreed. "I wouldn't let him lick me in the face either. That dog's not discriminating in what he eats." He playfully bumped his wife's arm.

Sulundik rolled her eyes.

"But what do I call him?" Rabbi Elisha asked excitedly.

Bollard shrugged, "Nothing."

"Nothing?"

"Nothing. We don't call him anything. He's never had a name. You name him."

"Then I'll call him *Nichevo*," the rabbi said. "Nothing!"

They returned to their seats and the celebration continued. The leadership wished the trio safe travels and Rabbi Elisha prayed for God's protection. The hookah was then taken away with the same amount of gravitas as it had arrived.

As they walked back to the holding building, Bollard was incredulous. He had smoked a brick of marijuana with an enclave of Gorsky Jews in the middle of the Soviet Union. He was reminded of similar customs from other cultures, such as the use of *peyote* among some native Americans, or hashish among certain groups of Baluchi. It was obvious the marijuana was ceremonial only; too many partakers and not enough marijuana to be concerned with any consequence, but just enough to maintain the customs and traditions of the people. He understood they had just participated in an age-old Persian-Jewish ceremony that few if any outsiders would ever know or experience.

Chapter 28
Armenia

In the morning hours, before any of the Gorsky population began their normal daily routine, a truck loaded with lumber pulled up beside the holding building. There were no farewells, no goodbyes. Everything that needed to be said had already been done. Three figures emerged from the building and crawled into a compartment separating the truck's cab from the lumber.

From a distance, it looked like nothing more than a stack of lumber; large enough for Bollard, Grigori, and Sulundik to sit, but far from comfortable. They positioned their packs uncomfortably in their laps, each one now stuffed with three days' worth of food and water. The trio had traded their rifles for pistols. Armenia was not Chechnya, and anyone seen carrying a rifle would only draw unwanted attention.

They bumped along steep, rocky roads for several hours until the truck jerked to a stop. They heard the crunch of footsteps on gravel, and the driver opened the compartment. The three compatriots stepped outside and stretched. The driver pointed to some distant hills to the east.

"This is as much of a detour inside the Armenian Republic as we can go. It will attract too much attention if we go any further."

"Is this the location you were supposed to drop us off or did you have to alter it?" Bollard asked.

"No, this is the location. We're moving northwest now to drop off the lumber." He pointed in the opposite direction, then shook their hands one last time.

Grabbing their packs, they moved into the tree line where they would wait until dark. Once in position, Bollard opened his pack and prepared his radio to signal an update: "Operational; Armenia."

***

The trio traveled for three nights. Moving through Armenia presented a different kind of challenge compared to the

Caucasus; the terrain was more exposed, the larger population was more interspersed across the region, and towns and villages were abundant.

Bollard studied the hand-drawn copy of the map he had made while with the Gorskys. He sensed he was in familiar territory. There was nothing about the map or terrain that captured his attention, but the sounds did. Large trucks moved constantly back and forth in the valley below. Those moving west to east lumbered slowly with the downshifting of gears under heavy payload; those moving east to west drove more quickly with the engines at high RPMs and no indication of a payload.

If he was right, these were the same trucks he had heard when the guerrillas originally smuggled him through the ratline in the back of a coal truck. If so, the trio was just southwest of where he had inserted into the Armenian ratline.

"I fear the border between Armenia and Azerbaijan will be watched, given their age-old animosities," Grigori said as the three of them huddled over the map.

Sulundik agreed. "If we continue east or northeast and find a crossing point, I have contacts who will arrange our transit to Baku." She then touched the bottom of her pack. "I also have papers to document I'm a resident of Azerbaijan."

"You're just now revealing this?" Bollard asked.

Sulundik met his flat gaze. "These papers are useless except in Azerbaijan. If the authorities discover the papers before we get there, they wouldn't be of any benefit to us." She guided the conversation back to the plan. "Once across the border, I could arrange your passage as well, but you would still be inside the borders of the Soviet Union."

Bollard gave a crooked smile. "I appreciate your offer, but I have a home and a family. I need to move southeast for extraction, and I have to go it alone," he told her. "We're nearing that point when we'll have to go our separate ways." He pushed a stick along the southeast portion of the map.

"We're out of options," Sulundik said. "We're almost out of food unless we steal, and that is extremely dangerous."

Bollard paused, then offered slowly, "There's an option we might be able to play."

"What is it, Matvey?" Grigori asked.

"I have an emergency contact," Bollard lied, not wanting to reveal the presence of a ratline. "If I approach alone, and the contact believes me, they may help to move you two across the border and get me where I need to go. It's a hell of a long shot, but I can't think of a better option."

"What do you think, Sulundik?" Grigori asked, taking her hand.

"What did you ask me earlier?" she said to Bollard with a smile. "You're just now revealing that point?"

"Touché." He returned the smile. "There's no guarantee. This could be a deadly mistake," Bollard warned, smile fading.

Sulundik made a helpless gesture. "We've little choice but to try it."

"Then, it's agreed. We'll identify a hide site and alternate site an hour from my contact. I'll depart for the linkup tonight. If I'm successful, I'll be back within two days. If not, you'll anticipate I failed and go alone. Okay?"

"Agreed," they replied in unison.

Bollard's next request was both perplexing and intriguing as he instructed them to hold out their arms and expose their shirt sleeves.

Chapter 29
Back to the Well

Phiroza's heart hammered against her ribs as she ran, the adrenaline roaring in her ears drowning out every other sound. Panting, she found her father repairing the wheel of an old push plow. She forced herself to take deep breaths so she could speak.

Phiroza's father tossed his hammer to the side and stood to meet her, instinctively knowing something was wrong. She waved her closed fist at him and motioned for him to follow her toward the house. Safely inside, Phiroza began a breathless description.

"Three threads!" she exclaimed.

"Slow down! Take your time and tell me from the beginning."

"Three threads! At the well! I went to the well to draw water like I do every day. When I dropped the rope into the well, I checked the rope at the top to see if it might be loaded. You know, to determine if a thread was attached."

Her father was struggling to catch on. "Right."

"But Papa, look!" She opened her palm. "There are three threads!"

Her father plucked the strings from her hand to examine them. "Three threads," he repeated, almost in wonder.

"Yes. What can this mean?"

The old man rubbed the back of his neck and shook his head. He wondered if their entire organization, operational for so many years, had finally been compromised.

"But we're supposed to be notified in advance and by other communications if we're to activate the ratline."

"But that's not always the case!" Phiroza protested. "Papa, do you think three people are waiting to enter the ratline?"

"I don't know, Phiroza." He placed his hands on his hips and considered the situation warily. "This is incredibly dangerous. Get my pistol. At dusk, I'll go to the hide site and see who's there."

Phiroza hurried out of the room and returned with his gun. "I'll go with you," she said.

Her father took the gun and shook his head. "No. It's too dangerous and could be a trap. I don't want you anywhere near it."

Phiroza frowned but did not argue. "How will you approach them?"

"I'll use the standard challenge and see if they know the password. If they don't know it, I'll leave. Otherwise, I'll have to work my way through the situation."

The hide site held enough food and water for one person. If there were three people and they needed help, then Phiroza needed to prepare more food, water, and wine. She assembled the supplies and placed them in a basket as her father contemplated what he might have to do. It would take a couple of days for his contacts to confirm any additions to the ratline, and there simply wasn't time. He had to determine if the ratline was compromised.

At dusk, Phiroza's father set out toward the well. Chambering rounds in his pistol, he did not think to check behind him as he crept up the trail. If he had, he would have seen Phiroza following at a safe distance with basket in hand.

***

Bollard was waiting in the hide site when a voice came from the entrance, "Hello inside."

"Hello Igor," Bollard replied – the alternative for Anna.

"How's the family?"

"All are sick."

Once Bollard finished supplying the necessary code phrase, he expected the contact to enter the hide site. However, this time, a gruff voice ordered him outside with his hands raised.

The man appeared to be middle-aged, with a tan weathered face. He held an old pistol in experienced hands, aiming directly at Bollard's head.

"Who are you and what are you doing here?"

Bollard was going to answer when he looked beyond the man and saw Phiroza sprinting toward them.

"Papa, it's the American!" she called out. "The one I took through the ratline." Phiroza paused to catch her breath when she was closer. "Tamaz! Why are you here?" she asked when she finally held out her hand to shake. Bollard waited for the father to allow him to lower his hands.

Wasting no time, Bollard replied, "I'm in a bad way. I was ultimately taken to Chechnya and things have gone poorly. There was a lot of in-fighting and I barely escaped with my life. You're the only people I can turn to."

"You mean you've traveled all the way from Chechnya?" the father asked disbelievingly.

"It wasn't easy, but yes. We had to call on Adyghe Habze among the people. I suppose I'm asking for that from you."

"Habze? Ha!" The old man scoffed. "The mountain tribes might adhere to Habze, but we have a different code. The Turks nearly wiped out our people, which has made us not so accommodating. We have historic ties, and we have a Christian ethos, but everything is balanced with our survival."

"I think I've proven I'm not a threat," Bollard said gently.

Phiroza held up the three threads. "You said, 'we'. What does this mean? Three threads on the well? What was your intent?"

As she asked, her father took the threads and pulled Bollard's arm up to match one.

"There are three of us," Bollard explained. "We're traveling as a group and we're out of food, water, and options. I had to reach out to you."

"I thought that was the case, so I brought extra food and some wine," Phiroza said as she lifted the basket.

Her father was less conciliatory. "You may have compromised us," he said angrily.

"I haven't compromised you. The others, a married couple, know only that I've gone to find help. I took a thread from their shirts so you could identify them in case something happens to me, but they know nothing of you or the ratline. They're an hour away, and we aren't even asking to enter the ratline."

"So, what do you want from us?"

"We have a two-fold request. They must reach Azerbaijan, where they will find protection. I'm going in another direction, southeast of Yerevan. We'll take any assistance you can provide, but transport would get us out of the region more quickly."

Phiroza's father thought for a long time. Phiroza's youthful enthusiasm would not wait for him. "Father, DyaDya could do it," she said referring to her uncle. "The bus crosses the border once a week. Once a month he takes people to the capital."

Phiroza's comment drew her father's harsh glare, but it was too late. Bollard pounced on the lead. "The sooner we get away, the better it is for you."

The man returned his attention to Bollard, grip tightening around the pistol again. "How so?"

"I know you want reliable and trusted contacts in Azerbaijan, especially given the volatile situation in Nagorno Karabakh. My friends could be those contacts if you help them." Bollard was gambling, but he had to play it out. "Also, your daughter speaks excellent English. I may be able to work something out for her in the future."

Phiroza's father grabbed him by the arm, and they walked out of her earshot. A few minutes later, he returned and said loudly enough for Phiroza to hear, "Then it's settled."

Phiroza wasn't quite sure what was settled, but her father departed to make arrangements with his brother for the clandestine transport. He would return with the details as soon as possible. In the meantime, Bollard would remain at the hide site. Once coordination was complete, they would link up with Grigori and Sulundik.

***

Bollard and Phiroza's father crashed through the woods at a near trot as they made their way toward Grigori and Sulundik's location. Bollard worried he would not be able to locate the spot where he had left them. After all, it had been thirty-six hours since he left, and now the darkness, thick brush, and unfamiliar setting complicated his return. He had hoped late-night truck traffic might help orient him to the valley below, but he could hear nothing. He stopped, caught his breath, and held his watch steady.

They had hiked for three-quarters of an hour. He must surely be nearing the hide site. If so, there should be a draw just ahead that would lead back up the hill to their position. Five minutes later, they clambered down a short slope and started back up the opposite side. It was the draw.

Bollard felt he was now within hearing range of Grigori and Sulundik and stopped. He paused, then whistled three times. He waited, then was about to whistle again when he heard a response; two whistles.

Both Sulundik and Grigori were standing with their weapons drawn further up the draw.

"Good to see you! We were wondering if we might have to set out without you," Sulundik said, then quieted when she saw the man following Bollard.

Bollard quickly introduced Phiroza's father as their guide and directed the two to hold out their sleeves so he could inspect each with the remaining two threads. Even with Bollard's assurance, it was a necessary procedure. Once Phiroza's father confirmed the threads matched each sleeve, Bollard handed each a bag of food to stuff in their packs. He explained they must make haste, put on their packs, and depart to a pickup point for getting into Azerbaijan.

"What's the plan?" Grigori wanted the details.

Bollard put his hand on Grigori's shoulder and whispered, "Not a lot of time. He will guide you there and put you on a bus."

Grigori blinked. "A bus?"

"Yes. It's a regularly scheduled one. You'll board as passengers. No one will ask questions, and you should interact with no one. The bus will have no problems at the checkpoints; it's taken care of. It's a standard route. The only issue that might arise once in Azerbaijan is if locals attempt to intercept the bus, but that's unlikely."

"Where is it going?"

"Nagorno Karabakh."

"What?" Grigori asked. "I thought that region was heavily controlled, both its access and egress."

"It is," Bollard confirmed. "But don't worry. You'll be off the bus well before then. The driver will tell you when and where;

all he knows is he's picking up two passengers and has no specific details for delivery."

"This is incredible," Grigori exclaimed as he picked up his pack. He'd operated all around the Soviet Union both covertly and overtly but never knew the regions were so porous.

Bollard said. "You'll get on the bus just after daylight. He'll lead you there."

The three quickly embraced for a final time.

Chapter 30
The Road to Yerevan

Bollard had been in hiding for twelve days since splitting off from Grigori and Sulundik. Twice Phiroza delivered food and drink, as well as new batteries for the radio. He hoped the long downtime was due to detailed planning over his exfiltration and not to more unfortunate alternatives.

It was morning on the thirteenth day when Bollard heard someone advancing towards the site. Instead of Phiroza, as Bollard was expecting to see, it was her father. After an exchange of passwords, he directed Bollard to come outside.

Phiroza's father greeted him with a sack of food and two bottles of wine to place in his pack. "You'll be getting on the same bus as your friends did. However, it's going to the capital in Yerevan, and it'll have a different kind of passenger. Mostly hacks, and local apparatchiks," he explained.

"How was my friends' drop off? Were there any issues?" Bollard asked, searching the man's face in the darkness for any tell.

"There were no issues. They got off the bus in a little town near the Nagorno-Karabakh border."

"That's good." Bollard breathed a sigh of relief.

"I fear their ride was more comfortable than yours will be."

"How's that?"

"You'll be hiding on the bus. The driver keeps a large steel toolbox at the rear. You'll be locked inside it until time to drop you off. The driver will pretend to have engine troubles to delay arrival in Yerevan until after dark. Once he's dropped off the apparatchiks, he'll take you within six kilometers of the town you identified. That's where he'll let you out. Your town will be due west."

"How long is the trip?"

"Until it's over," the man said dryly. "My point is, you're going into the toolbox and not coming out until it's late. It'll be cramped and uncomfortable."

Bollard thought for a moment. "If I'm in a steel box, I'll need something to cushion the ride."

"You can take one of the blankets. It's likely to be cold as well."

Bollard got a blanket from the hide site and the two set out to link up with the bus and its driver.

***

As Phiroza's father and Bollard emerged from the dirt road onto the main road, the driver turned on the bus lights. Both men hurried toward it as the driver swung the door open.

"Do your best to honor our deal, no matter how long it takes," Phiroza's father said as he shook Bollard's hand.

"No matter how long it takes," Bollard echoed with a smile.

Bollard stepped onto the bus and following his instructions, he walked to the back of the bus and opened the toolbox. It was smaller than he anticipated. He laid the blanket along the floor and edges of the box, then stuffed himself inside, curling up with the backpack in his arms, his head almost tucked between his legs. There would be no latrine breaks and there was little room to move in the tight quarters. If he did, it would have to be out of necessity and done quietly. Just as he reached up to shut the lid, the driver appeared and handed him an empty plastic coffee can.

"Here, you'll need this. I don't want you pissing your pants in my toolbox."

Bollard moved his pack out of the way. After unfastening his pants, he placed the can in the area of his crotch where he could get to it easily without spilling. When Bollard was situated, the driver shut the lid and locked it.

***

They promised Bollard the ride would be miserable, and they delivered. Each bump of the road rattled the suspension at the back of the bus with a sharp bounce and firm landing. Bollard half-suspected the bus might not even be equipped with shocks. He was glad he thought to bring the blanket, or it might have been even worse. He tried to reposition the blanket to protect the side of his head but once in place, nothing budged in the tight quarters.

Bollard listened to the hiss of bus doors as passengers boarded. As far as he could tell, most of them sat towards the front. He assumed it was to avoid the bumpy rear of the bus. It didn't take long to realize there was another, more dangerous reason. The smell of cheap fuel and exhaust from a broken muffler seeped its way through every crevice of the bus. Anxiety panged in Bollard's gut. The fumes became so bad, that one of the passengers eventually lowered the windows for several rows. One problem was traded for another, as the fumes were pulled outside and Bollard could breathe again, but the cold air made the temperature plummet inside the toolbox.

Shortly, the driver announced he was having an engine problem and got out to open the hood. He advised everyone to get out and stretch. Bollard wished he could join them. The feigned repairs of the bus took an hour before he started it again.

After what seemed to be an eternity, the bus entered a city. Bollard presumed it was Yerevan given the volume of traffic sounds and the number of stops. In the center of the city, the bus pulled into the bus station and everyone disembarked. A couple of passengers complained to an official about the long stop and repair that made them late.

Bollard could hear the official step onto the bus to discuss the vehicle's issues with the driver. The driver assured him he had a friend who could repair it for free and was on his way to the friend's location. After the official got off the bus, the driver backed up and left the station.

They were soon out of the city, and well after dark the driver stopped the bus. He walked to the back, unlocked the box, and opened the lid. Bollard started to rise, but he couldn't make his muscles move. The driver reached in and helped pull him to his feet. Bollard's legs collapsed and the driver propped him up until he could regain circulation. As soon as he could stand and step off the bus, the driver sped away.

Bollard could see the reflection of the town's lights to his west. He would have to walk well south of the town to where his new hide site should be located.

***

He walked six kilometers south of the target town until he came to a large field that paralleled the border with Turkey. Eight large haystacks stood in the field. From the dirt road, Bollard walked to the far end of the field to the last haystack.

He stomped his foot around until he heard a hollow thud. Dropping to his knees, he found the edge of a concealed board. He lifted the hatch. Bollard lowered himself inside and found a light on the dirt floor. He shut the trap door, then followed the tunnel to a short ladder that led up to a concealed room under the haystack. It was an ingenious layout.

Bollard flashed the light around the room. It contained some canned food, wine, and a blanket. He focused the light on the cargo pack that was key to his extraction. He opened the large bag to ensure he had everything he needed. It was all there, and he needed to send a radio signal immediately.

Chapter 31
Combat Talon
Extraction

Lieutenant Colonel Thad Thorpe and Major Dave Austin had three things in common. Both had flown airplanes since they were teenagers, island-hopping from their homes in Florida throughout the Caribbean. Both had turned down positions flying with commercial airlines for the more exciting life of a military pilot. They were the two best special operations pilots in the military and perfectly suited for piloting the MC-130E Combat Talon.

Normally parked in a hanger, the Combat Talon was rarely seen and only brought out at night for special missions and training. It now sat ready with all four engines revving and a top crew eager to commence operations. Using sophisticated terrain-following radar or nap-of-the-earth (NOE) flying, Thorpe and Austin often flew this aircraft on low-level, special operations missions; just sixty-five meters above the ground to minimize visual or radar detection.

Parked across the runway another specially configured C-130, an EC-130J Volant Solo, revved its engines. Every night, for over a month, Volant Solo took to the skies and flew a circuit paralleling the Soviet border along the boundary of the Armenian Republic. In addition to their other clandestine mission capabilities, they were tasked with transmitting and receiving messages. One of those messages included a repeated codeword intended specifically for an American operative and signaled an extraction confirmation. Tonight's mission would be no different than the previous with one important exception, Thorpe and Austin would be joining them on a different mission, one of their most dangerous.

As Volant Solo began its takeoff, Thorpe and Austin pulled on their night vision goggles and paralleled it on the adjacent runway at the same speed. Lifting off at the same time, the Combat Talon followed Volant Solo like a shadow. When Volant Solo turned northeast toward the Soviet border, Thorpe accelerated. He flew the Combat Talon a hundred meters directly below it; dangerously close, even for a trained pilot. The tight vertical formation painted a single radar image, simulating a single aircraft.

As the two aircraft, flew in the direction of Yerevan from the southeast, Volant Solo commenced its racetrack while the Combat Talon rapidly dropped altitude and disappeared.

***

Over the past forty-eight hours, Bollard left the hide site only to use his radio. His first time out was to send an initial radio signal indicating he was ready for extraction within the prearranged window. Twenty-four hours after sending the extraction request, Bollard sat outside one of the haystacks nearest the middle of the field and set up his radio. He took a moment to appreciate the night sky and fresh air after dwelling underground for so long. Given the stillness of the night and the clear skies, he was confident he would receive the go-ahead message.

He tuned the radio and turned the volume down low. He received the last letters of the coded message and waited for it to loop again. The message confirmed they would extract him the following night. He then sent an acknowledgment.

The next night he was back in the field with the large cargo pack. The weather conditions were perfect, with a clear starry night. His extraction was set for 0300 hours and he could have no delay. He checked his watch. He had exactly two hours to prepare. Everything would be timed to the minute, and there could be absolutely no mistakes.

He methodically emptied the cargo pack and carried each piece into the middle of the field. He took particular caution moving a critical piece of equipment, a dirigible-style balloon. He placed it forward of the other components. An infrared light was affixed atop the balloon. Bollard flipped a switch that activated the large pulsating light, invisible to the naked eye, but appeared as a strobe to anyone with a night vision device. The balloon was connected to a one-hundred-and-fifty-meter nylon rope that served as the lift line, with all of it but the first forty meters precision coiled in a tarp container. The trailing end of the rope at the bottom of the tarp was attached to a harness and jumpsuit.

Bollard double-checked the balloon and lift line attachment point, confirmed there were no entanglements, examined the harness, then satisfied everything was in order, he donned the jumpsuit. He monitored his watch and ten minutes before extraction, pulled a pin on the helium cartridge that inflated the balloon.

The balloon shot airborne taking the lift line and infrared lights with it. Now sitting and facing away, Bollard felt the hard tug on the harness as the balloon reached altitude.

His extraction was now in the hands of others. All he could do was wait.

***

As Lieutenant Colonel Thorpe and Major Austin approached the extraction point inside the Armenian border, the Combat Talon mimicked the motions of a small boat moving among huge waves. Each time they crested a hill they looked for the blinking infrared light on the balloon and the stringer of infrared lights beneath it.

When the Combat Talon crested another hill Austin called out as he saw lights shining brightly in their night vision devices. It was their target, one and a half kilometers ahead. They were on course and continued their low-level approach. Once in line with the string of lights and increasing altitude to seventy-five meters, Thorpe, in a precision move, aligned the front of the aircraft with the balloon.

A wave of relief crashed over Bollard as the roaring of engines reverberated and thundered throughout the valley and off the adjacent mountains. He could see nothing, but the sound of the Combat Talon's engines was unmistakable.

Thorpe made the necessary minute adjustments and then flew the plane directly into the lift line, engaging the aircraft's yoke and sky anchor to both cut the balloon free and lock the rope to the aircraft.

"Whiskers engaged," Austin said.

365

Bollard disappeared immediately like a card in a magician's hands. In one instant he was sitting tethered to the lift line and idle; in another, the Combat Talon engaged the lift line and snatched him into the air at a hundred twenty knots.

"Altitude," Thorpe said as he pulled the aircraft up to avoid dashing his passenger across the trees and landscape.

At the rear of the aircraft, the crew activated the switch on a specialized winch having sensitive governors to compensate for the hard snag of the passenger that might break the rope. They quickly winched Bollard aboard the rear of the aircraft and helped secure him to the web seating, while the crew chief signaled the pilot. Thorpe again dropped altitude to sixty-five meters and turned the aircraft west; out of the Soviet Union and into Turkey. As they entered Turkish airspace, they linked up with Volant Solo again and returned to their shadow position.

Once the aircraft leveled out, the crew helped Bollard out of the jumpsuit. He shook hands and thanked them as they clapped him on the back, not even daring to imagine what he must have been through. The Crew Chief opened a cola and handed it to him.

"I suspect you've missed this," he said with a grin.

Bollard downed it gratefully.

The Crew Chief continued, "I saw a Learjet taxi into the airport yesterday. No markings. I'm guessing it's your direct flight home."

"Home," Bollard repeated. "What could be better?"

Epilogue

Three years had passed since Bollard exfiltrated from Armenia. The Soviet Union had collapsed, and its former republics had gained full autonomy, with embassies from around the world lining the streets of the capital cities.

Baku, Azerbaijan was awash with activity upon CIA Station Chief Richard Ward's arrival. He was eager to get to work. A flurry of communications from around the world processed through his office and thousands of files came under his review. Ward was keenly interested in one particular file on his new assignment.

He sat at his desk thumbing through a green folder simply titled, "Alpha." The document was Top Secret, but the portions that interested Ward were those sections labeled "Unclassified When Separated" from the main document.

The file included a hand-written note, recently inserted, and tagged with an attention-getting red page marker. The note contained three alpha-numeric letters, "A 10 7." They were action triggers. Ward immediately activated the associated notification plan that included a series of messages and a stateside phone call.

Back in the United States and balancing one of the twins on his hip, Bollard picked up the phone to hear the voice of an old friend. "Omar? This is Abdul."

***

The driver came to a screeching stop and double-parked in front of the airport in Yerevan. The diplomatic plates ensured no one dared approach the vehicle. However, as the doors opened, a plume of smoke came from inside. The distinct odor of American cigarettes, a luxury most elusive in the former Soviet Republic of Armenia, drew the attention of those nearby.

Ignoring those around them, the embassy official and his charge, ran up the entrance carrying a single suitcase. At the ticket counter, he flashed a black diplomatic passport and the staff scurried to ensure they expedited all ticket processing.

The official examined the ticket to Washington, D.C., where Armenian ex-pats prepared to receive their guest and facilitate enrollment at Georgetown University. The official smiled and handed the ticket to his young charge. As he did another American approached.

The official made introductions. "This is Michael," he said, "he will escort you to Washington. Michael, this is Phiroza."

Michael smiled warmly and shook her hand. "Phiroza, nice to meet you in person. I've read so many reports about you. We're very appreciative of what you and your family did to protect one of our people. We're happy to honor his promise to your father."

Phiroza smiled. "He would've done it without the promise."

***

Seven hundred kilometers due east in Azerbaijan, a commercial airplane made a gradual descent. Bollard leaned forward to peek over Molly's shoulder and out the window. The blue water sparkled as they approached the long peninsula of land jutting into the Caspian Sea. Another descent and the flat ground of Bina International Airport passed by quickly as the aircraft landed with a hard thump and then another. Bollard leaned back in his seat and stretched one last time. His memories of this region were not necessarily the best, but the people here were etched into his mind. He looked at Molly as she gave him a reassuring smile. He winked in return.

The airport was a busy hub. Languages from around the world merged into a cacophony of discordant chatter, overpowered intermittently by the garbled public address system. A waiting crowd stood in anticipation at the international arrivals area. An opaque glass door separated the travelers from their waiting friends and relatives. Each time it opened, the crowd craned their necks to scrutinize the long lines of fatigued passengers waiting to collect their baggage. Many of them held flowers, some held signs, and all revered the mighty door that promised the flood of new arrivals and loved ones.

Standing with a family, a colonel in a starched, stiff uniform and beret kept vigil. The occasional passing military member rendered a snappy salute.

As the door swung open, the colonel and family searched for the American and his wife, grinning and waving when they spotted them. Bollard noted the couple had an addition to the family; an infant adorned in lace. Held in a loving embrace, the infant peered up at her parents. Her dark almond eyes shone with the same brilliance as her mother's – the colonel.

Character List

Abdul – codename for Bollard's CIA contact
Adlan – leader of the militant faction of Chechen guerrillas
Alpha – Bollard's codename, from Seven-Alpha
Alyena – codename for Bollard's contact in Georgia
Anna – Phiroza's codename
Aynurova – Azeri recruit to the Inter-Service Intelligence (ISI)
Captain Karakas – ship commander of the Faik Ali
Chief Kevin Dixon – Navy SEAL supporting isolation team
Colonel Khan – Pakistani ISI
Colonel Stevens – Bollard's Special Forces Commander
Colonel Todd Jacobs – Bollard's isolation team chief
Dariga – Sulundik's younger sister
Janet Jennell – CIA operative supporting isolation team
Dimitri – Grigori's brother
Dr. Blood – Russian abortionist
Dukvakha – Four's nephew
Dayan Mattathia ben Moshke Nadki – Gorsky Jews' Dayan
Erasyl – Uncle Bolat's oldest son
Five – codename for Chechen Area Command Auxiliary Chief
Four – codename for Chechen Guerrilla Chief
Georg – Sulundik's childhood friend
Gershon ben Schmuel na-Katan – Gorsky Jews' enclave leader
Grigori, Major Grigori Asimilov – Spetsnaz operative; guerrilla
Igor – codename for Phiroza's father at hide site
Imam Shamil – historic Caucasus leader against Tsarist forces
Jerry – duty-buddy to Technical Sergeant Gonzalez
Lieutenant Colonel Thad Thorpe – Combat Talon pilot
Lors – Third in charge of the MRNC
Major Bob Townsend – briefing lead supporting isolation team
Major Dave Austin – Combat Talon copilot
Massoud – Mujahideen guerrilla chief
Medved, Colonel Victor Medved – Soviet officer betrayed USSR
Michael – Phiroza's escort
Molly – Bollard's wife
Mrs. Syed – Pakistani ISI
Nadyezhda – babushka, friend of Dr. Blood
Nick – Four's deputy and Chechen guerrilla leader
Nol – Senior Chechen leader, targeted by the GRU and Grigori
Omar – Bollard's codename when working with Abdul
Phiroza – Armenian teenager and operative

Private Nemtsev – Soviet soldier, member of the helicopter assault
Private Petrov – Soviet soldier, member of the helicopter assault
Rabbi Elisha ben Schmuel ha-Kohen – Gorsky Jews' rabbi
Richard Ward – Baku CIA Station Chief
Saud – Saudi operative
Seven – codename for liaison and representative to Area Command
Seven-Alpha, Alpha - codename for Bollard among guerrillas
Seven-Bravo – codename for Saud among guerrillas
Six – codename for Chechen Area Commander
Starshina Davidov – Grigori's cover name in Chechnya
Stork, Angry Stork – Ossetian Area Commander
Sulundik – Afghan guerrilla
Tamaz – Bollard's codename, during initial insertion
Technical Sergeant Pablo 'Pancho' Gonzalez – USAF comms tec
Ten – codename for supplier to Chechen guerrillas
Three – codename for Area Command Underground Chief
Two – codename for Area Command Intel Chief
Ugroza – Chechen guerrilla leader
Ulbolsyn – Sulundik's sister, returned to Chimkent with Sulundik
Ulzhalgas – Sulundik's older sister
Ulzhan – Sulundik's actual name
Uncle Bolat – Sulundik's uncle; caravan leader and black marketer
Vsadnik – muleskinner
Warrant Pavlick – Soviet warrant, leader of helicopter assault